NO TRUCE WITH THE VAMPIRES

Book Three

NO TRUCE WITH THE VAMPIRES

Those Who Endure

Martyn Rhys Vaughan

Cover Design By:
Terry Evans: www.terry-evans.com

AUTHOR'S NOTE

This novel is set in Australia and makes reference to the culture and beliefs of the First Nations Of Australia.

I am not an expert in such matters and if I have inadvertently caused offence to the members of such nations, may I apologise in advance.

FOREWORD

There came a day when the humans could no longer be trusted with the stewardship of the Earth. Those who had watched them from the shadows for millennia, and occasionally feasted upon them, knew it was time to act swiftly and decisively.

And so the vampires came out of the shadows wherein they had abided for so long, and wrested control of the planet from those who had proved themselves unworthy and had come close to destroying it with their insane weapons of destruction.

Humans were deposed from all positions of real authority and turned into a subject people. Or perhaps less than a subject people, for many were placed in Blood Farms where they regularly supplied their new masters and mistresses with the rich warm fluid the new rulers desired so much.

A small group of free humans attempted to shake off the yoke of vampire rule and launched an insurgency in the period immediately prior to the Third Vetusian war. However, despite allying themselves with the immensely powerful enemies of the vampires, they shared their defeat and their subjugation continued.

Regarded by the vampires as no more than a commodity, human history appeared destined for an inglorious conclusion.

But even the vampires cannot foretell the future.

BOOK THREE: THOSE WHO ENDURE

There was a small hillock not far from the settlement, and he stood upon it as the people gathered below him. The sun had set, but a tawny shading still lingered in the west, while above in the clear desert sky, the first southern stars were appearing. All was still.

He stood there like an Old World preacher, ready to deliver the Law to recalcitrant followers. His arms were raised, his face unreadable in the gathering dusk.

'Now, you know the truth. I hear you ask what must you do to escape. The answer is you must trust me. A place, a world, has been set aside for you and I can send you there. Life there will not be easy, but when have you expected it to be otherwise? You are strong men and women who have survived in this most unforgiving land. You do not expect gifts to be handed to you. You are used to doing things for yourselves, finding your own proud ways. These strengths will serve you well in your new home, where you will finally be free of your oppressors.'

He conquers who endures

Aulus Persius Flaccus

PROLOGUE

G reg Ferguson sat on the floor, his back to his mother's cot, staring down, unwillingly listening to his mother's moans and whimpers.

He studied the lines and whorls in the grain of the wooden planks, noticing that one area looked a little like a kookaburra viewed from the side. Another, he thought, looked a little like the incredible red rock that was rearing up into the sunset, not far from his hut.

But nothing could blot out the cries of pain coming from his mother.

Nothing.

His vision misted over as his eyes became moist. She had been crying for so long now. It felt like the whole world had shrunk to the hut and the cot that held his sick parent. In between her moans, he could hear the sound of her covering of rough hessian being periodically thrown off her twisted body before being gently placed back by his silent father.

Suddenly, he decided he could take it no more. He would go out into the cool evening and look at the stars, somehow finding solace in the idea that out there in the darkness, there was no suffering.

He rose to his feet without looking in his mother's direction, only to find the way to the door barred by his father.

'Where do you think you're going, son? Your mother needs you; she needs to know you're here with her.'

Greg shook his head desperately. The tears were flowing freely now.

'I don't want to leave her. It's just I can't bear the thought of her being in pain.' For the first time, he looked up, meeting his father's kindly gaze. 'I'm not a bad boy, am I, Dad?'

His father smiled. It looked like he was finding it hard to smile, as if it had been a long time since he had smiled and had almost forgotten how. He reached down to put a hand on the boy's shoulder.

'No, not you, Greg. She knows you love her. I know you love her. It's just that she doesn't want to be alone. It helps with the pain.'

'Can I go out just for a while, Dad? Just a little while?'

His father glanced at the cot. The figure under the hessian sheet had stopped thrashing around and was quiet. He knew it would not be long before the moaning began again. He nodded toward the door.

'Out you go. Don't go far. Don't be long.'

Greg took one lingering look at the figure under the cloth and then left. Maria watched him go and gave a small, sad smile.

The evening air was chilly, and immediately, he began to shiver under the thin rags that served as his clothes. He felt the coldness sinking down into his lungs and wondered momentarily if he should go back in.

No, he would not do that, not yet. The thought of the pain his mother was suffering was too great for him to face again just yet. If only he could absorb some of that pain, take it into his own thin body for as long as he could bear, until he was forced to give it back.

But he could not; the pain was hers and could not be shared; the burden could not be lifted however much he wanted, needed, to spare her.

While these thoughts had raced through his mind, his body, without him noticing, had adjusted to the evening air. There was a large, flat-topped rock close to his hut, and he often sat upon it and looked at the sky. Usually, the evening sky, when the stars first began to show, or better still, the nighttime when the sky was filled with a blackness that could be found nowhere else, dotted with seemingly millions of hard, still stars, ranging from brilliant points to ones that were so faint that the eye could not be certain they were really there.

And there was the great band of milky radiance, hanging like a frozen river in the darkness. He had once asked his father if it had a name, and his father had said it was indeed milk, spilled from the cup of some great god. And not far distant from that river were two cloudy patches, one noticeably larger than the other. His father had said they were just splashes of milk made on the black floor of the sky as the god had moved his cup.

Greg had listened dutifully, not sure if his father really believed these tales of milk-drinking gods. He had always felt there was a deeper, more significant explanation. But he had nobody to discuss the topic with. His mother, even before the sickness had claimed her, had never been interested in the mysteries of the sky, she had always said it was the world which mattered. The *real world*, she had said, but left that phrase undefined. And so the true nature of the celestial river and the little clouds had remained unrevealed.

Gradually, he became aware that he had been sitting on his rock for too long and his extremities were starting to tingle with cold. He rose slowly and took a look around the sky, preparatory to re-entering the hut of sickness.

Of the moaning.

The last streaks of crimson had faded from the dying sunset, and the deep blue dome above was well on its path to absolute blackness. The one star that was brighter than all the others was now shining almost directly overhead.

He sighed once and made to go back.

And stopped.

There had been a sound. He stiffened. There had been reports recently that the big Cats had returned to the area, and there had been reports of sheep being eviscerated on the nearest farm, about eighty miles distant. Such a distance was nothing to one of the great Cats, he knew very well. He prepared to run for his life.

And then a nearby shadow moved and he could see the slim silhouette of a young girl.

It could only be Allira. She came up to him.

'Hello, Greg. It's cold tonight. You should be inside.'

Her dark features were difficult to discern in the gathering gloom, but he easily recognised her voice. She was no big Cat, although her movements sometimes suggested the easy motion of a feline creature.

'I can stand the cold better than you,' he lied. 'I'm a man, don't forget.'

She laughed musically and came nearer,

'I might believe that, if it wasn't for the fact I can see you shivering from a mile away.'

They were almost the same height, and as he looked at Allira, he felt an odd admiration for this girl growing inside him. He remembered the last time he had seen her in daylight, remembering hair as black as the nighttime sky, brown eyes, and skin a soft, supple brown that never became red under the fierce sun, unlike his own pale covering. She claimed to be one of the Old People, people who had always been in this land; indeed, had sprung from the land itself, unlike Greg's people, whom she referred to as "Colonists". Neither she nor Greg knew what that name meant, but he, in particular, didn't like the sound of it. When he was with Allira, he often wished he too had sprung from the land and was one of the Old People. She sat next to him on the rock, and instantly, he noticed a pleasant, musky odour flowing from her.

It made him feel excited in a strange way he was not familiar with.

'I saw you looking at the sky,' she said. 'What were you thinking?'

He shrugged, not sure of what to say, and then: 'I thought it looked so peaceful. There are no problems up there, no pain.'

She spoke again, apparently not responding to his thoughts.

'What do you know of us Old People?'

He hesitated, not wanting to show his ignorance or offend her somehow.

'I know you say there are two sorts of people in the world: one people who always lived here and another who came after. And you belong to the ones who were always here. And I don't,' he added, feeling very slightly annoyed that he appeared to be of inferior status.

'That is all true.' She smiled in the fading light and briefly touched his hand. 'But no need to feel ashamed; I like you.'

He smiled. It was good to be liked. But she had only just begun.

'Once, long ago, we Old People were divided into different tribes who lived in different parts of the World. We spoke different languages and had different legends. Sometimes we even fought each other. But then something happened, and we all merged together, like raindrops coming together to make a pool. We learned to speak the same language as you Colonists, even though it was not as rich or melodious as our native tongues. But we kept our ancient stories about the World and the Sky, legends that you do not have. Look,' and she pointed to the Milky Way, (for such it was) now taking on the form of a misty river in the darkening sky, 'we know the great god Nepelle, ruler of the heavens, lives there in the river and watches us here. I suppose, Greg, you know of the Lady Of The Night?'

He shook his head, and she laughed.

'What do you Colonists know! The Lady Of The Night is the lesser great light in the sky, the one who changes shape. And you must have noticed the great star that shines just before the Sun rises.'

He nodded, and then, realising she probably could not see the motion in what had become true darkness, said, 'Yes. I have seen it. It is very bright.'

'He is the husband of The Lady and together they made all the people in the World.'

'What, even us Colonists?'

She laughed again.

'Some people doubt that, but I don't.' She touched his hand again. 'I think we're all the same, Old People, Colonists—what does it matter?'

He thought for a second. He liked the idea of being of the same people as Allira. But then the grim facts of his situation hit him, and he turned from both the night sky and Allira. He wiped his eyes and even in the deepening darkness Allira saw it.

'Greg, you spoke of problems, of pain. It's your mother, isn't it?'

He looked askance at her dark silhouette.

'How do you know that?'

'I just do. We know of many things out there in the Bush. We know the needs of the goanna, the thoughts of the kangaroo. And I know about your mother and her pain.'

He felt the need to share his sorrow, the need for someone to hear his distress.

'Yes. She just lies there. She is in pain that never stops. I wish she could give me some of the pain so she would feel better, but she can't, and I can't take it from her, much as I want to!'

Allira remained silent for quite some time, as if unsure whether to reveal her thoughts. Then: 'There is a man.'

Instantly, he was alert.

'A man? What sort of man? Why did you mention him?'

She spoke again slowly, with odd gaps between the words.

'There is a man, a strange man. He is not of us Old People but neither is he one of yours. Oh, I know that doesn't make sense. You and me, our kind are the only ones who live in the World, but, but there is something different about him. He has strange eyes, and the few who have been near enough to be touched by him say his flesh is cold—icy cold.'

Greg stared at her. A man who was not one of the Old People or of the Colonists? That was impossible. What was he—a talking kangaroo? No, that was impossible: kangaroos had red blood that was warm to the touch; he had done so.

'So, why are you telling me this? What's he got to do with my mother?'

Another pause, and then Allira said, 'Sometimes he helps people. People who are sick, I mean.'

Greg's entire body tensed with the shock of hope.

'Then I'll go and see him! Where is he—is it far?'

'No, not far. But I have never heard of him helping Colonists; just my people.'

Greg leapt to his feet, the blood hammering in his arteries.

'Then I will make him help her! I will!' He stared down at her. 'Where is this man? How do I find him?'

'I can take you. It is a long walk.'

'I'll walk to the Lady Of The Night if I have to! When do we start?'

'We can go tomorrow. But will you find the time? You will be away most of the daylight hours.'

Greg's mind whirled madly. *Most of the daylight hours.* He hadn't banked on such a long journey. He knew the Old People thought nothing of such treks, but he was not one of them. Water would be needed and some food.

He would have to ask for his father's permission.

***

'No, of course, you can't go!' his father yelled. 'You have chores! Do you think the farm runs itself, boy!' Greg held his father's enraged stare in a calm, steady one of his own.

'Allira thinks this man can help mother.'

His father snorted.

'Some Blackfellow's daughter! And you believe her, do you? You're just a child!'

'So, you won't let me go?'

'Of course I won't. Who would look after your mother while you're on some crazy walkabout?'

Greg's father had persuaded an elderly woman of the Old People to help around the house since his wife had gotten ill. She was looking at Greg and gave him a reassuring smile.

'Maria could do it,' Greg said. 'You could give her another leg of mutton.'

Maria clapped her large hands together and her wide face split under a broad grin.

'Leg of mutton! Praise be!'

His father ignored her.

'Of course. I could give her the whole flock as well.' He glanced at the open doorway, seeing a blindingly bright stretch of blue above the dusty red landscape. 'The sun is well up. Get your hat and get out there.'

Soon, Greg was plodding up the dusty slope to the pen where the sheep were kept; Sky, his border collie bitch, walking faithfully alongside. The heat was like a tremendous hand pressing down upon him as he forced his legs to carry him away from the family hut, the bag of feed feeling like a boulder on his back. His companion seemed sense his inner turmoil and looked questioningly up at him several times during the walk.

They reached the top of the rise, and the tremendous dusty plain of the Red Centre was stretched out below him, mile after desiccated mile of arid, rust-coloured sand and stone, sparsely dotted with withered thorn bushes. It reached out to the far horizon until red sand met electric blue sky. It was beautiful in an austere way, but it was unkind to people. That is, it wasn't kind to the Colonists; the Old People appeared to regard it as Paradise.

The sheep were waiting for him and as he came into their sight, they pressed against the fence, desperate for the food he brought. Since the latest drought had taken hold, there was not enough out in the Bush for them to feed themselves. The two guard dogs ran towards Greg, tails wagging furiously. He looked at the thin sheep, counting them carefully.

They were all there. One of the local pride of big Cats had not carried some off during the night. He had, of course, known that for some time: there had been no smell of blood on the furnace air.

He began throwing the feed into the troughs, without paying much attention to his aim. He had done this so many times he rarely missed. The feed was the only thing keeping the flock alive; the current drought was so fierce that there was nothing they could eat out in the Bush. That done, he sat on a rock and pulled the brim of his wide hat down to shade his eyes from the brilliance of the shimmering land. Sky nuzzled his hand questioningly until he told her to sit somewhere else.

He knew he should remain alert. The Cats were big, big enough to take one or two sheep, but they would not stand up to the combined forces of a teenage boy and three snarling dogs. But he wondered how long that would last; the old folk said the Cats had been smaller in the earlier days. Every year now, they seemed to be bigger than the previous one. There were already tales of them taking down big buck kangaroos, although no one he or his father knew had seen that happen.

Against his will, his head nodded, and he was suddenly asleep.

He was awakened by a hand shaking his shoulder and his eyes opened in terror. *His father would be really mad he had fallen asleep on watch!*

But, looking up, he saw that the intruder was Allira.

'I waited,' she said simply. 'I waited but you did not come.'

All three dogs had gathered around her, nuzzling and licking her legs. She was rubbing their heads as they looked up at her. It was almost as if she had some power over them, Greg thought, normally they were very hostile to strangers.

'I can't go.' Greg stopped and thought for a moment. 'I can never go. Father won't let me.'

She reached down and gently lifted his chin with one hand.

'Then you must come today. Now.'

'Didn't you hear what I said! I can't!'

She turned and looked at the sheep.

'I will tell the guard dogs to protect the sheep while you are away. Then we go. Together.'

Greg stood and stared at her.

Tell the guard dogs to protect the sheep? Was she mad?

But she had already left his side and was walking around each dog in turn, bending close to their ears and whispering something. Then she returned to the puzzled boy.

'The dogs understand. They will do their duty.'

He stared at her, open-mouthed.

She smiled.

'Stop that. If we go now, we will be back before sundown.' Seeing that he remained immobile, she ran a hand down his cheek and repeated: 'Now.'

***

They walked side by side through the bush. The blistering air was like a red-hot skein thrown over the land, air that felt as if it did not contain a single molecule of water vapour. The ground on either side of the track shimmered through curtains of heat haze, occasionally fooling the eye with images of fictitious pools. He was nervous, and somehow she knew.

'What is the matter?'

He hesitated; he did not want to upset her.

'This journey you've persuaded me to go on. I don't really know you, and I've abandoned the flock I was meant to take care of. I could be in a whole lot of trouble.'

She considered that and touched him again, briefly.

'I understand. It is possible something will happen to your sheep. Every year, the Cats get bigger and more fierce. One day they will take down a man. But Greg, this is the only way to spare your mother more suffering; isn't that worth the risk?'

He thought for a moment. He was still far from certain—he really didn't know Allira that well. Could it be she was leading him into the outback with some scheme in mind? A few old folk maintained the Old People had murdered the occasional Colonist as some kind of reparation for past wrongs—whatever they had been. He looked at Allira, tall, slim, black of hair and skin of warm mahogany. She smiled, showing teeth that, for a moment, seemed dazzlingly white against her skin.

And he doubted no longer.

They walked on, Greg seeming to trudge, Allira seeming to glide over the rust-coloured track. Greg saw something dart off the path in front of them and disappear among the thorn bushes.

'What was that?'

She laughed.

'You are jumpy, Greg. It was only *ngiyari*—the "thorny-devil", as you call it. It will not harm you.'

He felt foolish; it was not as if he had never seen a thorn-devil. A few yards on, they came across a blue-tongued lizard, unconcernedly sunning itself in a patch of fierce sunlight. *Lungata,* she called it, and it sat motionless and watched them as they passed.

'How much longer?' he said. His lips were beginning to blister, and all the water was gone. She had let him drink most of it. Sky was definitely both limping and panting, with her tongue hanging motionless from her mouth.

Allira pointed ahead.

'We're here.'

He looked. He saw a wall of red rock like a thousand others. But there was something he had never seen before in a rock.

A door. A grey, featureless door.

What was this? he thought. Rocks didn't have doors.

The three of them stopped before the door, and Greg inspected it. It looked odd. It wasn't wood, or stone, or metal. He touched it, and then pulled back, looking at Allira. The substance was smooth as glass and—and *cool*.

'What is this?' he said. 'What have you brought me to?'

Once again, his mind whirled. Many said the Old People had strange powers. Was this the lair of some sorcerer?

'Don't fear. I have been here before. You will not be harmed.' She looked at the top of the door, although nothing was visible there, and waved a hand.

And then there was a voice, a voice Greg did not like. It was deep and resonant, the voice of someone certain in its authority, sure of its power. But there was something else about the voice.

It was cold, impersonal, uninterested in its visitors.

'Allira. You have come again. And brought two with you. Which of the creatures needs my help?'

Creatures? thought Greg. That did not sound inviting.

'Neither,' Allira said. There was an edge to her speech as if she, too, was disturbed by the voice. 'This is Greg Ferguson. It is his mother who needs your help.'

'Very well. It has not been long since I helped another one of your race, but I must adhere to the plan.'

To Greg's astonishment, the door opened, but completely unexpectedly: instead of opening outwards or inwards, it slid upwards into the rock. Alarmed, he looked at Allira and it was only her composed expression which kept him there. But there was soon another reason to stay, as the air flowing out of the interior was soothing to his baked skin. They entered a narrow corridor which was not carved out of the native rock but was the same unidentifiable material as the door. And once he had adjusted to the coolness of the air, he noticed it carried a similarly unidentifiable odour. Once again he looked at Allira and she squeezed his hand. Twice.

They came to another door and this time it opened by sliding horizontally and soundlessly into the surrounding material. And behind the entrance was a desk. And behind the desk was a man.

Greg entered warily, all his senses now on high alert. He knew he was now an indeterminate distance inside a rock face, in the company of someone he did not know well, and confronted by a stranger.

He stared at the seated individual and what he saw did not allay his fears. Even though the man was sitting, Greg could tell he was unusually tall, almost freakishly so. As Greg reluctantly approached, he saw a clean-shaven, oval face with prominent cheekbones. No, the man was *not* clean-shaven: there was not the slightest sign of possible beard growth. His face looked like it was completely hairless. His scalp, however, was covered in thick, jet-black hair. And the skin! It was so pale it was almost white, the white of the recently deceased.

There was a transparent tumbler containing a deep-red liquid in front of the man's unpleasantly long-nailed hands. Greg did not like the look of that liquid; it reminded him of something he did not like thinking about.

The man spoke.

'Welcome to my consulting room,' he said, with no welcome in his voice. 'Allira, I know. But you are?'

Greg was about to speak when Sky gave a strange, deep-throated growl, and the hair on her neck and back lifted into stiff bristles. Greg had only seen that posture and heard that sound when a Cat was near. He was about to stroke the collie when he heard the man say, 'Allow me.' He turned to see the man rise from his chair and walk towards them. Instantly, he recoiled slightly; the man was indeed freakishly tall and cadaverously thin. He walked to the growling animal and extended a hand, held horizontally with the palm uppermost.

'Silence,' he said.

Sky relaxed instantly, slumping into an almost boneless heap, and attempted to lick the hand, her tail wagging weakly. Greg looked down at this sudden reversal with disbelieving eyes.

The man ignored the dog and returned to sit behind his desk. His pale, long-nailed fingers interlocked.

'You may not know my true name, but you may call me "Renfield". What is your identifier, boy, and what brings you here?' he said.

Greg shook his head. None of this was making any sense. He tried to bring things back into the disappearing world of normality.

'Why can't we know your real name? Why must we call you Renfield?'

'Because it amuses me. Now answer my question.'

Greg glanced at Allira but her face was impassive; she seemed familiar with this approach. And so, he identified himself and explained the reason for the visit. Renfield's face did not alter in the slightest. If it carried any recognisable expression, it was one of boredom and indifference. He asked several questions about Greg's mother but took no notes. Eventually, he raised a hand and said, 'That is sufficient. I will visit your hovel and administer some pain relief. Goodbye.'

'Wait a minute. I haven't told you where we live.'

'I know where you live. I know the location of every human within my zone of operation.'

Every *human?* Another example of peculiar wording.

'But what if we're out? What if we're tending the flock?'

'Your mother will not be out, I believe.'

'But how would you get in? We don't leave the hut open to anybody. A Cat might get in!'

'None of your people could keep me out if I wanted to come in. You have invited me: that is enough.' He raised a hand. Even the palm was oddly white. 'Now go. I have expended enough time listening to your problems.'

Greg gave Allira another glance, but this time she nodded, to show she agreed with the strange man. It was time to go. Greg looked down at his dog and clicked his fingers. Immediately, she snapped out of the odd trance she had been in, and started wagging her tail in a very happy manner.

The journey back was silent for some time. Then Greg could bear the silence no longer.

'Who was that awful cobber? How did you meet him?'

Allira looked down at the yellow grit and gravel of the path before speaking.

'He came to my father many years ago.'

'Many years ago? He doesn't look old enough for that!'

'Are you calling me a liar—or worse still, my father?' she spat, her eyes blazing. 'That's what my father told me!'

Greg was sensible enough not to press the issue and, after some time trudging under the westering sun, he changed the subject and they talked about farming matters.

Eventually, they came up the slope to the sheep pen and Greg looked around nervously to make sure all the sheep were still there.

They were not.

All but one was there, but where there should have been a pregnant ewe there were clumps of red-stained wool lying on a patch of dry blood.

A Cat had gotten in.

Greg felt his heart begin to hammer and his palms go sweaty. The worst had happened. Things were bad enough on the farm without him wandering off and losing an animal.

But it was even worse than he had thought, for only one guard dog came warily to meet him, its tail limp and motionless. Not far off, lay the torn corpse of the other on its own patch of dry blood.

'Cat,' he mumbled to himself. 'Cat got them.' He whirled around to glare at Allira. 'This is your fault, dragging me off to see that weird man! Go away!'

She stared at him, hardly blinking.

'You don't mean that,' she finally said, her voice dry and cracking.

'Yes, yes! Go away! I never want to see you again!'

She turned and descended the slope into the lengthening shadows of the Red Centre, not looking back. Greg thought he had heard a muffled sob. Then all was silent.

***

Greg's father whipped him good and hard after his stumbling attempts to explain why he had left the sheep unattended. Even his mother was moved to protest from her sick bed at the boy's cries. Eventually his father's arm grew tired, and Greg was allowed to go to his room.

Supperless, of course.

The next day, his father made a halting apology and explained it wasn't just the ewe but the loss of a good guard dog. Dogs like that were hard to come by, and he would have to dig into the family's reserves to get a new one.

Greg had nodded silently, his eyes downcast. He knew he had screwed up badly and made no further attempts at self-justification. He still couldn't believe he had been so stupid as to go on a long trek with Allira for absolutely nothing.

Later that day, the two of them returned to the sheep pen to see how the Cat had gotten in. But there was no break in the fence.

'Damn thing must have jumped over the fence. And then jumped back over with the best cuts of the sheep. Damn thing, damn, damn thing!'

Greg knew his father was deeply angry and bitter for he rarely heard the man swear. But one thing occurred to him, even in the depths of his misery: people said the Cats were getting bigger every year. Didn't that mean they must once have been small, basically harmless things, small enough to rest on your lap? But what would you use a small Cat for? They would be too small to do any herding of the sheep. He put the puzzle from his mind: he had other problems.

And so it was a miserable return to the miserable hut. Maria had made them some mutton chops, but Greg could hardly eat his, feeling as if he didn't deserve them. His mother tried to eat some small slices but could not keep them down and vomited back some barely chewed pieces onto her covering.

They gave their goodbyes to Maria who had spent all the time with them she could spare. Fortunately, her own dwelling was not far away, otherwise Greg and his father would have had no help at all. Greg's mother's moans made an unwelcome accompaniment to thoughts which circled aimlessly, getting nowhere, accomplishing nothing.

Suddenly, he stiffened, instantly alert.

There had been a movement, a shadow. He whirled around on his chair and stared in disbelief at what he saw.

It was Renfield, dressed in a long black cloak, wide-brimmed hat and shades, standing a yard or so away. Greg heard his father curse and rush between Greg and the intruder, an axe in his right hand.

'Who are you? What are you doing in my house? How did you get in?'

Renfield raised a hand as if to brush away some annoying gnats.

'Do not waste my time with questions. Your son invited me in. That is all you need to know.' He turned from the astounded parent and moved in a sinuous, boneless fashion towards the cot in which Greg's mother had managed to pull herself into a sitting position, her eyes wide and terrified.

'The patient, I presume,' Renfield said in his usual toneless manner. 'Be still. I will not hurt you.'

Greg's father made a sudden movement toward Renfield, axe raised. Renfield did not turn around at his assailant's approach but merely said, 'Put that foolish implement down, or there will be two patients in this hut, one of whom I shall not be treating.'

Greg rushed to his bemused and angry father and pulled at the arm holding the axe.

'I think it's OK, Dad. This is the man Allira took me to. He's a healer—I think,' he added. Greg's father stood in obvious indecision as Renfield leant over his wife, but Greg pulled at the arm again.

'We've got to trust him! Allira wouldn't have tricked me, I'm sure!'

Greg's father lowered the axe but moved closer to Renfield.

'If you hurt her…'

'No empty threats. Surely you can see I'm busy.'

As he said those words Greg saw Renfield had a small rectangular object in one hand. It looked like it was made of metal and had several lights blinking on its silvery surface. A soft glow was coming from a small panel on the upper surface.

It did not resemble any object Greg had ever seen before.

His mind was in turmoil at this development. *Allira had not lied! Renfield really was a healer! And if he was a healer, could he actually help…*

Renfield straightened and turned from the cot, his face, as always, cold and impassive. He could have been looking at rabbits in a trap.

'I ask myself how many more decades of this I have to endure,' he said, apparently to no one actually present. 'But I have to conform to her plan. After all, she saved us all.'

Silence followed that mysterious remark. Greg and his father stood as if transfixed by their strange visitor, waiting for something to happen. There was a thud as his father's hand lost its grip on the axe.

'The female is suffering from one of the many degenerative diseases which afflict you people,' Renfield said. Once again, Greg noticed the odd phraseology; the implication of *otherness*. 'It is not necessary that I attempt to cure her, for she will soon be dead, if not of this condition, then of one of the many others.' Still his audience remained motionless; Greg had the feeling it would be impossible to move, even if he tried. 'But I can take away her pain.' Renfield reached into his cloak and took out a box. Amazingly, it was perfectly transparent, more so than regular glass, and Greg could see it contained a large number of small blue balls. Renfield returned to the cot and gave the box to the trembling woman. 'Take one of these every day with a little water. The pain will stop a few hours after your first dose.'

His mother took the box, looking between Greg and her husband as if seeking permission.

Renfield turned back the two males.

'You will not see me again. Do not look for me; I have done enough to fulfil my obligations. If, by some chance, you come across me and tell me of your pain, I will give you more. Farewell.'

And with that he left through the open doorway. Greg was relieved; he had more than half expected the stranger to turn into a vapour and creep under it.

But his father had crossed to his wife and tried to snatch the box from her.

'Don't you take any of those things! We don't know what they'll do to you!'

But Greg suddenly found his voice. He, too, crossed to the woman sitting in the cot.

'No, Dad! I trust Allira now! I was wrong to doubt her. She says that man was a healer and I believe her!'

Greg's father looked back and forth between his wife and his son, his indecision plainly written on his face. Then, his decision was made for him. His wife spoke in a dry, cracked voice.

'Tom, get me a cup of water.'

Greg watched his father's silent battle with his conflicting thoughts and then saw him go outside to the pump, returning shortly with a chipped cup clasped in a hand that was slightly trembling. He watched his wife swallow one of the blue balls, washing it down with the tepid water. 'We're fools,' he said. 'Damn fools. It won't do anything.'

***

'I feel much better,' she said as she came in from the heat of late afternoon sun. 'A lot better.' She sat on the three-legged stool and looked around, smiling.

Greg was also smiling. It was two days since she had started the strange man's treatment and the difference was verging on the miraculous. He could still remember the shock of seeing her swing bare feet onto the floorboards and hesitantly stand erect, waving her husband away as he rushed to steady her. From that moment on, everything changed; her voice returned to the melodious tones he had almost forgotten, and the only time she evidenced pain was when she had stubbed a big toe against a chair. And today there had been yet another wonder when she ventured into the open air and stood for many minutes just looking at the red landscape and the brilliant sky.

Greg hugged himself in his joy: he had his mother back! What a fool he had been to doubt the strange man! Despite his peculiar manner, he had been shown to be a kind, compassionate healer. And there was no way of thanking him as he had warned them not to look for him; no doubt he was crisscrossing the Bush looking for more suffering people to heal and could spare no time to reminisce. Greg was not aware he had pushed part of the man's words into his deep subconscious, the part about his mother simply being released from the pain.

And nothing else.

***

From the moment she had taken the blue pill, Greg's mother rapidly became free of the esurient pain that had been eating away at her humanity. Greg would never forget the day when she walked calmly out of the hut and came back with a pail of water from the well. Such a thing had been unimaginable only a few days earlier. Maria had taken the pail from her and hugged her until it seemed both women would burst!

But there was something else: now that she could speak again, there always seemed to be something she wanted to say to Greg and to him alone. Greg would often catch her looking up at her husband when he stood near the open door, apparently wondering if he would be going outside to leave the both of them alone.

And then there came the day when her husband picked up his woomera and best-throwing spear, strapped a slingshot to his waist, and looked around with an air of finality.

'Well, Greg, are you coming? Those rabbits out there are getting mighty fat. I'm sure Maria could make a good stew out of them!'

Maria was not, in fact, in the hut at that moment; as Greg's mother gradually regained her abilities, she had begun to reassert her primacy in matters culinary, although she still left the basic cleaning to the woman of the Old People.

Greg was wondering if he should get his own, much smaller spear, when he felt his mother's gentle touch on his back. Taking the hint, he said, 'Sorry, Dad. My stomach's playing up today. Sorry.'

His father looked annoyed, but he shrugged and simply said, 'One less rabbit for the pot, then,' and went off on his hunt.

Greg waited until he was sure his parent wouldn't be coming back for some forgotten item and then spun around to face his mother.

'Well?' he said. 'I know you want to say something. So, say it.'

'Sit on the stool,' she said. 'This may take some time.'

He obeyed, and they sat facing each other. The silence grew. And then she smiled and said: 'This is so difficult. Where to begin?'

Greg gave the customary reply, and she laughed.

'You're right. Best to dive right in, then.' Somewhat to Greg's alarm, she leaned forward and held both his hands. *Oh no!* he thought. *She's going to tell me where babies come from, and I already know about that!*

But her face became still and serious. Her words were not about the mechanics of reproduction.

'This land is not the whole world, Greg.'

He looked at her in total bafflement. Not only was she not talking about babies, but her words made no sense. Finally, he simply asked: 'It isn't?'

'I know what I am about to say will sound like utter nonsense. But, trust me Greg, I am not raving. I am not suffering from some kind of seizure. I feel better than I have for years. I wanted to wait until you were older, but I realise now I may not be around when you are older, so it has to be now, this minute.' She took a deep breath, took a quick look at the doorway to see if her husband was standing there, and then looked back at Greg.

'This land is not the whole of the world. There is much, much more. Many centuries ago, they gathered us up from all the different parts of the real world and placed us here.'

'Who are you talking about? Who are *they?*'

'I don't know. Maybe we knew right at the beginning, but the knowledge is lost. All I can be certain of is that they must be very powerful, or they could never have done what they did.'

Greg thought about that. His father often referred to the gods when something unexpected happened, but Greg was certain he didn't really believe in them. The Old People were different; Greg was sure some of them believed in actual gods, but he had never heard a tale about them "gathering people up". He gave up, and nodded to his mother that she should continue.

'Not only did they put us all in this place, but—for some reason—they wanted us to forget that our forced migration had happened; they wanted us to think that what we know is all there is to know, that the land we see is all the land there is.'

'If it's not, what is it?'

'It is just a part; probably a very small part. But at the time of the collection, a few very brave people managed to bring some books, some records of where they were being taken from. It must have been a terrible risk, for all such things had been forbidden. Or so the oldest tales say.'

'Who forbade them?'

'*They* did.'

Greg took his hands from his mother's, noticing they had become unpleasantly clammy. He fixed his mother in a stern gaze.

'What does Dad think about all this?'

She sighed.

'Your father is a good man. He still feels guilty for the way he beat you a while back. But he carries such a load, looking after the animals, looking after you, and lately looking after me, of course. But he only believes in what he can see, what he can touch, and so he does not believe in what I have told you. And when he began to get angry when we spoke of it, I stopped saying these things to him. But it did not stop me from loving him, Greg; you must believe in that, at least.' She took another strangely deep breath. 'But I have proof, Greg, proof.'

Greg, like his father, wanted this woman to stop babbling these worrying, disquieting stories, but another part of him wanted her to continue. She was his mother; she would not lie to him. And so, he said: 'Proof? What sort of proof?'

'I have some of those ancient books. I had others, but they crumbled into dust when I tried to turn the pages. But these ones were in a kind of envelope, a very peculiar envelope: you could see straight through it. And there was a map!'

'What's that?'

'It's a kind of picture, one which shows the world—the real world! And it shows where we are. On an island!'

She had to explain what an island was, as Greg had never seen a body of water large enough to contain one. 'Your father threw them out, saying he had no use for fairy stories, but one night I went out and gathered them together in a box, and hid it.'

Against his will, Greg found himself believing; he had to see this box!

'Where is it?'

'I can't tell you yet. You have to tell me you believe every word I have said. Otherwise, you might destroy the books and the map.'

Greg's conflicting thoughts chased each other through his brain. He wanted to say he believed. He looked up into his mother's face and was about to tell her he believed her, when she turned away, her face twisted with sadness.

'You don't believe me. I will have to wait a little longer.'

And with that, she turned from him and lay down on the cot, something she had not done in the daytime since taking the pills. Greg did not dare raise the topic again after somehow proving unworthy of his mother's trust, and so the rest of the afternoon was spent in an awkward silence, broken only by the triumphant return of his father with a collection of large rabbit carcasses over his shoulder. Greg shuddered slightly; he liked rabbit stew but was not so keen on the preparatory skinning.

Still, it had to be done, and all three had a pleasant supper.

And so the peculiar day ended. As he lay in his bed, Greg spent no little time thinking over his mother's strange words, trying to make sense of them.

But nothing came of the arguments he had with himself, and he was soon asleep, with no thoughts of the mysterious *they* to trouble his dreams.

***

A few days later, Greg heard his parents arguing about Maria. His father wanted to dispense with her services, saying that his mother was now fit and well enough to resume all of her duties as a wife and mother. But Greg heard her say, 'No, Tom, let's not be hasty. Let's wait a while to see how I get on with what I am doing. You never know.'

He heard his father snort.

'Nonsense, woman. You're as fit as I am. And Greg needs his mother; he's still a very tender little boy.'

Tender little boy—hah! Greg thought. *One day I'll show you!*

And he had noticed one occurrence his father had not—the supply of pills was gone; his mother had taken the last one three days ago.

And that worried him; he did not want to hear her crying out in pain ever again. But he forced himself not to think about that, for a busy day lay ahead. The drought had at last broken and the sheep needed to be brought back to their pen after their freedom out in the Bush. Fortunately, his father had finally managed to get a new guard dog, after much bargaining back and forth with one of the nearer neighbours. At last, it finally looked like they were getting back on their feet again.

And so, it was two tired, but contented males who came back from their labours as the shadows were lengthening. Approaching the hut, Greg cast a glance at that stupendous rock to the north, marvelling at how it always seemed to change colour at sunset. Only the upper part was above the horizon at their distance but, even so, the sheer might of that mass of stone was clearly evident. Now it was glowing in burnished bronze, burnt umber and fiery crimson against the deep blue of the northern sky, cloudless as usual. The great milky river in the sky would be very prominent tonight, but sadly, he thought he would be too tired to admire it.

Indeed, they both decided they were too weary to eat after they had come home and taken off their heavy boots. Unusually for him, Greg's father said he would take a nap, and disappeared into the marital bedroom, leaving Greg alone with his mother.

He thought she seemed agitated as they looked at each other, and a little worm of worry began to stir in his mind.

'What is it, Mom?' he said, hoping her reply would be an everyday observation.

She crossed to him and, to his dismay, clasped his hands in the same manner she had done earlier.

'Greg, we didn't finish our talk.'

'Mom, I'm not sure I want to hear it.'

'You must, Tom. This illness of mine has put everything out of joint. I was going to tell you all this when you were older, but now I can't take the risk. I have to tell you—now.'

Greg gave a reluctant nod.

'OK.'

She moved so her face was only inches from his. It looked to him as if a strange feverish light was burning in her eyes, and her grasp on his hands was becoming painful.

'I told you that this land is not all there is. Once we were spread all over the world, the real world, not just this fragment of it. But something happened, a power we could not resist swept us up and deposited us here. But they did more than that, Greg, they deprived us of our history, took away our memories and burned them, reducing us to the level of children, eking out our existence with simple childish tools that once we had seen only in museums.'

('What's a museum?' he said, but she ignored the question.)

'But a few people kept some pitiful fragments of our history, the knowledge of who we are as a people, of how we owned and ruled the world.'

('But we do rule the world,' he said, but she ignored the interruption.)

'Such courage. But we do not remember them, their names are lost. That was our jailers' intention, to infantilise us so we would not be trouble to them.'

Greg could not sit meekly anymore. He rose and turned his back on her.

'You're doing it again. Who did all this to us, and why? We're happy here; we have all we want. Sure, the Cats are a nuisance, but we can handle them.'

She rose and clasped him to her, forcing him to turn to face her.

'But that's not what we were made for; that's not how we used to be. They took that from us, Greg!'

He was becoming angry now.

'Stop this, Mom! Show me the evidence, show me this box you keep talking about—or never mention it again!'

'Alright, Greg, I will. You're younger than I hoped you would be, but you must know. I…'

She stopped. Greg waited for her to start again, but she did not. Then he heard a thump from behind him and spun around to see her lying full-length on the dusty floor. She raised her arms to him.

'Greg, Greg, I feel strange! Get your father!'

Immediately, he turned to obey, his heart hammering. But then he heard her cry out, 'No! No more time! Come back, I must tell!'

He ran back and lay down beside her so their faces were level. Her face was contorted with pain.

'Greg, the box, it…' A spasm hit her, and she went silent.

'Yes, Mom, the box?'

'It…the goanna, the tail, nothing changes, sun, it…'

And she died there, as he lay helplessly beside her.

***

The burial was a simple affair, not long after the death. There were no priests of any sort to hold any kind of ceremony, so it fell to Greg's father to say a few words over the grave. He was not a man to whom emotional words came easily; he was a simple hunter and farmer, happy to wield a woomera or wool shears—but not grand-sounding or complex words. In the end, the emotion overcame him and his trembling voice spluttered into wordless sobs. Greg held his father to prevent him from collapsing. Then his father nodded and gave a weak smile.

'I'm alright now, Greg. But she was so young—so damn young!'

'Yes, I know.'

Greg looked at the grave. The soil was thin and rocky, and a linear mound starkly revealed where the body was.

We are of the land, Greg thought, *and must return to the land.*

His father was speaking again, and his voice was firmer now; he had overcome the tears.

'I'm going to rely on you now, Greg. You'll have to do a lot more around the farm. You're going to have to become a man sooner than you may have liked. But I'll see if Maria will stay for longer, to help around the house.'

Greg nodded: he accepted all that. The sun was low, and he had to squint to keep the grave in focus. But then he looked up into his father's lined and leathery face.

'I will do all I can, Dad. I won't let you down. But on the day of my eighteenth birthday, I will leave you and go out into the world.'

His father was taken aback.

'So soon? Why, Greg, why?'

Greg hesitated; he knew it was difficult to explain his reasons. But times had changed and he had made his silent vow.

'I know you don't want to hear this, Dad, but Mom told me some things I have to sort out in my mind.'

His father snorted.

'I know what you're going to say. Fairy stories!'

His father's airy dismissal did not disturb Greg; a vow was a vow. And he had made his.

'It's OK, Dad; I understand you don't want to think about the things she said. But if she was right—what then, Dad? What if we are living in some kind of prison?'

His father did not look at him and raised a hand as a shield against the westering sun.

'Don't want to think about it, Greg.'

'But I do. It was important to her, and I will do all I can with this life of mine to find out the truth.' He squeezed his father's sad hand and turned away, looking to the horizon, looking beyond the horizon into an unknown world, an unknown future.

'If there was something, some power that did in fact imprison us here—I swear I will find them!'

ONE: The Red Centre

Greg Ferguson's biceps bunched into granite hardness as he swung the pickaxe down onto the stone-peppered ground. A wicked sliver of stone flew up, embedding itself in the flesh a few millimetres above his left eye. He wiped the blood away and continued with his wearisome task.

He was burying a sheep, one that had not survived a nocturnal visit from a Cat. The dogs had driven it off, but not before the sheep had been eviscerated by the predator. Ferguson swore as the pickaxe jumped in his calloused hands as it hit yet another buried stone. He stopped and looked down at the trench he had dug with axe and spade, and then at the corpse of the sheep. He shook his shaggy head: he was wasting too much time out here with a vertical unshielded sun blasting its power onto the back of his neck. He reached a decision: the trench was too short to accommodate the sheep; he did not want to spend any more energy on enlarging it. Therefore, he would have to make the corpse smaller. Ferguson picked up his spade, turned the blade ninety degrees and brought it down on one of the sheep's legs. The bone was still fresh, so it did not shatter immediately, and by the end of his task, he had expended almost as much energy as if he had continued excavating.

He threw the spade down in disgust after shovelling enough sand and gravel onto the corpse to cover it. It was not that he invested the burial with any kind of emotion, other than irritation; the sheep meant nothing to him except as a way of making money out here in the wilderness. No, he simply wanted to ensure that the smell of decay did not attract scavengers. Of which, each passing year seemed to produce more of the blighters.

He unscrewed his canteen, took a deep draught of its contents and then rubbed the tepid moisture over his dry and cracked lips. Flies buzzed around him, trying to get at the salt which was now in plentiful supply upon his bronzed skin. He swung his head so that the corks that dangled on strings from his wide-brimmed hat disturbed their aerobatics.

It did not seem to make much difference. And then his dog Sky came up to him and nuzzled his leg, pleadingly. Ferguson grinned as he looked down at his companion. The tawny-haired animal, named after his beloved childhood pet, of course, was at least eighty percent dingo, but tolerated humans—or one particular human, to be strictly accurate: she wasn't too friendly with strangers. He sat on a rock, smiling as he ran a hand over her coarse pelt. Ferguson's hands were not much smaller than dinner plates when the fingers were spread, but there was no sign of their power as he stroked the animal. He looked into her dark brown eyes and said, 'OK, you're right. I've done enough here. I'll get us both a proper drink.' And so, he collected his tools, swung them over a massive shoulder, and began his descent to his farmstead. It was quite near to his old family home as distances go in the Outback, and even nearer to the tremendous sandstone monolith which he could see lying on the horizon like some sleeping creature from mythology. He had left the area after his father died, glad to escape the long silences that had characterised his father's latter days and then wandered far and long in the Outback while becoming a man but, after one too many failed relationships, had returned to the shadow of the great rock to build his own homestead from stone and timber.

It was a small dwelling, but big enough for one man—even one of Ferguson's bulk.

After stowing his tools, he gave Sky a quick drink of water, for the public house was some distance away and the day was hot. He did not lock the door; everyone, for many dusty miles around, knew and trusted each other. They were all in it together, man and woman against an arid and unforgiving land.

In the distance, he spotted the spare outline of Maurice Delgado, the only person who lived near enough to him to be actually visible on a clear day. Despite being very old, he was a nice enough guy. Ferguson returned his wave and took a look around prior to undertaking the dusty journey to get his drink. Everywhere he looked were the same basic landforms: shattered and splintered masses of reddish stone, seemingly carelessly dropped onto the moistureless soil by a bored god. One largish pluton, vaguely reminiscent of a crouching animal, had suffered a landslip recently and had lost what would have been its snout, revealing a sheer, unclimbable wall of fresh grey granite.

Then man and bitch set off for the township that had developed since he had left the area, seeking fame and fortune. He had found neither, but had accepted that a quiet life was to be his destiny. And what better place to spend such quiet days than near the shadow of the monolith?

The public house had a sign over the door which had once read "Kookaburra" above a badly executed portrait of said bird, but both had been scorched by the sun into near invisibility. But as it was the only place of entertainment within a day's trek, such issues were minor indeed. And it was a quiet, friendly place. The *friendliness* came from the clientele; the *quiet* came from the patrolling Mozzies, which did not tolerate any kind of disturbance.

The barman immediately recognised him, as much from the fact that his shape momentarily cut off the sun as he paused in the doorway, as from his shadowed features.

'Greg!' he called. 'Good to see you. The usual, I suppose?'

'Yep,' Ferguson said, as a stool groaned under his weight. 'One for me, one for Sky, my old friend Schwartz.' He pushed some metal disks across the counter. It was a new development, which some people said could replace the usual barter, but Ferguson had little faith in the idea. Why would anyone choose a metal disk over a freshly-killed rabbit? As Schwartz stood in front of a row of beer barrels perched almost out of reach on a high shelf, Ferguson called, 'Hey, how come I never see you out in the sun, old friend Schwartz? Are you still an albino?'

'Doesn't make you a bad person,' the barman, called over his shoulder, risking being overgenerous with Ferguson's beer order.

A few minutes later, Ferguson was gazing into a chipped tankard containing what he and others called "beer." That weak, thin liquid would not have been recognised as such by earlier generations, but it was sufficiently different to water to merit its own name.

He poured Sky's beer into a plate and watched the animal lap up her drink with apparent relish. He grinned and rotated on the stool to face the barman.

'Is that beer ever going to get any better?' he said, careful to keep his tone sociable. He didn't want anyone getting alarmed.

The barman responded with his own grin; this topic of banter was familiar to both men.

'It's the best the house can offer,' he said. 'It's my only special brew: *Schwartz's Best Ale*, I call it.'

'Well, if it gets any worse, old friend Schwartz, you'll have to give *me* one of those disks to persuade me to drink it.'

Both men laughed. Sky had finished her beer and looked up at her owner with pleading eyes. Ferguson shook his head, but proceeded to order another tankard of Schwartz's Best Ale for himself.

'Don't want you getting drunk, do we, Old Girl?' was the only comfort he offered to the disappointed animal. Sky accepted the inevitable and, with her head between her paws, went to sleep.

Ferguson's tone became businesslike as he continued talking to Schwartz.

'Can you take any more of my mutton?' he said, between sips. 'I could do with the trade.'

Schwartz had also switched modes.

'You and a dozen others, Greg. I like you, and do as much business with you as I can, but I like other people around here as well. That's the trouble with me—I like everybody!'

Ferguson nodded. Schwartz was right; the township was too small for the number of sheep ranchers that had sprung up lately. Someone would have to go out of business. Although he knew it was unwise, he ordered a third beer and sat with his thoughts, morosely sipping his drink from time to time, wondering why life was so difficult, so repetitive and unrewarding. Then he frowned: that was the thirteen-year-old Greg Ferguson—not the man he was now.

He realised Schwartz had been talking to him for some time. 'What?' he said, suddenly appreciating he was slightly woozy from that third beer.

'I said, I was wrong to say I liked everybody,' the barman repeated. He jerked his head toward an unseen person over Ferguson's right shoulder. 'That's Karl Gottlieb. Best to keep on the right side of him.'

Ferguson half-turned and was surprised to see a man who was at least as big as himself. The man's clothes were torn in various places as if his bulk was escaping from clothing far too small. His face was sunburnt to almost the shade of the Old People's skin; or at least the part not hidden by a tangle of black hair was. He had two smaller men behind him; presumably his henchmen.

Ferguson returned to the last of his beer. It was a man, just a man. Gottlieb strode up to the bar, brushing against Ferguson as he came.

'Watch where you're sitting, mate,' he said as he passed. Ferguson said nothing. His beer was almost finished; he would soon be returning to the farmhouse to think about his future; or rather, trying to decide if there was any future. 'What about your men?' he heard Schwartz say, 'are they drinking?'

'They drink when I say they drink,' was the reply. Gottlieb held up a metal disk and pushed it just under Schwartz's nose, forcing him to pull his head back sharply. Ferguson noticed it was a peculiar yellow colour; a metal he had never seen before. 'Know what this is? No? Well, it's gold. Gold, my little friend. You haven't heard of it here in this arse-end of nowhere, but it's the future. Soon no-one will be using those stupid lead coins anymore, and miners like me will be kings. And you, my little friend, will be one of my serfs. Got that?'

Schwartz did not reply and went to one of the barrels on the shelf behind the bar, but not the one containing his eponymous ale, Ferguson noticed with a wry smile. Gottlieb took a deep draught of his beer, frowned and then spat it over Schwartz.

'What in the hells? Did I ask you to give me what you pissed out this morning, you bloody toad! Where's the beer I ordered?'

Ferguson decided enough was enough. He carefully rose to his feet, adjusting his stance to compensate for his wooziness.

'That's enough, cobber. No need to speak like that to someone just doing his job.'

Gottlieb spun around. His eyes betrayed a momentary surprise to see another pair on a level with his own, but he soon regained his swagger.

'What's it to you? I ordered a beer—not that midget's piss! Get back on your stool before I make you eat it!'

Ferguson shook his head. Fortunately, it was clearing rapidly from its fog.

'There's no need to speak like a bastard. I think you owe Mr. Schwartz an apology.'

He glanced at the bar counter to see how Schwartz was taking it, in time to see that gentleman disappearing below it.

'It's time you yokels learned who's in charge now,' Gottlieb said and took a step towards Ferguson. But in so doing, he stepped on one of Sky's sleeping paws. She yowled and leapt up, only to receive one of Gottlieb's boots in her ribs.

'Who let that mangy dingo in here?' he bellowed. 'This is a bar, not a bloody kennel!'

Ferguson grasped the collar of Gottlieb's dust-encrusted check shirt.

'Now you have to make two apologies.'

Gottlieb's expression was one of utter amazement; obviously no one had ever manhandled him quite so boldly before. His mouth worked furiously, but no intelligible sounds came out. Ferguson glanced back at the bar counter, but Schwartz had not yet surfaced. He turned back to Gottlieb and said, 'First apology is to Mr. Schwartz and the second is to my…' and then he stopped talking.

He stopped talking because a ham-sized fist had just crashed into his face, catching him expertly on the point of the chin. Ferguson felt as if he had just been struck by a sledgehammer, and crashed back onto the counter, the impact knocking a few tankards onto the floor and rattling some bottles stacked behind it. Ferguson wiped his hand over his split lips, tasting the metallic tang of his own blood. He looked up from his bloodied hand to see Gottlieb hurling himself at him and stepped aside just in time. His assailant, unable to adjust his trajectory, also crashed onto the counter, but this time, there were no more tankards to dislodge. With a roar, he turned to face

Ferguson but with the element of surprise having been lost, immediately experienced the sensation of someone else's ham-sized fist contacting a face at a high velocity.

The two men staggered into the centre of the room, the terrified clientele pulling back like a ripple in a pond, fleeing from a tossed stone. Gottlieb's cronies stayed nearest, obviously wondering whether their boss would praise them or blame them for interfering in the fight. In the end, they decided not to intervene, which was probably for the best because neither looked as if they could receive one of the blows being handed out and live.

Ferguson had not been a participant in that many fights, but was not completely inexperienced either. However, none of his previous opponents had been of Gottlieb's size and build. But he was learning fast. Tables and chairs were sent flying as if made of papier mâché, and both men's faces were taking on the appearance of crimson masks. But Ferguson realised that Gottlieb's fighting style was based entirely on his size and power, and he had not met another who could match him before. Gradually, Ferguson was finding his way through his opponent's guard more and more frequently, sending his rival's head snapping back under pile-driver impacts. Dimly through the tumult, he heard Sky madly barking. Then, through the grunts of laboured breathing and the thuds of blows, both men suddenly heard Schwartz yelling, 'Stop it, you idiots! The Mozzies will close the place down! I'll be out of a job!' The fight continued unabated. 'There'll be no more beer!'

Ferguson lowered his fists, deflected one of Gottlieb's punches with his forearm, and said, 'This is stupid. We can't lose this place. Let's continue this outside.'

Gottlieb, his breathing reduced to desperate gasps for oxygen, looked uncomprehending for a moment and then lowered his own fists.

'You're right. The beer is a wombat's piss, but it's better than nothing.'

Ferguson jerked his head in the direction of the open door.

'Outside?'

Both started for the exit, but one of the cronies shouted, 'No, Boss! We gotta meet that guy about the shipment!'

Gottlieb halted, wiped some blood from his mouth and looked back and forth between Ferguson and his underlings. He returned to Ferguson, who had decided to extend a hand to indicate "No Hard Feelings" and contemptuously knocked it away.

'I can't finish this now, whatever your name is.'

'Ferguson, Greg Ferguson.'

'I'll hunt you down, Ferguson, and I'll finish this. And you.' He looked his opponent up and down, measuring the muscles and tendons. 'You're a big man, mister, but I'll find a way to hurt you.' He looked around at the wreck of the bar room and the nervous throng of punters, slowly returning to their earlier positions. 'And when I hurt you, Ferguson, you will feel pain like you never believed you could.' He turned his head slightly toward the relieved sidekicks waiting behind him. 'Let's go, boys.'

TWO

Ferguson soon forgot about the incident in the Kookaburra: he had much more important things to think about, like what he was getting for his lamb and mutton. Sure, his face ached, and the blue and purple bruising took quite a while to fade away, but both disappeared eventually, returning his skin to its standard weather-beaten tan. His teeth had felt loose as well, but all had remained in their sockets and in the fullness of time they felt fine as well. And Gottlieb did not reappear at the pub, no doubt dissatisfied with the quality of the beer. Ferguson was both relieved and sorry: everyone needed to pull together in this savage land, and Gottlieb did not fit that pattern. But Ferguson was sure he could make the man see sense. When two men have fought each other to a standstill, a camaraderie born out of mutual respect often develops. But what really puzzled Ferguson was how they had fought so violently without the Mozzies intervening; they must have been busy elsewhere, he supposed.

Today, there was the promise of rain in the air, and a few nervous clouds had dared to intrude into the brilliant blue dome above him as he sat in his chair, surveying his territory. The chair, inexpertly constructed from bloodwood and red river gum timber, threatened to collapse at any moment. Sky had taken up position several yards away in case both man and chair crashed on top of her—an event she would be unlikely to survive.

However, he beckoned her to him and spent some minutes rubbing a hand over the coarse hair on her neck. Her eyes closed in silent pleasure.

'You know, Old Girl, I think it's time we did the neighbourly thing and paid a call on Mr Delgado. He's even older than you.'

Ferguson had not seen the man for several days, and Delgado had become something of a totem animal due to his age, for the elderly were not common in the cauldron that was the Red Centre. Ferguson was no more superstitious than the average farmer, but he had the nagging feeling that bad times would follow if Delgado was no more.

'Up we get,' he said and withdrew his hand from Sky's neck, much to her displeasure. It was a short walk for someone possessed of a stride as long as his, and he knocked gently on his neighbour's weathered and splintered door, fearing the worst. But after a few seconds, he heard the welcome noise of movement within. The door's top hinge had pulled away from the jamb, leaving it at an angle, and the occupant was having some trouble opening it. Ferguson decided not to help, in case the entire thing came away in his hands.

Delgado stood there momentarily, blinking in the savage sunlight, but the size of Ferguson's silhouette soon identified his visitor.

'Greg! Come on in! What brings you to my humble abode?'

Delgado was using his standard self-deprecating greeting, but in his case it was amply justified, for his abode was unquestionably humble. The walls had fissures and rents through which powerful beams of light, thickly populated with dust motes, were blazing. The furniture comprised two chairs and a table too lopsided to risk putting anything on it. Ferguson looked at the ancient chairs and then sat cross-legged on the floor, not wishing to deprive the old man of one of his items of furniture.

'I was worried about you,' he said. Even though he was sitting on the floor, his head was not much below his host's, who was now occupying one of the chairs.

Delgado waved a hand.

'Oh, I'm fine, just aches and pains. They mean I tend to stay put a lot these days. That's why I never visit you anymore. But can I get you some water? For the dog, if not for you.'

Ferguson knew better than to accept the offer: water was too precious to waste on social calls. But he was too curious about one aspect of Delgado to let the chance pass.

'Aches and pains, you say. How old are you, Mr Delgado?'

Delgado waved a hand again.

'Tush! We've known each other too long for that nonsense. The name's "Maurice".' He stopped. 'What was it you asked?'

'Your age, Maurice. How old are you? If you don't mind me asking.'

Delgado looked up at the ceiling, as if looking for the answer written there.

'How old am I? You know, I haven't thought about that for a long time. A long time.' Ferguson thought there was something birdlike in the quick, jerky movements Delgado was making as he thought. He studied the other's face, noting, even in the gloom, the crazed pattern of lines and wrinkles on the face, carved there by a pitiless sun as much as by age.

Delgado had reached a conclusion.

'Why, I must be sixty. Sixty. What do you think about that?'

Ferguson was impressed. He hadn't expected a number that large. A silence fell, one Ferguson found a little awkward. Delgado was the only old man he knew; Hells, he was probably the only old man anyone knew! Always at the back of Ferguson's mind were the mysterious words his mother had said to him during her last days on this earth. Had they been nothing more than the ramblings of a sick mind? Somehow, he could not believe that; his mother had spoken clearly and matter-of-factly on everything else during that period; why would she have been deranged on one particular issue? Could someone with Delgado's knowledge of the past also know something about the unknown *They*? And in so doing, also prove that his mother had not been raving.

But how to broach such a peculiar topic? He decided to ask, anyhow.

'Maurice, you've been around a long time, seen a lot of things come and go.'

Delgado raised a quizzical, snow-white eyebrow.

'Yes,' he said slowly. 'You're not getting personal, are you? I've already agreed I'm an old timer.'

'No, no, of course not. It's just you're a…a,' he searched his limited vocabulary for an appropriate word. '…a *unique* person. You must know a lot about things we youngsters don't.'

Delgado leant back with a near-toothless smile, obviously mollified.

'Yes, I have. Lots of things. Look, I can remember when the Cats were no trouble at all, just furry little things. So small you could make 'em scoot just by frowning at them.'

Ferguson smiled politely. He knew all about the supposed time when the Cats were just harmless annoyances, and half-believed it.

'Really? I didn't know that. But what about us, we people, we *humans?* Where did we come from?'

Ferguson's heart sank as he saw Delgado's expression; he obviously didn't understand the question.

'Well, you'd better ask the Old People that, Greg. They tell stories about the Great Father Spirit and the Young Goddess, who's supposed to have made us. You can believe that if you want to. I always say I do, if some of those people bring up the story. At least, I do if it's a nice young Sheila telling the tale!'

Ferguson sighed as quietly as he could. Dead End. His mother had never mentioned the Great Father Spirit, and from what he dimly remembered of the stories, it had only been the Old People who had been created in that mystic time.

Time to go.

He stood, but Delgado waved his hand again and said, 'Sit down, Greg. I have some old bits and pieces from when I was a boy. I don't know why I kept some of them as I threw most out. Space is very limited in my little house, you see.'

Ferguson sat down. It would be rude to leave now he had been asked to stay. Delgado went to the back of the room and started throwing some sheets around, muttering to himself. Ferguson heard him say, 'I could have sworn I left it here.' Minutes passed, but eventually, he returned carrying a small wooden box. It was chipped and splintered, so it was at least as old as Delgado.

Delgado sat with the box on his knees and, after struggling for a while, opened the box. He looked into it, squinting in the half-light.

'No, that's not it. Now, how did that get in there? Ah, how about this, Greg?'

He handed his guest a small, thin cylinder. Ferguson placed it on his palm and was amazed at how light it was. The translucent material stirred an almost buried memory from long ago, about a short tunnel that had been made of an unknown substance, smooth to the touch. He and a girl had traversed it and found a strange man at its end.

Who had helped his mother.

This small tube, however, was chipped along its length, with a ragged end as if the tip had been broken off. It looked hollow, but whatever had been inside it was long gone.

'What is it?'

'No idea. I was hoping you could tell me, as you're interested in the past.'

Ferguson handed the tube back. It was unusual, but told him nothing. The thing was just another object that defied an easy explanation. It really was time to go.

But Delgado hadn't finished. He handed Ferguson a bag that obviously held several small objects. This time, the contents were heavier.

'It's OK. You can open it.'

Ferguson loosened the drawstring and tipped a number of the objects onto his palm. They were small, grey metal disks. All but one, which was a dull yellow. Delgado pointed to it.

'That's my favourite. Pretty, isn't it?

Ferguson stared at the metal disks. They were almost identical to the ones he had seen in the Kookaburra, even the one Gottlieb had called "gold". His eyes narrowed in suspicion as he looked across at Delgado.

'You said these were old. But I've seen things that look just the same only recently.'

Delgado pulled himself straight, obviously stung by the implied doubt in Ferguson's words.

'They are old. My father gave me them, and he got them from his father. I don't know how my grandfather came by them.'

'But what are these things?'

Delgado shrugged.

'Not sure. My father said people used them instead of barter, but they didn't catch on. People went back to exchanging chickens and such like.'

Ferguson became still and silent. A long time ago, people had tried to introduce the concept of *money* but nothing had come from that innovation. They had even used gold.

And now people were doing it again—with no knowledge of it having been tried before, and abandoned. No one had ever mentioned money before its recent appearance; even Delgado knew nothing of it. Could everybody be living in a society which had not made any progress? How many times before Delgado's grandfather had the same thing been tried, abandoned, forgotten?

What else were people doing over and over again, without knowing they were trapped in an endless cycle? Had an earlier version of Ferguson walked these sands with an earlier version of Sky?

And so on—endlessly?

And then Ferguson shook his head, his mind recoiling from the possibility it had briefly entertained. It was too soon to reach any such ridiculous conclusion; perhaps there had only been one earlier attempt to develop a money-based economy. That would not be too unlikely. And he knew one thing: he had to get out of Delgado's hut and the unwelcome, disturbing concerns the old man was unknowingly creating. With some difficulty, he succeeded in standing upright again, trying not to hold onto the furniture for fear it might come apart in his hands. He avoided Delgado for the same reason.

'Going so soon? You've got a Blackfellow to help you now, haven't you? What's the matter, Greg? You look worried.'

'I'm OK. But there've been reports of those Devils out in the Bush, near my flocks. Better check them out.'

Delgado chuckled.

'They're well-named, those things. Have you ever heard them devouring a 'roo? They can strip it to the bone in minutes. I don't know which is worse—them or the Cats. Funny, we call them "Devils", but my father says that word used to mean something else when he was a boy. Some kind of evil spirit, but the Old People hadn't heard of it.'

Ferguson nodded politely. He knew if he stayed any longer, Delgado would begin an interminable series of stories about his father or, even worse, his grandfather.

And so he shook his head at Delgado's increasingly desperate pleas for him to stay, and emerged back into the cruel blaze of the sun. He had a lot on his mind and needed time to think.

The sheep could take care of themselves for a while.

THREE

Ferguson could not understand why Delgado's ramblings had disturbed him so intensely. It was as if the old man's words had been some kind of key that unlocked a fear that had lain slumbering in his subconscious for all of his adult life. Yet the man's words had been simple enough: why had they caused such a reaction?

He forced his mind back to the workaday world. There were real, not imaginary, problems for him to deal with. His fellow farmers had reported a troupe of Devils had moved into the area. And that was genuinely worrying. The carnivorous creatures were, on average, smaller than Sky but were fierce and implacable hunters. They could tear a sheep to crimson shreds in minutes. He shuddered to think what such creatures could do if they invaded his territory.

As he approached the homestead, he spied Wygu descending the slope from the sheep pens. He was carrying his usual spear and woomera, but there was no trace of red on the spear.

'Everything all right?' Ferguson called. 'No sign of them?'

Wygu knew exactly what the term referred to.

'No, Greg. All is quiet.'

As the two men came together, Ferguson saw before him a fine example of Old People manhood: not much shorter than himself, well-muscled and with no trace of superfluous fat anywhere on his body. Wygu had straighter teeth than Ferguson— after the latter's unfortunate encounter with Gottlieb—and they flashed almost pure white in his mahogany features as the two men slapped each other on the back.

'Glad to hear it. I don't know who named those creatures, but he did a good job. I don't want them anywhere near my land.'

Wygu nodded his partial agreement, but said, 'Yes, but they are of the land. They belong here. Sometimes I think we don't.'

Ferguson shrugged and made his way into the farmhouse, Wygu following.

'I think you mean the Colonists, as you call us, don't you?'

He tried to keep his tone light, but was aware a slight edge had entered it: he didn't want anyone defending those creatures. Or implying that the Colonists weren't of the land.

The older man sat, divesting himself of the weapons.

'I don't mean to be disrespectful. I know some tribes believe you pale men are not of the land, but I am not one of them. And even if you are less ancient than my own kind, what does it matter? We are all one people now.'

Ferguson grinned as the tension evaporated. He didn't know why he had taken Wygu's words so badly; it wasn't as if he was unaware of the other man's views. What he did know was that Wygu was the last man he should pick a fight with—two strong men were better than one in this savage land.

'Sorry to be so snappy. I've got a lot on my mind. Look, I'm going down to the Kookaburra, seeing as you say there's no danger. What say you join me this time?'

Wygu looked doubtful.

'That drink you call "beer". I think if we sprayed it on the Devils, we'd see the last of them.'

They looked at each other and then burst out laughing.

And when they were in the Kookaburra together, Wygu did have a little beer, though not without much face-pulling—not all of it for comic effect.

'You Colonists must have done something very bad to be punished like this,' Wygu observed, leaving a substantial amount of liquid in his tankard as he pushed it away. 'My people ferment honey. You should try it.'

Ferguson found he had no interest in starting a debate about the differences between alcoholic beverages. Instead, his new concern returned to trouble him.

'Have you, or your people, noticed many changes in the way things are done around here? How our way of life has changed?'

Wygu looked surprised by the sudden change in conversation.

'No. Have you?'

'No. But the Cats, they are bigger—that's a change, isn't it?'

'Yes. But we have a story that the Cats became too large and fierce and Nepelle killed all the big ones and just let the little ones live.'

Ferguson stared at the other.

'What—you're saying the Cats started small, became big, went small, and now they're getting big again?'

Wygu shrugged.

'That's the story.' He looked deep into Ferguson's eyes, only slightly above his own. 'What is this? Are you laughing at my people's legends, because if you are…'.

'No, of course not! It's just…just.' *How to explain this new obsession?* 'Just something I started wondering about, that's all. No offence intended.'

He broke eye contact and stared down at the worn and chipped counter where his own drink rested.

The wrong answer. Once again, a lack of any real change had been the message hidden within Wygu's simple reply.

Nothing was changing, except in a cyclical fashion.

Big—small—big again.

No currency—currency—no currency…

Why had no one else noticed this?

Ferguson felt his worry squirming in the base of his mind like a grub preparing to burst out of a flower bud. He turned from Wygu to the barman. Perhaps Schwartz would be more helpful.

'You were here when I first started drinking. How long have you been here?'

Schwartz shrugged.

'Oh, a long time. I can't remember.'

'What did you do before you were a barman?'

'Oh, I don't know. I've always been a barman.'

'Seen many changes here?'

'Like what?'

'New ways of doing things. New ideas.'

'New ways of doing things? Why would we need them? What's wrong with what we've got now?'

Ferguson sighed.

'OK.'

'You know what's wrong with you, Greg?'

'I know you're itching to tell me.'

'Big strong man like you. Surrounded by nothing but sheep. You need a woman. Preferably a big strong woman, so you don't crush her.'

They both laughed, but Ferguson's rang a little hollow. Schwartz had expertly changed the subject. He looked hard at the barman and then turned to face the rest of the clientele. Blank stares met his own questing stare. Suddenly, he felt he had wandered onto a stage in the middle of a slow-moving play and all those meeting his gaze were simply characterless actors.

Abruptly, he felt no interest in any more beer. The barman looked surprised as Ferguson pushed the tankard towards him, without indicating a refill was required. Schwartz opened his mouth to enquire after Ferguson's health, but his erstwhile clients, including Sky, were already heading for the door. Schwartz picked up the tankards and looked at the departing figures. Two powerful men, one powerful dog.

He looked long and hard.

But his face was without expression.

***

Wygu tapped Ferguson on the shoulder.

'I think we should stop for a moment.'

He indicated a large, flat-topped boulder nearby with his spear point. Ferguson looked surprised, but complied.

'What is wrong with you, friend Greg? There is something preying on your mind; I know it.'

Ferguson shrugged.

'It's nothing, really. Nothing at all.'

He gestured to Sky to come to him, and sat, stroking the animal and looking out over the red desert.

'Come on, Greg. We've known each other for long enough now. Tell me what is troubling you.'

Ferguson sat silently for a while and then, still without looking at his companion, took a deep breath and began to speak.

'I've been thinking about what my mother said to me long ago; twelve years ago, in fact.'

'And?'

'She said we were put in this land by some powerful force, something that keeps itself hidden from us, but still watches and controls us.'

Wygu nodded.

'Yes, of course, we also believe that. I am of the Anangu people and we know we have lived in this land since what you call the Dreamtime, which we correctly call Tjukurpa, many, many thousands of years ago. There is nothing to trouble anyone in such knowledge. We know that was when we were put upon this earth and given the duties of protecting Uluru and Kata Tjuta. But the powers that did those things are not hidden, Greg; they are everywhere— in the sky, in the clouds, in Kata Tjuta. We are never without them.'

Ferguson frowned, his eyes focused on infinity.

'Yes, I know of the Dreamtime. But Wygu, were all of us brought onto the earth at that time? We Colonists—there is something different about us.

Why do we have a different name to you? Have we also been here for many, many thousands of years?'

It was Wygu's turn to frown.

'There are people who say you are not of the earth, that you came to this land not long ago and tried to dispossess us, but I do not believe such tales. They are put about by bad men who seek to drive barriers between us. We are all the same people: two legs, two hands, two eyes. What differences there may be are nothing. Would you say a thorny Devil is not a true one of its kind because it has a different number of spikes from another? Of course not.'

Ferguson finally turned and looked at his companion.

'I'm glad of your words, Wygu. We are all the same people at root, just as you say. But there is another reality, and it is not captured in your Tjukurpa. And I say that not to insult you; the Old People's memories go a long way back. But there is something hidden from us. Every day, I am more certain of that.'

'But why do you say that? There are powers greater than men, but they do not hide themselves from us, to trick us and make us fools.'

Ferguson grasped the flesh on Sky's neck as he struggled with his thoughts, more strongly than he had intended, causing the animal to yelp and look at him reproachfully.

'Wygu, I realised recently that this world of ours is static: nothing changes, nothing develops. Ideas are created, forgotten, and then created anew. There is no memory of past achievements because there are no past achievements.'

'Now, you are indeed talking like a Colonist. Why should things change? We Anangu have been living the same lives as our ancestors did when they first awakened. We are at peace with the land to which we must return, and that is the life we are meant to live. Anything else is foolishness.'

Ferguson shrugged again, and a brief smile played on his features, betraying an inner struggle.

'You must be right. Perhaps I've been placing too much importance on the words of a woman who was about to return to the land. As you say, it is foolishness.'

Wygu was about to reply when Sky suddenly gave a deep-throated growl and leapt to her feet, hair bristling, teeth fully displayed. The men also jumped up and stood scanning the landscape with eyes shielded from the westering sun.

'What…?' Ferguson said.

Wygu pointed at a nearby bush.

'There. Something…'

He did not have time to complete the sentence. Without further warning, a black animal shot from the bush like a thunderbolt, accompanied by a terrifying screech. Big though he was, Ferguson was knocked aside by the onslaught. He soon understood that he had not been the target of the attack, and also realised the identity of the assailant: the ruthless carnivore known, for good reasons, as a "Devil."

Fierce though the creatures were, they did not normally attack grown humans. But this one apparently had not heard of that particular rule for it had decided to make Wygu its evening meal. The force of the impact had knocked him onto his back and only his spear shaft, jammed between the ravening jaws, had saved him from fatal injury. But that would not be for long; the Devil's bite is one of the strongest known and the shaft was already splintering. Ferguson regained his balance and rushed at the creature, hands spread wide to grasp the stocky neck. A putrid stink assailed his nostrils as his fingers sank through the coarse, wiry black hair onto and into the flesh below. Immediately, the Devil bucked and thrashed under the piston-like driving force of those hands, but suddenly it twisted and Ferguson was looking into its enraged face. It was like trying to hold living lightning as it fought to free itself.

Abruptly, it succeeded and its explosive power knocked Ferguson backwards onto the stony ground. Now it would be his turn to feel the crushing strength of those mighty jaws. He raised his arms to catch the animal before it reached his face.

But it was not to be.

Another creature flashed into his view as Sky leapt at the Devil as it was completing its trajectory onto Ferguson. There was a dreadful crunching noise as the Devil's skull gave way under Sky's closing jaws. Another terrifying screech from the creature, and then it lay lifeless at Ferguson's feet.

Neither he nor Wygu moved for some minutes, so sudden was the return of quiet normality after the horror of those few minutes that they could not truly believe that the incident was over. Then, both men rose unsteadily, checking themselves for wounds.

Amazingly, there were none.

Wygu looked at Ferguson and showed him the spear with its useless, splintered shaft.

'That could have been me.' He crossed to the other and reached for a hand. 'Thank you, friend Greg. You saved my life.'

Ferguson shook his head.

'I did nothing of the sort.' He turned to Sky, who was prodding the Devil's corpse with her nose, checking for signs that the creature was shamming. 'It was Sky. Come here, girl.'

The animal obeyed and Ferguson squatted in front of her.

'You saved both our lives, Old Girl.' He rubbed the bitch's head, looking deep into calm brown eyes. 'I'll never forget what you did. Woe betide any man who tries to hurt you. I'll kill him without a second's thought!'

They left the Devil to the buzzards and kites and resumed their journey to their farm. In the hazy distance, the dying sun spread subtle tints of ochre over the tremendous rock.

FOUR

Months passed. Wygu warned Ferguson that he would soon have to return to his tribe, for his eldest son was about to undertake the ceremony of Walkabout and would soon become a man. He also missed the musicality of his native language and wanted to hear his true name spoken.

But because of his imminent departure, he continued his teaching of those parts of his people's traditions which were permissible for the ears of a Colonist. And so, Ferguson slowly found himself more and more at peace, knowing that each and every event and action was bound up in laws created before the foundations of the earth were laid. He learned how, on passing from an earthly life, a human could become a star, the curve of a cloud, or a flicker of light from the ripples of a windswept billabong.

But he also knew that his desire to understand, to *know*, was not fully met by these teachings, that his hunger for the truth had only been pushed down into the depths of his subconscious where it circled endlessly, like a brooding predator in a deep darkness. And although he did not consciously rake over the words of his dying mother and tried to think no more of the unknown *they*, he knew the need to do so was only slumbering.

But with the powers of four strong arms, the farm thrived and Ferguson added pigs and poultry to his flocks. Life was good. The locals had banded together and driven the Devils out of the area. People had come to accept the new monetary system of commerce.

Even Schwartz's beer seemed to taste better.

'So, tell me more,' Ferguson said one evening. The sky had taken on a purple cast and the great rock glowed like a dying coal on the horizon. 'I want to hear more about Liru and Woma. The role of the Rainbow Serpent in Tjukurpa.'

Wygu shook his head.

'No. I have told you all that is fit for your ears. But my silence is not because of anything you have done. It is because you are not Anangu.'

'Then I can never hear all the stories you could tell me.'

'No. I am sorry, friend Greg.'

The pair fell silent. A bright star appeared in the darkening sky.

'Then perhaps I can't find what I need to know in your teachings. I had hoped I could. That my mind would finally be at rest.'

'I don't understand.'

Suddenly, Ferguson violently clenched his fists and turned in his chair so he was looking full face at the other.

'What do you know of goannas?'

'Goannas? You mean *tinka*. I have told you of their legends. That was not forbidden.'

Ferguson's eyes were holding a stare Wygu had not seen for some time; his features had become drawn and tense.

'Is there anything special about goannas in this part of the land? Anything at all?'

'I've told you all I know about tinka. I have no more. You must remember I come from many miles away.'

Ferguson turned away; it was as if Wygu no longer existed, that he was alone with his fierce yearnings. His eyes sought the sky.

'Why did she mention the goanna? It was almost the very last thing she said. Then she said "Tail." Why mention that particular part?'

Wygu was silent. He knew the questions were not directed at him. In increasing alarm, he watched as Ferguson leapt to his feet, bringing a mighty fist down on his chair. Splinters flew.

'What was she trying to tell me?'

Hesitantly, Wygu rose and carefully placed a hand on the other's shoulder.

'Friend Greg, I thought you had conquered these demons.'

Ferguson continued to look up into the darkening sky.

'So had I. Oh, don't get me wrong, Wygu: your words have been a comfort to me. Knowing that everything is connected, like parts of a tremendous tapestry, there is comfort in that. But for all our friendship, you have made it clear that there are many things you can't tell me, that it is forbidden to tell me. Although I am your friend, I will always be an outsider. I can't be born again as one of the Anangu.'

Wygu bowed his head.

'I wish you had not said that, Greg, for you force me to speak the truth. And that truth says there will always be a void between us, one that cannot be crossed.' He motioned to Ferguson's chair. 'Sit down, my friend; there is something I wish to ask you.'

Ferguson complied and then raised an eyebrow.

'And that thing is?'

'This is not easy for me, friend Greg, but you are a strong man at the peak of his physical powers. But you are alone in a way that I am not. When I return to the tribe, there will be a woman waiting for me. But you do not have a woman of your own. It is not right that a man like you should not have a woman.'

Ferguson was silent.

'Is it possible that you do not like women? That is a choice that many make.'

Ferguson gave a short, dry laugh.

'Oh, I like them all right. I am not totally unfamiliar with what a man and a woman can do together. But as for one of my own—there is no one in this area that I could want to always have with me. And so I must remain alone, taking my pleasures where and when I can.'

Wygu sighed.

'Then I can help you no longer. A few more of your weeks, and then I must leave you. I am sorry, friend Greg.'

There was no more conversation, and for a while the two men sat together, watching as the stars emerged from their hiding places.

And then they said goodnight to each other.

***

The time for Wygu's departure came ever nearer. Ferguson found himself thinking about his future once again. Although he had spoken the truth to his companion, he still felt that his life was missing some vital element, without which he would never be whole. Still, the mystery of his mother's last words often stalked his dreams and forced him to wake in the darkness, leaving him red-eyed and irritable in the morning. Wygu knew when it was best to say as little as possible during those periods, and the men would attend to their chores in a strange silence.

But now, they were staring at a sight that had shocked them both into silence. It was a ewe's head, crudely torn from its bloodied body and stuck on one of the enclosure's fence posts.

'Not the work of a Devil or a Cat,' Wygu said.

'Please don't state the obvious,' Ferguson snapped. 'This is the work of a man. And when I find him, I'll stick his head on a pole.'

'But who would do this? Not one of my people. We have no great love for these farm creatures, but we have too much respect for all life to do such a thing.'

Ferguson removed the head and stared into its dull eyes. A suspicion had formed, but he wanted more evidence. He looked around, searching for some clue, some evidence of who the perpetrator might be.

And found it.

On one of the barbs of the enclosing fence was a small piece of fabric. He examined it—clearly a piece torn from a check shirt.

He whirled around and commanded Sky to sniff it.

'Can you find the piece of shit this piece of shirt belongs to?'

The animal could not respond in words, but her whole body stiffened as she pushed her nose into the cloth. Then she sat on her haunches, looking up at her master with eyes that were bright.

That was enough for Ferguson.

He jerked his head toward the sweltering lowlands and said simply, 'Let's go, Old Girl.'

'I'll come with you,' Wygu said, but Ferguson raised a calloused palm toward him.

'No. If it's who I think it is, it's between him and me. You've got enough work to keep you busy here; get on with it.'

And with that, Wygu was left watching the man and animal descend the slope until their figures blurred into the desiccated red landscape. And then he shrugged and returned to his chores.

Sky led the way through the hardly-yielding thorn bushes; her nose held an inch or so above the parched dust. Ferguson had often wondered at her near-miraculous tracking powers, but never had he wanted more for her to succeed than he did that day. They crossed mile after mile of the pitiless terrain until a pile of grey granite boulders came into view, many times the height of a man. Sky's pace immediately sped up, forcing Ferguson into a near run. His face itself took on a granite hardness.

His quarry was close.

Ferguson and his tracker climbed slowly into the mass of rocks, forcing themselves between gaps only just big enough to permit Ferguson's bulk to pass through. They reached the top of the little hill, cloven in two by a narrow but deep ravine. Squinting against the sun's blaze streaming from the naked granite, he searched for his foe.

It was then he heard Sky give a deep growl, and was instantly aware of something behind him.

There was a flash of pain and then darkness.

He could only have been out for a few minutes, but he awoke to find his hands and ankles crudely bound with some plant twine. A voice behind him called, 'It's OK, boss! He's back.'

He rolled over from his supine position and managed to shuffle into a sitting stance. A pair of legs moved into his vision, and looking up, he recognised one of Gottlieb's goons.

'You!' Ferguson said. 'Where's that fucking swine of a boss of yours?'

'Here I am, Ferguson!' a voice called from the other side of the narrow ravine. 'I knew your mutt could track me down from that piece of shirt I left behind. Good plan, eh? And you walked right into it.'

Ferguson turned his aching head—and there was Gottlieb on the other side of the cleft. But he had one foot on Sky's head as the animal lay before him.

And that head had the tinge of blood on it.

Even though she was still breathing, Ferguson's vision swam into a red mist.

'You let Sky go or...'

'You'll *what*? You're doing nothing, pal, but watch me and the boys have a little fun. At your expense, of course. Now watch this.'

In cold horror, Ferguson watched as Gottlieb withdrew a long-bladed knife from his shirt sleeve and held it triumphantly above his head. The light blazed from the bright metal like a second sun.

And then he drove the knife deep into Sky's neck

And then into her chest.

And then her abdomen.

The unconscious animal made no sound, but shook and twitched.

And then was still.

Ferguson's cry of grief and impotent rage echoed among the boulders. Then his head slumped onto his chest. He dimly heard three sets of laughter; two near, one slightly farther away.

'What now, boss?' he heard one of the voices ask.

'Just hold him there. The dog's a goner. I'll be over now.'

But the penetrant grief subsided in Ferguson's skull. Sky was dead, and he would never walk with her again. Now, there was only rage and hatred. But it was a controlled hatred, a planning, calculating rage.

He tested his bonds. Just the simple, twisted fronds of some desert plant. Little tensile strength. The knots were loose and amateurish, obviously done in a hurry. He drew in a deep breath, down into the very ends of his alveoli. He tensed his muscles in preparation. Then he drove the full power of his great body into opening his legs and arms.

His bonds parted like tissue paper, and the next second he was on his feet, staring at his horrified captors. One hurriedly lifted a knife.

A rock-like fist sent him spinning away. The other turned to flee. Ferguson caught him from behind, one arm clamped around his scrawny neck. Another hand descended onto his skull. There was a violent twisting motion, then the unpleasant noise of tissue and fascia and vertebrae yielding under the applied force.

Ferguson dropped the corpse and spun around to face his real opponent. But Gottlieb had already crossed the gap and was directly behind him, knife descending in a killing strike. Ferguson jumped backwards, and the knife cut only through air, not flesh.

The two men stared at each other. Was there a glimpse of doubt in Gottlieb's eyes, now that the plan had gone so terribly wrong, now that he faced an unchained opponent?

As for Ferguson, a tremendous heat was blasting through his arteries. He felt power building in him like the first tentative shock of the coming earthquake. Power to toss boulders like thistledown and rip them into dust seemed to have been granted to him.

Gottlieb raised his knife arm again. Ferguson watched it descend, seemingly in slow motion, and casually reached out and seized the other's wrist, slamming it against the nearby boulder with almost superhuman power. Gottlieb's hand opened and the knife fell to the dust. Ferguson kicked it away.

There would be no swift end for this foe.

Gottlieb sent a barrage of blows toward Ferguson; some did not connect, some did. It mattered not; Ferguson did not feel them.

His own replies were blows to shame a sledgehammer, and each one sent Gottlieb reeling backwards toward the waiting ravine. As the other tottered on the lip of the cleft, Ferguson grabbed him by his tattered collar and raised a killing fist above Gottlieb's head.

'This is for Sky.'

But then the conflict was abruptly ended. Ferguson's fist did not crash into the other's face. Both men turned their heads to one side, with uncertain, questing expressions.

There was a loud humming, buzzing noise coming towards them. Ferguson released Gottlieb, and both men stepped away from the ravine.

'Mozzie,' Gottlieb said, wonderingly.

And so it was. They saw a man-sized black object, with wings blurred by their rapid motion, rise above the edge of the hill and come directly towards them. They fell back, away from the intruder. Ferguson backed into a cleft between two massive boulders, but Gottlieb stood motionless, staring up at the invader, apparently mesmerised. Ferguson watched as the Mozzie halted a few yards above Gottlieb's upturned face. Its wings were just a grey blur as it hovered. Then there was a flash, and for an instant, both man and Mozzie were connected by a thin line of green radiance.

Gottlieb fell like a dead man.

The Mozzie turned and Ferguson realised it knew exactly where he was, and because he had backed into the cleft, he could not escape.

It flew towards him.

There was a green flash.

FIVE

Ferguson's eyes flickered open: someone was calling him from far away. He closed his eyes again. It was too much trouble to keep them open. Now someone was shaking him and calling his name!

'Greg! Greg! Wake up, what's happened?'

Ferguson finally managed to force his eyes to stay open. He saw it was Wygu who was shaking him. *What did the man want now, for gods' sake?*

'What do you want?' he said. His mouth felt parched and his lips seemed to be swollen and reluctant to part.

'*What do I want?*' Wygu gasped. His eyes were wide with astonishment and, perhaps, concern. 'You went looking for the man who beheaded the sheep, didn't you? Did you find him? You've been gone for two days! And where's Sky?'

Ferguson closed his eyes.

Why didn't people mind their own business and just leave him alone? He didn't have time for all this bother.

'Just leave me alone,' he mumbled, and adjusted his position in the chair, turning away from his interrogator.

The shaking resumed.

'Wake up, damn you! What's happened to you, man?'

Ferguson stretched and accepted that he would not have any more sleep.

'What's it to you? What are you—my mother?'

Wygu reached for the other chair and drew it closer so he was sitting directly in front of his friend.

'Greg, this isn't right. You're not right. Something has happened to you. Why didn't you call for me when you returned?'

Ferguson waved a hand, nonchalantly.

'Questions, questions. Always with the questions. Don't you have some work to do?'

Wygu reached over and clasped the other's arms, forcing the men to face each other.

'You went to find a man. You took your dog. Now, you're back without the dog and behaving as if none of that happened. But something did. What was it?'

Ferguson gently removed Wygu's hands from his arms.

'Please don't do that again; I'm not a child. As to what happened...' His brow crinkled. *What had happened?* He thought deeply for a minute or two. 'I...I found him—I think. Yes, I found him.' He paused. 'Oh no—I think we fought. I think I hit him. I hope he isn't hurt.'

Wygu's eyes widened to their absolute maximum.

'You hope you didn't hurt him? When I last saw you, you were going to tear him apart!'

Ferguson shook his head.

'Oh no, I would never say that. That's not nice, not nice at all.'

Ignoring Ferguson's prohibition, Wygu clasped the other's arms again.

'Greg—*where is Sky?*'

Ferguson thought for a while. Then: 'Oh, yes. I've got it now. It's dead.'

Wygu rocked back. His face had become a hideous mask of horrified disbelief.

'Dead? *Sky is dead?* And you don't care? You should be tearing the stars down in your anger, not just sitting there, half asleep!'

Ferguson shrugged.

'It was only a dog. One must keep a sense of proportion, don't you think?'

Wygu jumped to his feet and backed away, his narrowed pupils surrounded by the stark white of fear.

'You are not Greg Ferguson. You can't be. Some spirit must be controlling your body!'

Ferguson also rose, though slowly and calmly.

'Well, that's enough of that. Is there anything to eat?'

Wygu strove to control the turmoil swirling within his skull and eventually succeeded. This was not his friend. Something had happened to him. The Anangu knew of such happenings, and there were procedures that could be taken to drive the evil spirit out. It was the only explanation. But what to do? He had no direct experience of the rituals necessary to cleanse the soul. His people were too far away. To seek their help would mean leaving Ferguson alone in this state for weeks. But then his face lightened, as if a thought had come to him.

'I'll get us something,' he said, disappearing into the galley kitchen.

After some time, both men were working their way through a stew of mutton and kangaroo. Ferguson said it was tasteless, something Wygu knew was untrue, as it was a meal they often enjoyed together. Afterwards, Ferguson started to rise, stating that it was time for another nap.

But Wygu stopped him.

'Wait. You have forgotten dessert.'

Ferguson stared at him. His lethargy did not extend to cloudiness of mind, apparently.

'I don't know that word. But whatever it is, we don't have it.'

'We do now. Here.' And Wygu handed him a small, greyish cylinder of some pliable material. 'Put it under your lip or against your cheek, and chew it slowly.'

Despite looking extremely doubtful, Ferguson complied. Then, his face contorted, and he inserted a finger to remove the object.

'It's horrible!'

'No, Greg, trust me! Keep chewing; you'll like it soon, believe me!'

Ferguson stared at Wygu with a motionless face for perhaps a minute, and then began to chew slowly. He sat in his usual chair, facing the window, and chewed the strange dessert for another half hour.

Then he was asleep again. But a sleep with unusually deep and steady breathing.

Wygu disposed of the wad that Ferguson had spat out, drew his chair nearer his friend, and sat close to him, waiting.

The shadows lengthened.

✳✳✳

Greg, can you hear me?

Yes, I can hear you.

It is Wygu. I want you to think back to what happened two days ago. Can you do that for me?

A PAUSE. THEN:

Yes, I can do that.

You left here with Sky, searching for the man who had killed the sheep. Did you find him?

Yes. It was Gottlieb.

I thought as much. What happened when you met him?

He was there with his two underlings. I killed one. I'm not sure about the other.

And Gottlieb?

We fought.

And you killed him?

No. Something happened.

What happened?

A PAUSE.

Come on, Greg. You can do this. What happened?

It was... A Mozzie. It came over the edge and did something to Gottlieb. Then it came to me. And did something to me.

What did it do?

There was a flash, and I couldn't move. I couldn't even move my eyes. But I knew it had picked me up somehow, and we were flying.

Flying? What, like a buzzard?

Yes. I could see the ground a long way below me. The thornbushes were just little grey patches. Just them and the desert.

A PAUSE.

And then?

We came down, and the side of a hill opened and we went in. And there was... there was...a bright light in my eyes and something on my head. And I could hear a voice in my head, telling me something.

What was it telling you?

'No fighting. No struggle. Just be peaceful. Be quiet. Do not struggle. Do not question. Just accept. Everything will be right in the end. All is as it should be."

And Greg, do you believe everything is what it should be? What about Sky? Where is she?

Ferguson screamed.

***

Wygu stared down at Ferguson. His friend was covered in sweat and trembling. His eyes were wide and wild.

'What did you do to me?'

Wygu helped him to his feet and guided him back to his chair. He could feel the muscles beneath his fingers rapidly clenching and unclenching, rippling down Ferguson's body in waves of clonic shock.

'What did you do to me?' Ferguson repeated, a pleading look on his sweat-streaked features.

'Take it easy. I did what I had to do.'

'I repeat: what did you do to me?'

'What I had to do. I brought you back.'

Ferguson's head drooped to his chest, as if it had suddenly become too heavy to hold upright.

'Explain, before I get up from this chair and kill you.'

Wygu grinned. That was more like the old Ferguson!

'There have been tales of Mozzies taking people away, but I did not believe them. Usually, they simply knock people out and leave them to recover, as if they have taken too much of your dreadful beer. But the Elders of my tribe have said that sometimes people disappear after a Mozzie has visited them, and when they come back—they are different. Different like you, friend Greg.'

Ferguson's head rose so he could look directly at Wygu.

'Like me? What do you mean?'

'Not wanting to do anything. I'm more educated than you, Greg, so here is a word you may not know: *Apathetic.*' Seeing his friend's puzzled look, he continued, 'Synonyms are *dispirited, indifferent, emotionless.* You were all of those things. Your lack of concern for Sky told me something bad had happened to you. I used her name to lever open your mind.'

Ferguson's lips appeared to tremble for a moment.

'Sky. She really is dead?'

'I assume so. I was not there.'

Ferguson took a deep breath.

'Yes. It was Gottlieb. He killed her. He and I have unfinished business.'

'Sky was the key I needed to unlock your mind.'

Ferguson shook his head.

'No, there was more to it than just Sky. You did something to me. Was it that revolting thing you made me chew?'

Wygu smiled tolerantly.

'That "revolting thing", as you call it, was *Pituri*—a herb we Old People use to lift the curtain that hides this world from the next, and allows us to venture into it for short periods. We mix it with the ash from certain trees, whose names I shall not give you, and chew it. I gave you a particularly strong mixture, so strong in fact, I now have none to give my son. But it allowed me into your mind and helped me to undo the bad thing that was done to you.'

'*The bad thing*,' Ferguson mused. 'But why was it done to me?'

'I do not know, friend Greg.'

Ferguson rose to his feet. He was steady again, and the twitches had ceased. But as he looked at Wygu, his hands balled into fists of awesome power. 'But much more importantly: *who* did it to me?'

'I cannot answer that, Greg.'

'No. Neither can I. But I will find out.' He gave a sudden roar and brought a fist hammering down onto his chair. It splintered. 'I will find out!'

SIX

'There is a great mystery here.'

Ferguson looked up.

'No shit. What part of my story do you find the most mysterious? That I couldn't kill Gottlieb?'

'Please don't be facetious, friend Greg. My people have known that sometimes Mozzies take people away, but when they return, they can never tell where they have been.'

'Neither can I. I saw no one. Neither Colonist nor one of your people.'

'You're missing the important part: you said the hill "opened up". What exactly did you see?'

Ferguson stopped trying to repair the chair he had broken and sat back on his haunches, looking up at Wygu.

'It's difficult. I couldn't move my head. I only saw what was directly in front of me. The Mozzie held me still in a tight grip as we flew. But as it turned I saw a hill and then, suddenly, a black shape appeared on its side. I took that to be a kind of door. It must have been, for a few seconds later we were inside a sort of cave. Then everything went fuzzy.'

'What kind of cave? Like ones the river makes, with stalactites hanging down?'

'If that's what they're called, then no. It looked like a space men could have made; smooth walls, flat floor.'

Wygu was silent for a matter of seconds. Then: 'There is something badly wrong here. Such caves should not exist. My people have not made them; neither has yours. Perhaps all of us have accepted too many things as natural, as normal, when they are not.'

An odd silence followed Wygu's words; the air felt as if it had suddenly cooled and now held an undischarged electric potential, one searching for a way to ground itself in a blinding flash. Wygu's gaze followed Ferguson as the latter rose slowly from his squat by the ruined chair.

'You know what I am saying, Greg. You have told me your own thoughts about the way things are, on many occasions. That you think something is hidden from us.'

Ferguson's features displayed a hunted look, as if he were being confronted by thoughts he wanted no part of.

'Yes, you're right, of course, you're right. A Cat or a Devil just wants to eat me, but the Mozzies—what do they want? They are not like the other animals.'

'In fact—not like any animal at all,' Wygu finished for him.

Ferguson stood silently for a while, reminding Wygu of an extremely overlarge child confronted with a problem beyond its years. Ferguson opened his mouth but had just begun to speak when both men heard a thin, piping voice calling from the doorway.

'Hello, Greg? Are you there? Are you alright?'

It was Delgado, and Ferguson welcomed him in. As only one chair had survived Ferguson's outburst, he sat down while the others stood before him.

'I'd heard you'd gone missing, Greg, and came to see if your Blackfel...' He caught Wygu's disapproving glare and hurriedly changed tack, 'if your serv... I mean, if...'

Ferguson took pity on the old man and said his words for him, changing his phraseology to a more acceptable version.

'If *Wygu* knew where I was.'

'Yes, exactly! That's what I was trying to say; sometimes, I forget there are so many different ways of saying things these days. Everything's changing.'

Wygu brought a packing case from the back room and the younger men positioned themselves on it. Ferguson raised a quizzical eyebrow as he studied Delgado.

'*Everything's changing?* That's not what you told me a while back.'

Delgado looked flustered, giving off the air of someone who had become unused to long sentences.

'It's ways of speaking, I mean. Mainly about the—uh—Old People. Words we can't use about them anymore. That's all I meant to say.'

Wygu leaned forward.

'I understand you talked to Greg some time ago and came to a different conclusion about the modern world. Is that right?'

Delgado looked at Ferguson, seemingly seeking permission to relate his previous talk. Ferguson gave him an approving nod, and a relieved Delgado turned back to Wygu.

'Yes, that's right. Greg came to my place and we had a nice chat. But he asked me a lot of very strange questions. Got me thinking about things I hadn't before. You see, the old brain these days is...'

'And what did you think?' Wygu interrupted. Ferguson was staring at Delgado as if expecting him finally to solve many mysteries.

'Greg asked me about the old days…' He broke off, looking back at Ferguson. 'Greg, is it alright...?'

'Carry on, Maurice. You're not in any trouble. Wygu's just giving my voice a rest.'

Delgado looked relieved, and continued: 'Yes, he asked me if I knew of many changes in the way things are around here, and that got me to thinking, you see. And I realised things are exactly the same as they were in my father's day, and, as you know, I'm a very old man. Why, I can remember the day when I thought I'd discovered a new type of knot—for fishing, you see—and Dad didn't like it at all, said I should leave things alone, that the old knots were good enough for his father, and I could get into trouble.'

'Into trouble?' Wygu said, wonderingly.

'Yes. He was always going on about the Good Old days and how modern people should leave things alone.'

'And this was when you were a boy?'

'Yes. You see, I can remember the old days better than the things I did a few hours ago!'

Delgado laughed, but the others did not. He looked nervous once more, but continued his tale.

'And after Greg's visit, it came to me that what we call "New Ideas" are things brought back to life by people who don't know they're just the same old ideas that people have forgotten.'

Wygu and Ferguson exchanged meaningful glances. Delgado leaned forward excitedly, as if about to reveal a hidden truth.

And he was.

'And another thing: when did you last see a baby? Fewer births happen than when I was a boy. And you know what that means...'

Ferguson shook his head.

'No.'

'It means we are dying out. The human race is going...going...' He looked at Wygu for help. 'What's the word? Funny sort of word.'

Wygu showed no emotion; his face could have been carved from warm mahogany as he completed Delgado's sentence.

'The word you're looking for is *Extinct*. The human race is going extinct.'

***

The day finally came when Wygu had to take his leave of Ferguson. Wygu stood with the great arid sweep of the Red Centre framing him as he shook hands with his erstwhile employer.

'It's going to be strange without you,' the latter said. 'Do you think you will ever come back?'

'Probably not, friend Greg. Once I am back among my own people, it will be difficult to leave them again. There is much I will have to catch up on, perhaps even to relearn.'

'I had hoped you would be happy here.'

'I was. But being among Colonists is not good for one of my kind; you think too differently, you do not see things that we see.'

A silence fell, and both men stood awkwardly looking at each other, unsure of how to end the encounter. Then Ferguson continued, 'The things Delgado said; the things I have said: if I am right and there are events happening beyond our control, your people are no better off than mine. We both might be just pawns in a game we don't understand.'

For some moments, Wygu looked away at the tumbled rocks and the uninterrupted sky and his face became troubled.

'I fear you are right, Greg, and that is another reason why I cannot stay. I need to talk to the Elders, to discover if they have been able to see beyond this veil that you believe wraps around us. I think there is something about you, friend Greg, that marks you as different to the other Colonists. They go about their business, not thinking about anything beyond the next meal, the next beer. But somehow, you want more. If you are right, then your kind are not masters of the land—as a Colonist would put it—but neither are my people the land's true guardians. That is what worries me. No, that is not strong enough—that is what frightens me. For that reason, amongst others, I must go back to them.'

Ferguson nodded. His face was impassive.

'Some of what you say is true, but you give me too much credit. It was my mother; she knew things that other people didn't, but more importantly, she said she had proof that we live in a different world to what everyone thinks.'

'Then you must show people this proof. Perhaps then they will believe you.'

Ferguson's face twisted into a mask of angry frustration and his hands balled into massive fists.

'Yes! Yes! She was about to tell me! A few more seconds before I lost her; that was all I needed, all I wanted! Twelve years, that's how long her last words have haunted me, and I'm still no nearer!'

And so, they parted. Silently, Ferguson watched his friend descend the slope, out of his life, returning to a people almost as old as the surrounding rocks.

Wygu never looked back.

SEVEN

Ferguson felt more alone than he had for years after Wygu's departure. Conversation with another man at any time of the day had become natural, and his talks with Wygu had helped convince him he was not losing his sanity by dwelling on his strange obsession.

Now, all that was gone, and his only company was his fellow drinkers at the Kookaburra, none of whom was famous for deep discussions on the nature of reality. Besides, he could tell Schwartz didn't like his halting attempts to instigate such discussions; Ferguson had seen him casting odd looks at him on the rare occasions he had tried to begin such a conversation. When deep in his beer, he sometimes entertained the idea that perhaps he was the only living individual and that the others were just puppets, with nothing behind their eyes. But when sober, he was now certain that the world was not as it appeared. Wygu's drug had restored his memory of the time with the Mozzie. Over the years, he had met several people who had had close encounters with those creatures, including some who had been snatched up and then returned, but they had no memory of their time away; only he, Ferguson, could remember the abnormal cave and the strange voice.

Wygu had said the cave, as described by Ferguson, could not be natural—and so, it had been dug out by the work of men. But who were these men? Why did nobody know about them?

Answer: *no one knew about them because they did not want to be known.*

And that was a very disturbing thought.

Round and around, those thoughts and many like them, would chase each other through his mind, but nothing ever came of those chases.

He was alone in his doubts, and that in itself was terrifying.

And so, he had contented himself with his work; work that was much more demanding now he was alone. But at least the Devil problem was over, and no one had seen a Cat in the area for quite some time, so gradually he relaxed, even to the extent of leaving his spear and woomera behind when he went out.

And, of Gottlieb, there was no sign. Perhaps he, too, had been taken up by the Mozzie, but in his case had not been returned.

But soon, his thoughts of hidden men who dug caves and had Mozzies as their servants faded, if only temporarily. He was looking at the sheep pen, or more accurately, at the rent in the wire which formed the pen's boundary. He examined it closely; no blood or animal tissue, so a Cat or Devil attack was unlikely. But there were a few scraps of wool on the exposed ends, showing that at least one sheep had forced its way through. Rapidly, he counted them, and with a relieved sigh, saw that only one was missing. Straining his powerful arms, he pulled the wires back into close proximity and drove a new post into the resulting gap. Sometime later, with a new reel of wire and a cutter, he had the fence back into a sheep-proof state.

Now to find the escapee.

The stony ground held no markings to show which way it had gone, but Ferguson knew there was only one place it would have headed to, a patch of green vegetation maintained against the midday heat by a temporary pool. It had still held water when he had last seen it, and so the vegetation would still be green.

That's where the fugitive would be.

Leaving the bail of wire behind, he set off on his mission of recapture. As he wound his way between the rocks, he reached the conclusion that he needed someone to replace Wygu, and the only way to do that would be to find an encampment of the Old People and look for a strong man who would be prepared to work with him. That would not be easy; Wygu had been unusual in having no prejudices against the Colonists.

The land became level, although no less rocky and arid. Thornbushes became more common and several times he was cut when trying to push between them, rather than skirting around. Eventually, the heat was too much and he sat on a vaguely chair-shaped boulder in the shade of a huge slab of reddish rock, waving his hat over his face to cool down. But after only a few minutes of rest, he felt a sense of unease seeping into his mind.

Someone or something was watching him.

Instantly, he was alert. Out in the Bush, it was wise to trust your instincts; it could be the difference between continued existence or an early death. Few creatures would be content simply to study him; another man perhaps, but out here it was normal to call out to strangers rather than watch them from afar. The other possibility was much more alarming.

A Cat.

He cursed himself for having come out defenceless; he had spent too long puzzling over insoluble mysteries instead of practicalities. This was how people were killed, by underestimating the dangers of the Bush.

Slowly, carefully, he raised himself from the stone, looking around as he did so, casting rapid-fire glances at every shadow, every rock in the vicinity. His search was over for today; never again would he venture out without a weapon.

There! In a shadow cast by an even more immense pillar of rock, there had been a movement. Automatically, his hands balled into fists as his eyes strove to identify the shape in the shadow.

It was a woman. She came out of the shadow towards him, smiling and with palms outstretched in greeting. Ferguson saw a tall, slim woman of the Old People, well-proportioned and with a long sweep of jet-black hair reaching almost to the small of her back.

'I'm sorry if I frightened you,' she said. 'I saw you jump when I gave myself away.'

'I wasn't frightened,' Ferguson said, annoyed at the implication. 'I wasn't expecting to see anyone out here, that's all. What are you doing here?'

She came nearer. He saw deep brown eyes holding his gaze and found it difficult to look away.

And she looked vaguely familiar.

'I left my tribe. Or rather, they asked me to leave.'

An odd response, but he did not follow it up.

'I was looking for a sheep, but I suddenly realised I was taking a risk being out here as I don't have a weapon. And neither have you,' he added, taking the excuse to look her up and down.

She smiled.

'I have my own weapons, but you won't find them by staring at my breasts.'

Ferguson grinned self-consciously. He hadn't realised he had been so obvious.

'Sorry about that. But I think I'd better get back. I've been a bit of a fool; in more ways than one, it seems.'

She raised a slim hand.

'Wait. I know you, but it is obvious you don't recognise me.'

He looked at her again; this time mainly at her face.

'I thought I might have seen you before. Who are you—and how do you know me?'

She was so close now he could have raised a hand and touched her.

'It's been over ten years since we saw each other. I haven't changed that much, but you seem like two men merged together. It suits you.'

'Cut to it—who are you?'

Now, she reached out and lightly touched his shoulder. For some reason, he felt a reaction like a mild electric shock race down his spine.

'You are Greg Ferguson. I am Allira.'

Involuntarily, he took a step backwards. It was as if the years fell away and he was sitting next to a young girl in the twilight, watching the great milky river come into focus above them. And he remembered how their relationship had ended, with him ordering her away, for a wrong she had not committed.

'Allira,' he whispered, his eyes wide, despite the killing sun. 'Is it really you, or am I heat-struck?'

'It's really me.'

'Where have you been? It's been twelve years, for gods' sake!'

'You told me to go away, and so I did, back to my own people. We moved away from you and your little hut and your sheep. But I am glad your mother was well, for a while, at least.'

'How do you know she got better? I never saw you again.'

'I knew, but this is not the time to explain, because you're right; it's not safe out here. A Cat is nearby.'

Her words did not shock him as much as might have been expected, because he was thinking of something else.

'Wait! Where are you going? Will I see you again?'

She gave a half smile.

'You told me to go away. Are you now telling me to stay?'

'Yes! I mean, no, I'm *asking* you to stay! There's so much to catch up on! I was a thirteen-year-old boy when you last saw me, and I got things wrong. I was worried sick about my mother, and I thought you'd tricked me. You hadn't, but how was a boy supposed to know that?'

Allira touched his shoulder again, with the same effect upon Ferguson.

'Of course. It wasn't just you, Greg. I needed to spend time with my own people; I was turning into a Colonist, and who would want that? I'll come back with you for a while. If that's what you want,' she added, playfully.

Ferguson momentarily stared at her, unsure of what he should say. For some reason, he was now extremely eager for Allira to accompany him back to his farmstead, but he couldn't put it into words. After all, she didn't look as if she could be much help with all the farm chores. So, in the end, he just grinned and nodded his head.

They set off but hadn't gone far when he put out an arm to block her progress.

'This way is full of thorn bushes. I know another way; it's longer, but likely to be less painful.'

She gave another smile, revealing perfect teeth of warm ivory.

'How considerate. We Old People are quite used to thorn bushes, but I understand Colonists are a little worried by them, so we will take your longer way.'

Ferguson was unsure of whether or not he had just been gently mocked, but he grinned again, and they set off.

The silence between them disturbed him; he felt he should be saying something to keep his new guest interested. He glanced sidelong at her, hardly believing she would still be there.

'You didn't say why you left your tribe.'

She returned the glance, once again a mischievous expression playing over her features.

'No, I didn't, did I?'

'I...'

He stopped. They had come across a hollow between the mighty boulders, a kind of bowl with a small scummy green pool at its centre.

And by the pool was the dead body of a sheep, with its guts spread out in a bloody fan from a gash in its side.

And by the carcass was a Cat.

It lifted its red-stained muzzle and stared at them with pitiless yellow eyes. The two humans were shocked into immobility. Ferguson had never been this close to a live Cat before.

And he had left his spear and woomera at the farmstead.

'Back,' he whispered, 'back.'

Keeping their eyes fixed on the predator, they moved very slowly backwards. Ferguson saw that the animal was slightly shorter than he was tall, discounting the tail. Apart from the bloody jaws, it was a nondescript sandy colour, ideal for melting into the landscape.

They continued their slow, silent retreat into the shelter of the tumbled boulders.

It began to follow them.

'We're in trouble,' he said. 'Get ready to run. Find a boulder you can climb up.'

She did not reply.

Ferguson cursed his stupidity. His relationship with Allira, so exciting a few minutes earlier, looked like it was going to be a very short one, with a tragic ending. His retreat came to an end as he backed blindly into a mass of stone.

The Cat charged.

Instantly, Ferguson's world shrank to contain only the charging animal and the need to survive. Allira, the blazing blue sky, the great rocks—all vanished. He saw only saliva-dripping jaws which promised a sudden end to his existence. The Devil had just been a toy compared to this killer.

At the last instant, he threw himself to one side and the animal crashed into the boulder, spitting and hissing. No point in running—it would be on his back in a heartbeat; his last heartbeat, that is. And at that moment, it had its back to him as it angrily reared up against the stone. He threw himself behind it, away from the bloodied teeth and the bloodied claws, his arms encircling its throat, and he threw all his power into desperate constriction. Ferguson's strength was great, much more than that of an average man, but never had he held such an engine of destruction. His great arm muscles felt like they would be ripped from his bones as the Cat threw its own strength into escape and terrible vengeance.

It was no good. Ferguson had held the thrashing creature prisoner for many seconds, an eternity more than most men could have achieved, but it broke free and whirled around, claws raised high. He threw himself to one side as the paw came down, but he was not fast enough, and great parallel gouges were carved along his left arm. The impact and the shock of pain threw him onto his back, and a moment later, he was staring into yellow eyes, a handbreadth from his face. The jaws opened and a gust of death swept over him.

But the jaws did not close on him.

Instead, the great head turned, looking at something off to one side. It moved away slowly, still looking at something out of Ferguson's visual field. He took the opportunity to push himself away, still on his back, his free-flowing blood turning the dust under his arm into a crimson paste. Now he could see what the predator was looking at.

It was Allira.

She was standing nearby, with both arms raised, as if in some ceremony. The Cat continued retreating from Ferguson. It stopped and looked longingly back at him as if it were a child denied a treat. It growled, then turned back to Allira.

And silently loped off into the boulder field.

Ferguson's mind reeled. What had just happened? Was he safe?

Allira was suddenly by his side, her face calm and resolute. Without a word, she tore a strip from his shirt and wound it around his arm, tightening it savagely above the wounds.

'This will stem the worst of the flow,' she said. 'But you will need help. And soon.'

EIGHT

'**C**an you walk?'
Ferguson winced as Allira pulled him upright, using his right arm as a support. The red blotch on his arm had spread to discolour all of Allira's makeshift tourniquet, which was now worryingly wet.

'Yes, of course I can. We should head back to the farm. I can get proper bandages there. I'll be alright.'

'You will not be alright! A Cat's claws are covered in filth. Your wounds will go bad—and quickly. If we don't get proper help—and soon—you could lose the arm. What kind of farmer would you make then?'

Ferguson stared at Allira. Reaction and shock had set in, and he was feeling increasingly dizzy. He was fighting a terrible desire to lie down and sleep; sleep for a very long time.

'Where could we get help? We're miles from the township. I'll bleed out before I get there.'

'There's somewhere nearer than that, under a mile. We can make that. Hold your arm above your head.'

'Why?'

'Just do it, you stupid man!'

As Ferguson finally obeyed, Allira tore a strip of fabric from her own clothing, exposing her full breasts. Ferguson hardly noticed; the world seemed to be turning into a blurred monochrome painting. She wrapped the strip over the original tourniquet, her face twisting with effort as she strove to tighten it to the limits of its strength.

'Put your other arm on my shoulder and let's go!'

Ferguson was now too confused to ask where they were headed, and the pair set off into the yellow undergrowth with fitful, halting steps.

If the Cat comes back for us, we're finished, she thought, and then drove the defeatist thought away. Ferguson gradually rested more and more of his considerable weight onto her as the journey continued, and his pace slowed; dangerously so.

'Not long now,' she said, hardly daring to look at him. But she did; his head had dropped onto his chest and his eyes were closed. 'Not long now,' she repeated, willing the distance away.

And then they were there.

'Look!' Allira said, giving her almost comatose companion a shake. His eyes flickered open, and he saw a wall of red rock like a thousand others. But there was something he had only ever seen once before in a rock.

A door.

Allira looked at the top of the door, although nothing was visible there, and waved a hand. A deep, resonant voice filled the furnace air around them. It was a voice which would have been emotionless had it not carried a slight tinge of anger.

'Allira. You have come here again. This is trying my patience. Go away.'

'No, please, don't send me away!' Allira almost screamed. 'I promise I won't come again, but this man is dying! I won't come again, I promise!'

There was a silence, then: 'Very well. But if you break your promise, I will punish you most severely. Bring the creature in.'

'I can't,' Allira said, and this time she was sobbing. 'He can't walk and he's too heavy for me to move! Please help me, please!'

Another silence, and then: 'This is more than she contracted us to perform.'

Silence.

Allira lowered Ferguson to the ground; he was unconscious. She lay beside him and raised her face and arms to the unseen observer.

'Please! I'm begging you!'

Silence.

Then, after two minutes of Allira's agony, the door rolled upwards into the rock and a figure emerged. It was a freakishly tall male, with long, lustrous black hair. His eyes had an odd reddish cast, and his fingernails were unpleasantly long. He bent over Ferguson and picked him up without displaying the slightest effort.

All three then entered the tunnel that had been revealed. It opened into a room containing two couches and a desk. Behind and to the side of the desk, was a door of the standard type. The strange man deposited Ferguson on the nearer couch and spent some time staring at him. Allira attempted to get nearer to Ferguson, but a long-nailed hand waved her away.

'Can I help?' she asked.

The man did not look at her.

'No, of course not. Don't come any closer.'

The man continued his silent study of his patient. Allira heard him mutter, 'This should be the last time I deal with these creatures. My tour of duty is finally over. It has been a long, miserable time.' He suddenly remembered Allira and turned to face her. 'The procedure won't take long. Lie down on the other couch, girl. You must be tired. Very tired.'

'No, I'm...' Allira stopped. She *was* tired, why she could hardly keep her eyes open! It took all her willpower to keep herself awake as she walked, almost staggered, to the other couch. She lay on it, feeling the warm, velvety fingers of welcoming slumber caress her body. She stretched herself out and felt her eyelids begin to descend like leaden curtains. But then:

No! she thought. *I will not sleep! I don't trust this man. He seems different from last time.*

Raising her eyelids felt as if she were trying to stop a great boulder from crushing her. But somehow, she managed it. Through narrow slits, she saw the man open a compartment in a nearby wall and wheel out a device. It had a flexible rod protruding from its centre, terminating in a kind of box that glowed with pulsating greenish light. The man did something to the device's side, and the rod bent like a cobra's neck, the glowing box stopping a few inches above Ferguson's bandaged arm. She saw the man run his fingers over the other's body and heard him mutter to himself once again.

'Why, what do we have here? This human is an uncommonly fine specimen. Such sumptuous flesh. It really is very tempting.' He suddenly looked away from Ferguson, fixing his gaze on a random point on the ceiling. 'Should I? She will never know—why not? It is what we are meant to do, meant to be.'

The rod moved back to its initial position, and he lowered his head and unwound the two strips of fabric. The arm was still bleeding, though not as strongly as when Allira had last seen it. And then the man did something totally unexpected. He lowered his lips to the arm and began to slurp the blood, as if he were one of the desert Cats!

Allira's scream was silent.

And then she was finally, deeply, asleep.

***

Allira awoke and spent some seconds trying to remember where she was. Then she remembered Ferguson and the Cat and the terrible walk to the Healer. Yes, that's where she was: in the Healer's cave.

But there had been a very strange dream. She had dreamt the Healer had licked the blood from Ferguson's mangled arm!

Utterly ridiculous! She had seen this man before. He had an unpleasant manner but was a true healer. Obviously, the strain of recent events had caused a kind of hallucination.

The man was still in the room, next to Ferguson. And he was looking at her.

'Ah, you're finally awake. Come girl, and look at your friend. See what I have achieved.'

She crossed to the other couch, her tired limbs protesting at the sudden movement. Ferguson lay there, naked from the waist up, his great chest and arms bathed in green-stained light. He appeared to be sleeping as the chest was gently rising and falling. She looked at his left arm.

It was whole again! Where there had been great rents in the flesh, there were now parallel bands of new paler skin, as yet unburned by the sun. She whirled to face the Healer.

'Oh, thank you, thank you...it's Renfield, isn't it?'

'Yes, well remembered girl. It has been some years, and I know your kind does not have minds like ours.'

'Is he alright? I mean, he is going to wake up—isn't he?'

'Yes, of course. He will be at least as healthy and strong as he was before his accident.'

'So, can we go now? His sheep...'

'No. I won't let you go, just yet. This is a remarkable example of your males. A type I had not seen before. I would like to spend some more time with him.'

Allira nodded and smiled.

But she felt a cold hand seize her heart.

NINE

'Why do you want to keep us here? You've done what I asked, and I am very grateful. As Greg will be, when he wakes up. Please, we would like to go now. We have much work to do.'

Renfield did not smile; in fact, he had the type of face which seemed incapable of smiling.

'I believe you when you say you have much work to do; no doubt dealing with those animals you depend upon. But that is of no interest to me. What does interest me is your companion. I was not aware that your species was capable of producing such a specimen. My time here is almost over, and so I want to spend the remaining days getting to know your companion.'

Allira stared up at Renfield. The coldness around her heart was intensifying.

'I'm sorry, but I don't understand. What do you mean by "getting to know"?'

Renfield did not bother to reply and turned his back on her, walking back to the couch and Ferguson. She briskly walked after him.

'And where are you going? Why is that so important?'

He whirled around to face her, and the redness in his eyes was fiercer, glowing like red hot coals.

'Your questions are not merely annoying; they are impertinent. I did not ask to come here—I was sent by a higher authority. And I have hated every minute of it. You have your animals to deal with, I have had mine!'

Allira quailed under the sudden change in the Healer's attitude, but she did not retreat.

'You are a healer. You care for people. Imprisoning them is not caring.'

'Enough!' Renfield shouted. The instruments in the room trembled. He walked directly up to her, staring down with eyes that were now undeniably a dull crimson. 'You are feeling tired. Very tired. All you want to do is sleep. Go to the couch.'

Once again, Allira felt exhaustion break over her with the power of a great roller, far out at sea. Immediately, she obeyed and lay down on the couch she had so recently quitted.

But once again, she felt some strength within her, fighting the tiredness.

She fought long and hard. But eventually, darkness claimed her.

***

Ferguson awoke. He felt immensely better, as if new strength and power had been poured into him while he slept. Then he remembered his arm and, looking down, was amazed to see it was whole and unblemished. He sent a mental message to bend the fingers, and immediately, they curled into a massive fist. He spent a minute or two examining the arm from all the angles his frame allowed and, apart from some pale streaks, everything looked great.

Ferguson became aware that someone was standing not far away and, looking up, saw the tall figure of the Healer.

'I guess I have you to thank, cobber,' he said, swinging his feet onto the floor and standing up. 'Put it there.' He extended his right hand.

The Healer ignored the hand.

'I am glad you are feeling better. I can provide some simple food items for you. I expect you are hungry after all your adventures.'

'Simple food items? No, that won't be necessary. I've got to get back to the farm now I know there's a Cat in the area. But thank you again, sir.'

Then Ferguson stopped. His face lost its expression of friendly gratitude and became emotionless. He was examining the other's features intently.

'I feel I know you. You remind me very much of a man I saw about twelve years ago.' He looked around, the blank expression changing into wary bewilderment. 'In a place very much like this one.'

The Healer showed that his face was indeed capable of displaying a smile. But it was not the kind of smile one would wish to remember.

'Perhaps it was. I'm not sure you people have the mental capacity to recall that clearly.'

Ferguson took one step backwards.

'I do remember. How could I forget? It was the last chance of saving my mother. Allira was there with me.' He glanced over at Allira's sleeping form. 'We were just children.' Then his face twisted into a mask of alarm. 'And you were there! *Renfield*—that was your name! But that was twelve years ago—but you look exactly the same. That memory is clear in my mind, how could I forget you! You came to the hut as well. It's you! But you are unchanged, exactly the same! Not a white hair, not an ounce of fat added. It's like I was back in that cave twelve years ago!' Ferguson looked wildly around as if looking for an escape. Then back to Renfield: 'What's going on, mate? Is this some kind of trick? Are you wearing a mask or something?'

'No trick. It is I, Renfield. Your memories are surprisingly accurate. For a human.'

'*For a human?* What in gods' names are you gabbling about?'

Renfield had clearly lost interest. He pointed at the couch Ferguson had just left.

'You are feeling sleepy. Lie back down.'

'I've just bloody wo...'

Ferguson stopped. He *did* feel sleepy!

Unsteadily, he made his way to his couch and lay back down. This was ridiculous, he had only just woken up! And not long after stretching out, he felt hands running up and down his chest. Those hands were cold, strangely cold, given that the cave was not particularly chilly. He fought to stay awake, but knew he was succumbing.

And then, from a short distance above his face, he heard someone laugh.

A cold, humourless laugh.

After an unknown space of time, he was awake again. And so was Allira, for she was standing over him.

'At last,' she said. 'I thought you were going to sleep forever!'

He swung his legs onto the floor.

'I could say the same about you.' He looked around, like a prey item searching for a predator. 'Where's Renfield?'

A jerk of her head indicated the cave's other door.

'He went through that some time ago. Looks like he's busy.' Suddenly, she grasped his wrist. 'I think we should get out. There's something badly wrong here. I've had several dealings with Renfield over the years, but he's never behaved like this before. Let's go while we can!'

Ferguson stood.

' "Several dealings over the years",' he quoted. 'Did you never notice how he hasn't aged?'

'No. Most of the times I met him, I was still a girl. But now I've seen him again, I agree: he does look completely unchanged.'

Ferguson stretched; his muscles felt stiff and unused.

'And your explanation?'

'I have none. Some tribes tell of people who have come back from the dead and prey on the living, but my own tribe does not have that legend, so I know no more than what I just told you.'

'Big help,' Ferguson grunted. 'But you're right: there is something screwy about this guy.' He looked at the tunnel leading to the outside. 'Let's go.'

As one, they headed into the tunnel, Allira casting a fearful glance behind her. It seemed longer than it had on their first traverse, but they were soon at its far end. They faced a wall of the same smooth, almost slippery, material which characterised Renfield's lair.

And absolutely no mechanism for opening it. With growing concern, they searched every square inch, but there was nothing.

'Looks like we'll have to fall back on Renfield's mercy,' Ferguson said, and they traipsed back to where they had started. This time, they sat side by side, looking at the other door, awaiting the return of what had been their healer and who now appeared to be their jailer. Suddenly, Allira hugged Ferguson and whispered, 'I am starting to feel very frightened.'

He did not reply but maintained his watch on the door. She ran her fingers over his neck in a way he found exciting, even in the bowels of the hill.

Then she pulled her fingers away with an exclamation of surprise.

'Greg, have you noticed any insects in this place?'

'No, just you, me and our host.'

Her fingers returned to his neck, but this time their touch was questing, not arousing.

'You have two small holes in your neck, not far apart. They look like puncture wounds. Like a bite.'

His own fingers found the marks.

'You're right. But there's no pain or even soreness. I would never have noticed them.'

'There must be something in here with us. Some kind of animal.'

'How? We would have seen it.'

'Perhaps it only attacks when we are asleep. Renfield must have some kind of pet.' She ran fingers over her own neck, and half-turned to Ferguson. 'Do I have any bite marks?'

He studied her mahogany skin.

'No.'

'Just you then. It must find you tastier than me.' She assayed a smile. 'I feel insulted!'

Ferguson did not smile.

'That clinches it. I think I'm going to have to get rough with friend Renfield.'

As if on cue, the other door opened and Renfield's spare form was revealed.

'Ah, you're both awake. Now, this is ridiculous; you need your rest, both of you. In fact, I think you're both feeling extremely sleepy. Very sleepy indeed.'

At once, Ferguson felt the seductive comber of somnolence crash over him. He fell backwards, away from Renfield, whose thin lips now held what could possibly be described as a smile.

But he heard Allira beside him.

'Greg, fight it! I feel it too, but I think I'm holding him. Whatever you're going to do—do it now!'

Like an unwisely awakened bull, Ferguson shook his great head to clear it. He took several steps towards Renfield.

'Are you going to let us out?

Renfield's rictus of a smile broadened.

'Now, you are being ridiculous. You are truly delicious, much better than that artificial slop she makes us drink in these benighted days. She can't see me here, so I can do what I like. And what I like is you.'

Ferguson only understood about half of Renfield's words, but what he did understand he didn't like. He raised his fists. Renfield's eyes followed the movements, and he laughed, his usual cold, unsettling laugh.

'I see you are determined to provide me with harmless amusement. This day is turning out splendidly. You fool, I have five times your strength.'

Ferguson crossed the distance between them in a blur and one fist swept up onto his opponent's pointed chin, while the other powered into Renfield's belly.

Whatever Renfield had been expecting, it was not exactly what he received. The first blow knocked his head backwards, the other doubled him up. He staggered back; his crimson gaze now directed at the floor.

Ferguson, however, was not encouraged by the sight. When he had hit the other, it felt as if he were punching the wall. Renfield had felt solid, unyielding, in a way Gottlieb had not. He realised his opponent was not one who could be brushed away so easily.

Renfield proved that a second later, as he straightened himself, rubbing his chin in wonder.

'Remarkable. I was right: you are an exceptional human. Not in brain, of course, that is obvious, but most certainly in brawn. But not enough to better one of the Elite. And I'm afraid once I start to retaliate, I will almost certainly lose control and kill you. That is a great pity; the live stuff is so much sweeter.'

Ferguson realised that his opponent was much more of a threat than he looked, but he also knew that having gone this far, there could be no retreat. He studied Renfield, looking for an opening.

But there was no need: Renfield stood there, hands at his side, smiling that smile.

'I am ready for you now,' was all he said.

Ferguson needed no further invite and gave the Healer a swift One: Two.

No effect.

Renfield's head jerked back slightly, but that was all; his smile never wavered.

'Thank you for that demonstration. I would truly like to take you back to the real world to show the others, but that would never be allowed. Here you are and here you stay.'

And suddenly, he was on top of Ferguson, who found himself lifted high above the other's head. Renfield threw him against the wall, and he crashed down on his sofa, rolling off onto the floor. Fortunately for Ferguson, the wall was made of the same mysterious material he had puzzled over before, not inflexible stone, and his internal organs survived. Even so, he heard Allira scream.

Renfield strode over to administer further punishment but received a heavy boot to his face. This time, the force made him stagger away and he had to steady himself against his desk. He felt his jaw, while glaring at Ferguson. He was no longer smiling.

'That is enough. You have really annoyed me now. I warned you I would lose control and kill you, and now I will.'

Ferguson pushed himself upright. He knew he would be dead in a few seconds' time. Whatever Renfield was, he was no ordinary man. An ordinary man would have been writhing on the floor by now. He straightened himself, fists raised.

He would make sure Renfield remembered this battle.

And that was true.

As the erstwhile Healer crossed to Ferguson, hands twisted into clawed instruments of death, a great voice blared out, carrying power that almost knocked all three off their feet.

'Agent 427! Stop! You have broken the ordinance I established for treatment of the humans!'

Ferguson listened in awe to the voice. It sounded female, but not like those he had met outside the cave; it carried the chilling demands of absolute obedience. It was as if an earthquake could speak with a woman's voice.

Renfield had stopped immediately. Had he been other than he was, his face would have turned pale, but it was already as pale as it could be. Even so, it looked as if he had been turned into a life-sized statue. Even his eyelids did not move.

It looks like he was under observation, Ferguson thought. *But who was watching him?*

The voice continued, even though the cave felt like it was not large enough to contain it.

'Your presence is now required. You are to present yourself to me as soon as you arrive. You can then attempt to explain yourself before I administer your punishment.

'Now!'

Renfield did not say anything more, nor did he look at Ferguson or Allira. He turned on his heel and went into whatever lay beyond the second door. A few seconds later, a flash of purple light was briefly visible in the gaps of the door jamb.

Ferguson and Allira were alone.

She rushed to him.

'Greg! For gods' sake, are you alright?'

He gave a weak grin.

'Just about. A few more rounds with that cobber would have finished me. What in the names of the hells was he made of?'

To his amazement, she said no more but leaned in and kissed him fervently.

As they broke away, she whispered, 'I don't want to lose you!'

'I didn't know you had me,' he said, 'but I'm not complaining!'

But as the terror faded and their adrenaline levels sank to more typical values, the reality of their situation returned.

'Well, he's gone but we're still stuck here, inside a hill,' Ferguson said.

Allira nodded, but before she could give her own view of the situation there was another purple flash behind the door. They whirled around as it opened.

And a woman came out.

Or at least, a female of some kind, for she was dressed in a garment neither of them had ever seen before. It was tightly figure-hugging and made of a fabric which glowed softly in the cave's jade light. However, there was no smile of reassurance on her sculptured features. Indeed, the look she directed at them was one of indifference, which could have easily slid into contempt. She was not as tall as Renfield, but once again, considerably taller than what one might have expected for her gender.

She approached the astounded duo, who had unconsciously reached for each other's hands.

'So, you are humans. You look like the pictures I have seen, but perhaps better fed.'

Allira spoke first.

'That's not the greeting I expected, but who exactly are you? And have you been behind the door all this time?'

The woman's cold expression did not alter.

'I am Agent 558. You don't need to know my pseudonym as you will never see me again. In fact, that is all I wish to tell you.'

Ferguson rose to his feet.

'And are you going to hold us here, to torment us like Renfield?'

The woman pointed to the tunnel behind them.

'Of course not. I have better things to do. Go.'

TEN

Allira took another sip of her drink.

'Nice tea. Where do you get it?'

Ferguson took another look at the young woman sitting a short distance away. His gaze lingered a few seconds too long for politeness, and she gave an understanding smile.

'We were talking about tea. Remember?' she prompted.

'Ah, yes, it's...' He stopped, clearly flustered. For a moment or two, for the life of him, he could not remember where he got his tea. Then: 'Schwartz. At the Kookaburra; he sells me some of the best stuff.'

Members of an earlier generation would not have identified the drink as tea, but Ferguson and Allira knew no better.

The journey from the Healer's cave had been uneventful and Ferguson was greeted by his guard dogs with excited barks and much tail-wagging. It had taken them the briefest of times to accept Allira, which surprised Ferguson, as normally they were very suspicious of any newcomer. He had told his guest about Sky's sad demise, and she told him how she had loved the original animal to have borne that name. He had smiled at the fond memories.

And now he had a whole sheaf of not-so-fond memories. Their imprisonment by Renfield still made him feel cold and uneasy, especially the man's incredible resilience under Ferguson's blows. He should have gone down after the first one, but had hardly flinched. And the strange woman—had she been behind the door all that time they were in captivity? Was it her voice that had summoned Renfield away to meet his punishment? Yet, when she had spoken, her voice had been cold and authoritative, but not the klaxon that had demanded Renfield's attendance.

The pleasant feelings Ferguson was enjoying from Allira's company drained away, and he was forced to face the fact that the world he was used to had gone missing somehow. And the cave and its two inhabitants were not the only mystery.

'Allira,' he said, and the coldness of his tone snapped her into attention. 'There are a few things I don't understand.'

She did not reply but merely waited to hear his words, her hands folded demurely in her lap.

He began, hesitantly at first.

'The Cat. It was going to kill me. But for some reason, it didn't. I can't think why it didn't; I was helpless.'

'I'm glad it didn't, Greg.'

'Thank you. But when I looked across, I saw you, standing with your arms held high. And the Cat was looking at you. And it went away—like a lamb.'

'There's no mystery, Greg. I tried to distract it, and I succeeded. That's all it was. Obviously, it wasn't that hungry. After all, it had just eaten half a sheep.'

Greg nodded. That sounded reasonable. But he needed more explanations.

'When I was fighting Renfield, you said something like, "I'm holding him." But you weren't; you were nowhere near him.'

She shook her head, smiling at him in a way that made him feel like a brute to question her.

'Greg, Greg, do you expect me to explain everything I said? I was terrified out of my mind. You were about to fight Renfield to get us out of that terrible place. And I don't remember saying those exact words; I could have said anything, I was so frightened.'

He returned her smile. Everything she said made perfect sense. Just one last thing.

'You said you were forced to leave your tribe. Why was that?'

The smile vanished.

'Greg, you must not ask me that. It was something very important to us Old People; you Colonists would not understand. All I can say is that it was something very important in our beliefs. You must never ask me again.'

Ferguson spread his arms wide.

'I'm sorry. I didn't mean to upset you or insult your people. I'm sorry.

The smile returned.

'Apology accepted, you big lunk. Now, let's have some more of this wonderful tea.'

***

Ferguson shielded his eyes from the morning sun with one hand while stroking the head of one of his guard dogs with the other. The animal was gazing lovingly up at him, but he didn't notice; he had other things on his mind. It was later than he would have liked. Allira had slept in Wygu's old bed, of course, but, unlike Wygu, she had seemed reluctant to leave it.

Finally, she appeared at the doorway, smoothing her hair.

'I should have known there wouldn't be a comb in this place. You're obviously not used to overnight guests. Of the female variety, that is.'

If Ferguson had blushed, it would have been undetectable under his tan. As it was, he merely pointed into the distance and said, 'I'm afraid you have to earn your keep while you're staying with me. I've got more important things to worry about than combs—whatever they are.'

She laughed and, joining him, slipped an arm underneath one of his.

'I can't believe you don't know what a comb is. But anyway, what are we doing so early in the morning?'

Ferguson was thrilled by the intimate contact, but, keeping his voice steady, replied, 'We're taking the sheep down into the Bush. That feed I give them is no good in the long run. Makes poor milk.'

'Some people put it in tea, I've heard. What a waste of two good drinks!'

He laughed, enjoying the easy banter, and whistled to the dogs, using the device his father had given him, so long ago. Soon all four of them were walking behind Ferguson's flock as they made their way down the slope. Allira walked close beside Ferguson, but did not touch him again.

'Were you far from here when you were with your tribe?' he said, anxious not to let a silence develop.

'Yes, very far. But this place has always been my home. I loved being with my own kind, but I'm afraid

I've spent too much time with Colonists. You could say I'm a kind of mixed-up girl.'

'I like the mixture.'

She looked up at him, wide-eyed.

'Greg Ferguson! I do believe you're flirting with me!'

He felt a sudden desire to reach for her, hold her and kiss long and hard, but he was not sure if he had been mocked, and so did none of those things.

Allira appeared to have forgotten the moment and was looking around at the red and ochre landscape.

'I love these hills. Not all of them are sacred, of course. They don't all have names.' She stopped and raised an arm. 'See that one over there. It had a bad landslip some years ago.'

Ferguson looked across the parched land to the low hill she was pointing at.

'Yes. My family home was right next to it.'

'Yes, I remember. Some people said it looked like a big lizard before the landslip.'

Ferguson looked away. The sheep were getting too far ahead.

'Is that right?' he said, the disinterest in his tone evident even to him.

'Yes. They used to call it the goanna.'

Ferguson took a step toward the flock while her words were mulled over by the part of his brain not concerned with sheep. Then the import of what she had said hit like a physical blow and he almost stumbled onto the rocky path. He whirled around to face her. She, in turn, stepped backwards at the sight of a terrible hunger burning in his face.

'What did you say? What did you call it?'

She replied in a meek voice, thinking that somehow she had angered him.

'*Goanna.* I said people used to call the rock the goanna, before the landslide.'

He looked past her at the rock, mentally trying to replace the missing section and see what earlier people had seen. Suddenly, the past twelve years evaporated, and he was back in the family hut by the side of his dying mother. What had been her exact words?

'*It…the goanna, the tail, nothing changes, sun, it…*'

But earlier, she had said something that was very important to her: the proof that the world was not what everyone else thought it to be, before *they* had done something, taken something away. She had the proof! What had she done with it?

While Allira stared at him in concerned amazement, he closed his eyes and lowered his head in an agony of concentration.

It came to him.

'*Your father threw them out, saying he had no use for fairy stories, but one night I went out and gathered them together in a box, and hid it.*'

Were the two statements connected? Had she been trying to tell him where she had hidden the box before death had robbed her of the opportunity? Was the box hidden somewhere near that great rock?

He opened his eyes and stared at the now seriously worried Allira.

'The goanna rock, did it, does it, have a tail?'

She turned and pointed.

'Yes, of course. Look at the southern end, see how a spur of rock sticks out. That's the tail.'

Ferguson followed her pointing finger, screwing up his eyes against the glare, willing himself to see a vast, crouching lizard.

And he could! And in that instant, he became convinced that the answer to the mystery that had haunted him for over twelve years was within his grasp.

He turned away, all thoughts of his flock, his farm, his livelihood, swept away by the surging demand of his need to know. Unconscious of Allira, of anything other than the mystery, he began to stride towards the great mass of ochre rock.

Allira stopped him.

'Greg, slow down, stop it! You can't just go marching off into the Bush like this; you'll ruin your whole life!'

For an instant, she thought he was going to strike her in his madness. Hurriedly, she placed her palms on his heaving chest and whispered, 'Greg, take it easy. It's me.'

He looked down at her and she saw recognition return to his eyes, and knew she was safe. He shook his head to clear it.

'Yes, yes, of course. The sheep. I can't leave them, can I?'

'The goanna will still be there tomorrow, and the day after. You've waited twelve years; what's another day more? You and I will go there tomorrow after the flock has been fed and watered.'

'Yes,' he said. 'We will.'

ELEVEN

The ground was treacherous with splintered and shattered stones, clutching at their ankles, threatening to snap them at any moment. Ferguson looked up, seeing a tremendous finger of stone thrusting out directly above him, blotting out a significant fraction of the cloudless blue beyond it. Surveying the grim boulder field around him, he felt his heart sink. To go through this area, turning over stone after stone, would consume a lifetime! Perhaps he had placed too much emphasis on the stuttered words of a dying woman; seeking meaning where there was none.

Allira caught his mood.

'We mustn't give up, Greg. We must go over the area in a methodical way, marking where we've been so we don't do the same area twice.'

He sighed. Allira was right—but he had expected more. He had thought there would be an obvious cairn, or stones laid out in an arrow, so they could go straight to the spot and, after a few minutes of frenzied digging, retrieve the longed-for box. But it was not going to be easy; what had seemed small from a distance had turned out to be a jumbled labyrinth of rocks, stones, and boulders of vastly different sizes and shapes. Had his mother's dying words been just an outpouring of jumbled, meaningless sounds, after all?

He thrust the thought away and, tensing his muscles, rolled over a boulder, revealing untouched sand and gravel that had not seen the sun in perhaps a hundred years.

'Greg,' Allira chided gently, 'think it through. It was an ordinary woman out here, hiding something, not a great lummox like you turning over boulders like they were sheepskins. It would have to be an area of small stones.'

'First, find your small stones.' Ferguson tried to subdue the anger he felt growing inside him. This was not working out as he had expected, and the reality was stark. They could spend a year out here and not find a thing. 'Let's take a rest. And maybe we'll see something.'

They found a boulder with a flat, slightly sloping top and sat side by side. Allira knew better than to make any comments, encouraging or otherwise, and waited for Ferguson to speak.

'I'm not giving up,' he said, eventually. 'That damn box is out here somewhere.'

'And what do you think will be in it?'

'Answers. Answers to problems that clearly haven't bothered you. There is something hidden from us, I'm sure of that. Renfield is the best example of that. How could he heal me so completely? Even your people, with their herbs and tinctures, couldn't have gotten rid of those wounds. I mean, can you see any scars?' he added, thrusting out an arm.

'No. Just small pale streaks. I agree; my people could not have done that.'

'And he stood up to my punches. I swear I could have punched through the farm wall with them, but he hardly flinched.'

'Just a strong man.'

'Nonsense. Did he look strong? He had the build of a dry twig. He should have snapped. But he didn't.'

A baffled, frustrated silence fell. Allira waited for Ferguson to break it. The minutes passed. Eventually, he stretched and rose to his feet.

'Let's get back to it.'

He looked around, seeking some sign that another human had passed this way: a group of stones piled in an unnatural way, a scrap of faded cloth...

He stopped and shaded his eyes. His expression went from angry boredom to a keen arousal.

'Can you see it?'

Allira joined him and followed the line of his stare.

'Yes, a dark patch in the rock wall. It could be...'

'It is! The entrance to a cave! That's where she would have put it. We should have guessed she wouldn't have been out here, turning over boulders with her bare hands! Let's go!'

Allira carefully navigated the treacherous gaps between the rocks and soon found herself far behind Ferguson. Fortunately, he paused at the entrance to allow her to catch up. Together, they stared into the shadowy orifice.

'I would say this cave was here before the landslide. None of the rock faces look sharp,' she said.

'Even better. My mother was out here when the whole thing looked like that bloody lizard. She would have known of this cave. I bet we'll find the box just inside; I mean, why would she go further in than she needed?'

Allira made no comment and followed Ferguson into the cave.

The light dwindled rapidly and Ferguson fell several times in his haste. Ignoring the blood on his knees and hands, he strode on, eyes flicking left, right, and down as he went. But gradually, he slowed as the scattered stones below his feet showed no sign of any hiding place.

And then he stopped. Wearily, he turned to Allira's dim shape and said, 'Nothing.'

Allira joined him and grasped an arm, making a turning motion on his immovable mass.

'You're wrong. Look.'

Ferguson turned and, eyes straining, looked down the tunnel of blackness.

'Yes,' he breathed. 'I see it.'

'A light. But what is a light doing here, at the end of a tunnel in a rock?'

Ferguson had learned from his misplaced confidence.

'Probably just some kind of shaft. But we'll take a look.'

They walked, slowly this time, into the darkness, seeing a very faint greenish glow at the tunnel's vanishing point. Inch by inch, their surroundings became clearer, although the light gave them a disturbingly necrotic cast. Then their journey ended; the way was blocked by a sheer, featureless wall. The light was coming from a small gap at the left-hand side of the wall. Ferguson touched the wall.

'It's the same stuff as Renfield's cave. Smooth, slightly slippery.' Ferguson stopped his inspection. A memory had come to him: the tube Delgado had shown him, that had also been made of a smooth, featureless substance. Was he dealing with the same type of material? Something neither ceramic, nor stone, nor wood, nor metal? Something completely strange and unknown to either Colonist or Old One? He looked at Allira.

'Touch this wall. Do you know what it's made from?'

'No.'

He ran his fingers over the wall again until they came to the gap along one side.

'Wait a minute: this is no wall—it's a door! A door that hasn't closed properly.'

Allira put her eye to the gap.

'Yes, there's a breeze coming from inside; very cool. Odd smell.' She turned to Ferguson. 'Greg, whatever this is, it's nothing to do with your mother. It reminds me of Renfield. We should go.'

'Not yet.' He turned from her, back to the wall which was a door. 'Hasn't closed properly,' he said to himself. 'I wonder.'

The gap was wide enough to insert a hand. Then the other. Allira realised what he was going to do. 'Greg! Don't! We don't know ...'

Too late. In the green gloom she saw his tremendous biceps bunch into rounded masses as hard as the stone below his feet. His face twisted into that of a tormented gargoyle under the strain.

And the door moved.

Jerkily and with a grinding protest—but it moved.

When Ferguson finally stopped, the gap had grown wide enough for someone to get through by turning sideways.

'Can't do any more,' he panted.

'I still think we should go.'

'Not now. I want to know what's going on.'

He exhaled strongly and pushed himself into the gap. He struggled for a moment and Allira, heart in mouth, thought for a moment he was stuck. But then, with a final effort, he disappeared into the void beyond.

She followed—with no struggle at all. Ferguson had not gone far and was looking around in wonder and bewilderment. She joined him and was soon doing precisely the same.

They were in a cavern whose roof was far above them. All around were frameworks of shelves, one behind the other and stretching far into the cavern. Allira touched the wall nearest to where she was standing.

'Metal. This is not a natural cave.'

'Definitely not. But what's on these shelves?'

They approached the nearest. There was something lying on it, about as big as an average man. Ferguson partially lifted it out of its cradle. It was streamlined, with a head vaguely reminiscent of a bird but bearing two forward-pointing hemispheres, patterned like the compound eye of an insect. And folded along its back were sheets that could only be wings of some kind. As Ferguson examined it, he gave a sudden grunt of surprised recognition and turned to Allira.

'It's a bloody Mozzie. I've never seen one this close up, but definitely a Mozzie!'

Hesitantly, Allira ran a hand along its upper surface.

'Yes, but more importantly, look at it carefully, Greg. It's not a living creature—it's made entirely of some kind of metal!'

Greg looked blankly at her.

'Not a living creature? That's rubbish—how can metal move? These things fly, for gods' sake!'

Allira shook her head.

'Not sure. But we have to believe our eyes. These things are definitely Mozzies. And they are definitely not some kind of animal.' She looked at him, her eyes wide with alarm. 'We are in too deep here, Greg. This is out of any experience of either of our peoples. This is dangerous. We must leave before something happens to us.'

He shook his head.

'No. This has something to do with what my mother told me. We haven't found her box, but this is proof she was telling the truth about some kind of hidden world.' He looked around. 'Have you seen anything like this before?'

'No. But that's why it's dangerous.'

But Ferguson had gone deeper into the cave. She hurried to catch up with him. The frames with their motionless Mozzies ended, and they stood before a gently sloping ramp that rose from the floor and ended at a far wall. A great circle was carved into its metal and the ramp met the wall at the exact centre of the circle.

'I wonder...' he said, but did not explain his words.

'Wonder what?'

He turned from studying the ramp.

'My workmate, Wygu, gave me a drug called pituri.'

'Yes, I know of it.'

'It opened my mind, and I was able to remember what happened after I was attacked by a Mozzie. It flew away with me and took me into a cave. One very much like this one. Perhaps this exact one.'

'All the more reason to get out now.'

Ferguson glared down at her.

'What is wrong with you! This is living proof of what my mother was trying to tell me. Does any of this look normal? I've got to find out more!'

Allira glared back but said nothing and followed her companion as he moved further into the cave, stopping by the side of the ramp.

'I wonder if...' Ferguson began. He stopped. There was a grinding noise from the wall which had the great circle inscribed upon it. The astounded pair watched as a line of light appeared within the circle, forming a vertical diameter. The line widened rapidly as the two halves moved apart, revealing the brilliant sky beyond.

'Get down!' Ferguson hissed. 'I know what's coming!'

Almost immediately, a dark object became visible in the centre of the circle of blue and rapidly resolved itself into a flying Mozzie, carrying something below it at the end of four spindly legs. Dumbstruck, they watched as it landed at the top of the ramp, which immediately began moving, transporting the Mozzie and its cargo to floor level. As soon as they were at the base of the ramp, the Mozzie released its load, which revealed itself to be an unconscious man. The section of the ramp bearing the man then detached itself from the remainder, sprouted wheels and moved off into an unseen part of the cave. Ferguson's face hardened into barely suppressed anger.

'This is what happened to me! They're going to pump that guy's brain full of crap! Make him forget everything!'

'Keep your voice down, Greg! Why would they do that?'

'It doesn't matter why; all I know is they turned me into a shell of a human being; one who had no will to do anything. Just sit and daydream and play with themselves.'

Allira pulled at his sleeve.

'Whoever is doing this is someone we don't want to meet. Greg, please let's go!'

Ferguson straightened himself from his crouching position and shook his head.

'No, I'm going after them. Whatever they're up to, they can't treat people like this, as if we're farm animals!'

Allira also stood and, together, they took one step in the direction that the unconscious captive had been taken.

And stopped. There had been an ominous buzz behind them.

They whirled around to find that the recently-arrived Mozzie had noticed them, and was hovering in the air just a few yards away. It rotated vertically, revealing four appendages protruding from its underside. It flashed towards them and Ferguson saw it clasp Allira and begin to lift her off the floor. He grabbed it from behind and clutched the legs that were imprisoning the woman. The Mozzie buzzed angrily as he threw his strength into breaking its hold. The legs lost their traction on Allira and she dropped the few inches to the floor. But Ferguson did not release the Mozzie; instead he continued to bend the thing's legs outward so they could no longer turn into a grasping position. Its buzzing grew louder as its legs ground ever outward. Ferguson concluded it was calling for help and so he lifted the creature high above him and then brought it crashing down, headfirst, onto the hard floor. The head buckled and the buzzing stopped. He looked at the gasping Allira.

'Time to go,' he said.

TWELVE

Ferguson and Allira cast many fearful glances behind them as they fled from the Goanna Rock, expecting to see the sky darkened by a horde of vengeful Mozzies.

But none appeared, and eventually, they were back at the farmstead.

Ferguson slumped onto the packing case while Allira sat in the one surviving chair. They looked at each other in nervous bewilderment.

'I've seen Mozzies before, but it's hard to believe they aren't natural creatures,' Ferguson said at last.

'I knew nothing about them, except I knew they carried people off, but I've never met one of those people. Until you, that is. Why do they do it? Some people thought it was to feed their chicks, but obviously that's not true.'

'They don't do anything to the body. I'm proof of that. They do something to your mind.'

'I didn't understand what you said in the cave; say it again, please, Greg.'

He glanced down at his interlocked hands before returning to his companion.

'I can't remember too much about it. The memory of being in the cave was buried until the drug released it. But Wygu said I was—some long word—"apa"

133

something.' Allira nodded to show she understood, and he continued: 'I didn't want to do anything. All I wanted to do was sit and daydream, like I'd been turned into Delgado, long before I should have been.'

'But why do that to you? What did the Mozzies get out of it? It would have made more sense if they'd eaten you.'

'I don't know.' He stood up suddenly. 'I'm sick of saying those words! It's all I ever say these days! Sometimes, I wish I'd never heard those words from my mother; my life would have been a lot simpler!'

She stood and kissed him on the forehead.

'I'll make some tea.'

But he grasped her wrist and held her there.

'No, you don't. You don't make sense either. You went away, and now you're back. And you haven't given a good explanation for either.'

She waited for him to release her and then sat again.

'I didn't know who I was: Old One, Colonist—or something else.'

He frowned.

'There is nothing else.'

'I hope you're right.'

'Stop being so damn mysterious. I hate mysteries.'

'Sorry. But this life of ours is mysterious. I think we've proved that. Anyway, I went away. I blamed you, but that wasn't really true. We were both children. And so I spent a long time with the first tribe that would take me in.'

'You don't really belong to a tribe?'

'No. I never knew my parents. I was found wandering by some of the Old People, but I never underwent the ceremonies that would have made me a full tribe member. So, in the end, I thought maybe my destiny was with the Colonists after all. So I came back to be with them.' She paused. 'And perhaps be with you.'

You don't know me.'

She smiled.

'Something tells me I will.'

The evening was well advanced. The sky was shading from blue to a rich purple and the brightest star was already visible. In the distance, the great rock glowed like fading fire.

They looked at each other.

Ferguson said, 'Come here.'

She obeyed, and without saying more, sat on his lap, one arm draped over his neck, the other holding him tightly. They kissed slowly, exploring each other's mouths and then their bodies. From her position she could feel his developing masculine demand. The kissing became faster, more frenzied. Then, without any words, he stood, carrying her in his arms as if she were made from nothing more substantial than the desert breeze that was ruffling her hair.

He took her to his bedroom, and she stood there smiling as he gently removed her clothes before removing his own. She gasped as she felt his weight press down upon her and then again, more ardently, as he thrust into her.

Then she placed her palms on his chest and gasped, 'Greg, you must do something for me!'

'I am,' was his only reply as he prepared for another thrust.

'No, please listen! You must not finish inside me!'

He stopped, his face a patchwork of conflicting emotions.

'Why? It's what I want!'

'No, not yet, Greg! I'm sorry, but you must promise! We can't risk bringing a child into this world when we don't know what problems we might be exposing it to.' Her face became still and resolute. 'Promise, and we will make real, proper love. Refuse or say nothing, and you will be raping me, and we will part forever and I will hate you forever!'

He was silent for the briefest of moments.

'I promise.'

She smiled, and raised her head to receive his kiss.

And then they made love.

***

For the next few days, they were lost in their newfound intimacy, exploring each other, thrilling at each discovery. Eventually, they remembered the needs of their livestock, and their headlong pace slackened.

But did not stop completely.

As they lay together on what was now their joint bed, Ferguson stroked a willing breast and murmured, 'I now understand why I was so obsessed with finding out what my mother meant with the last thing she said to me. I was trying to fill a hole in my life; trying to rid myself of an emptiness.'

Allira smiled as she looked up into a face that was also smiling.

'I'm so glad to hear you say that, Greg. This constant questioning, trying to look behind the curtain, it's been consuming you, making you unhappy. There are some things we shouldn't worry about. We don't know why the sun rises; why should we care about the Mozzies? They're just another part of life we have to accept.'

'What about Renfield?'

'What about him? Greg, we all know you're big and strong, but you're not the toughest man in the whole world. Renfield wasn't built like you, but he had—what's the word?—resilience. You dished it out—and he took it.'

'The woman?'

'She was in the other room. There were probably lots of rooms in that place we never saw. No mystery there. Greg, let's face it: maybe you've been looking for answers to problems that don't exist. Perhaps there are no mysteries."

He nodded, but she saw a swift shadow pass across his features at her final words. Perhaps her blunt statements had somehow disturbed him, perhaps his quest had not been abandoned after all. But his next actions reassured her. Flinging off the thin sheet that had been partly covering them, he left the bed and stretched, letting the morning sunlight warm his muscles. He turned.

'Well, much as I'd like to spend the rest of the day on the bed, we have a farm to run. And lambs to take to market.'

She swung her feet onto the floor and pulled a face.

'Those poor lambs. I don't like the thought of their kidneys ending up on somebody's plate.'

He laughed.

'I thought you were the one who said we had to accept life as it is. That Cat certainly wanted my kidneys!'

She looked at him with a mischievous glint in her eyes.

'Well, I don't particularly want your kidneys, but there is a part of you I really do mean to have!'

Sometime later, after they had both put on their shorts, they set off for the auction, the dogs driving the lambs in front of them. Ferguson and Allira were holding hands when he suddenly said, 'I'll have to get some condoms; I really can't carry on like this much longer. It doesn't seem natural.'

She gave his calloused hand a quick squeeze.

'No, of course not. I understand your need and I'm proud of you for going along with me. But I really don't want to risk a child.'

His lips pursed.

'OK. But I don't see why you're so dead against it. Life's not too bad around here, and I'd like a boy to help on the farm—just like my father had.'

She laughed.

'Just like a man! Has to be a son, doesn't it!' She kissed his neck, the only part above his shoulders she could reach, and said. 'We'll see about that one day, Greg, but not yet. Get the condoms.'

Laughing, she reached for his groin but missed. Her hand grazed a thigh and he winced.

'Hey, that hurt!' He looked at the offending hand and said, 'Can't you get those nails cut?'

'I could, but I like them this way. They grow so quickly and then stop. They won't get any longer.'

'Just as well. It would be like living with a Cat.'

The farmers' market was held in a large rectangular shed with an open central space where the animals were paraded. They sat near the front, watching the bulls and rams pass in front of them. The air was full of the earthy smells of animal flesh and excreta, along with the grunts and bleats of the livestock.

He looked at her.

'Are you getting used to all this? I know the Old People don't have farming in their lives, preferring to hunt and forage. They don't know what they're missing.'

She laughed.

'And you won't know what you've been missing until you try a honeypot ant!'

The auction ended, and Ferguson was pleased with his payment, which included several chickens and pigs' trotters. They were leaving when Ferguson stopped and stared across the enclosure to the other rows of benches.

'What's he doing here? That's Schwartz. The barman I told you about.'

He waved, and Allira and he made their way through the rows of benches to where Schwartz was still sitting. Schwartz's face was neutral, as if not particularly pleased to see them. Or perhaps to have been noticed.

'Greg, good to see you,' he said as he rose. He spent some time staring at Allira, his gaze flicking up and down her body until Ferguson began to get annoyed. Fortunately, he turned to Ferguson and said, 'And this lovely young lady is...?'

'Allira,' the young lady said, extending a hand, 'My name is Allira.'

'Pleased to meet you,' Schwartz said, and immediately turned back to Ferguson. 'You got a good price for those lambs, Greg. Well done.'

'Yes, I did. But what are you doing here? You're not a farmer.'

'No fooling you, Greg! No, I thought you might be here at the market, thought I might bump into you.'

'Well, you have. Any news? Has your beer become drinkable?'

'Ha, ha! Very funny! No, I heard you've had a rough time; thought I might bump into you, see how you're getting on. Just being friendly to one of my best customers, as I haven't seen you for a while.'

'Yes, some people might say it's been rough. But I'm still here.'

'Yes, that problem with the healer. Very nasty.'

Ferguson's eyes narrowed.

'The Healer? How do you know about that? I haven't been down to the Kookaburra since I got back.'

Schwartz's face went blank.

'Ah, you haven't, have you? No, I heard about the Cat from one of your neighbours and as you're still alive, I guessed you'd had some medical help. I just guessed it was a Healer, you see.'

A silence fell. Both men stood looking at each other. Then Ferguson shrugged and said, 'Very clever of you. I didn't know you cared so much about me.' He looked down at one of the chicken carcasses. 'Well, Allira and me will probably come down to the Kookaburra soon and celebrate—we're together now.'

Schwartz's expression did not change, but he said, 'That's wonderful. Yes, come on down and I'll get the Special out and the first two will be on me.'

With that, he was on his way. Ferguson stared after him.

'That's funny. I'm sure no one knew about us and Renfield.'

'Lighten up, Greg. All that's behind us now. You know how people in communities like ours love to gossip.'

Ferguson was quiet for a moment and then, 'Well, our only close neighbour is Delgado, and I haven't seen him since we got back.'

'Greg! Leave it alone; you're worrying about things again! I thought we agreed you wouldn't do that. Come on; let's get back and make some chicken soup! That should put hair on your chest!' She laughed. 'Well, more hair, I should say. Perhaps I could cuddle close and hide myself in it!'

Ferguson smiled a great smile, wide enough to reveal the crooked teeth Gottlieb had given him.

'You're right, as usual. What would I do without you?'

They kissed.

THIRTEEN

It was late evening and the dome of the sky was transitioning from a rich purple to deep ebony. Ferguson had finally managed to hammer a replacement chair together but, gallantly, had given the original to Allira in case his workmanship should be found wanting. They were sitting together on the veranda, looking up at the starry sky.

'So, tell me more about your legends,' he said, gently stroking her abundant hair. In response, she pointed at the Milky Way's misty thoroughfare.

'As I understand it, you Colonists see patterns in the sky by connecting the stars with imaginary lines. You see things like scorpions and make-believe creatures that are both man and horse. We do not see those.'

Ferguson pointed at a small group of four bright stars.

'Surely, you recognise that as the Southern Cross?'

Her nod was just visible in the gathering darkness.

'Of course, everyone knows that. But tell me this, O Wise Man, if that is the Southern Cross, where is the Northern?'

He looked at her in amazement.

'Good gods, I never thought of that.' He looked around the sky, obviously seeking the complement of the Southern star group.

She laughed.

'You won't find it, you silly man; there isn't one.'

'But why call something "Southern" if there isn't a "Northern"?'

She placed a warning finger on his lips.

'Now, Greg, don't go looking for mysteries again. It's a name; just a name.'

'OK. So, tell me more about your view of the night.'

She pointed again at the hazy highway.

'You join the stars together; we do that as well, but we do more. We also see dark constellations. Look at your Southern Cross, do you see a black patch near it? Yes, you do? Well, that is the head of the Emu in the Sky. Now, take your gaze down the celestial river and see the dark lanes against the milk. Those are the legs of the Emu.'

Ferguson stared, and for a thrilling moment, he was able to see the emu.

'Yes, Allira. A great emu. What does it do? Peck the stars, thinking they are seeds?'

'Don't mock, Greg. The Emu in the Sky holds great importance for many groups across our land, as it is deeply connected to our spiritual beliefs, cultural practices, and daily life. The Emu is often seen as a Creator Being, responsible for shaping the landscape and bringing life to the Earth. Many Old People communities have their own stories and legends about the Emu, which have been passed down through generations as part of their oral tradition. The Emu in the Sky is not only a significant part of our spiritual beliefs but also plays a crucial role in our understanding of the natural world. You see, its appearance and position in the sky are closely linked to seasonal changes and the availability of food resources, making it a tool for survival. The Emu's presence in the sky also serves as a reminder of the deep connection between us, the land, and the cosmos, reinforcing our identity and sense of belonging.'

'Hmm. I don't understand any of that, but you puzzle me, Allira. One minute you say you are not really one of the Old People, and the next you are solemnly reciting their traditions. What are you, Allira?'

There was a silence which Greg thought might never end, and then he heard a sigh in the darkness.

'I wish I knew, Greg. I am searching for an identity, somewhere to truly belong. A place I can finally call my home.' She paused. 'Have I found it with you, Greg?'

He reached for her, attempted to kiss her but missed in the darkness, brushing against her hair instead.

'Of course. I've been searching as well. And so we have found each other. And we will stay together, believe me.'

'I am so glad to hear you say that. I want us never to be parted.'

But after she said those words, she turned her face from Ferguson and stared long into the starry abyss as if hoping for confirmation from the Emu in the Sky of future happiness.

But there was none.

***

Ferguson wiped the sweat from his forehead and pulled the wide-brimmed hat tighter. Heat was rising from the ground in great wavering ripples, distorting the landscape into something from a dream.

There was still no sign of water. The spring near the farmstead was not as vigorous as it should be, and that was a terrifying thought. If it should dry up, he and Allira would have to move. The two of them could survive on much less water than at present but his animals could not. Delgado had said there used to be another spring in this area, but Ferguson was damned if he could find it. He sat on a rock and took a slab of dried meat from his tunic. He chewed it morosely, occasionally glancing around in case he had missed something. Vegetation should be stronger and greener near a water source, but everything looked grey, dry and dust-covered. He finished the meat and stood, wiping his hands on his khakis. Time to move on.

He stopped, cocking his head, listening.

Could it be...?

It was. The ominous buzz of a Mozzie.

Searching the sky, he felt his heart jump when he saw a black dot in the distance.

No, worse than that—three black dots: three Mozzies. Coming straight at him. Looking for him. Hunting him.

It looked like the Mozzies were after revenge for his demolition of one of their comrades. He knew this time he wouldn't escape so easily. Images of Allira frantically searching for him flashed through his mind, images of his livestock starving and dying.

He looked around desperately. He had to hide, hide from these aerial hunters! There was a jumble of rocks some distance away; he could wedge himself

145

between the boulders; even if they could see him, they wouldn't be able to get at him. But if they hit him with that flash of light, like the first time...

The mass of stone was his only hope. He dodged around the first boulder and tried to continue further into the jumble of rocks, but a wide patch of deep sand and gravel slowed him down. The buzzing was getting louder. He stumbled and fell into a deep depression in the ground; sand slithered down its sides, partially covering him. He coughed as the harsh material began to fill his eyes and nostrils. Then he stopped fighting as a thought came to him: how intelligent were Mozzies? They could not have seen him disappear as he had gotten behind the boulder, out of direct sight. When they reached it and he was not there, would they abandon the hunt or deduce he must be hiding? But how long could he hide inside this shroud of sand? The flow of sand had stopped; he could only be some inches down, less than a foot, but quite enough to suffocate him. Keeping his eyes firmly shut, Ferguson wriggled onto his back and felt for his father's whistle and placed it in his mouth. He took a breath through it but received only a thin shower of sand. It had not broken the surface, but it was essential that he did not lift his head high enough to mound the sand and betray his hiding place. Ferguson slowly lifted his head slightly, praying he could just reach the sweet spot where the mouth of the whistle would be high enough to break the surface, but not enough to be recognisably an unnatural feature. His closed eyes then received the tiniest glimmer of light, and he instantly lowered his head to half of the distance it had just covered. His heart was thundering and a terrible need for air was beginning to torment him. He had to hope the whistle had just broken through, and risk breathing!

He breathed and received a blissful mouthful of air; the same air that only a short while before had been like an exhalation from a raging bushfire but now felt cool and sweet.

He waited as long as he could.

Then breathed again.

Time passed. Seconds? Minutes? Hours?

He could not tell; all he knew was that he was not getting enough air, and the enclosing sand was starting to cook him.

Ferguson erupted out of his sandy coffin with fists clenched and ready. Sand was in his eyes and he could not stop gasping and spluttering as he threw himself full-length on the ground. Through streaming, grit-filled eyes, he looked around as best he could, searching for his pursuers. He saw nothing and dared to push himself onto his knees, reddened eyes darting from spot to spot.

Nothing. Ferguson crept to the edge of the boulder that had sheltered him earlier and peered around. In the blue distance, he saw Mozzies flying away, defeated.

Then those sore eyes saw something was wrong. He blinked desperately, not daring to rub his eyes for fear of scarring them. But his burning vision was even more blurred than the heat ripples were causing; he could not be sure that there was still danger!

Then he was: there were only two Mozzies in the sky—one had stayed. He flattened himself against the rock.

'Where are you, you bastard?' he hissed. He realised that the things had, indeed, some level of intelligence; one had stayed behind to check for deception. And somewhere, it must be watching him, realising that the deception was over.

Ferguson ran their earlier encounters through his memory. In the cave it had attempted to capture Allira; it had not used its flash-of-light weapon. But when one had caught him in the open, it had used that weapon.

He was in the open now.

Therefore, it would use that irresistible weapon when it saw him.

There was only one hope, one slim possibility: maybe, just maybe, the energy of the flash had to be transmitted by the eyes to the brain to be effective. Ferguson did not think in exactly those neurological terms but the conclusion was the same as if he had.

And then there was no time to weigh probabilities, to think, to ponder. There was a brief flutter of strong metal wings, and the Mozzie was before him, its compound eyes boring into his own. Ferguson leapt towards it, turning his head away from those eyes. He grasped its hard vibrating body, feeling power surge in appendages that instantly began to close around him in a steel trap. Even if it could not knock him unconscious, it could still transport him to its cave where his nightmare would begin again! But keeping his eyes firmly shut, he strove to create a mental map of where the nearest boulder was in relation to his current position, while one hand located the Mozzie's head. Ferguson blindly lifted the now loudly buzzing thing and oriented it horizontally with the head pointing away from him. His muscles tensed and he whirled around, driving the thing headfirst onto the unyielding stone. Ferguson heard the satisfying crunch of an imploding head, and the power vanished from its clinging legs. He released the dead Mozzie and collapsed.

An unknown time later, his eyes flickered open. He lay there, wondering why they hurt so much. Then he remembered. Lying next to him was the weird and now silent form of the Mozzie.

He lifted it up, glanced into its compound eyes for a second and immediately looked away. Nothing happened, so he returned to studying it. To his wondering eyes, it lay revealed as a thing of a hard metal, but smooth to his touch and lustrous to his vision, completely unlike the crude tips of the local spears, or the irregular grey wires that formed the fences of the animal pens. And now he had time to really study it, unlike the time in the cave when its details had been obscured by the low lighting. His fingertips marvelled at the smoothness of its surface, and he was startled to see his face looking up at him from its shining hide, his eyes screwed up with the pain of the sand. It suddenly came to him that he must be the first person to be this close to one of these things while still conscious and with time to study it. And so, Allira's initial conclusion had been horribly correct, and he, Ferguson, was now the first person to fully understand that the Mozzies were not weird living creatures, but some type of *device*.

How could anyone of the Colonists, or still less the Old People, have made it? The conclusion was overwhelmingly obvious: neither it, nor the cave from whence it came, could be the work of any tribe known to him. From which only one conclusion followed.

This was the work of his mother's *they*.

And the fact that no less than three Mozzies had been sent to hunt him down proved another thing: the mysterious *they* were angry with him.

He scowled and sat wearily back on his haunches. His life had just gotten a whole lot more complicated.

FOURTEEN

They sat together, wrapped in an oppressive silence.

'We have to leave,' Allira said. 'We can't stay here.'

Ferguson looked up.

'No. This is my land. This is all I know.'

She reached over to touch his arm; he did not react, continuing to look into the corner of the room, away from Allira.

'Greg, Greg, I know this is difficult for you, but things have changed. Somehow, you've become involved with the Mozzies, and they're out to get you. Three times you've met them, and you've been lucky to escape. That can't last.'

'I didn't know what to expect the first time, and the second time I was too busy rescuing you to think much about my future plans.'

'Yes, you did, and I am forever grateful to you for that. I don't know why they went for me that time and not you. But if they're after me as well, doesn't that make it imperative we move?'

'I wish you'd stop using words like "imperative". It makes me feel awkward. Did all the people in your tribe talk like that?'

Her head drooped.

'I'm sorry. It's just the way I speak; I thought you knew that.'

Ferguson finally turned to look at her.

'I'm sorry to snap at you, but you're asking me to run away, something I've never done before.'

'You've never faced Mozzies before. Look at it my way; normally, they just knock people out cold and leave them to recover, like they've had too much of Schwartz's dreadful beer, but they abducted you and took you to one of their caves and messed with your head. You said Wygu hardly recognised you as his friend.'

Silence.

'Don't you see what that means?'

'No.'

'It means there's something about you they don't like, something they want to change. And perhaps me, as well,' she added, after a few seconds' thought.

'There have always been Mozzies; they've never been that much trouble. The Cats are far worse; should we leave because we might run into a Cat?'

'You're twisting my words. What a Cat wants is obvious: it wants to eat you. Why would Mozzies want your mind—not your body?' He did not reply. 'Greg, remind me: what was happening just before the first Mozzie took you away?'

'I was about to kill Gottlieb. And I knew I was going to do it. He's a big guy, but I had the strength of ten men when I saw what he'd done to Sky. I would have taken him apart slowly.'

Her face went completely blank; a sure sign, Ferguson knew, that she was thinking. Deeply.

'Anger. Imminent violence. Perhaps that is what they don't like.'

He snorted.

'Hah! So, they want us to be meek and mild, do they! People who wouldn't squash a fly if the bugger bit him!'

Her face carried no emotion as they looked at each other.

'Yes, Greg. That is exactly what they want.'

***

Ferguson drained the last of the beer, felt the bitter liquid at the back of his mouth for a moment, and then swallowed. He pushed the tankard back to Schwartz and said, 'Another.'

The barman tightened his lips and shook his head.

'I don't know, Greg, you've had more than a few, and I really don't need any more mutton.'

Ferguson stared at the other for a moment and said, 'I'll throw in a kidney. Another beer.'

As he began to gulp his drink, Schwartz said, 'Whoa! Take it easy, pal!' As Ferguson reluctantly complied, Schwartz continued: 'What's eating you, Greg? You don't usually drink like this.'

Ferguson shrugged, and then said, 'Woman trouble.'

'Oh, that old story. What's the problem?'

Ferguson explained about Allira's plea to move out of the area.

'I can't do it. My father farmed this land, and his before him. It's in the blood.'

Schwartz nodded in agreement.

'Yeah, everyone around here feels the same way. I can't see it myself; one patch of scrub looks like every other patch of scrub as far as I'm concerned.' His expression became serious. 'So, what's the old ball-and-chain been saying now, Greg?'

'She's worried about the Mozzies. Seems they don't like me.'

Schwartz laughed.

'Come on—everybody likes you, Greg!' He leaned over the bar, nearer to his customer. 'What's there to worry about? They've never killed anyone, to my knowledge. How about you: have you heard of anyone being murdered by a Mozzie? No? Then what's for her to be worried about?'

'I was—what's the word?—*abducted* by one and I came back sort of different. Kind of meek and mild, just sitting around, daydreaming.'

Schwartz laughed again.

'Yeah, that's you, alright! Tell me, did it last? Are you still "meek and mild"?'

Ferguson shook his shaggy head, resulting in a triumphant look from the barman.

'There you are! Seems to me these Mozzies are just playing with us; they mean us no harm. Now the Cats—they're different. It's them your Old Lady ought to be worried about.'

Ferguson felt his worries lift somewhat under Schwartz's affability, but there were still problems with the latter's sunny analysis.

'The Mozzies—they're not flesh and blood, you know...say, what is your first name?'

'Felix. I thought you knew.'

Ferguson did not display any further interest in his host's nomenclature, but continued, 'They're metal. All metal.'

Schwartz leant backwards, shaking his head.

'Now, that's plain silly. You can't have animals made of metal, Greg. You must have had a touch of the sun.'

'Well, I'd just been fighting one, so I wasn't thinking straight, I know that.'

'Exactly. If you go around kicking animals, you've got to expect them to kick back. And as for that metal nonsense, there are lots of desert creatures out there with really tough, scaly bodies; hides you couldn't get a knife through. Am I making sense?'

Ferguson smiled, his relief evident.

'Yes, yes you are!'

Schwartz returned the smile, although an alert observer might have noticed the smile looked a little theatrical, as if a troubling thought had entered his mind.

'Sense at last! Have another beer, Greg—I think you need it!'

Ferguson left the bar feeling at peace with himself, for the first time in quite a while.

***

Allira looked at Ferguson in wide-eyed amazement.

'Mozzies are nothing to be worried about? Who in the name of all the hells told you that?'

'Felix—if you must know.'

After Ferguson had explained who that entity was, Allira turned away from him and sat down, staring at the wall.

'This is ridiculous,' she said, apparently addressing the wall. Then she looked up at Ferguson. 'So, a few words with a barman, and you're prepared to deny the evidence of your own eyes.'

Ferguson shifted uncomfortably.

'He said a lot of sensible things.'

She leapt to her feet, eyes blazing.

'He said nothing of the kind! Anyway, sit down; you're drunk.'

Unused to merely verbal lacerations, Ferguson complied and sat looking at his companion, silently awaiting the next onslaught. However, it was not forthcoming; instead, Allira stood and began pacing back and forth.

'Perhaps if we could make an end to this box thing, we could move on,' she said.

'No, I'm not forgetting about the box.'

'I'm not asking you to.' She whirled to face him. 'I've been thinking while you've been out drinking yourself stupid. Your mother's last words: say them again so I can be sure.'

After Ferguson had done so, she repeated them, and then: 'Perhaps we have been overlooking an important clue. She said "tail"—and we know what she meant by that. But she also said "sun".'

Ferguson nodded, unsure if he was expected to speak.

He was not, for Allira continued, 'A tail. And the sun. What do you get if you put them together?'

Ferguson thought for a moment and then said, 'I don't know.'

'A shadow, Greg, a shadow! The box will be where the shadow falls.'

He leapt to his feet.

'Let's go!'

She waved him back to his seat.

'No, not yet. You're in no condition to go digging, and I need to think it through.'

'Why?'

'Because the shadow moves. She must have meant a particular time.' Her face lightened, becoming unlined. 'It would have to be midday.' Then it became concerned again. 'But midday depends on the time of year. It would be at one particular place in winter and another at the solstice.'

'What's a solstice?'

'But the shadow would move along a particular path. One end in the winter, another in the summer. So, we don't know the exact spot—but we do know that spot will be along a line, a line marking out the two extremes.'

Ferguson found that his head had cleared and jumped to his feet, his own eyes now carrying some of Allira's fire.

'So, we dig along the line until we find it!'

'Exactly.'

***

The midday sun burned down almost vertically upon the backs of the man and woman as they scrabbled among the small rocks and loose stones of the ground. Rivulets of sweat were coursing regularly down their faces as hands with black-rimmed, torn nails turned over stone after stone. Occasionally, Allira would look up and scan the sky with fearful eyes, as if expecting danger to descend upon them from above. Only part of that sapphire dome was visible, appearing as a rectangular segment; the rest was blotted out by the vast overhang of rock that loomed ominously above.

'Don't look for Mozzies,' Ferguson grunted as he turned over a particularly large rock. 'Just keep looking. That way, we'll be out of here sooner.'

Allira nodded nervously, bent over the accumulation of stones and resumed her searching.

An hour had passed since they had arrived, and Allira calculated that they must be two thirds of the way along the line the sun tracked on its annual migration. She thought how bitterly Ferguson would react if this search also ended up blank. Would he be downcast and depressed, or would he be angry with her for raising false hopes? She shuddered even in the baking heat; she did not wish to witness either reaction.

'Come on, come on,' Ferguson said. 'These stones aren't going to move by themselves!'

She noticed the stones were getting smaller; large areas of black, fine-grained gravel were appearing between them, ideal ground for concealing something. Hope fluttered in her mind, but she said nothing. There must be no more false hope.

On and on they went, in what was rapidly feeling like some kind of eternal punishment. Several times, ignoring Ferguson's commands, she thought she had heard Mozzies approaching from behind, but each time the land behind them was empty. There were no sounds other than their laboured breathing, cursing, and the dry noise of stones rubbing against stones.

Eventually, she stopped, straightened her aching back, with some difficulty, and wiped the trickling sweat from her forehead. She had made a decision.

'I think...' she began.

But she did not complete the thought, for Ferguson gave a sharp cry and then he also straightened up. He was facing away from her and she could see the huge dark stain of sweat, almost filling the fabric of his shirt. From his posture, he appeared to be holding something.

'Greg!' she cried. 'Greg...'

He turned.

He was holding a box of dented, pitted grey metal. He smiled.

'I've found it.' Holding the box by its handle with one hand, he came to her and wrapped the other mighty arm around her, pulling her onto him. 'I've only gone and bloody found it!'

They ran out from under the tail of that colossal goanna, away from the danger, away from the endless piles of broken and shattered stone. From time to time, Ferguson would let out a whoop of victory, but Allira was too tired to tell him to be quiet. Soon, she could not keep up with him and had to call to him to stop, as in his excitement, he had not noticed she was no longer beside him. But, even at their walking pace, the journey finally ended, and they sat opposite each other, with the mysterious box between them. She saw the glow of excitement almost streaming from his face.

'Well,' she said, 'are you going to open it, or just sit there, grinning like a fool?'

He picked it up and studied it.

'It's locked,' he said. 'We must not have noticed where the key was.'

'Maybe there was another riddle as to where the key is, and your mother never had the time to tell it to you. So, what will we do now?'

'This.'

He reached over for his spear and, inserting the tip between the lid and the side of the box, turned the blade. The lid lifted slightly.

'I don't want to damage that spear. So, I'll do this.'

The gap he had made was wide enough for him to push his large fingers into it. He pulled at the lid and, with a groan of failing metal, it flipped up. There was a small shower of ochre dust. Allira felt her heart jump. Would there be nothing inside, except scraps of brown, faded papers? Would all of this have been for nothing, after all?

Ferguson reached in and removed several packages, all consisting of sheets of paper inside a pliable covering of an unnatural transparent substance. In a frenzy of excitement, he tore the covering open with his teeth. A sheaf of papers fell to the floor. He picked up the top one and started reading it, his hands shaking slightly. But Allira saw a frown develop, replacing the excitement. He dropped the paper and picked up another. Once again, she saw incomprehension appear. Eventually, he sat back and handed the sheaf to Allira.

'Too many words. You read it, Allira.'

And she did.

FIFTEEN

It is not necessary to know my name; (*Allira read*) it is only necessary you read all my words and understand them. I cannot know what you are like, the people who are living after I have gone; I cannot know how far you have sunk into ignorance and quiet acceptance.

You may think my words are harsh, but your world is harsh. Listen to me: the world is not what you think it is! You may believe the world is a beautiful place, you may even consider it to be a kind of paradise. Perhaps it is beautiful, but it is not a paradise.

No, it is a prison. You are prisoners.

For we humans have not been alone in our world. We have shared it with another race, who have lived alongside us, always in the shadows until recently.

Some of us knew of this other race and gave them a name. Learn this name, for it is the most important one there is. These others are **The Vampires**.

They watched us and lusted after us, for we had something they wanted, something that they needed. That something was our blood, for without it they sicken and die. And so they preyed on our kind, becoming nocturnal predators in order to hunt us, mocking us as they sank their fangs into us, draining us. Few people saw a vampire and most of those who did found it was the last thing they would ever see. But enough victims survived for knowledge of our dreadful enemy to be held by many.

But even then, they tricked us. Most people believed that the story of the vampires was simply a myth, a perverted fairy story, to give people a frisson of harmless fear, before they moved onto another type of entertainment. Stories about them were everywhere, on printed pages and in stories displayed by pictures that moved. Towards the end, the notion of vampires had become a kind of joke, a worn-out tale that only adolescents and simpletons took seriously.

That perhaps was their greatest achievement, before what happened next. You see, our people had made great strides in understanding how the world works, but some of us, regrettably, used this knowledge to create terrible weapons of unbelievable power that would have turned the entire world into a graveyard. Mark me well: we created those weapons in our stupidity, but we did not use them, save for one sad episode. But the vampires used the existence of those weapons as an excuse to leap out of the shadows and wrest control of the earth from us in one blindingly swift attack.

And then they did the unthinkable to us: they turned the majority of the human race into farm animals, literally kept on farms where they were forced to give up their lifeblood for their new masters to enjoy. Oceans of blood must have been given up in those early days after all human resistance had been obliterated.

Shameful it is to tell, but some people collaborated with the new rulers, and were given menial jobs as a reward. Some kept watch on their fellow humans in low-grade positions in organisations that policed the surviving population for any signs of resistance.

And worst of all, far worst of all, some were given authority over the enslaved people who were being robbed of their blood. Those wretches were kept on what the vampires termed Blood Farms. Your minds may recoil from this and believe it to be just a sick fantasy of mine, but it is true.

But the flame of resistance was not completely extinguished for a group of our people discovered that the vampires themselves were not all-powerful. They had an enemy, one with immense strength, and who regarded the vampires with the same hunger as the vampires did us humans. Several times these two had fought, and the vampires had driven their enemies off, but only at a terrible cost to themselves. I am not sure of the name of this enemy because only the leaders of the resistance knew it, but I do know the vampires were terrified that they might lose the next war, for a new war there would assuredly be.

Our leaders made contact with this enemy and we joined them in their most recent attack upon the vampires. Or at least, we thought we had, because the supreme leader of our people was eventually revealed to be a traitor, working for the vampires.

And so, our last attempt to regain our freedom failed. And in so doing, we were delivered into the cold hands of a cruel and merciless tyrant called Serafina Ginevra, who had become their supreme leader during the war. It was she who delivered the final blow against us.

You see, by now the vampires had discovered a way of generating artificial human blood, indistinguishable from the real thing. At once, they no longer had any need for us, and we know that Ginevra intended to exterminate us completely. Somehow, someone persuaded her otherwise, but she had another plan.

All the humans, whether farmed or free, were rounded up and shipped off to their prison—the one you are living in now. Those people were truly heroic; they knew exactly what was happening to them, and what their future would be. For Ginevra intended to wipe out all memory of the civilisation that had been stolen from us, and reduce us to the status of ignorant peasants. But some people learned what her plans were, and in a way I do not understand, managed to smuggle some books and documents along with them. Those heroes knew that word of mouth would soon be discounted and that memories would fade, swiftly. First, our past would become a series of legends, and then it would be forgotten entirely. In my day, I can see that is already happening, but I have been given the honour of guarding the remaining texts. And I will do all I can to keep our memories alive.

The vampires collected all the defeated, downtrodden remnants of humanity into one miserable band of refugees and transplanted us onto an isolated landmass, there to mingle peaceably with its original inhabitants. They called the land "Stralia", but we know and still remember its true name. One we must never forget.

So, what of you, the one who lives an unknown time after me? Decades? Centuries? What hope can I offer?

The answer is none: I must tell you I see little hope of escape from this prison. I have done all I can do, in keeping the records safe from those who believe them to be sacrilegious. You must make your own hope. Perhaps you have not lost all of the knowledge and technology we once had. Perhaps Ginevra's plan has not been a total success.

Whatever your state, you must find a way to retrieve our past status, our past happiness.

We are not farm animals.

We owned a world once.

We must have it back.

SIXTEEN

Allira finished reading. The paper fell from her nerveless fingers as she stared at Ferguson, who read the horror in her eyes, knowing that his own held the same stunned emotion. He looked away from her, down at the box, the box that he now wished he had never opened. How better it would have been never to have heard those words, so he could have continued his ordinary life. Now the veil he had longed to tear away had indeed been removed, but what lay behind was something he did not wish to see. His own words came back to him, the vow he had made: '*If there was something, some power that did in fact imprison us here—I swear I will find them!*'

Now he knew the truth, but a truth vastly more horrific than he could possibly have been prepared for. He had only half-believed his mother's story when he had made that vow. In his inner mind, he had thought that if he did find the mysterious *they*, he would discover a group of powerful, ruthless men. Dangerous men, men it would be wise not to confront, but still *men*.

But that threat now seemed ridiculously trivial against this now-revealed reality.

Vampires.

He had never heard the word before, but he could have no dispute with the testament for which he had been searching for so many years. It must be true. So, there were no men he could confront and hammer into submission with his fists of flint. Only—*vampires*; creatures who treated humans like beasts of the field but also wielded powers unimaginable to the simple folk who tended their sheep on the arid red plains. His jailers were creatures who, virtually overnight, had overthrown the worldwide civilisation built by human beings.

He realised he had been staring at nothing for a long time and his head jerked upwards to see Allira standing a short distance away. She crossed to him, her eyes shining with the moisture of unshed tears.

'Greg, Greg, I'm frightened!'

He held her, her head resting against his upper arm, for she was not quite as tall as he was. But as he did, he wondered what words of comfort he could give the woman; words that could only be hollow for he, himself, was also frightened.

He took her back to her seat and pulled up the original, sturdier chair to be close to her. He looked at Allira, holding her hands.

'Greg, what shall we do? What *can* we do?'

Suddenly forced to make a decision, his mind whirled.

'This is too much to understand all at once; we can't make any plans. We've only read the first document. Maybe there's something that will help us in the others.'

She shook her head.

'Greg, I don't want to read anymore. I can't face it!'

'You must. Only then can we be sure of what we're up against.'

She gave a dry laugh.

'Up against? We're not "up against" anything, no more than a quokka is up against a Cat.'

'I'll read them, then.'

She considered that, and then: 'No, we'll be here all night. I'll do it.'

She picked up the remaining documents with the air of someone expecting an electric shock, and together, they studied them.

Ferguson saw his first map. It showed a great, vaguely rectangular landmass surrounded by a blue colouration he took to denote a large body of water. Underneath was a long word beginning with "A", and he finally learned the true name of his home. There were other maps as well; one displayed two adjacent circles showing other landmasses as well as Stralia. His home was in one of the circles, but much smaller. Allira realised that this map was showing them the entire world, and that their home was only a small part of it, and somewhat isolated from the other land areas. Another map showed a close view of an area far distant from theirs. It contained symbols that indicated places of habitation; one, near the coast, was called "New Marinetown" and was in bold, capital letters, as if it were important for some unknown reason.

There was a long text that detailed the achievements of human beings before they were enslaved. He saw names like *Leonardo da Vinci, Shakespeare, Einstein*, amongst many others, but they were just groups of letters, and did not improve his understanding, and so were worthless. Eventually, Ferguson tired of having the documents read to him, as he only understood parts. The central message was only too clear.

He spread his hands in a gesture of bafflement, and said, 'So what now?'

'What now?' Allira repeated. 'What now? We get out of here and start a new life. It all makes sense now: Renfield must have been a vampire. And that strange woman, do you remember what she said?— *So, you are humans. You look like the pictures I have seen.* She was a vampire as well.'

'So, they look like us, do they? I hadn't expected that.'

'It doesn't matter what they look like, it's what they can do to us. Don't you realise that they must be behind the Mozzies? And that whoever is controlling them doesn't like you? We've got to get away from here, far away.'

'My animals...'

'Give them to another farmer. Nothing matters more than getting you away from those monsters.'

Ferguson was lost in thought for some seconds, then: 'Perhaps. Move far away. Start a family in a new place.'

She looked away.

'Perhaps.'

He noticed her reticence.

'Why do you say that? Don't you want to be with me?'

She looked down at her interlocked hands.

'I'm not sure why I say that. There's something inside me telling me I shouldn't take that step—a family, I mean—not you. It's a woman thing; I can't explain it.'

'Well, you'd better grow out of it; I don't intend to be the last of my kind. I may not have much of a life, now I know what the world is really like, but surely you wouldn't deny me that piece of normality?'

Again, she looked away, saying nothing.

Ferguson slowly rose to his feet, his head spinning. How had all this suddenly happened? What had he done differently? He ran his mind over the jumble of recent events; the only thing that stood out was his interaction with the Mozzies; they had taken him away and done something to him, and he, in turn, had followed them to their lair. Despair took him then: Allira was right; he had angered them—whatever they were. And his discovery of the hidden texts had indeed given him a greater understanding of his world, but one he wished he had not uncovered. He made a decision.

'Allira.' Her head jerked up at the commanding note in his voice. 'You're right—we're leaving. But there's something I have to do first.'

He disappeared into the other room and returned, holding his tinder box. Allira realised what he was about to do.

'No, Greg! You can't burn those papers! Your mother kept them hidden, especially for you to read!'

'Then she would be happy I have read them. And now I have no intention of ever reading them again. What good has reading them done me? I now understand I'm just a helpless prisoner in a mad world, so thank you, Mother!'

Allira watched in silent misery as Ferguson set fire to the documents, saw them fold in on each other as they blackened and then burst into flames. She watched as the only record of the heroism of the first people to be transported here was lost forever. Suddenly, the memory of an old legend burst into her mind, the story of another group of people who had been exiled to this land. What was the name of the place where they had been imprisoned?

Suddenly, she had it. She remembered the name, even though it was not of a place she knew; a name that was simply meaningless.

Botany Bay.

SEVENTEEN

Allira looked up as Ferguson entered the building, but the look on his face told her he had not received good news.

'No good?'

'No. Delgado says he'll take a few lambs, but he's too old to take on all the animals.'

'Are you surprised? Anyone can see he's just a weak old man.'

Displaying a weary expression, Ferguson sat down heavily, in his depression not noticing he had chosen the newer chair, and it groaned disapprovingly under the unexpected load.

'I had to try. I thought I might be doing him a favour. All that stock would have made him a rich man, but it looks like he prefers sitting in his chair, talking about the Old Days.' He looked at his hands and grunted scornfully. 'Hah! The Old Days! What does he know about the *real* old days? Who does? Me, only me!'

'And me,' Allira reproved, in as gentle a manner as she could. 'So, what now?'

'I'll have to give the animals away to people I don't really like—people I'd rather see eat dirt. But I can't just let my stock starve, not after all the care I've given them. So, those good-for-nothing bastards get the result of all my work, just because I know things they don't!'

Allira made no attempt to console him, knowing it would be fruitless. Better to stick to practicalities.

'How long will that take? When do we go? Where do we go?'

For the first time, he looked across at her. She saw the anger in his face, but strove to ignore it, hoping it was not for her.

'Three days, I guess. There's no way I can hand over my animals without actually going there, is there? I'm not one of your bloody vampires, with all their magic powers. Once I've seen the animals are safe enough, we get the hells out. As for where, I'll have to find another farmstead where I don't know the owner and he doesn't know me, and sign on as a hand. Right back to the bottom of the pile!' He brought a fist down on the chair arm. It snapped off, but in his rage he appeared not to notice. 'Bottom of the fucking pile!'

***

They stood before the farmstead, looking at it for one last time. Allira felt her eyes suddenly sting with incipient tears. She had not lived there for long, but it was a special place; it was where she and Ferguson had first made love. Now, she would never see it again. Perhaps someone would discover it and set up home, or, more likely, it would simply fall apart, its timbers rapidly covered by drifting sand.

For once, Ferguson saw her distress and gently pulled her closer.

'This is not the end. We'll have another place one day. I'm big and strong and I'll make a good farmhand. I'll have my own farm again before too long.'

She nodded. She wasn't sure she believed him, but this was not the time for doubts. She shouldered her bag of possessions and turned to her partner. He was carrying a much larger bag. He smiled.

'Let's be on our way; we have a whole new life to discover.'

'Do we have to go far?'

'Who knows? Does it matter? Didn't you go Walkabout?'

She did not answer. They began their walk.

Hours passed and still they had not reached any unfamiliar area; even the Goanna Rock was still visible, although much diminished by distance. Ferguson noticed her disquiet.

'It's alright; we're heading south. I know the cobbers to the north and they're just wasters. We'll find somewhere soon.'

She nodded and adjusted her bag strap, which had begun to chafe. *One foot in front of the other,* she thought, *then the other foot. Just keep walking.*

They stopped for a short meal of beef jerky, washed down with the absolute minimum of warm water from their canteens, and then resumed their trek. But after perhaps another hour, Allira suddenly stopped, dropping her bag into the dust.

'Come on,' Ferguson said. 'We must keep going if we're going to get anywhere.'

She shook her head.

'Something wrong. I feel odd. There's a tingling going up and down my legs, in my arms.'

Ferguson shook his head with obvious irritation.

'I thought you Old People could walk for days, going without food or water. We have to go on.'

She nodded weakly and they resumed their walk, but after only a few more yards, she stopped again.

'It's getting worse. I'm sorry, Greg, but I have to stop.'

Ferguson glared at her and picked up the bag she had dropped.

'I'll carry both, if I have to. Come on!'

He strode off, with Allira, divested of her load, following a few yards behind.

Then Ferguson felt it. A slight tingle along his nerves, just above the threshold of detection, just a mildly annoying tickle.

But it held the threat of stronger sensations if he continued walking. He glanced back at Allira, seeing that her face was now showing the unmistakable sign of stress, perhaps of pain. He went to her, smiling.

'It's just all this walking; we're not used to it. Here, I'll help.'

And with that, he grasped her and laid her across his arms, as if she were no more than a collection of feathers. He strode on.

But as he walked, he felt the tingling feelings change insidiously. Each step produced an increase in the sensations; gradually they moved from being irritating, through disturbing, and finally into pain itself. His nerves felt as if they had changed into red-hot wires, carrying stinging, burning feelings into every part of his body. He staggered, almost dropping Allira. They sat together, looking at each other with fear-filled eyes.

'Greg, I can't stand it! What's happening? What is it?'

He shook his great shaggy head, closing his eyes.

'I'm not sure. Every time we walk, it gets worse. It must be that our muscles are not used to all this movement.'

'Greg, that's nonsense! We're both young and fit. You walk everywhere, tending the flocks. It's something else, not just aching muscles.' Then her expression changed; uncertainty was washed away by a wave of terror. 'Greg! I know what it is! It's them— they don't want us to leave this area! We're trapped!'

He rose groggily to his feet, pulling her with him.

'If that's true, we've got to break through. Come on!'

She followed, unwillingly, and they carried on in the direction they had been following. A large rock with a flat, sheer face loomed in front of them. Ferguson made that his target and walked briskly toward it. Instantly, the flame in his nerves brightened to yellow-white horror, and he cried out as if the jaws of a Cat had closed on him. Dimly, he heard Allira screaming behind him. He fell, unable to break his fall, and the ground hit his face like a punch from a giant. He rolled onto his back, seeing Allira on all fours, her face twisted into a repellent mask of pain. He was unable to move, even to retrace his steps, and involuntarily curled into a foetal position, trying to hold out against voracious agony. It was then he heard it: the low, repetitive humming of a Mozzie, distant at that moment but closing rapidly. No, not a Mozzie, two, three—perhaps four. This time, they were determined he should not escape! Despite the fire licking his bones, he managed to raise his head and saw how right he had been: in the distance were the dark silhouettes of no less than four Mozzies, arrowing straight toward him. Beaten, he lowered his head. Whatever they had planned for him—this was it. 'Allira,' he gasped, 'I'm sorry. Sorry I got you into this.'

She said nothing, but managed a twisted smile.

And then it was over.

The pain was there.

And then it was not.

Bliss beyond description flooded his body as even the memory of his ordeal vanished. He felt strong again, strong enough to rip the head off of a Cat! He stood and looked into the distance from where the Mozzies were coming. And saw a wonder: even from their distance, he saw the dark shapes shake and quiver and then plunge powerlessly into the ground and out of his sight.

Allira was beside him.

'Greg, what happened? They're gone and so has the pain. What happened? What was that pain?'

'It was a confined microwave field,' said a familiar voice behind Ferguson. He whirled around.

And saw Schwartz.

EIGHTEEN

Ferguson gawked at this unexpected apparition. So astounded was he that he took several steps backward, away from the barman's stocky form.

'Felix! Is that you! What in all the hells are you doing here?'

'Looking after you,' was the terse reply. 'Now, follow me.'

'Follow you—where?' Ferguson asked, but Schwartz had already turned away. The trio were standing in front of the large rock with the flat vertical face they had espied earlier. Ferguson saw that the other man was holding a small rectangular metal object. Schwartz pointed the object at the stone and immediately a portion of it slid upwards, revealing a void beyond.

Another door in a rock, Ferguson thought. He hoped that Renfield or a thing like him was not waiting for them inside. But what was inside were banks of machines, gently humming to themselves while their coloured lights blinked on and off. There was an unpleasant, acrid sting in the air. They walked farther into the hidden room. There was a susurrus of moving air and the illumination in the room dimmed momentarily before returning to its original brightness. Ferguson turned around, looked past a nervous Allira, and saw that the door had closed. For better or worse, they were once again inside a mass of stone with what was now revealed to be a total stranger.

Schwartz indicated some chairs, situated a short distance in front of a large raised platform. There were two others on either side of it.

'I suppose you'd like an explanation,' Schwartz said, his normal genial expression returning momentarily.

'Sounds like a good idea,' Ferguson said, as he sat. He turned and waved Allira to sit beside him. And then both looked up at Schwartz like schoolchildren about to receive a difficult lesson.

'I'm not sure exactly how much you know,' Schwartz began. 'So let me know if I'm not telling anything new.' He waited for an acknowledgement, but receiving none, continued: 'I am a vampire.'

Allira spoke up.

'But you look like an ordinary man. I was expecting something different, something more...'

'Impressive?' Schwartz laughed. 'A vampire bartender; it's a joke, right? Not very frightening, am I? But I *am* a vampire. This is a long story, so I hope you're comfortable.' He began to walk back and forth, only occasionally glancing at them. 'You see, humans and vampires shared a common ancestor in the Pleistocene.' A quick glance. 'Sorry, let's just say "a long time ago." At root, we're not that different. And by methylating certain key genes, the overt vampiric morphology can be suppressed.'

Ferguson and Allira looked at each other and then back at Schwartz. He spread his arms apologetically.

'Sorry, it's very difficult to explain what is happening without the necessary terminology. I keep forgetting that Serafina Ginevra has infantilised you.'

Ferguson stared at his tutor.

'I know that name. *A cruel and merciless tyrant*, my mother's documents said.'

'Yes, some would agree with you. But a great vampire once said that history is written by the victors. And, I'm afraid to say, you humans lost. To us, Serafina Ginevra was the greatest hero our race ever produced, one who, when all seemed lost, defeated the Vetusians.'

'Vetusians?'

'Not relevant at the moment. Best we don't talk about them, and I certainly hope you never meet them. Back to me. Let me explain a bit more about the situation here. This will take some time; are you sure you're comfortable?'

'We are not. We need water. Desperately.'

After their needs had been seen to, Schwartz continued his lecture.

'Serafina Ginevra was determined that the humans would not cause us any more trouble. You see, you had fought against us in a great war, the war which she won. So, she transported you out of vampire society to this remote island. It's a very big island, so even though there were people already here, there was enough room for an influx of refugees. But she determined it was best you forgot all about us, so she destroyed all of your records, all of your history.'

'Not all of it,' Ferguson said, trying to control the cold fury that was building inside him.

'So I understand. That was a remarkable achievement. She is very thorough, but must have delegated too much.'

' *Is very thorough?*' Allira said. 'I thought all of this happened a long time ago.'

'It did. She's quite an old vampire now.'

Once again, his students exchanged glances, but Schwartz did not elaborate.

'Anyway,' he continued, 'Having transferred you here, she was determined that her plan would be maintained and that you would devolve into a basic agricultural society, losing nearly all of your science and technology. But she sent vampires to live among you, without them revealing who and what they were. Some would provide a basic medical service. You see, she had developed a level of affection for your kind.'

'Renfield,' Ferguson said, turning to Allira. 'That explains Renfield.' He returned his gaze to Schwarz. 'I see what Renfield did, or was supposed to do, rather, but what do you do—apart from push tankards of beer across the counter?'

Schwartz looked a little sheepish.

'Yes, I must apologise for that. Us vampires don't really understand alcohol; it plays no part in our society. We prefer another beverage.'

Ferguson's face twisted.

'Our blood. You treat us like farm animals.'

'That is true. But it was just a trick of evolution. We developed many traits that make us a superior race: our physical strength, our lifespans, our ability to control mentalic fields...'

'Mentalic fields?'

Schwartz waved a hand.

'Not relevant at present. As I was saying, we have many advantages but, in our evolution, something was lost and we needed a co-factor which can only be obtained from blood. Your blood, unfortunately.'

'Very "unfortunately",' Allira said, in acid tones.

'Yes, it's easy to condemn us, but you have a similar problem with Vitamin B12, I believe.' Noting their incomprehension, he continued. 'She was determined to keep a tight rein on you, so we could basically forget about you and concentrate on our real problem. But being the vampire she is, she sent a number of methylated vampires here to note if any humans showed signs of understanding and, if so, report back to the Controllers. These adjusted vampires would serve a term of duty, just like the medical vampires, and then return to society to be restored to their real nature. My job was to keep you in this small area and convince you to just get on with your ordinary farming life.'

'But you haven't done that,' Allira pointed out. 'You've done the opposite by showing us what the real world is. That will surely get you into trouble with this Ginevra woman.'

Schwartz's face looked stricken for a moment, as if a suppressed memory had resurfaced.

'Yes, I'm afraid it will.'

'So, why have you done it?'

Schwartz fetched a chair and sat facing them. Allira had the feeling the main part of the lecture was over.

'I've been tricked by biochemistry. Apparently, I should not have been chosen for the methylation procedure. The longer I looked, felt and acted like a human, the more I thought I was a human. You could say I've gone native.' It was obvious they did not understand the phrase, so he continued: 'I came to identify more and more with the people here; especially you, Greg. I liked you.'

'That's very nice,' Ferguson said. 'I'm not yet sure if I feel the same way, but you haven't explained the Mozzies.'

'Yes, that's partly my fault. I don't control them; that's done remotely from Amerika. But I do alert their Controllers if I suspect one of you people starts showing signs of mental alertness, shall we say. And one thing the Controllers don't like is aggressiveness, or any kind of violence within the population.'

'They like a calm, placid population,' Allira said, and then glanced at Ferguson. 'A population of sheep. And you're not anyone's idea of a sheep.'

Ferguson nodded, and then glared at Schwartz.

'A slave population: ignorant, harmless. And you expect us to be grateful; grateful to this Ginevra thing.'

'Hold on; I didn't set this situation up and I've put myself at some risk from helping you. You see, you're top of the list for re-education. When they scoop you up, they take you to one of their bases and there you're given a dose of mentalic field.' He held up a hand. 'Stop. Don't ask me about them; you'll never understand them. The fight between you and Gottlieb attracted them, and you were given a heavy dose. It made you passive, lifeless, submissive. Just the kind of person the Controllers want. But somehow you threw it off and were worse than you were before the treatment. I'm not sure exactly how you managed that, but I suspect it was something to do with the pharmaceutical knowledge of the native Stralians.'

Ferguson said nothing in reply. Perhaps some secrets should be kept.

'So, what happened to them? Why did they suddenly fall to the ground?'

'I cut off their control frequencies. Very simple—for me, that is,' Schwartz added. 'But you tell me you found some records of the population transfer to here. I would like to read them.'

Ferguson said nothing.

'All right; I see you don't trust me. That's understandable, given the trick that's been played on all of you.'

'You look like a man,' said Ferguson, 'but you're still a vampire. You would like to drink my blood, if you could get away with it. Renfield did.'

'Yes, I know. He has been recalled and no doubt punished.'

'Which just goes to show we can't trust you,' Allira said, her eyes compressed into hard slits. 'Whatever you say, we must be like fat little honeypot ants, just waiting to be sucked dry. Why don't you just reach out a hand and take us!'

Schwartz's head drooped.

'I do feel like that. But I control it.'

'As long as you're not a full vampire, I suppose,' Ferguson said. 'So, nothing's really changed: I know what the Mozzies are and why they're after me. But what good is it to know that? Am I to just accept my lot in life, and expect to be dragged away to some cave every time I appear to be thinking for myself? What kind of life is that? I'd be better off dead.'

'Yes,' Allira added. 'You've told us lots of things which have just made our skin crawl, but are we to stay in this cave with you for the rest of our lives?'

'I can send you somewhere else,' said Schwartz, 'somewhere far from here.'

'What, this Amerika you mentioned?'

'That's possible, but it would not be wise to go there. There are some nearby islands; they would be much safer for you.'

'What, help us build a canoe and paddle it?'

Schwartz's face showed a sadness, the face of someone much older than he looked, and who had seen too many things.

'Now, you're just mocking me. That's not fair; I have put myself at risk by helping you. Anyway, escape from Stralia without vampiric technology is impossible; there is a Barrier around it.'

'A what?'

'Never mind. I'm tired of all this explaining. What I can do is transport you to another part of this continent, or even to an offshore island, as long as it's within the Barrier. Don't ask me how: it's something called teleportation. You don't need to know any more.'

'But you said teleportation could get us off— Stralia.'

'It could. But you are only safe somewhere on this continent. And, believe me, if you ever got off it, you would assuredly not be safe.'

'I still don't understand all that's happened,' Allira said. 'What is this place? It looks like a natural rock from the outside—but not from the inside. And you can't possibly live here and work at the Kookaburra as well; they're too far apart. Are there two of you?'

'No, just one. This is a teleportation station. There are many all over Stralia, disguised as natural features. They allow rapid transfer between points. Not exactly instantaneous, as it's restricted to lightspeed, but it feels instantaneous.'

'I don't understand most of what you said,' Allira continued, as Ferguson appeared to have been struck dumb, 'but I think you're saying these transfer stations allow you to move between two different places very quickly. And somehow, without crossing the space between them. Is that right?'

Schwartz beamed.

'Yes, very good, excellent in fact! You are remarkably quick. For a human, that is.'

Ferguson looked back and forth between the two of them, obviously feeling he was being left out of the conversation. He decided to reclaim the initiative.

'Enough of these stupid words. Are we staying here or are you going to get us out?'

'Yes, of course. This base is shielded, but it's best not to take unnecessary chances. The Controllers will have noticed the loss of the Mozzies. I need to get out of here just as much as you do, but I'll send you first.'

'Where to?'

'The east coast; you'll like it there; the climate's better, more greenery.'

'And you're going to...' Allira paused. '*Teleport* us?'

'Of course. You're not planning to walk, are you?'

Allira and Ferguson gave each other a swift glance.

'Is it safe?' she asked.

'Don't be ridiculous! I use it every few days, and I'm still here. Now, stop wasting time and get on that platform.' Schwartz pointed to the central dais. 'Hurry along; we've spent enough time talking.'

Reluctantly, the pair stood on the platform. Unconsciously, Allira reached for Ferguson's hand.

'It will take a short while to scan you, and then, in the blink of an eye, you'll be standing on a beach with blue sea before you.'

Ferguson and Allira felt a sudden vibration in the floor beneath them, and a deep humming noise began, so deep they could feel it in their bones. It gave the sensation of being merely the overture to a display of immense power that had been newly awakened. To their alarm, two curved transparent panels emerged from the floor and closed on each other, cutting them off from Schwartz, whose speech became muffled.

'You'll be underway in a moment. Have a good life, you pair!'

Ferguson noticed his surroundings had become suffused with an uncanny purple glow. Schwartz had crossed to an instrument panel, his hands making small motions on its surface. As Ferguson watched, those motions became slower and everything outside the panels became blurry, as if seen with weeping eyes.

Schwartz spoke, but his voice had become slower and deeper so that it took an effort on Ferguson's part to understand him.

'*H-e-r-e w-e g-o.*'

But even as the bemused pair struggled to understand what was happening, the podium next to them flashed into life. Its panels were already raised and there was a sudden blaze of purple brilliance within them. The panels slid apart and a man-shaped being stepped out of the weird radiance. He pointed a small metal object at a terrified Schwartz. There was a barely perceptible flash and Schwartz crashed to the floor.

Then everything disappeared, replaced by unending nothingness. They heard a female voice.

'*Yes, I have them.*'

NINETEEN: THEY

For an instant, the world dissolved into a kaleidoscopic blur of contrasting colours; they felt a slight kick in their guts and then the colours stabilised and solidified into a meaningful scene.

They were in a large room with antiseptic white walls and no windows.

And two figures were looking at them, with eager, almost hungry expressions. One appeared to be a tall, clean-shaven man with long black hair. Even in his confusion, Ferguson noticed he bore a disconcerting resemblance to Renfield. Standing next to him was a slim female figure. She was almost as tall as the male and wore glossy shoulder-length hair the colour of a winter's night. They glanced briefly at each other.

'They are perfect, Gronz, simply perfect. Look at the male, what a specimen he is!'

The man—if *man* he was—smiled. With a start, Ferguson saw that the parted lips had revealed long, brilliantly white fangs. A sick feeling swept over Ferguson as he realised who these people must be: not people at all.

Vampires.

And he very much doubted that he and Allira were safely in another part of the island continent that the vampires called Stralia. He had seen Schwartz slaughtered in front of him an instant before the transference had begun. Schwartz had claimed to be their friend; it was unlikely that these people would also claim that status.

The male vampire, whom the female had termed *Gronz,* raised his wrist to his lips and spoke into a small metal object attached to it.

'Excellent work; you can stand down now that the traitor is dead. We have them, and no parts have been cut off during the transference.' Gronz lowered his hand and approached Ferguson and Allira, his gaze fixed on them all the while. In his eyes, a reddish fire appeared to be smouldering. The transparent covers surrounding the platform slid away, and Ferguson and Allira were exposed to the air of the room. It was cold and carried an unidentifiable acrid tang to their nostrils. Gronz stopped within touching distance of Ferguson and ran a hungry gaze up and down. Then he reached across and clasped Ferguson's right bicep. Ferguson jerked away, shocked by the coldness of that uninvited grasp.

'Get off me,' he said. 'Who are you? What do you want with us?'

Gronz glanced briefly over his shoulder.

'Listen to him, Theondra, listen to the defiance in the creature's voice.'

The female joined Gronz, but her stare was directed at Allira.

'Humans, real live humans.' She turned to Gronz. 'It always amazes me how they look so much like us.'

Gronz's lips twisted, showing the alarming expression that passes for a smile among vampires.

'Only on the outside, my dear, not the insides, as you will soon see. Simply a trick of evolution; a cosmic blind alley, if you will.'

189

Theondra turned to Ferguson and gave him a close view of her dentition.

'But what a joke. These examples are much more interesting than the others. Those are just walking vegetables, but these are unconditioned, just as nature intended.'

Allira looked down at the female in growing horror.

'What are you going to do to us? Are you going to hurt us?'

Theondra laughed a humourless laugh.

'I'm afraid we are. Oh, not intentionally, of course; we are not Vetusians, after all. There will be pain, but it will not be inflicted as an end in itself; no, simply as an unavoidable side-effect, shall we say.'

Gronz gestured to them to step down from the platform and, reluctantly, they stood in front of their captors. Gronz spent some more time studying them.

'I should have done this earlier instead of wasting my time with those conditioned wretches. I've been something of a fool.' Then he gave an unwelcome smile. 'Now, I'm doing it again, wasting your time listening to my self-deprecation. What kind of host am I? I'm sure you haven't eaten properly for a while or made use of sanitary facilities.' He turned. 'Theondra, take our guests to the eating area and attend to their needs.'

Theondra bowed her head briefly and then pointed to a nearby door.

'Come with me.'

The bemused pair followed her and immediately were in a room containing a long table. Theondra sat at one end and indicated to Ferguson and Allira that they should sit next to her. That done, she clapped her long-nailed hands and another door opened behind them. Turning, Ferguson saw a figure appear in the doorway. It was a young woman, plainly dressed in a grey tunic and wearing unadorned sandals.

'Bring food and water for our guests.'

The woman nodded.

'Yes, at once, mistress.'

After she had disappeared into whatever room lay beyond, Ferguson said, 'Was that one of us—a human?'

'Surely you can tell without asking, Greg? No vampire would ever carry a blank expression like that; no vampire would ever be a humble servant.'

Ferguson said no more and shortly thereafter the human woman returned, carrying a tray loaded with fruit, a jug of water and drinking glasses.

'Eat and quench your thirst,' Theondra commanded, 'we do not like people who do not show sufficient gratitude for our generosity.'

Ferguson and Allira obeyed. The fruits were of a type they had never seen before: large, soft and luscious. There were also brown strips of something which appeared to be a type of meat, although, once again, neither of them could identify it.

Ferguson felt a little more in control of himself after the meal and looked questioningly at Theondra. She smiled a mischievous smile, spoiled only by the prominent display of wicked fangs.

'If you are going to ask me more about your situation here, Greg, you will have to wait for my lord.' Hearing a door softly open, she turned and smiled a more genuine smile. 'Ah, here he is now.'

Gronz sat at the other end of the table, forcing Ferguson and Allira to turn in their seats.

'You must have a lot of questions, so to save time, I will give you a little lecture. Forgive me, if there are things in it you don't exactly understand; you will learn more in your stay here.' He leaned back, averting his gaze from the others. 'I am, as you already know, a vampire with the informal name of Gronz. I am a very important vampire because I am the supervisor of Stralia, your erstwhile home—one you will never see again, I'm afraid. You are currently resident in my dwelling, which is located in an opulent part of New Marinetown.'

'I saw that name on a map,' Ferguson said.

'Excellent. We say "new", of course, as the original was destroyed in the Third Vetusian War. But no matter; please do not interrupt me again. To continue: It is I who controls the devices you humans term "Mozzies". I use them to seek out and control humans who diverge from the desired state of inert acquiescence; the authorities here like their humans to be dull-eyed beasts of the field, not looking beyond food, drink and reproduction.'

'But *you* don't,' Allira suddenly said, as if something had just occurred to her.

Gronz nodded his approval.

'Well said; I have not erred in my choice of human subjects. But I would prefer if you simply listened, as I have already instructed your companion. To continue: I use the—uh—Mozzies to collect any human who diverges from that ideal of submissiveness, and they are taken to bases scattered across Stralia where my devices alter their brains to return them to the desired state of quiet acceptance. I became aware of Greg not that long ago, and dispatched the Mozzies to collect and condition him. To my amazement, he avoided collection, even after he had infiltrated one of the bases. That has never happened before. So, I decided to study him more closely. I had already observed his interaction with Renfield and how he successfully manhandled him. Renfield annoyed me, so I reported him to Serafina Ginevra, who immediately replaced him. And punished him, I might add.'

Ferguson stiffened at the sound of that hated name, a movement which did not go unnoticed by Gronz.

'Don't worry, Greg, you're not going to meet her, in fact you will never leave this building. Poor Serafina is not the power in the land she once was. To be perfectly honest, she was never quite the same after the death of her human lover. But I diverge; I was explaining how honoured you are to be in the company of so eminent a vampire as I.'

Ferguson pushed his empty plate away and glared at Gronz.

'Why do you speak in such a strange way, Gronz? I can hardly understand you.'

'I apologise, Greg. Sometimes I forget that despite your great talents, you are, at heart, a humble rustic. And you must remember that Ingliz is not my native tongue; I speak it merely as an intellectual exercise and I forget that I'm probably more proficient in it than you.'

Ferguson was not sure whether he had just been insulted but said nothing.

'Once again, I must continue. You see, not only am I the Supervisor of Stralia but my residence is one of the control nodes for the Barrier.' Gronz paused while he studied the uncomprehending faces of his captives. 'Oh, this is most annoying; you know so little it is difficult to communicate! I will be swift—

we have a Barrier which prevents the Vetusians from overrunning the world and it is generated by clones of the heroes who won the previous war.' Ignoring their blank faces, he pressed on. 'But the clones have developed a genetic malformation which shortens their lives. As a result, our scientists have developed machines which take over some of the load of the Barrier generation. I have one such machine here.' Gronz leaned back and gave a self-satisfied, fanged smile. 'So you must admit I am indeed a very important, no, *illustrious*, vampire and you are very privileged to be spending some time with me.'

'Thank you for the honour. Now, let us go.'

Gronz's smile vanished on the instant.

'No. I will never let you go. Whilst you live, that is.'

TWENTY

Ferguson leapt to his feet.

'Do you think you can keep us here?' He balled his fists. 'I know what you things are! Blood-sucking monsters! Allira and I would rather die than be your slaves!'

He glanced down at Allira as he said those words. She looked startled but then gave a short nod, turning her head to glare at Gronz. Suddenly, there was a tinkle of feminine laughter behind them. They turned to see Theondra laughing behind her delicate hand.

'Oh, they are priceless, Gronz! You really have excelled yourself with this couple!'

Ferguson ignored her and strode towards Gronz, who rose to meet him, smiling and shaking his head with amused pity.

'Greg, you are being very foolish. Do you think I am a fantasist when I say you can never leave? Many of those who have preceded you have said exactly the same thing. I repeat: you will never leave—as living creatures, that is. You must understand that the fish are always hungry.'

Ferguson planted himself directly in front of Gronz; he was slightly taller than the vampire and distinctly wider.

195

'Here's my answer to that!' he said and delivered a blow to the vampire's chin that would have knocked an ordinary man to the ground. But Gronz stood unmoved. His head did not recoil under the blow and his lips remained unsplit. He gave another smile, one of sorrowful understanding.

'You can't hurt me, Greg. A butterfly would be as much of a threat to me as you are.'

Ferguson was not entirely surprised; he remembered how Renfield had withstood his onslaught. He drew his fist back and struck again, this time putting every atom of his strength into perhaps the mightiest blow he had ever delivered.

This time, did Gronz's head jerk backward, just the slightest, perhaps?

It mattered not, because Gronz replied with a blow of his own and Ferguson found himself lying on his back, his head spinning. Through blurred vision, he saw his attacker reach down to help him to his feet. Gronz patted him on the shoulder, gently, fatherly, as if admonishing a badly behaved child.

'I'm sorry I had to do that, Greg, I really am, but you have to be shown, you have to be trained, that you cannot beat me. Why, Theondra is not a strong female by vampire standards, but you would have almost as little of a chance with her as you have with me.'

Ferguson sat down heavily and spent some time looking at his open hands. He looked up.

'What is it you want?'

Gronz sat beside him.

'I am something of a scientist, Greg, and I have a particular interest in humans. You see, we share a common ancestry; if one goes back far enough into the geologic record, it is certain that we are brothers.

Very different brothers, of course, but that is not unusual. Long ago, we discovered that methylation of certain genes suppresses vampiric morphology. I want to learn more; I want to discover what exactly it is that makes us now so different. And so I collect humans and test them, discovering what it is they can and cannot do when pushed to the extremes of experience. Only then can I know what I need to know. You see, Serafina spoiled all that. Because of her infatuation with a vampire who became a human, she ordered that we must stop preying on you, that humans should be placed beyond our reach and not interfered with. Hence, your exile to Stralia. But we will be the ones who triumph, for Kran already has his eyes on her. But Greg, surely you can see that her actions were wrong, so terribly wrong? Would you take a lion and force him to eat grass? Oh, she ordered the creation of synthetic blood to replace our consumption of your own beautiful fluid, but it is a very poor substitute.'

'You know that, do you?' Ferguson said, looking directly into the other's eyes for the first time since the fight.

'Of course. Do you think I would have all these lovely humans around and not indulge myself? Grow up, Greg!'

'I'm not a child; I'm a man, a person, a human being. Do you think you can treat me like some bloody goanna?'

Gronz smiled again, but Ferguson had become accustomed to the display of fangs and it did not disturb him as much as it had.

'Greg, you are not being fair to me. I am not someone who glories in suffering; no, I am a seeker after knowledge. I want to know why human evolution went so badly wrong, and you did not develop into vampires; what is wrong with that?'

'You're just playing with words, playing with me. Just let us go; we have done nothing to threaten you.'

Gronz stood, looking down on Ferguson.

'No, nor could you. Accept your situation, Greg. Many centuries ago, human so-called scientists experimented on animals, filling their veins with drugs, inserting electrodes into their brains, removing organs to see what they did. Those humans were not monsters and neither am I.'

Ferguson joined him in standing. To Allira's horror, Theondra had taken her hand and was gently stroking it whilst watching the man and vampire face each other. Ferguson spoke; his eyes were slits and his voice was low and crackling with hate.

'I am not an experimental subject. You are a monster.'

Gronz shrugged.

'Maybe I am.' Another fanged smile. 'But I am your monster.'

****

'What can we do, Greg? What can we do?'

They were sitting together on a cold, hard bench in another room, a room with white, antiseptic walls, floor and ceiling, and without windows. The air was still and, as before, carried sharp, unknown odours that attacked their nasal linings like invisible rodents. Ferguson was staring down at his hands, mighty appendages that had allowed him to defeat the attacking Mozzie.

But useless here, apparently.

'I don't know, Allira. I'm out of ideas. It looks like another group of humans are going to be abused by these blood-sucking creatures.'

Allira touched his head to make him look at her. When he did, he saw her eyes shining with unshed tears.

'We could kill ourselves.'

He laughed a dry, emotionless laugh.

'How? There's nothing here to help us do that. And in any case, I'm not ready for that. Not yet, at least.'

'You could kill me. You could do it very easily.'

Ferguson said nothing for quite some time, and when he finally spoke, Allira could hardly hear him.

'Yes, I could do it. Maybe it will come to that; it depends on just what they have planned for us. It will be some kind of experiment; Gronz made that clear. If it gets too bad, I promise I will kill you.'

'But you, Greg? What happens to you?'

Ferguson shrugged.

'Nothing lasts forever. They will kill me when they tire of me; I have that consolation.'

There was no more to say; their heads slumped, and they slept sitting together on the bench.

Ferguson awoke with a start: someone had touched him. He looked up.

It was Theondra.

'Greg,' she said in a soft, almost tender way. She smiled down on him, trying—and failing—to hide her fangs. 'I'd like to talk to you; come with me, please.'

Ferguson shook his head to clear it. He looked at Allira; she was still asleep, her head resting on one of his mighty arms.

'Just me? Allira?'

'Don't worry about her; she won't wake up for some time. A touch of low-intensity mentalic field will see to that.'

Ferguson strove with conflicting feelings; this was unexpected. Did Theondra have some plan for them which differed from Gronz's? He decided to see what was behind this visit and gently lowered Allira, so her head was resting on the bench.

'Come with me,' the female vampire said, turning away. Ferguson watched her as she walked towards the door, her smooth, fluid movements reminding him of the supple motion of a stalking Cat. She did not bother to look behind her, apparently knowing he had followed. They walked a short distance down a plain white corridor and into another room. As he entered, Ferguson stopped, astounded by what was before him. One entire wall was transparent and it was clear that it was part of a very high structure, for, beyond the window, he could see rows of buildings, shrunk by the elevation to the apparent size of a doll's house. She saw his amazement and laughed.

'New Marinetown. Of course, you've never seen any kind of city, have you, Greg? It's much more beautiful than the old town; Edward did us an unexpected favour when he destroyed that ramshackle collection of slums. Of course, we shared it with humans in those far-off days.'

Ferguson moved closer to the window and placed a questing finger on the transparent substance comprising it. He turned to Theondra.

'This is wonderful! I can see through it as if it wasn't there!'

She smiled with obvious amusement.

'Yes, we vampires have many wonders we could share with you, Greg. If you co-operate, that is.'

'Co-operate? I didn't think I had that choice.'

She sat on a couch covered in a plush fabric the colour of fresh arterial blood and patted it invitingly.

'Come and sit with me, Greg. We have much to discuss.'

He looked at her with mistrusting eyes, but eventually complied.

'That's better. It's nice to be close, isn't it? Gronz can be a bit of a bore sometimes, always talking about his theories and experiments. I'm not like that; I like to get to know people, to explore what motivates them, what their feelings are. What are you feeling at the moment, Greg?'

He stared at her before replying.

'That I want to get out of this prison.'

'I can understand that. This can be a terrible place for those who don't co-operate. But it's not just Gronz, you see; I have a say in what happens here, as well.'

'What *does* happen here?'

'Well, bad things usually; I guess you've already realised that. But it doesn't have to be like that.' She moved closer so that their thighs were just touching. 'You know, I could make your stay here a lot more interesting.'

Once again, he stared into her face, noticing that her pupils were now an intense green, as if they were the surfaces of untroubled pools glimpsed at twilight. He could taste her breath, which had an unidentifiable metallic tang on it.

'My stay? I thought I was here permanently.'

'That's what Gronz says. Perhaps you are, but there are many ways of spending your time here.'

'Such as?'

201

She looked away, turning her gaze to the window. The buildings were not visible from where they sat, but the sky was a bright, pale blue, generating the feeling that there was intense heat on the other side of the window. She returned her gaze to Ferguson.

'I'll be honest with you, Greg. I am a very emotional, physical vampire. I need excitement in a way that Gronz can't give me. He is too cerebral, too much of a measurer of things, rather than a free spirit that prefers to experience them directly.' She reached for a hand and held it tightly. 'Greg, let me share with you a lovely little fantasy of mine. I like the idea of taking pleasure with a non-vampire, something primitive, a creature closer to the earth, more driven by simple needs and wants. Something that acts impulsively and takes what it wants.'

Ferguson stared at her in growing horror. 'I'm not an animal,' he finally said.

She laughed.

'Now, don't be silly, Greg! That's exactly what you are, compared to me. That's why I find you exciting; the sheer wickedness of debasing myself with a thing like you would be so erotic!'

He stood.

'That's sick. You're sick.'

'Is it, now? Am I, now? There have been others before you who did not find it sick.'

'Then go back to them—if they're still alive.'

'They're not,' she said, almost pouting, 'but that's not the point. They were conditioned, just lumps of inert flesh that did whatever I told them; just robots of meat. But with you, it would be different. You're not conditioned; you're still a wild, untamed animal. It would be glorious, Greg—for you as well as me!' She stood and came up to Ferguson, reaching up to place her hands on his shoulders. 'Think how privileged you would be; how many humans do you think have ever had a vampire?'

He removed her hands.

'I have a woman of my own kind.'

Her eyes narrowed slightly.

'Yes, that Allira thing. There is something about her that disturbs me, something I don't like. I don't know what it could be.'

'I think we are done here, Theondra. Thank you for your interest in me, but on the whole, I'll just take what Gronz has in mind for me.'

She sat back on the scarlet couch and looked up at him. Her face now bore an unreadable expression.

'Yes, "what Gronz has in store for you." Has it occurred to you he has plans for Allira as well?'

A cold hand suddenly clutched Ferguson's heart.

'What do you mean?'

'Why, do you think he's only interested in males of your species? He hasn't had as many human lovers as I have; he's a cold, over-brained vampire, but Allira is good-looking in a human kind of way. In a dark room...why, who knows what might happen?'

Ferguson raised his fists and strode towards her.

She laughed.

'Now, you're being more silly than usual. I could pick you up and throw you through that window without drawing breath. And it's not me you should be angry with; I'm trying to help you.'

Ferguson stood still, baffled; thoughts clashed in his mind but came to no conclusion. Then Theondra was beside him again.

'And what do you think will happen to her when Gronz has satisfied his momentary curiosity? It will be back to experiments, and he will not be any more compassionate to her than he will be with you. I could spare her much pain.'

Ferguson's face twisted in his agony; still, he could not speak. Theondra laughed and turned away, looking down on the neatly ordered blocks of New Marinetown.

'You have not angered me, Greg. I cannot expect clear thinking from a simple animal like you. I can get that from Gronz; that's not what I want for us. And so I will not take your recent words as a rejection of me.' She spun around and Ferguson saw razor-sharp fangs fully exposed and blazing emerald eyes that were now backlit with an angry red fire. Involuntarily, he stepped away. 'But think well on this: if you refuse me again, you will have truly rejected me, and you will pay in despair and suffering. And so will Allira.' She laughed. 'Especially Allira!'

TWENTY ONE

Allira's eyes fluttered open. She looked around in a questing, anticipative manner, her eyes bright with hope.

Then the hope died in those eyes and her face became cold and expressionless.

'Still here then,' she said in a flat, dull voice. 'Still trapped with those dreadful creatures.'

'I'm afraid so. Nothing has changed.'

She sat up.

'Such a strange sleep. I don't think I've ever slept so deeply. All my fears seemed to go and I dreamt a lovely dream. Can you guess what it was?'

'No.'

She was sitting next to him and she shuffled along the bench until they were in contact with each other.

'I dreamt we were back in the cabin, you and me. We were entertaining Delgado, and he was telling us one of his long, boring stories about the Good Old Days. But we didn't mind.' She squeezed his arm. 'Do you know why?'

'No.'

'Because we were happy, Greg, you and me. We were in our home, together as a couple, facing the future together, wrapped up in our love, like we were under a big, soft blanket. And everything was alright;

there were no messages from the past, no Mozzies—and no vampires.' Her hand suddenly tightened. 'Why can't the world be like that, Greg? Why are there vampires?'

He shook his head sadly.

'There just are. Why are there Devils and Cats? Why are there months when it doesn't rain? It's just the way the world is. We have to live with that.'

She leapt to her feet, looking around madly.

'I don't want to live like that! I want to kill them! I want to kill every one of them for what they have done to us, what they are going to do with us!'

'Sit down, Allira, please. That won't help. I want to kill them just as badly as you, but wishing doesn't make it so. It never has and it never will. Somehow, we have to deal with the here and now. If there is some way I could take all the hurt and spare you, I would.' But even as he said those words, Theondra's promise echoed in the roots of his mind.

I could spare her much pain.

He did not continue with his words for fear he might betray what had happened while she slept.

Suddenly, there was a knock on the door and they looked at each other in uncertainty.

Vampires do not ask for permission, especially in their own lair.

Finally, Allira invited the unknown person in, and it was revealed to be another young human woman carrying a tray of food and drink. Ferguson watched her as she silently placed the tray on a small table, but as she made to leave, he clutched an arm and restrained her. She made no move to escape and just looked up at him with blank, empty eyes.

'What's your name?'

Her vacant, expressionless features displayed nothing in response.

'I have no name.'

'How long have you been here?'

'I do not know.'

Ferguson lifted her arms, noticing old scars upon them, scars that had once been small oval wounds.

'How did you get these marks?'

It seemed for a moment that her expression was in the process of changing, attempting to display some violent feeling, some half-forgotten terror.

'The fish. They are always hungry.'

'The fish? What about the fish?'

But abruptly, she was trying to break free from Ferguson's grasp and after realising she could not, rained feather-light blows upon his arm with a small fist.

He released her and without another word, without looking back, she left.

Ferguson and Allira said nothing until they had finished their simple meal and then Allira said, 'That poor girl. She didn't seem to be properly alive, like she was some kind of big, moving doll.'

'She wasn't a normal person. It was like she was the husk left behind after everything that made her real had been sucked out.'

Allira shuddered at the implication of his words.

'That's horrible. Don't say things like that.'

'It's what they do. I wonder how many captive humans they have here.'

'About twenty,' came a cold voice from the doorway. Allira and Ferguson turned to find the source of those icy tones.

It was Gronz, of course, and he entered the room displaying that smile they had already come to hate.

'I'm not quite sure of the exact number; it may be slightly above or slightly below twenty.' He sat on the bench, which the humans immediately vacated. 'But although they don't know it, your fellow humans in Stralia owe you a great debt. Because I find you such a splendid subject for my studies, I have halted all the abductions. Mozzies are still taking recalcitrant humans for conditioning, but I don't need to see any in person until I have finished examining you, Greg.'

'And then, have killed me.'

Gronz shrugged.

'What do you expect me to do? I could hardly return you to Stralia with what you know, especially after I have boosted your brain power. I could wipe your brain totally, but the essence that makes you *Greg Ferguson* would be completely erased. You surely wouldn't want to live on as a shambling, drooling idiot, would you, Greg?'

Ferguson did not reply, but Allira spoke up.

'And what about me? Don't you find me interesting as well, or is this some kind of a closed club for males only?'

Gronz took a long, slow look at Allira. Unable to bear that glacial stare, she turned away just as he answered.

'I selected Greg for two reasons: firstly, his unusually well-developed physique, which is rare in his low-calorie environment, and secondly, because of his astounding lack of knowledge and concomitant limited reasoning abilities.'

Ferguson wondered for a moment whether or not he had been insulted and was still considering that possibility when Gronz continued, 'You see, Allira, your body is not unusual for a female from your background and you are too intelligent for my experiments in cognition. It's true Theondra doesn't like you, but she can't explain why she has developed such an animus towards you.'

Allira was unsure whether or not she had been complimented and so said nothing. Further thoughts were abruptly cut off as Gronz stood and pointed to the door.

'Well, enough of this banter; time waits for no vampire and I must begin my experiments with Greg.'

Ferguson stiffened at the word "experiments" and balled his fists. Gronz, however, merely shook his head.

'Not this again. How many times must I remind you that you are helpless against me? Do you really want to make Allira watch while I rearrange your manly features into something resembling meat on a slab?'

Ferguson lowered his fists.

'Let's get on with it.'

Gronz nodded.

'Good boy. But let me take you on a little tour first.'

They left the room and entered another windowless corridor. Gronz led the way with his captives trailing behind him, neither making any attempt to attack or escape. They passed another room, and Gronz paused at its open door and pointed into it.

'What do you make of that, Greg?'

Ferguson looked in and saw a small platform inside a canopy of some transparent material.

'A teleportation device.'

'Yes, but not a standard one such as the one you arrived through. It is not only a communicator but can deliver its contents directly to the High Command. I told you I was an illustrious vampire, did I not?'

They did not reply and Gronz continued his tour. They had gone some way when Allira stopped, wrinkling her nose.

'Water. I smell water. But a different water-smell than I am used to.'

'Good, Allira, very good. My sense of smell is excellent, but I can barely detect it at this distance. Your native Stralian faculties have served you well.'

After some more wearisome minutes of walking down the corridor, it opened into a large space with a transparent roof, through which a merciless sun was blazing. In the centre of the space was a rectangular enclosure, full of dark green water. At the far end of the pool was a cylinder made of the ubiquitous transparent substance. It was empty.

'Take a look,' Gronz said. 'I dare say you've never seen so much water.'

'You're right,' Ferguson said. 'How big is this building?'

'Big enough. Most of it is underground. That's right, Allira, look into the water.'

Allira looked. The water seemed shallow but full of some sort of microscopic green algae, which made it barely translucent. Yet she could see dark shapes moving randomly about within it, sometimes nearing the surface, but then darting away as if looking for something they could not find. She turned to Gronz.

'Fish?'

'Yes, of course; what else would you expect?'

'*The fish are always hungry,*' she quoted.

Gronz smiled.

'Yes. Yes, they are.'

They walked on, but the rank smell of the pool followed them for some time. Then they entered another windowless room. This one was full of humming, motionless machines and had a man-sized table in its centre.

'Here we are,' Gronz said, a suggestion of animation entering his voice. 'Today's experiment, or, as I prefer to think of it, today's lecture. Lie on the table, please, Greg.'

'Why? What are you going to do?'

'Greg, your habit of continually asking for explanations is most annoying. But as this is your first time, I will forgive you. You and Allira can sit on those chairs while I explain.' After they had done so, Gronz stood before them. They looked up at him in the manner of newly enrolled students. 'One of my great interests is why humans and vampires are so different, given our shared background. It is obvious the structure of the human brain is at least part of the answer. We vampires are not only more intelligent, but the humblest of us have some degree of control over mentalic fields. Humans have known something of those fields and have given them names like "telepathy", "telekinesis", "clairvoyance", but were never able to definitively prove their existence, let alone how to control and use them. My people can use them almost from birth, although most vampires have only a limited ability. As a matter of fact, my own abilities are not great, but, of course, I compensate for that with my exceptional intellect. But, as a historical fact, it was through the use of these powers we were able to hide in plain sight from your people and disguise ourselves as a rather ridiculous fable until the time came for us to wrest control of the world from you to prevent you from destroying it.' He stopped, fixing his gaze on Ferguson. 'I see I'm boring you, Greg; I'm sorry for that, but, of course, you are merely confirming my view of your own mental status.'

'I'm a grunting simpleton, in your view. You know, I could almost accept that because it would mean I'm not a monster—like you.'

Gronz gave an almost human sigh.

'I understand your feelings, Greg. You feel trapped and helpless. But that is rational because you *are* trapped and helpless. You don't like those feelings, and that, again, is rational; I would feel the same if the roles were reversed. But they never will be, because I am a vampire. And unfortunately, your feelings have no weight with me; I am completely unmoved by your human emotions, and I record them simply as one datum among many. I would carry out my programme of investigation into your makeup even if you were indifferent or deliriously happy with my plans. As it happens, the opposite of the latter is true. But I will still conduct my investigations with you. Human scientists were uninterested in the feelings of their lab rats; surely you see the parallel?'

Ferguson looked down at his hands; they were clenching and unclenching involuntarily. He looked up.

'Your views are clear to me, Gronz. They simply emphasize that you are indeed a monster. I told Theondra I am not an animal, and I am telling you I am not a lab rat.'

Gronz raised an eyebrow.

'You told Theondra that you were not an animal? May I inquire into the context of that conversation?'

'Ask her yourself. Surely you have no secrets from one another?' Ferguson stood and planted himself directly before the vampire; his eyeline was slightly higher. 'And everything you have said confirms your inferiority to a human being. Your lack of—of...' He turned to Allira.

'Compassion, empathy,' she said, her voice almost a snarl.

'Whatever it takes, Gronz,' Ferguson continued, 'I vow I will kill you.'

'You will need to turn into a vampire to accomplish that,' Gronz said, showing no reaction to the threat, 'and now we shall begin my first experiment.' He glanced at Allira. 'You needn't worry, this particular investigation is painless.' He returned to Ferguson. 'On the table, please, Greg.'

Slowly, reluctantly, Ferguson complied. No sooner had he stretched out on the table than thin wires sprouted from it and attached themselves to his head. Two large hoops also emerged and enclosed him in bands of steel.

'Nothing to worry about, Greg. The bands are simply there to stop you wriggling around. The equipment is very sensitive and it is imperative to keep as still as possible.'

'I'll do my best,' Ferguson said. Gronz did not notice his dry insincerity and simply nodded. He turned his back on the humans and crossed to a bank of instruments that were giving off a gentle electronic purring.

'Oh, Allira,' he called, without turning around, 'don't try to release Greg; now that he's connected, the shock might kill him.'

Allira sat back down and gave an apologetic smile to her imprisoned companion.

'What exactly will this procedure do?' she asked Gronz.

'I've told you: it will stimulate his cerebral neurons. To put it in lay terms, it will re-plasticise them, opening them up to new experiences, in particular the insertion of new knowledge and, more importantly, it will clarify his reasoning processes.'

'And how will that help you?'

He returned to the table and looked down at Ferguson.

'Ah, he's unconscious; I was beginning to wonder why he was so quiet. All is proceeding as it should. And Allira, I will explain again why I am doing this: it is to test the differences between your type of brain and ours. I want to see just how many data I can cram into the human mind, how much I can improve the type, if you like.'

'Won't that make him more dangerous? I mean, he'll have brain and brawn.'

'My, you are a quick girl. I was right to choose Greg to experiment on because you're already halfway there. Well, to answer your question, obviously, I will stop before I have upgraded his mind too much; after all, I have more physical tests for him farther down the line. But for the moment, I shall just give him second-order logic and set theory, mathematical analysis and a touch of advanced physics. They are hardly any danger to me. Then after all my tests are complete, Theondra and I will suck him dry of that lovely blood you humans have, and I will then remove his brain, freeze-dry it, and, using advanced tomography, divide the brain into thin slices so I can see what changes I have wrought in Greg's neurons. He is the perfect subject, you see; the upscaling process is quite demanding and requires a strong constitution. At the same time, the baseline must be so low that the changes are obvious. Young Greg here is absolutely perfect in both criteria.'

Allira nodded.

'Yes, I understand now. Thank you. Do you mind if I take a closer look at what you are doing?'

Gronz smiled.

'Well, you really are a remarkable young human. It is surprising to see the spirit of scientific discovery so strong in someone from your impoverished background. Please join me.'

Allira did so, but walked past Gronz so she was staring at the bank of controls that controlled the procedure.

'Would you mind showing me what settings you used?'

Gronz looked confused.

'Well, that's hardly necessary, my dear...'

Allira returned to his side and looked up into his eyes, her own eyes strangely motionless, her lids unblinking.

'As one seeker after knowledge to another, I'm sure you would approve of my thirst for such knowledge. After all, you vampires are so vastly far ahead of us, it is difficult to get anywhere without detailed explanations.'

'Yes...yes, detailed explanations. Explanations. Detailed. Yes, that would be a good idea. Come with me.'

Gronz and Allira stood by the bank of controls and Allira asked a great many questions which Gronz answered slowly and carefully, often repeating his replies in response to supplementary questions from his human student. Eventually, Allira seemed satisfied and resumed her position on the bench, looking at the unconscious Ferguson. Gronz seemed to have shaken off the odd lethargy which had overtaken him and said, 'Now we begin.'

The machines' buzzing became louder and shriller, and Ferguson gave a single quick spasm as if he had received a mild electric shock. He was almost instantly motionless again and showed no further reaction of any kind.

The hours passed, while Allira strove to stay awake, watching every one of Gronz's motions.

Nothing appeared to be happening in the room that held the three, but that was not true of Ferguson's mind.

He was not awake but neither was he asleep.

It appeared to him that he was walking down a long corridor, punctuated by many doors. He felt a compulsion to open each door and go inside. Once inside, he heard voices speaking directly into his nerve cells, telling him things, making him learn things, concepts, ideas and data he had never dreamed existed. Sentences passed through his brain and he understood them all.

The concept of a function was first stated by Leibniz. The function can be understood as a relation between the domain and the range. The definitions of the independent and dependent variables are as follows...

In the General Theory, gravity is understood to be a geometric consequence of the warping of spacetime. From the concept of the Light Cone...

The complex plane can be envisioned as one which stands at right angles to the real numbers, crossing at zero. Therefore,...

The Heisenberg Uncertainty Principle is any of a variety of mathematical inequalities asserting a fundamental limit to the product of the accuracy of certain related pairs of measurements on a quantum system, such as position and momentum. Such paired-variables are known as complimentary variables. The principle requires us to understand that we can determine the position of a particle or its momentum, but not both. The idea of the collapse of the Wave Function...

Euler's Identity is a special case of Euler's Formula, which may be proven by...

But then Ferguson's mind could take no more and he began to jerk and quiver on the table and make a low moaning sound. Allira rose to her feet, but Gronz waved her back.

'He is alright. He has reached his limit, which was somewhat lower than I calculated. The procedure stops automatically when that limit is reached.'

Gronz removed the sensors from Ferguson's head and the steel bands instantly retracted.

'And what have you proved?' Allira demanded.

'Nothing as yet. I will only know that when I have examined his brain. I may perform another upgrade on him if he has responded well to this one. His level of understanding was so poor, it will be easy to measure how much improvement has taken place. And no, Allira, give up any hope you may be hiding from me: the knowledge I have given him is purely academic; it will not give him any new powers to overthrow Theondra or me.'

'Of course,' Allira said. 'I am not so stupid as to believe you are that stupid.'

Gronz studied her for a while.

'No, you aren't stupid, are you?' Gronz paused and then crossed to her. He lifted her hair away from her forehead and studied her for some seconds. He ran an ice-cold finger up and down one cheek, while staring with increasing approval. 'Theondra often lies with our subjects before she kills them, but I rarely do. However, "rarely" is not the same as "never." I think I may make an exception with you. But don't worry—vampires and humans cannot reproduce.'

Allira stared up at him, her eyes widening with horror.

TWENTY TWO

Ferguson groaned and then slowly raised his head, looking nervously around.

'Is it over?' he said.

Allira went to him.

'Yes, yes, it's over. You've been asleep for hours.'

'It feels like days; my eyes are gummed up and my lips are dry as sand.'

Allira brought him some water; they were back in their holding cell.

'Do you feel any different? Gronz said he'd given you lots of advanced scientific knowledge.'

Ferguson shook his shaggy head, moving slowly as if he feared he might lose it.

'Yes, I do feel different; my skull is splitting; it feels like Gronz drove an axe through it.'

Allira sighed.

'No doubt that will fade. I think that was probably the easiest of the procedures he has planned for us.'

Ferguson swung his feet onto the floor and stood.

'No doubt. Obviously, if vampires have any empathy, it must be approaching zero.'

Allira raised an eyebrow.

'Hmm. Are you sure you don't feel any different? The Greg I knew didn't use words like "empathy" or "zero".'

'What words should I have used? I tell you, I feel exactly the same.'

She decided not to pursue the matter; after all, Gronz's procedure must have made some difference to Ferguson. In any case, something much more important than an enriched vocabulary was pressing down upon her. She glanced at Ferguson and then away again. Should she tell him about Gronz's ominous comment?

But what would be the point? What could Ferguson do about it, what could he do about anything? They were like the sheep that he had kept on the farm, helpless creatures that were not masters of their own fate. The sheep had been fed, they had been watered, they had been protected from predators—but to what end? Only to be slaughtered and dismembered when their time came. There had been no rebellion of ovine freedom fighters, no clever escape plans executed under the noses of their captors.

Nothing.

And so it was with her and Ferguson. In the end, they were as helpless as the sheep. She felt tears well up as she contemplated the unfairness of existence, but she held them back. She would *not* weep!

Ferguson had noticed her distraction and enquired after her. But she did not have the time to reply as the door opened and Theondra entered. Her gaze locked with Allira's for a noticeable time and Allira felt as if some force was trying to worm its way into her subconscious, some probe that was looking for something, something incriminating. Then the feeling ended and Allira felt the questing power withdraw. Theondra then proceeded to ignore her, and turned to Ferguson.

'Greg, good to see you again. How are you feeling? Is there anything I can do for you?'

'Yes. Let us go.'

'Now stop that,' Theondra scolded. 'You're becoming boring, and it doesn't suit you. You're better than that.' She sat next to Ferguson, throwing Allira a quick, triumphant glance as she did so. 'As a matter of fact, I have a little surprise for you.'

Ferguson did not comment, staring blankly away from Theondra at the nearest wall. Unabashed, she continued, 'You must be feeling very lonely here, all alone in this terrible building. You must be missing the companionship of your fellow humans.'

'He has me,' Allira said, but Theondra made no acknowledgment of the comment and reached over to hold Ferguson's hand.

'So let's go and meet some of your human relatives, shall we?'

Ferguson instantly became alert.

'People? There are others here as well as that woman we saw?'

'Yes, of course there are, Greg. Scientists we may be, but we have needs and wants. So, we keep a little stock of your race for enjoyment.'

Ferguson's surprised expression was replaced with one of suspicious anger.

'Enjoyment? What some harmless game? A little soccer match, perhaps?'

'Now, you're being silly again. It's exsanguination, of course.'

Not entirely to Allira's surprise, Ferguson understood that unusual word. He grimaced and said, 'You drain them of blood.'

'Well, of course. What are we supposed to do? We're vampires, aren't we? Not all the people we harvest from Stralia are suitable for experimentation, so we just enjoy them for what they can give us. It's illegal, of course, after Ginevra's edict, but that only gives the act an extra *frisson* of excitement.'

Ferguson was silent but Allira could see his mighty hands clenching and unclenching. Theondra soon tired of the silence and snapped, 'Well, do you want to meet them or not?'

Ferguson stood.

'Yes. But Allira comes with us.'

'If you must have the tiresome creature follow you everywhere, like a faithful little bitch, I can't stop you. Yet.' She turned to Allira and curled a black-nailed finger. 'Come along, my dear.'

Ferguson could smell the people before he saw them. It was the smell of unwashed bodies who had little access to sanitary facilities. The door opened, and he saw them, cowering from the sudden influx of light. There were six, four women and two men, dressed in clothing that obviously had been worn far too long. One figure in the malodorous gloom was much bigger than the others. Ferguson approached.

It was Gottlieb.

For an instant, Ferguson was struck motionless with astonishment. Then, as he finally realised he was not hallucinating, he leapt at Gottlieb. One great fist connected with Gottlieb's chin, and he fell at his attacker's feet.

'Not quite the reunion I was expecting,' Theondra murmured, a pleased smile flickering on her lips. Gottlieb struggled to his feet, wiping blood from his mouth.

'That hurt. Why did you hit me? There was no need for that.'

'No need for that? You killed Sky, you bastard!' And with that, he launched himself at Gottlieb again. This time, his reluctant opponent deflected the blow with his arm, but still staggered under its force.

'Please don't hit me anymore, Greg. You're really hurting me.'

Ferguson dropped his fists and stared at Gottlieb with obvious incomprehension.

'What's the matter with you, man? Fight back for gods' sake!'

'No, no! No fighting. Please leave me alone.'

Ferguson took a step backward, his bemusement having robbed him of further action or even speech. He heard Theondra laughing and helplessly turned to her.

'Greg, Greg, have you forgotten the Mozzies? Gottlieb was abducted not long after you. You managed to shake off the conditioning somehow—we're still not certain how—but Gottlieb did not.'

'So this is conditioning: rendering a man helpless.'

'Helpless, apathetic, dispirited, incapable of action. I think a demonstration will make things clearer.' With that, she crossed to Gottlieb and slapped him across the face. He burst into tears and backed away, looking reproachfully at his assailant.

'Why did you do that? Why does everybody want to hurt me? I haven't done anything wrong!'

Ferguson felt a sickness in his stomach and then a growing anger. He turned to Theondra, his face suffused with angry blood.

'You've robbed him of everything that made him a man!'

She laughed.

'Listen to you! A few seconds ago, you wanted to kill him over an incident with a dog. Yes, we know all about that. The Mozzy recorded your little spat as it approached. You judge me for making him peaceful, while at the same time regarding a human life as of less importance than a pet.'

Ferguson said nothing but glanced helplessly at Allira, who showed no reaction. But Theondra had not finished.

'We have more humans, of course, but we operate a *First In-First Out* policy. These are the ones who have reached the First Out stage.'

' "First Out" to where?'

'I've already explained, Greg: Gronz likes his experiments, but few meet his exacting criteria. So we harvest them to enjoy what their bodies can give us.'

'My mother's document said there were artificial substitutes for our blood.'

'Yes, there are. But I doubt you would prefer synthetic meat to the real thing, Greg, so no lectures, please.' The thought had obviously excited her as her fangs had become very prominent as she smiled up at Ferguson. 'Now, because I like you, I'm going to give you a special privilege. You can choose a human for Gronz and me to enjoy.' She laughed at Ferguson's stricken face. 'Go on, Greg, choose! Gottlieb, I suppose.'

Ferguson watched Gottlieb move away, ending up cowering in a corner. He turned away, sickened.

'I refuse.'

Theondra laughed again.

'If you won't play my game with me, I'll choose without you.' For the first time, she looked at Allira, who felt a stab of cruel fear strike deep into her heart. 'Then I choose your cowering little bitch. Gronz doesn't want her for mental experiments, so I will have her for my pleasure. Ah, the rich, warm red blood jetting from her arteries! Oh, the fun we'll have together!'

Ferguson knew then that he would have to die defending Allira. Gronz had warned him of Theondra's physical prowess, but he knew there was no alternative. Better to die together than live in shame. He felt he was trapped in some dreadful nightmare as he watched Allira back away until she was up against a wall. Theondra's fangs somehow extended until they reached the length of her chin and gave off a pale glow in the gloom. She raised her arms high above her head; fingers, with their cruel black nails, crooked into terrible instruments of death. Ferguson readied himself to strike.

And then Gronz's voice rang out.

'Theondra! Stop this! I have plans for this female. Leave her!'

None of them had seen Gronz enter, but on turning, he was revealed as an evil silhouette in the doorway. He came further into the room.

'Theondra, you have angered me. I have already told you of the experiments I wish to perform, and Allira will play a central role in them. There may come a time when I will give her to you, but that time is not yet.'

Theondra dropped her arms, and her fangs returned to their normal length.

'Yes, Gronz. I'm afraid I became a little over-excited.'

'Clearly. Now, choose a human other than Greg or Allira, and we will resume work in the morning.'

Theondra whirled around, back to the cowering men and women.

'You!' she snapped, pointing to a young woman. 'Come with me! Now!'

After the pair had left, Gronz sent the remaining people into a separate room, and addressed Ferguson.

'I must apologise for that, Greg. I told you earlier that Theondra is a very passionate, physical female. She is not interested in the mysteries of the universe or the powers of the mind, as am I. Perhaps it is because she has greater control over mentalic fields than I, and believes she has nothing to learn. It is well the Vetusians have been driven away, for they would find her very interesting.'

Once again, Ferguson did not recognise the unusual word Gronz had uttered, but was not interested in discovering its meaning.

'Theondra is evil in one way, and you are evil in another. But you are both evil.' Then, some new thought struck him. 'You are responsible for maintaining order in our homeland—but abducting humans and consuming them is not part of your responsibilities. Does no one monitor your actions; do you not have a supervisor of your own? Am I correct in believing your little empire here is illegal?'

Did Gronz's expression alter slightly then? Ferguson was not sure.

'That is no business of yours,' Gronz said eventually. 'Whatever my status is beyond these walls, within them, I am your lord and master. Never doubt that.'

TWENTY THREE

As they made to leave, Gronz moved in front of Ferguson.

'We have unfinished business, Greg. I want to give you one last mental upgrade.'

'What, because I'm almost as intelligent as I'm going to be? Would you like me to prove Euler's Identity from first principles? Or peel a banana with my feet while scratching my armpits?'

'*Euler's Identity*; very good, Greg. The most beautiful statement in all of mathematics. You have indeed learned much. As for why the next session will be the last, I think it's likely you won't be around for much longer after that one. We will be moving onto the physical tests soon.'

Ferguson stared at the vampire.

'You have such a lovely way of putting things, Gronz. Oh, I'm sorry; I forgot: vampires don't have a sense of humour, do they?'

'I understand it's a variety of word-play, but my people don't have the time for meaningless frivolities. Language is for transmitting information. I'll call for you in the morning.'

Back in the holding cell, Ferguson looked across at Allira.

'Well, seems like we'll be saying goodbye to this place before too long. I can't accuse Gronz of sugarcoating things; he made clear from the beginning what was going to happen to us.'

'The maddening thing is that none of this needed to happen; we just chanced to fall into the grasp of the most vicious vampires imaginable. They have built themselves a little empire of pain here—just because they could.'

Ferguson nodded.

'In human terms, they would be called psychopaths.'

She gave a wry smile.

'And where did that word come from? You would never have said that a few days ago. Gronz is not a trickster; he has done something to your brain.'

'Yes, but I don't get to use it. All I have is a headache. And what he gets are little slices of frozen brain. Mine.'

To his surprise, Allira slid nearer to him and placed her head as close to his as possible.

'He lets me watch,' she whispered.

He looked at her in incomprehension.

'So?'

'I might learn something.'

His expression did not change.

'Like what?'

'How this place works. I think this "High Command" of theirs doesn't know what they're up to here. Perhaps we can contact them.'

'They're vampires, Allira. Have you forgotten?'

'No. But your mother's documents said nothing about humans being used for experiments—that's him and Theondra. Anything would be better than those two.'

Ferguson pursed his lips in thought.

'Maybe. He said that teleporter device of theirs is also a communicator. I have a strong feeling that if I could get near it, I would be able to understand how it works.'

'You feel that confident?'

'Yes. Everything is becoming clearer. Four-dimensionality is the key. My thoughts are interacting with each other, creating new ones as they spark together.'

Allira nodded.

'That mathematical example you used. I've never heard of it.'

'Do you think I had? I didn't know I knew it until I said it. And there it was in my mind, all laid out. I understood the symbols, but, more importantly, I knew how to derive it.' He sighed. 'But that doesn't get us out of here.'

Allira moved away slightly, looking into emptiness.

'We must look around, study everything. I have a rapport with Gronz that might help.'

'A rapport? What? How?'

'I'm not sure. There is a possible explanation, but...'

'But what?'

'Now is not the time to try to explain.' She turned back to Ferguson. 'But I will watch Gronz closely. Perhaps I will learn one little thing that will unlock this cage.'

***

'Hold steady, Greg,' Gronz said. 'Don't worry, this is the last time we'll do this.'

'Get on with it,' Ferguson said. 'I'm tired of looking up into your nostrils.'

Gronz made no reaction and carried on checking the sensors which had attached themselves to Ferguson's head as the latter lay supine on the examination table. Allira moved closer to the pair.

'Is it alright if I watch again, Gronz?'

Gronz looked at her, obviously puzzled.

'If you want to, my dear. But you know from last time there's nothing to see. There are readings on the screens, of course, but you couldn't possibly understand them.'

'It's just that my presence helps Greg relax. And I like watching a superior mind like yours at work. A kind of hero worship, I guess.'

Vampires don't understand humour, she thought. *Let's hope they don't know the difference between fact and flattery.*

It appeared they did not, for Gronz smiled and said, 'It is a strange pleasure to know you, Allira. Let me reassure you once again that anything I do to you and Greg is done purely in the quest to advance the boundaries of science.'

'It will be an honour to have served in that quest,' she replied, instantly wondering if she had gone too far in the flattery department.

But apparently, she had not, for Gronz was already studying the numbers which were constantly rolling up the screens of his devices. She moved nearer, so near, the metallic smell of cold vampire flesh infiltrated her nostrils.

'What are you giving him now?'

'More multi-dimensional geometry to start with. We learned a great deal in the last Vetusian war. We wouldn't have teleportation without it.'

Once again, that odd name; try as Allira might, she could not find a referent for it. Perhaps it would become clearer later. Hesitantly, she spoke again.

'Gronz, have you considered knowledge other than math and physics? Like history, how vampires came to rule the world. How things in this place work. Practical knowledge. Wouldn't that be a good idea?'

He turned. Allira's eyes locked onto his. They seemed to be pools of an unknown liquid, a very deep, unknown liquid. A minute passed.

'Yes. Why not? I was a little worried I might be running short on information to give him, but those topics will utilise different parts of the brain. Well done, Allira.' She smiled at the unexpected compliment, but did not speak. 'Perhaps I should study your brain as well,' Gronz continued.

She fought to keep the smile—and almost succeeded.

After an hour on the table, Ferguson awoke. The sensors automatically retracted, as did the restraining hoops. Ignoring Gronz, Allira went to him and helped him to his feet. There was a vacant look on his face, and he was having trouble focusing on nearby objects. Gronz caught her worried expression.

'It will pass. The brain, even of humans, is capable of remarkable feats. It can rewire itself if parts of it are damaged or removed. I have proven that many times with my own little experiments. And in the current experiment, I have done two things: I have created more neurons and replasticised the originals, and then crammed vast amounts of knowledge into those neurons, new and old. I can hardly wait to study those cells under laboratory conditions.'

'But not today,' Allira said, guiding Ferguson away from the experiment table. Gronz stood aside as they left the room.

It was difficult for Allira to get Ferguson back to their holding cell as he was having trouble co-ordinating his leg movements and, as a result, was placing much of his considerable weight onto her slim frame. Once there, he fell asleep again.

Many wearisome hours passed while she watched over him, watching his great chest rise and fall with his shallow breathing. Then, at last, his eyes opened, and he sat up, abruptly.

'I don't want to do that again,' were his first words. 'The headache I have now makes the first one feel like a gentle tickle.'

'You're still alive. That's all that counts. Are there any differences apart from the headache?'

Ferguson pointed to the water jug and drained it. Then he motioned to Allira that she should sit next to him.

'Yes. I got more science; mainly physics and math, but a great wodge of biology this time, as well. But I saw the recent history of this world, and now I understand so many things, Allira, so many things!'

'Like what?'

The blank expression had vanished, and his face was that of a man whose theories have all been triumphantly vindicated.

'I know how this state of affairs came to be. Listen, Allira, listen! For thousands of years, vampires had been living with us but not making themselves known. They lived among us, but we did not see them.'

'What? How?'

'Mentalic fields, Allira. I understand them now. They used them to cloud human minds, so they could operate alongside us. They lived a parallel existence. Many vampires lived disguised as humans, some reaching positions of great power and influence. Others lived humble, nocturnal lives, not drawing attention to themselves but regularly taking human beings for their blood feasts. Those who masqueraded as statesmen pretended to die so that their great lifespans would not give them away. They would then spend a few decades as nocturnal vampires, and then reappear to exercise power again under a new disguise. Those humans who suspected things or discovered them accidentally would end up exsanguinated.'

'But that's not how things are now.'

'Indeed. Several centuries ago, there was a crisis. We—humans, that is—had always been warlike, fighting each other; something vampires have never done. We developed more and more weapons, always deadlier than the previous ones. Allira, I can hardly bear to tell you this, but we built bombs which could destroy the planet, created diseases which could not be cured. We even built machines—robots, they were called—to kill our fellow humans.'

Allira pulled away, her face twisted with horror and shame.

'That's horrible!' She shook her head. 'My people are not like this; we live in harmony with the earth.'

'Yes, they do, but most of the world is not like your people. We built a terrible structure called Zee Zero Zee, which contained weapons that could destroy the world many times over. A war to end all wars could have broken out at any moment. In fact, it could have happened by accident if one of their

233

computers—their machines that could think, in a way—misinterpreted some random happening and fired the rockets, released the viruses.'

Allira did not understand all the new words Ferguson was using, but she understood enough to realise that humanity had stood on the edge of annihilation.

'Let me guess what happened next: the vampires couldn't risk being destroyed along with us and took charge.'

'Exactly right. We lost everything. Most of the population was put on farms where they were milked of their blood. A few people worked for the new masters in menial jobs, but they were a tiny minority.'

'But we, you and I, were not in farms, used like cattle or goats.'

'No, we were not. And this is the next thing I learned. I know now about the Vetusians.'

'I've heard that word several times.'

'Allira, listen: the vampires prey on us; that's why we fear them. But there is something that preys on vampires, something they are terrified of.'

'Vetusians.'

'Yes. They are not of this world, not even of this universe, but they are creatures of immense power. Three times, they have launched a war of conquest against the vampires, and each time, the vampires have only won after immense suffering. They are kept outside by something called the Barrier.'

'Gronz mentioned the Barrier.'

'Yes. It is the ultimate expression of mentalic fields and is generated—in some way I don't understand, yet—by living vampire brains. As long as the Barrier exists, the Vetusians can't get into our world. But they wait outside, constantly testing it. And there is a problem; it is weakening.'

'Then we will have two problems: vampires and Vetusians.'

'No. They are only interested in vampires. We are too lowly for their attention. And...'

Allira raised a hand to forestall him.

'I see it. You think we could ally with these Vetusians. To get our world back.'

Ferguson smiled a great smile.

'Yes. That is exactly what I think.'

Allira did not smile. Instead, in flat, defeated tones, she said, 'Just one flaw in your wonderful plan: we are trapped in an unknown building in an unknown city at the mercy of two psychopathic vampires.'

Ferguson's smile vanished.

'Yes, that is something of a problem.'

TWENTY FOUR

Time passes very slowly when one has nothing to do except wait for the next crisis. And so, despite the danger they were in, both Ferguson and Allira often fell asleep, unable to maintain a state of constant high alert. And so it was that Ferguson did not hear the door to their holding cell open.

However, he did feel a hand shaking him by the shoulder and heard a female voice say his name. His eyes opened to see Theondra looking down upon him, her eyes the deep, calm green that showed she was not angry.

Quite the opposite, in fact.

'Greg, I'd like you to come with me.'

Ferguson glanced at Allira, but Theondra continued, 'Don't worry about her; she won't wake for a while. I've ensured that, although the little sow fought me in a way I was not expecting.'

'I'm happy where I am, thank you, Theondra.'

Her eyes showed a momentary flash of back-lit crimson.

'It is for her own good that you obey me, Greg. And I don't like people who don't obey me instantly.' The fire disappeared. 'And I want to like you, Greg.'

Ferguson reluctantly followed her out of the cell and had not gone far when he realised they were heading for her private room again.

'Don't do this, Theondra,' he said.

'Oh, but I will, Greg. And more importantly, so will you.'

I think not, Ferguson said in the safety of his mind, but did not speak. Soon, Theondra had draped herself over the crimson lounger again, watching his every move. Ignoring her, he strode to the great window and drank in a welcome view of the sky. The horror of his incarceration struck him then as he watched the black dots of birds wheeling effortlessly against an electric blue backdrop. His gaze dropped to the neat rectangles of New Marinetown. He noticed that there were no parks, in fact, no greenery at all, just geometric arrays of buildings. The clinical, artificial nature of the design told him at once he was looking at a city of vampires, not people.

'Beautiful, is it not?' he heard Theondra behind him. 'Our cities are so much more elegant than your grubby collections of ramshackle hovels.'

'It's soulless,' he said, turning to face her. 'Soulless. And so are you.'

Again, a flash of fire.

'Greg, you must stop being so provincial. I understand you come from a pitiful, impoverished background, but you must try to appreciate the finer things in life. And stop using childish words like "soul." You're in the big city now.' She patted the lounger. 'Come and sit with me.'

He obeyed, but refused to look at her.

'What did you mean when you said Allira fought you? I didn't hear anything.'

'I used a touch of mentalic field to make her sleep deeper. She needed slightly more than I expected, that's all. Nothing more. I accept I called her an unpleasant name, but that's only because I don't tolerate rivals well.'

'She is not your rival because you mean nothing to me. Allira does not have a rival, and neither do you.'

'These are very foolish words, Greg, and I have explained why. Neither of you is going to leave this building alive, so why not take the opportunity of pleasure when it is offered you? There will be no more pleasure available to you soon, believe me.'

'Because it would not be pleasure.'

'Foolishness again, Greg. You are a young, virile man, that's obvious. You need to enjoy a female, now and then.'

'Yes, a woman—not a female vampire.'

'Yes, I am a vampire and proud of it. We are very different to women on the inside, but we look very much like them on the outside. But better, of course. Here, let me show you.' She rose from the lounger and planted herself in front of Ferguson. 'Look at me, Greg, or I will hurt you.'

He lifted his head just enough that he could meet her ardent gaze. She smiled and pulled the blouse over her long raven locks. She was not wearing a brassiere and had no need to, for her full and voluptuous breasts stood proud from an alabaster chest, defying gravity.

'You like them?'

He did not answer.

She made a quick movement at her hip and her skirt fell away. A few seconds later, she stood naked before him. She turned so she was full on to him and put her hands behind her head.

'Look at me, Greg. Am I not beautiful? Am I not better than that half-starved, brown-skinned wretch you have hanging around you? Come on, Greg, join me in nudity. I long to run my fingers over those muscles of yours. Such power; I could hardly believe you are just a human.'

He stood and removed his simple clothing, avoiding meeting her gaze as he did so. She slowly studied him from his mass of curly hair to his toes. Her vision lingered at his groin.

'Oh, Greg, you're not going to disappoint me, are you? Come, there's no need to be nervous.'

He sat back down.

'I'm not. Understand this, Theondra—I prefer my own kind to vampires.'

She shook her head.

'You must try, Greg. Have I not told you that Allira's fate depends on you pleasing me? Do what I want, and I will not hurt her. But you must understand that Gronz has no interest in her. If I ask him to give her to me as my very own plaything, he will do it. Allira will be very busy when I enrol her in my games; very busy, indeed. But I'm afraid the pleasure will be all mine. Let me give you a few examples of the games we will play.'

In growing anger, Ferguson listened as Theondra outlined her plans for Allira. His heart hammered, but not with excitement.

'You are a fiend, a sick fiend, Theondra! A vile monster, and you know nothing about humans! What you have told me makes me hate you even more. You disgust me!'

Theondra was silent for a moment; then she said—apparently to herself—'Yes, a miscalculation. A different way, I think.' She approached Ferguson and, placing her hands on his shoulders, gently pushed him back onto the couch. She sat next to him, thigh to thigh, and he felt the coldness of her skin begin to draw the heat from his body.

'Look at me, Greg.'

It was against his will, but for some reason he obeyed. He found himself staring into pools of deepest emerald, pools that were deep; very, very deep. Her hands reached for his and gently placed them on her breasts. At first, the coldness repelled him, but gradually, slowly, the sensation grew pleasant and he began to react. Then she began kissing him and he revelled in the icy touch of vampire lips. Soon he began to take the initiative and then, suddenly, pushed her down on her back. An instant later, he surged in, making Theondra give a high-pitched cry of mingled lust and triumph.

The morning passed in a whirlwind of sexual frenzy.

But towards the end, as Ferguson's third orgasm approached, a strange thought burst explosively into his mind.

Allira—forgive me!

***

'I awoke and you weren't here,' Allira said. 'Where were you?'

'I was out,' Ferguson said, not looking at her.

'Obviously. Had you gone Cat-hunting, or castrating a ram, perhaps?'

'No. Neither of those things.'

240

Allira stood over him.

'Greg, we may not have long left to go on this earth, so let's not play games. The sleep I had was peculiar; it didn't feel like our normal boredom sleep. So, if it wasn't normal, it must have been vampire-induced. There are only two vampires in this place; Gronz isn't interested in me, so that leaves Theondra. She must have intensified my sleep for some reason.'

'You know, Allira, I can understand you now. Words like "induced" and "intensified" would have baffled me not too long ago. Had you received a brain-boost before I met you?'

'Don't change the subject. You were with Theondra, weren't you? Remember, no game playing. There's no reason to lie to each other now.'

For some reason, the lines and veins on Ferguson's hands appeared to have become subjects of great interest to him, but eventually, he looked up.

'Yes, I was with Theondra.'

'Talking about vampire history, perhaps; how they enslaved our ancestors and put them on blood farms?'

Ferguson knew there was no longer any point in dissembling. He looked up at Allira and a great sadness swept over him; a desire to turn back time, to not have done what he had done.

'No, we had sex.'

Allira's face might have shown a brief sign of sadness as well, just for a moment; Ferguson was not sure. But she sat beside him and reached for a hand.

'I knew. Of course, I knew.'

'Do you hate me?'

She laughed.

'Hate you? Just for sex? No, of course not. We are about to be murdered in some ghastly way at the hands of creatures who can bend minds. Did you do it willingly, because you wanted to? Because you're tired of me?'

He reached for her and drew her closer.

'No, Allira, no! It was her eyes, something in her eyes! I didn't want to and then suddenly I did! She said she'd hurt you if I didn't do it! You must believe me!'

Allira smiled tenderly and ran a hand over Ferguson's lips.

'Of course I do. We are dealing with creatures way beyond our power. Our ancestors couldn't defeat, or even resist them when they had all the power of this world at their fingertips. They didn't go into the blood farms voluntarily, did they? So, whatever happens here is not what we choose to do; it's what we're *made* to do. We are helpless.'

The tension drained from Ferguson at her words, and she saw the muscles in his hands relax and his entire body become looser as if an internal hairspring had finally wound down.

He looked at her and she was expecting him to say some words of love. But he did not.

'We have to get out of this place.'

'How?'

'I have to kill them. Both. Gronz and Theondra. Especially Theondra.'

Allira did not reply; there seemed little point in discussing wish-fulfilment fantasies, and Ferguson did not elaborate.

And so they sat silently together, looking into emptiness as the remorseless hours ticked by.

TWENTY FIVE

Allira awoke with a start. She did not know how long she had been asleep. One hour was much like any other hour when they were not in the company of vampires. Was it the following day? She no longer knew.

She reached out to touch Ferguson, but her hand met only emptiness. She was alone. Allira sat up and put her head in her hands, fighting to withstand the tide of misery sweeping over her. Had he—despite all his contrition—gone back to Theondra?

But just as she thought of her enemy's name, the door opened and Theondra herself stood there, her lips, as usual, curved into a gloating smile.

'Ah, awake at last, I see. Come with me, my dear; Gronz has need of you.'

'Where's Greg?'

'You'll see him soon. And don't worry your pretty little head about him and me: I've satisfied my curiosity, and I have no more need of his services.' Her smile became wolfish. 'Which is not to say that I did not enjoy those services. He did not disappoint, Allira; I'm sure you'll be pleased to hear that.'

'You can go fuck yourself,' Allira hissed.

'No need for that, Allira. If I wanted such an action from Greg, I could get it by snapping my fingers. But I don't.' The grin vanished. 'No more delays, come with me. Now.'

Allira followed Theondra, but they had not gone very far along the featureless corridor when she detected the rank smell of the pool again. Soon, both females were standing at the poolside and Allira's eyes were once again drawn to the turbid slime-streaked water and its unseen inhabitants. Gronz was also standing at the poolside, looking into the water, but turned as he detected their approach.

'Ah, Allira, so glad you could join us.'

'Where's Greg?'

'My dear, open your eyes. There he is.'

She followed his pointing finger and then felt her heart jump. Once again, she saw the tall transparent cylinder at the far end of the pool, but earlier, it had been empty.

Now, it contained Ferguson. He was standing upright, his face impassive as he looked back at her. In her frenzied despair and anger, she faced Gronz and beat her small fists upon his chest.

'What are you doing to him!'

Gronz removed her fists, holding them tightly to prevent another futile attack.

'I am interested in human emotions, Allira. You see, the expression of emotions in the human is distinctly different to that in the vampire. You are far more emotional, far more childish in your attachments to others of your kind. You talk of "loving" another person. I want to study that, to see how far it overrides the normal instinct for self-preservation. Look at this.' He propelled her to the very edge of the pool and forced her to look into it. As before, she saw dark shapes moving in its depths.

'I have populated this pool with especially mutated fish, Allira. Now, the piranha of Sumerica is infamous for its ferocity, even though its behaviour is rather overrated. However, it has useful genes which can be incorporated into other water-borne creatures. This I have done, adding them to the genomes of some other carnivorous creatures. The slightest drop of blood in the water drives them to a feeding frenzy in which they can reduce a human-sized animal to the bone in a matter of minutes. They actually prefer vampire blood to human, but, of course, they rarely get the chance to enjoy that.'

'What are you going to do?' Allira said, in a dull, defeated voice. Theondra took over the explanations.

'If you look at Greg, my dear, you'll see he is trapped in that cylinder. You can observe his every movement, although he doesn't seem to be making many at the moment. Now, very shortly the cylinder will start filling with water. Like vampires, humans cannot live for very long underwater. Your task is to rescue him. The water is not very deep, so it is possible to walk through it, although your mouth will not be very far above the surface. Vampires cannot swim; our bones are too heavy, but I believe some of your people can. Whichever method of locomotion you prefer, you must get to the cylinder before it fills with water and poor Greg is extinguished. Do you understand?'

'Yes.'

Theondra pulled something out of a fold in her skirt. Allira saw that it gleamed dully in the artificial light.

It was a knife.

'Now,' Theondra continued, 'I am going to give you a small cut. It will be a very small one and it will not impede your ability to move. However, it will alert the fish, who will immediately attack you.'

'*The fish are always hungry,*' Allira quoted. She turned to Gronz. 'You said they can strip someone to the bone in only minutes. How am I going to get there in time? Can I walk around the pool?'

'Excellent questions. No, you must stay in the pool. If you try to get out, we will push you back in. As for the time taken to deflesh you, normally, you would be dead after the first few metres. Obviously, that would not be much of an experiment, so I have removed most of the fish. There are only three in there. They are most definitely able to kill you, but three will take some time to do that. I calculate that if you can exceed a certain speed, you can get to the cylinder before that happens.'

'And when I get to the cylinder...?'

'There is a manual switch at the base. Depress that and the water stops rising.'

'But the fish will continue to attack even after I have reached the cylinder.'

'Indeed they will. But I will send a small electric pulse which temporarily incapacitates them. I will send that as soon as I see you have reached the cylinder. I am a scientist, Allira, and I want you to survive.'

'So you can devise more experiments on me.'

'Yes. Once again, you have got to the heart of the matter. I am really beginning to think I must study your brain as well.'

'Thank you.' Allira looked down at the pool. 'When does this experiment begin?'

She heard Theondra say, 'Now!' She felt a sudden sharp pain as the knife punctured the skin on one arm. Then one of the vampires kicked her legs from under her and she fell headfirst into the pool. Instantly, her mouth was full of thick, rancid water. She broke through the surface and spat it out. Looking at her arm, she saw a thin red line of blood snaking down it. She lifted the arm as high as she could to try to stop the blood from spreading, but the wound produced a steady drip of scarlet droplets. One by one, the drops hit the water, instantly dispersing into spreading pink clouds. She started walking towards the cylinder, seeing Ferguson impassively watching her. Greenish water was swirling around his legs, just under the knees. The pool bottom was slippery, and the resistance of the viscous water also slowed her down. Then, she felt a sudden pain in her left leg, and a downward glance revealed a dark object making repeated lunges at it. She punched down through the water and the creature retreated but remained swimming alongside. At that point, she decided to swim. Allira had learned to do that in pools in eastern Stralia, but it had been several years since her last time in the water. But there was only one way to find out if she still had it in her. And so, she lunged forward and began swimming for her life. The only stroke she knew was a beginner's breaststroke, and her version of that was not much faster than walking, but every second counted for she felt another sharp pain, this time in her right calf. Almost at the same time, a wriggling thing attached itself to her right bicep. Allira saw jaws close on the flesh and felt that flesh separate under the pressure of razor-like teeth. A large red cloud bloomed around her.

And then suddenly, unexpectedly, she was at the base of the cylinder. Where was the switch? She could no longer see clearly in the red-tinged water and could only desperately paw at the cylinder's smooth surface, searching by touch alone for the switch that would save Ferguson's life. If he were still alive, that is. Then, her hands felt something protruding from the cylinder's surface—a handle. She felt the impact of another voracious fish on a breast while her fingers scrabbled to gain purchase on the switch's handle. She tugged.

It did not move.

Her lips were momentarily above the water, and she took a deep lungful of the stale air. Dipping under again, she pulled down on the handle with renewed power. It moved. Instantly, she felt an electric tingle in the water and the attacks on her exposed flesh ceased. Allira remembered nothing of the next few minutes, but awoke to find herself on her back on the poolside, with Gronz applying some cream to the gaping mouths of her wounds. Dimly, she heard him speaking to her, but it felt like he was a long way away.

'This ointment will heal these lesions. In about two days, you'll just have a few scars.'

Like the serving girl, she thought. *I wonder how she escaped.*

'Greg, where is Greg?' she finally managed to say.

A large hand caressed her shoulder.

'I'm here, Allira. You saved me.'

Ferguson bent over and he and Allira kissed, while the vampires watched in silent fascination, closely observing that display of human emotions. Ferguson straightened and spun around to glare at Theondra.

'You promised not to hurt her!' he thundered.

Theondra gave an almost human shrug.

'I lied,' she said.

TWENTY SIX

Ferguson lay by the poolside, breathing deeply but still tasting the foul bitterness of the water that had so nearly claimed his life. Allira lay by his side, her eyes closed, the red ovals of the fish bites lathered by the white substance that Gronz had applied.

The prurient gaze of the vampires had ceased after Allira and Ferguson had rolled apart, but now both were standing either side of the humans. Ferguson's eyes opened and he saw Theondra looking down at him.

'You really are a fiend, a monster that looks like a woman.'

'Not too much like a woman, I hope,' she said, pulling him upright. 'That would be something of an insult.'

For an instant, Ferguson toyed with the idea of striking her in the middle of those soft, cold lips, but thought better of it. It would achieve nothing, and his punishment would be swift in coming.

'Did you have to lie?' was all he said.

'Why not? We don't have to keep faith with you humans. At least it saved you worrying about what was about to happen to your mate.'

Ferguson decided further talk was pointless and turned back to Allira. She, too, was standing, but was visibly shaking as the reaction to her unspeakable ordeal swept over her. Gronz bent closer and applied more of his ointment, paying particular attention to her upper thighs.

'You have had a terrible shock, my dear. I think it's best you come with me for a few hours until your body finally realises it's no longer in danger.'

She looked at Ferguson, pleadingly.

'I want to be with Greg.'

'And so you shall. But I think it is best you stay with me for a while. After all, what could Greg do if you had some kind of seizure? You humans are not like us; you are far more fragile, and it is my duty to take care of you.'

She gave a bitter laugh.

'Take care of me? Until the next sadistic experiment!'

Gronz took her words at face value.

'Yes, that is correct.' He grasped an arm. 'Now, let us go. You will be back with Greg soon; after all, he's not going anywhere, is he?'

She gave Ferguson one last, almost despairing look, and followed Gronz out of the room. Ferguson was alone with Theondra. He turned to find her looking at him with a twisted half-smile playing on her lips.

'You humans. What a peculiar breed you are. That female can do nothing to help you; she is almost as helpless as you are, but you persist in displaying weak sentimentality when you are with her. What survival advantage can that give you?'

Ferguson stared contemptuously into her emerald eyes.

'I'm not answering any of your questions, you revolting animal. If you can't understand our feelings, so much the worse for you! Torturing us won't help you understand them—if that is, in fact, the only reason you are doing these things to us. I strongly suspect it isn't.'

She came closer. There was smouldering menace in her eyes.

'Careful, Greg. Just because Gronz has given you a few more neurons and a smidgeon of knowledge, don't think that makes you my equal or that you can speak to me in that disrespectful manner. I have total power over you.'

'Yes, that's how you destroyed our civilisation and turned us into farm animals.'

'You had no civilisation! You were just ignorant apes, happily playing with nitroglycerin! We saved you, Greg, saved every man, woman and child. And do we get gratitude? Enough! I am taking you back to your cell right now, otherwise I might kill you where you stand!'

Ferguson was certain she spoke in earnest, and they returned to the holding cell in silence, where she left him, impotent rage burning in every cell of his body.

Somehow, the cramped cell felt much larger without Allira, and he spent the wearisome hours staring at the door, willing her to come through it.

But she did not. Then, starved of all stimuli, he fell into an uneasy sleep. Visions of his homeland drifted through his mind; he saw himself under the nurturing sky of the Red Centre, walking with Wygu and with Sky at his side, always alert for the approach of a Cat. But once again, he saw himself sitting with Delgado, receiving the first ominous warning that the world was not what he thought it to be; he...

He heard the door open and snapped back into consciousness. A broad smile split his face as Allira entered, and he leapt up to greet her. However, she did not smile as he hugged her but seemed tense and distant. He sat her down next to him.

'What is it?' he asked. 'Is something wrong?'

She finally smiled, but it was one without warmth.

'What, something worse than being trapped with murderous vampires? There is nothing worse, Greg.'

'You have been gone a long time. Did anything happen with Gronz? Did he hurt you again?'

She shook her head.

'He didn't hurt me again.'

'Then what? What is the matter, Allira?'

Once again, she shook her head.

'I don't want to talk about it.'

And with that, she turned her face to the wall and fell asleep. Ferguson stood over her, stroking her hair and shoulders. He felt a growing shame that he had been unable to protect her. Twice now, she had saved his life; once when he had been close to drowning, and once when the Cat had been about to devour him. But what had he done for her?

She did not stir under his gentle caresses, and he sat alone again, staring at the wall. How long would it be before the next experiment? How long before one of them succumbed to whatever torment their captors had in store for them? He realised then he would gladly surrender his own life if he could take Gronz and Theondra with him. Was there no way he could contact the inhabitants of New Marinetown? Vampires they were, of course, but surely not as warped and despicable as the two who had enslaved him and Allira?

He had slept so much that, even with nothing to do but wait for further experimentation, he could not sleep. Behind closed lids, he watched his earlier life in Stralia, understanding now what a paradise it had been. He heard Allira stir.

'Is there any food?' she said. In response, he passed her the bowl of gruel, which was the usual tasteless sustenance supplied by the vampires. She took a few mouthfuls and then pushed it away.

'No,' she said. 'No more food. There is only one way out. I will starve myself to death.'

He went to her.

'No, we must keep hoping. There may be a better way.'

She did not look at him.

'There is no better way. Hope, without any grounds for such hope, is just an illusion; a drug which dulls our senses, prevents us from accepting reality. False hope is worse than no hope.'

Ferguson tried to turn her to look at him, but she resisted.

'Allira, are you sure nothing happened when you were with Gronz? I've not seen you so low.'

'I am not *low*. That implies there is a state I should be in, other than this. By starving myself, I choose the time of my own passing. That will be a victory. You could easily kill me with your strength, but you won't do it. So that leaves only my way.'

Ferguson sat silently, his mind whirling, trying to come up with some solution other than his partner's. Then, unexpectedly, an idea came to him; it all depended on the next experiment involving the fish...

His planning was cut short as the door opened. It was Theondra, of course, just as he had expected, but she was not alone. She had a human with her.

Gottlieb.

Theondra pushed him further into the room towards Allira and he obeyed, soundlessly.

'Greg!' Allira said, with panic in her voice as the large mass of the uninvited guest loomed over her. 'Get this man away from me!'

Ferguson studied his old adversary.

'It's alright, Allira. He won't hurt you.'

'That's right, isn't it, Karl?' came Theondra's permanently mocking tones. 'You won't hurt anybody, will you?'

'I won't hurt anybody,' Gottlieb said, in a flat monotone.

'Why is he here?' Ferguson said, addressing Theondra.

'He is a gift from Gronz. Well, he simply wanted to show you more of what a conditioned human is actually like, but it was I who chose Karl, as you and he are old friends.'

'And why does he want us to know more about conditioned humans?'

Theondra looked away from the two men and fixed the necrotic jade of her gaze upon Allira.

'It is to help Allira to decide. You see, Gronz has decided that the poor girl's cognitive abilities are significantly beyond what he would expect from someone of her upbringing. And so, he has decided he wants to examine her brain alongside yours, Greg. But to make life easier for her, he has offered to condition her first; that way, she will have no fear of the upcoming procedures. As you must by now realise, Gronz is a vampire of limitless compassion.'

'Yes, I had realised that,' Ferguson said, even though he knew that irony was lost upon vampires.

'Excellent. In which case, I'll leave you two to become reacquainted. Allira can observe and then decide if she wishes to accept Gronz's offer of conditioning.'

'I assume Greg will be getting extra rations, now that there are two big men,' Allira said.

'No, no need for that. All of you will be leaving us shortly, and so that would be a waste of food and water.' She paused at the doorway. 'So good to see humans making friends with each other.'

And she was gone.

Ferguson looked steadily at Gottlieb, waiting for him to say something. But it began to look as if he only spoke when spoken to.

'Gottlieb, sit down,' Ferguson finally said. Gottlieb obeyed, forcing Allira to retreat to the very edge of the bench to accommodate his width. Ferguson, in turn, became silent as he studied his old enemy. Gottlieb had lost some of his muscle mass, no doubt because of the inactivity he had been forced to adopt, but he was still a big, powerful man. Could the vampires have made a mistake in reuniting him with another powerful human? If Gottlieb could be recruited…

'Karl,' Ferguson began, 'how are you feeling? How have you been treated here?'

Gottlieb's face remained emotionless, passive.

'They give me food and they look after me.'

'They have imprisoned you, man! Don't you resent that? Don't you want to be free again?'

'I am happy with whatever the masters do for me,' Gottlieb said, and relapsed into silence.

Ferguson glanced at Allira, who shook her head.

'I don't think there's much left of the old Gottlieb you told me about.'

'There's got to be something left! I can remember parts of what I was like when I was conditioned, before Wygu rescued me. I knew who I was; I just had this terrible lethargy. I couldn't be bothered to do anything—but I was still me! Gottlieb must be the same; there's got to be something of the short-tempered brawler left, a core that the conditioning can't touch!'

'Perhaps there is, but how do you reawaken that core, make it the whole of Gottlieb again?'

'I must do it; he's our only hope. The two of us...'

Allira suddenly stood and crossed to Ferguson, ignoring the inert and silent mass of Gottlieb.

'Greg! I've just had a terrible thought! What if they are listening to us? You mustn't say too much! Or *think* too much!'

Ferguson shook his head.

'You mean reading minds? Well, I know now that some vampires can do that, but only in the ruling class. I don't think our two hosts qualify. But even if they can, I don't think they would be doing it. They are so contemptuous of us that they would see that as a waste of their valuable time. In any case, I've got to take the chance. Gottlieb might just be their first mistake!'

But even as he said those words, Ferguson was wondering about his liaison with Theondra and its unexpected culmination:

Did she just influence me—or did she read my mind?

TWENTY SEVEN

'You must remember the Kookaburra!' Ferguson almost screamed at the unresponsive Gottlieb. He glanced at Allira, but she merely shrugged. Ferguson returned to Gottlieb with gathering despair written on his face. Finally, the other man spoke.

'It's a bird, isn't it? Yes, I think it's a bird.'

Ferguson smiled; this was the first time Gottlieb had made any response to his increasingly frantic questioning.

'Yes, Karl, it is a bird. There was a picture of one just outside the inn door. Not a very good picture and faded, but it was meant to be that bird. Does that help?'

Gottlieb looked around uneasily.

'Why are you asking me all these questions? It makes me feel uncomfortable.'

'I'm sorry, Karl, I don't mean to upset you.'

Ferguson felt a growing sense that he was in some kind of dream; the idea that the Gottlieb he had known would have been made uncomfortable by asking him if he remembered a particular tavern was simply ridiculous. Here was a man, who previously had let his fists do the talking, acting like a child on his first day at school. He had to tread carefully; if

Gottlieb became really upset, he might refuse to be involved at all.

'Yes, Karl, it was a place where we drank beer. I usually gave some farm produce in exchange for my beer, but you had some metal discs that no one else had ever seen before. Do you remember?'

Gottlieb was silent, his fingers playing nervously in his unkempt beard. Then he nodded.

'Yes. Beer. It was terrible.'

Ferguson laughed out loud, the first time he had since his imprisonment began. The comment was so unexpected.

True, but unexpected.

'Yes, it was,' he said, as his laughter died away. 'Dreadful stuff. But that's all there was!'

To his relief, Gottlieb smiled as memories of unpleasant beverages returned to him. Ferguson wondered if he should let the man rest for a while; he was obviously finding it a draining experience to be forced to recall past events.

The cell was cramped and, even when talking to Allira, he was only a few feet away from Gottlieb. But he had learned there was no need to whisper when discussing Gottlieb's progress; being talked about in the third person did not appear to annoy him.

Worryingly, nothing seemed to annoy him.

'You mustn't push him too hard,' Allira said. 'he's already quite different from when he came in. Then he hardly spoke at all.'

'Yes, he is. But we don't know how long it is until the next experiment.'

'True. But we don't know if he'll be any help even when we do know. Can two men really overpower two vampires?'

'I'd like to find out. I really would.' Ferguson paused and gave Allira a hard look. 'Are you eating again?'

'Yes. I decided to see what the next test is. If we fail that one, I won't change my mind again. But it takes weeks to die of starvation. I probably won't be given that long.'

Ferguson reached for her hand.

'If everything fails, you must take the conditioning. That way, you'll be spared the worst of it.'

'And you?'

'I'll decide that when the time comes.' He saw her lift a hand to nibble on a nail and gently lowered the hand. 'Don't do that. I like them the way they are.'

She smiled weakly.

'If you like them, I'll keep them.'

Ferguson turned back to Gottlieb, who had remained motionless since the end of their conversation.

'Karl, what would you do if I punched you?'

Gottlieb looked startled.

'You're not going to do that, are you? I haven't done anything wrong!'

'No, no, I'm not going to hit you; it's just there are some bad people around, and they do like to hurt people. We must stand up to them or they won't stop. Do you remember when Theondra slapped you? You didn't like that, did you?'

'No.'

'Did you feel like slapping her back?'

A long pause, then: 'Yes.'

'Well, if you strike back when someone hurts you, usually they stop. You would want that, wouldn't you?'

A shorter pause, then, 'Yes.' Suddenly, Gottlieb frantically looked around, his eyes wide and staring. 'She's not here, is she?'

Ferguson realised it was time to quit his direct pushing. He patted the other man on the shoulder and said, 'No, she's not here, Karl. Everything's all right.' But having succeeded in establishing communication, he felt silence might be unwise, allowing Gottlieb to sink back into apathy again. 'Karl, you remember when we last met, back in the homeland. Tell me what happened, from your point of view. Please.'

Once again, Gottlieb did not meet Ferguson's gaze.

'I did a bad thing.'

'Explain. Please.'

'It was a very bad thing. I remember trying to hurt you. And...and...'

'Yes?'

'I killed your dog. I killed Sky.'

Ferguson took a deep breath. This might be a key moment.

'Yes, you did. But some time later, a Mozzy came. You remember?'

'Yes. It knocked me out, but I woke up and...and we were flying!' Gottlieb grasped Ferguson's wrist, and his eyes were wide and staring. 'You must believe me, Greg! We were up in the air and, looking down, I could see the ground, far below me! You must believe me!'

Ferguson felt the pressure on his wrist intensify, but did not attempt to detach himself.

'I believe you, Karl. But you didn't stay in the air, did you?'

'No. It was like a hole opened up in a hill, and the Mozzy took me inside. And then, and then...'

Ferguson felt Allira join him, and the two of them stared at Gottlieb, who appeared to be on the point of making a great revelation.

'Yes?' Ferguson said, as the revelation seemed a long time coming. 'Yes?'

Gottlieb lowered his head.

'I don't remember.'

Ferguson heard Allira exhale noisily at the anticlimax, but knew he could not give up the quest to reawaken Gottlieb.

'Karl, the same thing happened to me, but I know what happened. Inside the hill, the vampires messed with my mind. They changed me, Karl. They took away my manhood, made me a child again, afraid of everything, not wanting to do anything. These things you called "masters", Karl—they're vampires! Do you know what that word means?'

'It's a bad word. You mustn't say it.'

'It's a real word, a true word! Vampires aren't nice people who look after you; they've destroyed you, Karl. I hate to say this, I don't mean to hurt you, but they've turned you into a cowering little thing, afraid of the dark. They humiliate you, they strike you and you don't strike back! And sooner or later, they will kill you—but only after they've drunk your blood!'

To Ferguson and Allira's amazement, Gottlieb leapt to his feet, yelling, 'No, no! That can't be true! Why are you saying these awful things? I don't like you!'

Ferguson joined him and grasped the weeping man's shoulders.

'Karl, I don't say these things to upset you, to make you cry. The memories of what they've done to you—they're inside you, Karl. If you think long and hard, they will come back to you, and you will know where you are and what the masters really are. And what they are going to do to you.'

***

Ferguson knew he had pushed Gottlieb as far as he risked going. He and Allira had retreated as far from the big man as their cramped surroundings allowed, turning their backs on him to give him a semblance of privacy as he wept. Finally, the sobs had ended as Gottlieb fell into unconsciousness.

'What now?' she asked, sometime later.

'Nothing. I've done all I can. More pushing, probing, won't achieve anything. If I try too hard, I'll become the enemy, instead of the vampires.'

She looked at him askance.

'You really have changed, haven't you? The old Greg wouldn't have said that; he'd just have tried to beat Gottlieb into his senses.'

'I'd like to think I wouldn't have done that, but no matter: I can only be me—whatever that is.'

She squeezed a hand.

'Whatever kind of Greg you are is fine by me.'

Ferguson looked embarrassed, but she did not seek any kind of declaration from him; this was not the time or place for such feelings. Not when simple survival was at stake.

As was soon to be demonstrated.

TWENTY EIGHT

It was difficult for the prisoners to gauge the passage of time, seeing as they were confined in a windowless room with no means of relieving their endless monotony. Nevertheless, Ferguson estimated that it had been more than one day, but less than two, since they had last seen their captors. However, that situation could not last forever, and suddenly the door was flung open and Theondra appeared.

'I hope you have had a nice rest and made friends with each other. But Allira and Greg: Gronz is ready for his next experiment.'

Ferguson thought rapidly. If this was indeed the much-feared climax to their torment, it was vital that he and Gottlieb should not be separated.

'Please tell me Karl won't be with us,' he pleaded. 'I couldn't stand it if he were watching us. Please, Theondra, do this one little thing for Allira and me.'

Fortunately for him, the study of ancient human folktales had not been part of Theondra's education and she knew nothing about briar patches and mischievous rabbits, nor had he erred in his estimate of the female vampire's innate cruelty.

'Oh dear,' she said, her emerald eyes positively sparkling with pleasure, 'is that really important to

263

you, Greg? Why didn't you tell me earlier?' Her demeanour changed on the instant to one of haughty indifference. 'Well, of course, Gottlieb must accompany us, so he can see you finally taken off my hands.'

Ferguson had not warned Allira of this stratagem, restrained by a lingering fear that their conversations were being monitored, but after a moment's surprise, she too joined in.

'Please, Theondra. How can you be so cruel?'

'Very easily. Now, no more whining; you may be just humans, but please have some dignity.'

The stink of amines in the air told Ferguson that the fish room was to be their destination once again; Gronz obviously wanted to keep the rest of his building free from any unpleasant residues that might result from his experiments. He greeted the three humans as Theondra shepherded them into his presence.

'Ah, welcome, Greg and Allira. And I see you have brought Karl with you.' He shot an accusatory glance at Theondra. 'Why is that?'

She blinked under that gaze but collected her thoughts and replied, ''It gave me pleasure to do so. It will also be a test of Gottlieb's indifference to his fellow humans, should any such test be required.'

'Well, ensure he doesn't get in the way.' Gronz turned to the other two. 'This will probably be the final test of human emotions. The pattern is already clear to me and I am anxious to proceed with the examination of your brains.' He pulled Ferguson and Allira apart and made them face each other. 'This will be a joint study of so-called affection between humans. Stand a little nearer to the pool, please.'

After they had complied, he continued, 'What I want you to do now is to fight each other.'

'What!' Ferguson gasped.

'Yes. I know what you're thinking, Greg. The enhanced cognitive abilities I have given you have allowed you to realise that the test, as I have just described it, does not adhere to strict scientific protocols due to the great difference between your physical strength and Allira's. But I can control for that.' He withdrew a small object from his cloak and waved it briefly in front of them. Allira recognised a hypodermic. 'Greg, I will inject you in your right arm and left leg. The compound will disconnect your muscles from your brain, rendering those limbs useless. And once in your bloodstream, it will produce an intense feeling of lassitude in you, so it will be difficult for you to put up your normal resistance to an attack.'

'And what if we refuse to fight?' Allira said.

'Well, I hope it doesn't come to that, but should the need arise, I will cut the two of you and throw you in the pool. You know what will happen then.'

'There won't be much blood for you to enjoy if we are reduced to piles of bones.'

Gronz nodded.

'Excellent, Allira. But if I do have to throw you both in, I will consider the experiment a failure and I will retrieve you before too much damage is done. My techniques will soon restore the missing flesh, and then Theondra and I will enjoy you. I am sure it will be worth the wait.'

'Then why throw us in at all?'

Gronz looked puzzled.

'I can't let disobedience stand unpunished, can I, Allira? That is not the vampire way. But enough useless chatter; let us proceed with the experiment.'

Ferguson cast a quick glance behind him: Gottlieb was standing next to Theondra, his face blankly unemotional. Ferguson returned to Gronz.

As if from a great distance, he could feel his heart hammering wildly. This was it, the supreme moment of their incarceration. Everything depended on the events of the next few seconds. Once again, he had not told Allira of his plan. He would have to rely on her speed of thought in realising what had happened and what she had to do. He had reached a stage where he accepted escape was unlikely, but Gronz and Theondra must be given back some of the anguish they had so callously inflicted on their prisoners.

Gronz looked down at his hypodermic. The moment had come. For a second, maybe two, Ferguson felt he was already paralysed and incapable of action.

Then he acted. Vampires are powerful, but they are not immune to the laws of physics. Ferguson kicked Gronz's feet from under him and then shoulder-charged. Human and vampire crashed into the pool, sending up a great spray of evil green water. Ferguson twisted as he fell, so his feet crashed onto Gronz's back, pinning the astounded creature face down on the floor of the pool. He thought he heard a rib crack in the tumult. Instantly, he reached for Gronz's arms and twisted them behind the vampire's back, so he could not lift himself off the bottom.

'Allira!' he yelled. 'Join me! Now!'

Well it was for the human race that it was Greg Ferguson who battled Gronz on that dreadful day.

Few others could have held the raging vampire captive beneath the water's tumult.

Dimly, he knew Allira had joined him. He thrust his head above the stinking water.

'Allira, your nails! Slash his face!'

She dove under the erupting water, felt for Gronz's head, held her hand rigid and tore at his face. Vampire epidermis is tough, but she slashed and clawed and thrust, powered by anger, energised by hatred. And a red mist appeared around Gronz's face. His words returned to her:

They actually prefer vampire blood to human, but, of course, they rarely get the chance to enjoy that.

Ferguson felt Gronz's arms slowly slipping from his grasp; once the vampire experimenter had his hands free, he would be able to stand and then all would be lost. Grimly, Ferguson hung on, his muscles taught as bowstrings, awaiting the arrival of his allies.

They arrived. Suddenly, the water around Ferguson and Allira was full of small black fish, drawn by the irresistible flavour of vampire blood. Through a now red-tinged green opacity, they saw the fish dart in, rip a mouthful of flesh away, swallow it, and immediately dart in again. Bubbles came from Gronz's head as he tried to scream. Soon, a great spreading crimson cloud had formed around the scene as yellow-white spars of vampire bone began to appear between the ribbons of surviving flesh.

'Out!' Ferguson roared, 'before we get cut!'

They scrambled onto the poolside, their sparse clothing red-stained and sodden.

Theondra was waiting for them.

'You've killed Gronz!' she screamed, her now bright red eyes almost starting from their sockets.

'You killed Gronz!' She picked Allira up as if she were a rag doll and contemptuously tossed her aside. Ferguson kicked her feet from under her as he had with Gronz, but she twisted as she fell and narrowly avoided the pool of death. Like a tiger, she rolled upright again and charged at Ferguson. But he knew she planned the same fate for him as he had given her partner, and ran toward the entrance, as far from the deadly pool as possible. She met Ferguson there almost simultaneously and twisted him to the floor, crashing down on top of him with a force that knocked the breath out of his body. She reached with those long black nails to remove his eyes, but he held her hands motionless, inches above them, feeling her cold metallic breath sweep over him. He saw Allira's arm suddenly curve around Theondra's throat and tug backwards, but the rampant vampire turned like a Cat and flung her away.

Ferguson, however, had seized the chance and drove a boot onto his opponent's head. She shook that head, much as a human might when bothered by a fly, and stood to face him, her eyes blazing with vampire fury.

'For what you have done, I will devise a special death for you, Ferguson. I am not interested in science, but I am interested in pain and you will feel more pain at my hands than any other human has known during your disgusting history!'

With that, to Ferguson's horrified amazement, she reached for the doorpost and effortlessly tore a shard of metal away from it. One end was wickedly jagged and sharp.

'I will blind you first, and when you are helpless, I will break all your limbs, leaving you an impotent lump of flesh. Then I will spend quite some time devising an appropriate death.'

She charged. Ferguson turned as she passed, and clasped his mighty forearm around her neck, jerking the arm savagely back against her flesh. He felt the tissues yield slightly, and she went down, but still holding the makeshift weapon. Allira joined him in that embrace of death, and all three rolled across the floor until they hit an obstruction. Ferguson had a brief glimpse of Gottlieb's legs. And then he heard Allira yelling in a strange sing-song intonation, making the cry almost a chant.

'Karl, wake, wake! Join us! Help us!'

Ferguson heard Gottlieb make a peculiar guttural groan and then his huge hands descended on Theondra. Together, the three humans forced her upright and crashed her against the wall, forcing her to drop her weapon. Her face was that of a demonic invader from some forbidden realm, eyes blazing crimson fire, black-nailed hands curved into claws that struck out like obsidian stilettos against her attackers. Then she managed to twist in her tripartite trap and grasped Gottlieb's head. Theondra gave the head a violent twist and, with a wet ripping noise, tore it from his shoulders and sent it rolling along the floor and into the pool. But Ferguson now had the metal shard and swung it like a battle-axe directly into her leering face. She hit the wall again, but this time slid down it into a heap, her bloodied face bowed. Ferguson leapt upon the dazed creature, knowing her confusion would not last long and, picking up a limp arm, placed it across his knee at the elbow joint. He rammed down with all his strength and the arm fell away, useless.

The other arm followed shortly after.

'Kill her, Greg, kill her!' Allira screamed. 'We won't get another chance!'

TWENTY NINE

'**K**ill her, Greg! For gods' sake—kill her!'

Allira's desperate plea rang in Ferguson's ears as he straightened up from the ravaged thing that was Theondra. She was fully conscious and her scarlet eyes looked as if they would start spitting sparks at any moment. Deep red vampire blood was dripping from the many gashes in her face.

'Yes, you'd better kill me, Greg, for as long as there is breath in my body, I will find a way of paying you back for what you have done to me.'

'All in good time, Theondra. How does it feel to be at the mercy of humans; stupid, despicable, subvampire humans?'

'You were lucky, Greg, very lucky. But good luck doesn't last forever.'

He felt Allira tugging at his arm and he moved away from the crippled vampire.

'Greg, there's something worrying me.'

He raised an eyebrow.

'Surely not! What could possibly be worrying you in a lovely place like this?'

'We haven't seen all this building, have we? Don't you remember that a vampire came out of the teleportation device and killed Schwartz? And who was that vampire? It wasn't Gronz and it certainly wasn't Theondra.'

Ferguson frowned at her unwelcome comment.

'Yes. I had forgotten. And I know what that means: there are more of these rogue vampires. It wasn't just two mad monsters.'

'Maybe the third vampire is in this building, maybe he isn't, but we must get out of here and take our chances with the normal vampires.'

'*Normal* vampires!' Ferguson scoffed. 'Don't you dare honour them with words like that. They turned us into farm animals, remember!'

'Stick to the here and now, Greg. Keep focused.'

He turned to look at Theondra, who was still slumped on the floor, her now useless arms hanging immobile at her sides.

'She knows. That's why I haven't killed her. We've got to get her to talk.'

But the two surviving humans had their respects to offer first. Ferguson turned to check that their captive had not moved, and then walked over to Gottlieb's decapitated corpse and respectfully looked down at it. Allira joined him.

'He was a brainless idiot when I met him, relying on his fists to do the talking. But he saved us, Allira. I would never have gotten the better of Theondra without him. I hoped he would join us, but it was just a hope; I had no real plan. But he did join us, just at the last moment. But how did he suddenly make up his mind?' He looked at Allira. 'You yelled something at him. What did you say?'

'I just asked him to help us; a human helping other humans. You had done the hard work, Greg, in bringing him back, reminding him of his past and where his loyalties lay.'

'Yes, I did. And am I glad I did!' His look changed. 'And now for Theondra.'

But Allira touched his arm.

'You've forgotten something. There may or may not be other vampires here, but there are certainly other humans. I'll tell them the good news that they're free.'

Allira left the room, and Ferguson returned to Theondra.

'I would like you to tell me something about this building, starting with how we get out.'

'No doubt you would,' Theondra said, not looking at him. 'But why should I help you after what you've done?'

'You're helpless, Theondra. I could make life unpleasant for you.'

She laughed.

'Threats from a human! Do you have any idea how pathetic you are? I am a vampire; pain is nothing to us; that's why we despise you when we see you wriggling and squirming, trying to avoid it.'

'Is that so? Gronz seemed a little upset when the fish were eating him. No doubt you can control pain better than we can, but it's unlikely you're completely immune.'

Theondra suddenly lifted her head and stared directly at him. Ferguson noticed her eyes were now the piercing, shining green they had been when she had been seducing him. He found himself staring into those eyes, eyes which felt like they were growing bigger and bigger until they filled his entire field of vision, immersing him in a world of crystalline emerald. A voice that was not his came into his mind, whispering seductively.

273

Greg, all this has been a mistake. You hurt me earlier, but not with your fists, you hurt me because you turned against me, spurned me, cast me aside, the one who loves you, the one who will always love you. Return to me, Greg, bind my wounds, love me again.

The unspoken words stirred him, turned his world upside down. He suddenly realised what a monster he had been to treat this woman so cruelly, a woman who had done nothing but offer him unconditional love. He...

Another thought came into his mind, and this one was his.

A woman? This is not a woman!

Instantly, the world of crystalline emerald shattered into a million fragments, and the room of the fish came back into focus again. He shook his head, sorrowfully.

'Nice try, Theondra, but your soulmate, Gronz, gave me more than simple knowledge; he sharpened my thinking, made me able to see the connections between things. He sure as hell didn't intend to give me such a useful gift but, quite by accident, he did. And one of the things I can now do is detect mentalic fields when they're being used against me. That was a useful training exercise you gave me just then, but now I know exactly what an attempt to control me feels like. Thank you.'

She snarled like a cornered Cat and spat at him.

Ferguson looked around, his mind shaking free of Theondra. Where was Allira? What was taking so long? Then he heard strange muttering sounds, and about ten rag-clothed humans came into the room, herded by Allira, like a strange shepherdess. They looked around like frightened children, afraid that each corner might contain a monster.

However, in this case, they were not entirely mistaken.

Ferguson approached them, and they immediately went into a group huddle, clasping each other with stark terror writ large on their grimy features, half of them turning away so they could not see him. Ferguson guessed the reason for their fear; his clothing, though simply functional, was much better than their own, and they had taken him for a vampire.

'It's all right,' he said, trying to make his voice sound friendly, which was not as easy as it sounds, as he was sorely out of practice. 'I'm one of you; I'm a human.'

One man, bolder than the rest, said, 'You don't look like one.'

For proof, Ferguson opened his mouth as wide as he could; a few came cautiously nearer and examined his dentition—from a safe distance.

'You see? I'm like you—I'm from Stralia.'

'Prove it! Where from?'

Ferguson told the group, and he saw them relax.

The apparent leader approached again and offered a brown-streaked hand in friendship.

'Good on you; I'm from near the Snowies myself. Look, can you get us out of here?'

'Yes, I can,' Ferguson said, demonstrating an assurance he did not exactly feel. 'In good time.' He turned to Allira. 'Is this all? I thought there were twenty.'

'There are. The other ten wouldn't leave the room.'

They would have to wait. Ferguson turned back to his captive. It was not safe for her to be able to move around; Ferguson did not underestimate his foe.

'Look,' he said to Allira, 'you go to Gronz's lab and see if you can find something to tie her up. I'll stand guard.'

'I'll stay, Greg. You know what you're looking for.'

Ferguson's brow furrowed.

'Are you sure? You haven't had the Gronz upgrade; she might be able to influence you.'

She smiled.

'Trust me, Greg. I know what I'm doing.'

Ferguson hesitated. He knew how insidious Theondra's influence was and how it could make people do things against their will. A terrible thought struck him. Had Theondra already taken Allira over? Was this the next stage in her plan for freedom?

Allira smiled again, as if reading his thoughts, and placed a palm on his cheek.

'You have to trust me, Greg. I can do this.'

He nodded.

'OK. But keep these wretches away from her; they sure as hell couldn't resist her.'

'Yes, Greg,' came a mocking voice he knew too well, 'scurry away and do something big and bold and human. Why, you might find out how to make fire by rubbing two sticks together!'

Unwillingly, he turned.

'I will make you talk, Theondra.'

Her mocking smile matched the mockery in her voice.

'Unlikely. If you try hard enough, you will work out how to hurt me, but I will simply close my mind down so I will be unable to speak. If you try to starve me, I can go without solid food for months without much trouble. Months, Greg. How long have you got before your new admirers turn against you when they see you're a false, weak leader?'

'There will be a way.'

And with that, he left them. The last thing he saw was Allira standing over Theondra.

He felt a stab of unease as he entered Gronz's laboratory. That vampire's machines were still operating, their myriad coloured lights still glowing and occasionally flashing, their contented humming filling the air. He saw again the table that Gronz had strapped him to, prior to manipulating his brain for future dissection. Well, that at least, Ferguson thought, would not be his fate.

He searched for some time, opening many cupboards and drawers. Finally, an opened door revealed a storeroom, and there he found what he had been looking for: coils of strong black electrical cable. He tested his great muscles against the tensile strength of one length of cable and found it more than adequate. If Theondra could break out of that, she was far stronger than he had discovered during their battle together.

He returned to the main part of the lab and decided to open one large cabinet he had previously overlooked. As he opened it, a wave of cold air swept over him. He blinked and then saw what the cabinet contained.

Bottles; row after row of bottles, each containing a rich ruby-red liquid. He removed one and examined it directly under the ceiling light.

He smiled.

There was no doubt what this liquid was.

And with it, he had the key to controlling Theondra.

THIRTY

'**D**o you know what this is?' Ferguson said to Allira, as he held the bottle in front of her. She wrinkled her nose in disgust.

'I can guess. Blood. Human blood.'

'Exactly right. There's a whole cabinet of them in Gronz's lab; each one the result of a slaughtered human. How many people have passed through this hellhole, I wonder?'

'Too many. But how does this help us?'

Ferguson threw a swift glance at Theondra. He and Allira had completely swathed her in electrical cable, making her resemble a very unwelcome package delivery. She was watching the two of them—with unusually intense attention.

'Have you ever wondered why vampires prey on humans?'

'Because they like it?'

'They do, but that's not the reason. Human blood contains a compound which acts like a cofactor in vampire metabolism.'

'I haven't had the Gronz treatment. Explain.'

'A substance, other than the substrate, whose presence is essential for the activity of an enzyme. For instance, thiamine pyrophosphate is a cofactor in the essential activities of enzymes involved in carbon metabolism in humans.'

Allira gasped and then laughed.

'And I'm supposed to understand that?'

'You don't have to. We humans need thiamine pyrophosphate. Vampires need the substance which is in human blood. The pleasure they get from drinking it is just a secondary reaction, like you and I enjoy a leg of lamb.'

Allira nodded slowly as the import of Ferguson's words struck home.

'So, it's not just an item on the menu, but something they need to keep their body chemistry working.'

'Exactly. And without that cofactor, their bodies seize up quickly. Very quickly. That's why they need blood. A lot of blood.'

Allira gave an unusually gratified, knowing smile and slowly turned to look at Theondra. 'And how does this lack show itself, Greg?' she asked, studying Theondra as she spoke.

'It manifests itself in what the Vampires call "The Blood Hunger". An all-consuming craving for blood, a growing madness in which they will do anything to get hold of it. Literally anything.'

Allira finally laughed. It was the first time she had laughed for a long time—but it was not a pleasant laugh.

'I think we've found our test subject.'

Ferguson approached Theondra, bottle in hand.

'Do you know what this is, Theondra?'

She did not reply, but looked up at him with hate pouring out of her emerald eyes like a physical force.

'Well, you're not polite enough to give an answer to a simple question it seems, so I will tell you.' He

279

rotated the screw top until it lifted off. Crouching low, he passed the bottle just below her delicate nostrils. 'It's blood, Theondra, lovely, rich, delicious human blood. Smell it. Savour it. It's wonderful, isn't it? Would you like some?'

No reply. Just a gaze of raging, blazing hatred.

'Look, I'll put it here so you can see it.' He leaned over and carefully placed the bottle a few feet from the vampire. 'Now, every now and then, I will move the bottle farther away until I reach the fish pool. I'll then give you one last chance to tell us how to get out of here, and if you don't tell us, I'll give it to the fish. I'm sure they will appreciate it.'

No reply.

Ferguson and Theondra walked away from their captive enemy until they were beyond even vampire hearing.

'Will she give in, do you think?'

'Oh, yes. Vampires cannot resist the Blood Hunger any more than we could give up breathing. But she's no pushover; she'll take us to the limit. Which reminds me—we haven't eaten for quite some time. And I don't know where the larder is.'

'No problem. One of the ten is the girl who brought us our meals. She's more than happy to do it again.'

'Let's hope there's something other than the slop we've had up until now.' Ferguson paused as if unsure of his next words, but then continued: 'You know I was worried about leaving you in charge of Theondra; she didn't try to influence you, I take it?'

'Oh, yes, she did. I kept getting thoughts about what a useless rat you were and how I should chuck you in the fish pool. Like we did with poor Gottlieb.'

'Well, I'm still here, so you obviously didn't succumb. You clearly have a very strong mind.'

Her eyes sparkled as she gave him a mock punch on the shoulder.

'What, you've only just noticed!'

***

The food, they discovered, was just another version of the hated slop, and was as bland and unsatisfying as their prison diet. A long search did not reveal any hidden delights; Theondra and Gronz had seen no need to pamper their prisoners. But the food, poor though it was, had been enough to coax the remaining humans out of their timidity and out of their prison cell. Even so, they sat away from the others, casting the occasional mistrusting glance at Ferguson and Allira.

Those who were prepared to speak told basically the same story. Even though they all came from different regions of Stralia, the societies they described were virtually identical to Ferguson's. All were either stock herders or wheat growers or miners. There was nothing else; no concept of anything other than Stralia. All of them had gotten into some kind of trouble, involving behaviour bad enough to attract the Mozzies and require an in-person introduction to Theondra and Gronz. It was difficult to be certain of how long they had been incarcerated for the same reasons that Ferguson had been unable to mark the passage of time, but they all agreed it had not been very long. There were people already in the cell when they arrived, but, one by one, those original prisoners disappeared, never to be heard of again. The new arrivals had known where they had gone and what had happened to them, and had simply waited like lambs in the abattoir for their own time to come. All were conditioned, as Gottlieb had been, but some were less affected than others, and Ferguson put those ones to work on making the remainder accept reality—grim though that reality was. Progress was slow—but it was progress.

'We're gradually turning into one happy family,' Allira observed on one occasion, while watching Ferguson's "missionaries" in deep discussion with the "non-believers."

'Yes, but this family must split up soon and go our separate ways in the great big world beyond these walls.'

Allira gave a deep sigh, forcing Ferguson to look at her in some alarm.

'Yes, but what will that world have for us? Even if the vampires out there are more civilised than the ones here, they are still vampires. They have no love for us. The very best we can expect is to have our memories wiped and returned to Stralia.' She reached for him, moisture glinting at the corners of her eyes. 'And what if that wiping removes the memory of what you and I have become, Greg? What life will that be for us?'

He shook his head; he had no answer.

Instead, he looked across to Theondra. The bottle of blood was now halfway to the pool edge.

***

The answer came thundering up into Ferguson's conscious mind.

He gasped in shock. How could he have been so stupid! Maybe Gronz's upgrade was only a temporary affair! Allira was asleep at his side, and he roughly shook her awake.

'What—what is it?' she mumbled sleepily.

'I know what to do to get us out of here!'

She instantly shook off her drowsiness.

'And that is?'

'Allira, we were in Stralia. And then we were half a world away in New Marinetown. The teleporter! If it can bring us here, it can take us back, back to Stralia with our minds intact!'

She straightened up, the fire of excitement blazing in her eyes.

'Yes, it's so obvious! What fools we are to take so long to see it!' Then she sobered up. 'The teleporter. You know how to use it, do you?'

'No, but I think I will after a crash course from someone who does.' He looked across to where Theondra was lying. He observed she was now twitching and twisting within her bonds.

The Blood Hunger was upon her.

THIRTY ONE

'Greg,' Theondra said pleadingly. 'I know I've been very bad to you and I'm truly sorry. It wasn't me, it was Gronz; he made me do it. I told him it was wrong, but he was obsessed with his experiments, with learning about the human brain. He was a monster, and I'm so sorry I didn't do enough to stop him. Please forgive me.'

Ferguson was sitting next to her as she lay in her bonds on the floor of the fish room, so close the metallic sting of her breath was in his nostrils.

'I'm very glad to hear you say that, Theondra. It's good that you have finally learned the error of your ways.'

'So you'll let me up?'

'Not yet. Tell me, Theondra, you vampires are very intelligent, aren't you? Does your intelligence extend as far as the operation of the teleporter?'

'Of course. Why do you ask?'

Ferguson saw that her entire body was now trembling as she strained up against the cables, trying with increasing desperation to free herself. There was the sheen of sweat on her brow and her eyes had lost their brilliance, appearing a dull grey.

'I'm reasonably sure it was you, or Gronz, that captured us in Stralia and brought us here. Am I right?'

'Yes. It was I, in fact. Now, I've told you all you need to know, so let me up. Please.'

'Not yet. So, you could send us back, to Stralia?'

A glimmer of hope appeared on her twisted face.

'Yes, of course! Undo me and I'll do it right now!'

'Not yet. I'm very glad you've had this change of heart, but I don't trust you enough to give you control of the teleporter. No, you will teach me, Allira, and the rest of the humans how to operate it. Then, the last humans to teleport out will release you before they leave. How is that for a deal?'

Her excitement faded visibly, but she controlled herself, took a deep breath and said, 'Fine. I agree. But could I have some blood now, please?'

'Not yet. You teach us how to use the machine, and then you get blood. Not before.'

Ferguson called the leaders of the original group of humans and explained his intensions.

'Theondra teaches Allira, me and you. You then teach the rest of the people. Allira and I will go home first, and you can sort it out between you who will be the first and last to follow.'

Ferguson had no desire to become involved in determining the pecking order of the others; he doubted it would be achieved completely amicably. Theondra was calling again.

'Greg, you'll have to undo me so I can get to the teleporter.'

'No. We'll carry you.' Ferguson selected the fittest-looking men from the group, and he and they scooped the trembling vampire from the floor. Vampires are heavier than women of the same size, and it took three of them to carry her safely. She did not resist.

Fortunately, the room containing the teleportation machines was not far. Ferguson saw again the platforms on which they had materialised to be greeted by Theondra and Gronz. It seemed so long ago now! He felt Allira shudder beside him, and placed a comforting hand on her shoulder.

'We'll be out of this soon,' he whispered. 'The worst is over.'

She gave him a smile, but it was uncertain and fleeting.

Ferguson propped Theondra against a chair so she could see the controls on the nearest machine.

'I want you to return us to the building where you collected us. And give me the access code for that building.' He had no intention of being trapped inside another building for the want of some alphanumeric characters.

'I can do that,' she said in what was becoming an increasingly dry and hoarse voice. 'But give me a little blood first, please; I can't think straight.'

Ferguson had not let the bottle out of his sight after collecting it. He looked from the bottle to the vampire and made a decision. He unscrewed it, put some blood on his fingers and rubbed it onto Theondra's now fissured lips.

She licked it up like someone dying of thirst who had just found a waterhole.

'More. Please.'

'Not yet. Show us how to operate the machine. Show us Stralia.'

In a halting, panting voice, Theondra gave the instructions, and Ferguson carried them out. His heart lurched as a panel above the controls burst into full coloured life, displaying a landscape he knew so very well. He heard Allira's gasp of wonderment behind him.

It was the Red Centre. Just above the horizon was the uppermost flank of the great rock that had loomed so large in his childhood. He gazed at it in almost religious awe and devotion.

'Home,' he breathed. He whirled around to Theondra. 'Show me how to get there or I'll kill you!'

'Yes! Yes! There are writing materials over there; you will need to write down my instructions as you will never remember them.'

And so the teaching began. None but Ferguson could understand it all. Allira grasped a few concepts here and there. The others understood nothing.

Finally, after what felt like an entire afternoon to Ferguson and an eternity of purgatory to the others, Ferguson concluded he knew enough to operate the machine.

'I should test it,' he said, staring at his captive, 'just in case you have lied to us.'

'I wouldn't let you down, Greg. You can trust me. In any case, once the machine has sent something, it will take several hours to recharge. And the other machines need different instructions. Can you wait that long?'

'I know I shouldn't trust you,' he growled, 'but you're right, I can't wait that long.' He glanced at the other men, and waved some sheets of written material at them. 'It's all here; I can't do any more for you. You'll have to do your best.'

'We'll still have Theondra to help us,' their leader said.

'Of course. Now, let's get back and tell the others what they have to do.'

They carried the now violently thrashing Theondra back to the fish room and placed her perilously close to the side of the pool.

'Now!' she yelled, in an animalistic scream that betrayed her near madness, 'GIVE ME SOME FUCKING BLOOD!'

Ferguson signalled to the leader, and they picked her up and walked to the very edge. Ferguson nodded to the other man and took sole charge of the squirming vampire.

Theondra guessed his intent.

'No! You promised to release me!'

As she tumbled into the water, Ferguson gave a cruel smile.

'I lied,' he said.

THIRTY TWO

Ferguson was anxious to return to Stralia, but he noticed Allira seemed a little downcast.

'What's the matter, don't you want to go home?'

'Yes, but now it's finally going to happen I can't help but think of what we're going back to.'

'And that is?'

She sighed.

'We're exchanging one prison for another. Before all this happened, before we found your mother's documents, we were living in blissful ignorance. Our little world was all there was. As long as we kept our noses clean, we could live out reasonably happy lives. Now we know we're in a kind of open prison, watched over by creatures more powerful than we are.' She sighed again. 'There's an old saying about blissful ignorance...'

Ferguson was annoyed.

'So much for all my work! Perhaps I should leave you here; you could dangle your toes in the fish pool, just for fun!'

She put her hands on his shoulders and, standing on tip-toes, kissed him.

'I'm sorry, Greg. I'm just the kind of woman who doesn't know how lucky she is. Forgive?'

He grinned.

'Of course. We will soon forget the vampires when we are home; we have so much to do in the rest of our lives. Now let's get out of this shithole.'

Ferguson gathered together the most able of the original captives.

'OK, Allira and I are leaving you now. Watch exactly what I do, because I won't be here to help you when you leave. Watch how I set the parameters; it's vital to get those right, otherwise you could end up in vampire headquarters—and you wouldn't want that!'

One of the men was sufficiently recovered to give a short laugh at Ferguson's weak joke.

'After the parameters are set,' Ferguson continued, 'you'll have two minutes to get onto the platform. Then the casing will descend and you'll be off.'

The leader crossed to Ferguson and vigorously shook his hand.

'We'll never forget you, Greg. Thank you for all you have done.'

Ferguson pointed to Allira.

'I couldn't have done it without her. Now, enough of this—maybe I'll see you when we're all back home!'

With that, Ferguson, Allira and three of the others set out for the teleportation room.

'What will happen to the fish?' Allira said, *en route.*

He laughed.

'What, you're feeling sorry for them, now? The big ones will eat the little ones, and the last big one will die of starvation. Ah, here we are at last.' Ferguson turned to the men and solemnly shook hands with each of them. 'I've left Theondra's instructions; read them carefully before you try to follow. And don't fight each other for who's to be last to go. You're all going to make it!'

He looked around for a moment, as if memorising the details of their erstwhile jail, and then turned to Allira, smiling. He went to the control panel for the nearest machine and typed in the parameters with trembling fingers. One last glance at those who were remaining, and then Ferguson and Allira stepped onto the platform, ready to resume their lives in far-off Stralia. After some seconds, the transparent casing cut them off from all further communication.

A lambent purple glow encased them.

It was shortly afterwards that Ferguson discovered that Theondra had, even in her agonies, managed to trick him.

*****

Although the experiences of those who have undergone teleportation vary widely, there are clear patterns: some always feel that transition is instantaneous; Allira was one of those. A few unfortunates relate that they have spent days in that weird limbo. Others think that a few minutes pass whilst they are in a No Man's Land between source and destination. Ferguson discovered that, on this occasion, he was one of those. He felt he was in the centre of a whirling wheel of kaleidoscopic colours which danced and spiralled around him. But gradually, the colours became fainter and drabber, and he began to see the ordinary world as a monochrome background behind them. Then there was a jerk in the pit of his stomach, and he realised, with relief, his journey was complete.

He looked around, still slightly dizzy, and felt for Allira's hand. Despite his subjective feeling of time having elapsed, she had seen him materialise at the same instant as her, and so was also scanning her surroundings.

Ferguson's eyes narrowed. This was not the same room as the one they had left when Theondra had captured them. It was larger, and there were many rows of teleportation devices, in front of and behind them. The walls were farther away and the ceiling much higher.

And more importantly, there had not been a trio of figures standing before their platform, gazing sternly upwards.

And most importantly, he had not expected to be looking at vampires, for vampires the trio assuredly were.

'You are humans!' the central figure said. 'How did you get here?'

Both Allira and Ferguson were so shocked by this totally unexpected outcome that they could not reply. Their silence appeared to annoy the vampire who had spoken, for in an even sterner voice, he commanded, 'Stand down from the platform and do not move, if you value your lives!'

Ferguson descended from the platform and motioned to Allira to join him, then they stood together looking at the unfriendly trio. Ferguson noticed that the middle vampire was holding a metallic object from which a tube protruded. And the tube was pointed at Ferguson's heart. He had never knowingly seen projectile weapons before, but he guessed the object's function.

Which was to kill people.

One of the subordinate vampires glanced at the leader.

'You were right, sir. An unauthorised beam-in from Laboratory B1.'

'Yes. But I didn't realise just how unauthorised it was.' The leader looked back at Ferguson and Allira. 'You two—come with me!'

The vampires moved behind Ferguson and Allira, barking orders to them. They left the Teleportation Chamber and then discovered a new wonder: a small room which sped upwards into the higher portion of the building. It was only just big enough for them all, and Ferguson was again aware of metallic vampire breath spreading over him. There was an almost imperceptible jerk, and the door of the room opened, revealing a grimly functional room containing a desk and a few chairs. The subordinate vampires remained standing as Ferguson and Allira were ordered onto the chairs, the leader sitting himself down at the desk before them. That vampire spent quite some time silently studying a glowing screen that had risen out of the desk. Ferguson guessed he was not seeing things he approved of on that screen from the way his eyes narrowed and the development of a stern frown. He looked up.

'Well, I understand how you arrived here now. I am addressing Greg Ferguson and Allira, I believe?'

Ferguson found it disturbing that this individual already knew their names. It implied that someone had been watching them.

'Correct. How do you know who we are?'

The leader sent the screen back into the desk and leaned back, his eyes fixed on Ferguson. And they were not sympathetic eyes.

'Normally, I ask questions, rather than answer them, but you are new here, so I will tolerate that for the moment.' He leaned forward, his eyes now hard and interrogational. 'You have recently been in the company of two eminent vampires, Theondra and Gronz, I believe.'

Ferguson had a sickening feeling that the term "eminent" meant trouble for them. But he simply said, 'Yes' and waited for the bad news.

It was not long in coming.

'My name is Thron, Commander Thron. It might interest you to know that Gronz was my brother.' Ferguson felt a cold shiver rip through him. 'I say "was" advisedly, because not long ago, you murdered him. And also his consort, Theondra.'

'I would not say murdered,' Ferguson replied.

'Don't you contradict me, human!' Thron thundered. 'In your brutish ignorance, you were unaware everything that happened in Laboratory B1 was recorded. I have just finished watching your crimes on one of those recordings.' He leaned backwards again, placing fingertip on fingertip. 'We haven't had humans around here for a long time, but one of our most important laws is still on the statute book. The most heinous crime known to us is vampiricide by a human. That crime automatically requires the death penalty. There is no appeal. No trial is necessary. And so I find you and your woman guilty of vampiricide. Anything to say? Do you find the sentence excessive?'

'Your brother was a monster who cared nothing for the suffering of others.'

'My brother was a great scientist; his work on the brain is—was—legendary. It was he, and he alone, who first identified which areas of the vampire brain are involved in the generation of mentalic fields. What, do you think being a human means we can't experiment on you? You are sadly mistaken.'

'There are values other than scientific ones,' Allira said. 'Did your brother have a scale on which he measured our pain?'

Thron ignored her and continued, 'Let me explain how I see things, Ferguson. I am a patriot, a patriot of the old school. My only interest is the happiness and well-being of my race. You know what I feel when I look at humans? I feel sick to my stomach. It disgusts me that you look so much like us when, in fact, you are nothing like us. That's why Serafina Ginevra sent you away—so we didn't have to look at you!'

Ferguson felt an electric thrill pass through him at the mention of that name.

'Serafina Ginevra. Is she here?'

'No business of yours. I'm afraid you picked the wrong vampire to tangle with, Ferguson; as I said, I am a patriot. That's why I had no hesitation in executing Schwartz.'

'Schwartz! It was you! You are the third vampire!' Allira gasped.

Once again, Thron ignored her.

'Schwartz thought he had become a human, so I treated him like one. Like I will treat you. So, if you had any thoughts I might be one of those modern vampires who whimper that we should show more understanding of our human relatives, you can think again.' He stood. 'Well, I think I've said enough to make my position clear.' He looked over Ferguson's and Allira's heads. 'Take them away.'

THIRTY THREE

Ferguson's mind lurched. A short time earlier, he had expected soon to be standing on the welcoming sands of the Red Centre with his life returning to normal, and now he was under sentence of death—again! He glanced around the room—no, three vampires, impossible odds. Allira squeezed his hand, showing she accepted her fate without blame. He was glad; it was all he could expect now.

But Thron had not finished his orders. He was still speaking to someone behind them.

'Sran, do you think you are up to delivering these humans to the condemned cell all by yourself?'

Ferguson could detect the sneer behind Thron's words; apparently, Sran was being given a second chance to prove himself.

'Yes, Commander Thron. Thank you for your faith in me.'

'Don't fawn, Sran. Just get on with it.'

Sran moved into view, in front of the captives, pointing a small projectile weapon at a point midway between them.

'You two! Come with me!'

He waved the weapon at the door and followed Ferguson and Allira out into the corridor.

Ferguson turned to take another look at their guard. It is difficult to judge vampire ages, due to their long lifespans, but Sran certainly looked like a junior member of his race; little more than a teenager in human terms.

'Have you been in the force long?' Ferguson enquired conversationally.

'Keep your eyes front,' Sran replied. 'Don't look at me; I'm in charge here.'

Allira appeared to have picked up on Ferguson's approach, and said, 'I'm a woman; that's a female human. Have you seen many humans?'

Sran took a while to answer and then said, 'You're the first humans I've ever seen. I've read about you, though. Is it true you don't need blood?'

'Only what's inside us,' Ferguson said. *Which is where I intend to keep it*, he added mentally.

'Strange,' Sran said, apparently musing to himself. 'I regard myself as something of an expert on humans; I've read a great deal about them. But one source said you have three eyes; I can see that's not true.'

'Oh, but it is,' Allira continued. 'We are born with three eyes, but when we become sexually active, the middle one drops out.'

'That's incredible!' Sran said, sounding more and more fascinated. 'And it doesn't grow back, I suppose. Does it leave a scar? I can't see one.'

Allira threw Ferguson a momentary glance.

Get ready, that glance said.

'Yes, there is a scar,' Allira said. 'But it shrinks very quickly. But you can still just about see mine; it's a little bit above my nose.'

'Amazing. I didn't believe it when I read it, but humans really are that strange.' Sran prodded

Ferguson in the back with his weapon. 'You. Against that wall. Allira, stay where you are.' He brushed past Ferguson in his impatience to examine the scar. 'Lift your head, Allira. No, I really can't...'

Ferguson acted. One hand chopped hard into Sran's windpipe, the other tore the weapon from his hand. Then, before the choking vampire could recover, he propelled him headfirst into the nearest wall. He rebounded with a high-pitched scream and collapsed into a huddle, still conscious, but showing no signs of wanting to move.

'Now!' Ferguson roared. 'Let's go!'

'Where?'

'Anywhere but that condemned cell!'

They backtracked to where they had exited the moving room and leapt into it. Ferguson studied a panel beside the door, his lips moving silently.

'Yes, I can read it! Thank you, Gronz! "Ground Floor" sounds like a good place to visit!'

There was hardly any sensation, but Ferguson could tell the structure was plummeting downward. A slight jerk, a minuscule bending of the knees, and the door opened on a spacious plaza, framed by transparent walls. Through one, they could see the brilliant blue of the New Marinetown sky. The plaza was occupied by male and female vampires, all wearing similar uniforms to Thron. They had not turned to examine the newcomers when the door opened, and were busy about their business. It was not until Ferguson and Allira had crashed through their midst that they realised that something unusual was happening.

And by then it was too late, as the main door opened automatically as the fugitives approached, and then Ferguson and Allira were out beneath the cruel Fluridan sun. They looked around, their eyes trying to make sense of the mass of buildings that stretched in all directions, before them, to each side and behind. Some reared high into the blueness, not least the one they had just exited. Never had they believed there could be so much artificial stone, so much blindingly white masonry. Their sudden eruption into an urban world after lives spent among the rocks and sand of Stralia sent their minds reeling.

'What is this place? What do we do? Where do we go?' whispered an aghast Allira.

'As far away from where we are as we can get. Any direction's as good as any other. Come on!'

He grabbed Allira's hand, and they set off down a nearby alley, sheltered from the sun by its cliff-high sides. Fortunately, it was empty of any of the bustling inhabitants of New Marinetown and they made good progress.

'We've got to get out of this madness,' Ferguson said. 'Out into the countryside. Perhaps we can live off the land.'

'Perhaps. Oh, Greg, everything's going wrong! Why didn't we just accept the quiet life we were having, instead of trying to solve mysteries? Well, we solved this one, but we don't like the answer!'

'Perhaps. But we can't go back. Maybe there are vampires here that aren't trying to kill us. With Thron, it was personal; with others, they may not be so quick to condemn us.'

'We killed vampires, Greg. There's no escape from that one.'

He had no answer to that, but they continued onwards, moving from shadow to shadow, crouching low, hoping to be unobserved, like furtive rodents instead of humans. Then, suddenly, they were not alone in the shadows. One part of the shadows suddenly moved, revealing another vampire. Wearily, Ferguson raised his fists, ready for another, almost certainly hopeless, encounter. But the newcomer raised a hand, palm towards them.

'Stop. I'm not going to hurt you.'

Ferguson did not lower his fists and continued to look the stranger up and down.

'That would be a welcome change. Who are you?'

'My name is Larn, but we should not be standing here out in the open. It's only a matter of time before the authorities catch up with you. Come with me.'

He turned to go. Ferguson and Allira looked at each other. Then Ferguson shrugged, and they followed their new companion.

After a number of twists and turns down right-angled streets and alleys, they came to a low white building, dwarfed by the towering piles around it.

'My home,' the vampire said. 'Please come in.'

'Where you will no doubt kill us,' Allira said.

'I don't think you have any choice other than to trust me. A few more minutes and you would have been recaptured.'

'We'll trust you,' Ferguson said, but he raised his hand, showing what it now held. 'But I still have this gun thing.'

'You won't need it. Come in.'

After the heat, it was cool and pleasantly dim inside. A slim, female figure dressed in a long white gown rose from a couch as they entered.

'My partner, Cathrona,' Larn said.

'Ferguson and Allira, welcome,' Cathrona said, in a quiet, almost musical voice, unusual for a vampire.

'How do you know our names?' Ferguson demanded.

She smiled.

'Ferguson, everyone in New Marinetown knows your names; the authorities have been saturating the airwaves with accounts of your escape.'

Ferguson scanned his new mental databases.

'Some kind of beamed transmission. Electromagnetic?'

'No matter,' Cathrona replied. 'Who we are is more important. Please sit down; Larn will bring you some fruit and water.'

As they bit into their hosts' offerings, Cathrona began her explanation.

'Larn and I are a little different from the rest of our people you have met up until now. We are members of a group we call "Stronger Together." We are non-violent, and we believe in peaceful coexistence between human and vampire. Most vampires think we are idealistic dreamers; a few think we are traitors, but we are neither.'

Allira looked up at Cathrona with a face that was radiant.

'That is so good to hear! For weeks we've been hunted like animals; we simply can't take anymore!'

'Larn and I know you're not animals.' She stopped, cocking her head slightly. 'Ah, Brin is calling for me.' She disappeared into another room, and, after a few minutes, returned carrying a small bundle. She sat down, and as she did so, the fabric fell open, revealing a vampire baby.

'You have a child!' Allira exclaimed. She glanced at Ferguson and continued: 'I've always longed for a child, but now is not the time. Or place.' She moved closer, and tentatively held out her hands. 'May I?'

'Of course. Be careful; he's heavier than he looks.'

Allira parted the coverlet and gazed longingly down at the infant vampire.

'He looks just like a human baby. When do the fangs develop?'

'About the time they go onto solid food. They get blood mixed with milk up until then, of course.'

Allira returned the child; with some reluctance, Ferguson noticed.

'You're very lucky,' Allira said.

Cathrona smiled gently.

'You'll find having a child isn't all happiness, Allira. Little Brin is somewhat sickly and isn't developing as fast as he should. Larn and I are worried.'

'Sorry to hear that,' Ferguson said, preventing Allira from continuing with her conversation about babies, 'but can you tell us more about this group of yours? We really want to know if you can get us out of Marinetown. And why do vampires, in general, hate us so much?'

Larn sat next to his partner and, after a few seconds smiling down at Brin, looked up and began.

'Partly, Ferguson—or may I call you "Greg"? Partly, it's the contempt that the hunter feels for the prey. For millennia, we hunted you for that precious substance that defines us as vampires. And then, of course, there was the time when we were forced to come out of the shadows and take control of the world.'

'Yes, something called "Zee Zero Zee", I believe.'

'Yes, the most obscenely destructive collection of weaponry ever assembled. The world would be one giant cinder if we hadn't intervened. And then there was the Vetusian war.'

'Vetusian?' Allira said, breaking off from casting covetous looks at Brin. 'I don't know much about them.'

'It's a long story, but just as vampires prey on humans, so the Vetusians prey upon us. They are not of this universe, but come from a realm of higher spatial dimensions. For some reason we don't understand, they do not kill us outright but inflict unspeakable suffering first. They are kept out by a great Barrier, but occasionally it has been breached. And the last time that happened, the humans sided with the Vetusians. You must understand that was a terrible thing they did, and most vampires cannot forgive them for it.'

'Thank you; I knew some of that, but not all. I can understand that was truly a terrible thing to happen if the Vetusians are so vile.'

'Believe me, Allira, they are. In the aftermath, Serafina Ginevra banished the surviving humans to a place called Stralia.'

'I know it well,' Ferguson dryly observed. 'And I've also heard of Serafina Ginevra.'

'Yes, of course, I'm sorry. But we in Stronger Together believe it is time to put the past behind us and move on. You humans may not be fully sapient, but you are more than simple animals. We believe you should be allowed back into the rest of the world, and then perhaps we can find a way of finally living together in harmony.'

'Sounds wonderful,' Ferguson said, 'almost too good to be true. But until the majority of vampires believe as you do, we are in grave danger. To repeat myself, can you get us out of this town?'

To Ferguson's surprise and slight uneasiness, Larn leaned across and patted his knee.

'Of course, Greg. There are some farms on the east coast which would welcome a strong labourer like you. And no doubt Allira could find employment as a nursemaid of some description.'

Allira beamed.

'That would be wonderful!'

THIRTY FOUR

They continued to talk for some time until Cathrona noticed Ferguson's eyelids were beginning to flutter.

'I'm so sorry, Greg, you must be completely exhausted after all the terrible things you've been through. I'll get some beds made up for you at once.'

'Thank you, Cathrona. I am pretty beat up.' He started to stand, but Allira wished to continue the conversation.

'I'm right in saying that human and vampire can't interbreed, aren't I?'

Cathrona and Larn exchanged sharp glances, indicating to Ferguson that the conversation had taken a wrong turn. Cathrona spoke first.

'Well, Allira, that is a most peculiar question to ask, and somewhat offensive, I must say. The situation couldn't possibly arise, now could it?'

'No, of course not. I'm sorry, Cathrona, I didn't mean to offend,' Allira mumbled swiftly. 'It was stupid of me to upset you with all you've done for us. I'm truly sorry!'

That seemed to mollify the pair, and Larn said, 'Well, you're not used to vampire company; we understand that. Now, let's get you some rest.'

A short while later, Larn led them into a small room off the main living room. There were two simple beds, side by side, a chest of drawers—but no window. After Larn had left, Ferguson turned to Allira.

'That was a crazy question you asked back there! Why did you do it?'

She sat on one of the beds and held her head in her hands.

'I don't know. My head was full of babies, and I just wanted to know if it was possible.'

'It's not possible; I could have told you that. Why, are you thinking of getting a vampire boyfriend?'

She lifted her head and he could see the glint of early tears.

'No, Greg, no! Don't be horrible to me; my head's all mixed up. Everything that has happened is dragging me down!'

Ferguson was not to be placated.

'And if you're so keen on having a baby, why do you insist on me not finishing inside you?'

'Now, come on, Greg, would you really want a heavily pregnant Allira tagging along behind you with all this happening?'

'I could understand that, but you told me not to do it before we even knew there were vampires. So what's the real reason? Am I a stopgap until some better man comes along?'

She leapt to her feet and clutched him.

'No, Greg, no! There's only you! Who else has kept me alive? Who else *could* have kept me alive?'

'Gratitude is not the same as love. What is the real reason?'

She turned away.

'I will tell you one day.'

'And that's your answer?'

She said nothing more, and they lay on their beds in silence until sleep claimed them.

***

Greg, it's me. Can you understand me?

Greg, I can't wake up. There's something wrong.

Greg, Greg, please. There's something wrong!

Ferguson turned under the thin sheet. The night was warm and humid, quite unlike the cold, dry ones of the Red Centre. It felt alien, wrong; it was like being stroked in the darkness by fingers that were unnaturally hot and moist. Several times, he had felt himself rising almost to the surface of his sleep, but each time he had been able to turn back and descend into the dark depths.

Greg, something is wrong! Wake up!

There had been that insistent voice calling out to him, a voice that was not his but somehow familiar. It was begging him to wake up, but he did not want to. His brain was still aching as it strove to catalogue and organise the facts that Gronz had implanted into it. At present, the implant was still a mass of uncoordinated data, with no clear pathways from one subject matter to another. The links were forming, but the process was slow, tedious and a little painful. It was best done while he was asleep; when he was awake, he was too busy trying to stay alive.

Greg, wake up!

Now, he was becoming really annoyed. That voice was disturbing important work his subconscious had to do! He would have to wake up and silence it!

His eyes opened, and momentarily, he was unsure of where he was. It was a dark room, for there was no light and no window. He could no longer hear the voice, but he would have to find its source and ensure it did not trouble him again. Muttering to himself in his half-awake state, he swung his feet onto the floor—and immediately felt a tug on his arm. He felt along the arm in the near-total darkness and found something unexpected—there was a tube coming out from near his left bicep. Instantly, he was wide awake; the unknown voice had not lied: there was danger. He tugged at the connection between the tube and his arm, finding the effort painful. But he knew what to do; he had gone to sleep without a tube connected to his arm, so someone had attached it without permission. He gritted his teeth and gave a single powerful tug. There was a slight tearing of the flesh, and he felt the arm become damp with released blood. He flung the tube away, hearing a clatter as something on the other side of the tube hit the floor. Where was Allira? He searched his memory for the position of her bed relative to his and went in that direction, feeling ahead of him as he went. He found her warm body in the darkness and discovered she also had a tube attached. Unmindful of her pain, he tore it out. She awoke with a scream. He put a hand over her mouth.

'Allira, it's me. Wake up, we've got to get out of here.'

She nodded, and he removed the hand.

'Greg, I had an awful dream. I was trying to call you but you couldn't hear me!'

'I can hear you now. Be quiet; we're leaving.'

In their exhaustion, they had not removed their clothing or footwear prior to getting into bed, and so immediately moved stealthily towards where they knew the door to be. Ferguson opened the door, revealing a dark corridor leading past the living room to the outside door. He put one foot onto the floor.

Instantly, blinding white light flooded the whole house. A door adjacent to them opened, and Cathrona and Larn came out and stood blocking the way to the outside, terrible smiles on their faces.

'You shouldn't have done that,' Larn said. 'You have abused our hospitality.'

Ferguson blinked, his eyes trying desperately to adjust to the sudden change from near-total blackness to what seemed intense light to his sleep-heavy eyes.

'What were you doing to us?' he said, feeling his hands ball into fists, yet again.

Cathrona came slowly towards them, seeming to glide across the floor. As she did, her smile broadened until sharply pointed fangs became horribly visible.

'Little Brin is ailing; he needs blood, Ferguson. That Government stuff is useless; he needs the real thing so he can become big and strong. Bigger than you, Ferguson, stronger than you, a vampire amongst vampires, that's what my son will be! But he needs blood, real blood, human blood, your blood!'

'You welcomed us to your home,' Allira said.

Cathrona threw back her head as she laughed.

'Humans! You really are as stupid as the history books said! I couldn't believe how easy it was to trick you; it was too easy. You disappointed me; there was no game to play between us.'

'*Stronger Together*?' Allira asked. She drew herself up straighter, ready for the coming duel, but even as she did, she moved away from Ferguson, slightly further down the corridor.

Now it was Larn's turn to laugh.

'I really enjoyed coming up with the name. It's actually the exact opposite of what Cathrona and I and the rest of the vampire race really believe. We are loyal followers of Kran—the only vampire who knows how to put everything right! Serafina Ginevra could have swept you back into the Blood Farms, but she let you off because she is weak. But what Cathrona and I really want is an immediate invasion of Stralia and the extermination of all the old, weak, or degenerate humans and the immediate transfer of the good ones to new Blood Farms. We are sick to the bone of that thin stuff she makes us drink. We are vampires and we demand the right to live in the way our ancestors always lived—drinking things like you dry!'

Ferguson suddenly realised that Allira was no longer with him. His shoulders drooped. In this moment of crisis, she had snapped and deserted him, leaving him to battle these two monsters unaided. He straightened again. So be it.

But Cathrona had noticed Allira's stealthy vanishing act and called after her, 'It's no good, Allira, there's only one way out and that's past us!' She turned to her partner. 'How pathetic they are; no wonder it was so easy to conquer them!'

Larn's smile grew broader, revealing strong. broad fangs.

'Let's get these two back on the transfer machines; little Brin needs his sustenance.'

Suddenly, Allira's voice rang out.

'Yes, he does need you. Look.'

Ferguson and the vampires spun around as Allira came out of the nursery room. Cradling the vampire infant in her arms.

'He's a strong child,' she continued. 'You're right, Cathrona, he will be a great vampire when he grows up. Or, should I say, *if* he grows up.' She placed her hand on Brin's head. 'Stand away from the door and your son will live.'

Cathrona's face had become a strange mixture of rage and terror.

'If you hurt Brin, your death will be talked about with horror for a thousand years!'

'But that won't bring him back, though, will it? Stand away from the door. Last warning.'

The two vampire parents moved slowly away from the outside door, their red-shot eyes blazing at Allira and the whimpering child she carried. Ferguson moved alongside her. They backed toward the door, and his questing hand felt for the handle.

Did vampires lock their doors, if there was no vampire on vampire violence?

They did not. It opened under his fingers and the cool air of the early morning flooded in. Ferguson was the first out, leaving Allira inside, carefully holding Brin while the maddened vampires watched her every movement. Then she said, 'Catch!' and tossed Brin toward Cathrona. She joined Ferguson, and together they ran down the street.

The security forces were waiting for them, of course.

311

THIRTY FIVE

'So we meet again,' Thron said, looking at Allira and Ferguson on the other side of the desk. This time, they were wearing manacles around their wrists.

'So it would appear,' Ferguson replied. 'Where's Sran? I was hoping to catch up on old times.'

'He no longer works here.'

'You had him executed, I suppose?'

'No, vampire does not kill vampire. We are not humans.'

Neither Ferguson nor Allira could find any other words, nor feel any need to attempt to do so. They looked at Thron in bitter silence.

'Your escape last time put me in a very difficult position,' Thron said. 'It will take a long time before the stain on my record is forgotten. And so, I have no intention of putting you in a situation where you can perform another master class in escapology. Your sentence of death remains unaltered and will be carried out immediately. We have technicians present so your blood can be removed while you are still warm, and stored while it is pleasantly fresh. Due to my earlier blunder, I will not be allowed to consume any of it, which is extremely irritating.'

'I feel your pain,' Ferguson said, knowing the comment would not be understood.

Vampires have no sense of humour.

Thron merely looked puzzled and glanced at the guards standing like statues behind the prisoners. He shook his head.

'You humans. Nothing you say makes sense. But I won't have to listen to your gabble much longer.'

'And how are we to be executed?' Allira enquired. 'Another example of vampire sadism, I presume?'

'Of course not. We are a civilised people. It will be a simple firing squad, very quick, very compassionate.' He glanced at the screen before him. 'In fact, the squad have already assembled; they are ready for you now.' He stood, adjusted his uniform and looked over the humans' heads at the guards. 'Take them down.' He returned his gaze to the captives. 'And this time, I will accompany you to the place of execution. There will be no more of your human tricks.'

Ferguson and Allira stood on Thron's command. They looked at each other and stared into each other's eyes, unable to clasp hands.

Thron pushed them towards the door.

'Come along; the squad are eager to meet you, so don't keep them waiting. They rarely get the chance to actually kill things, so it's possible it may take more than one shot to finish you off, but I'm sure you will forgive their inexperience.'

Once again, Ferguson and Allira took the moving room to another level of the security building, but this time they entered a bare, bleak, windowless room with grey, unadorned walls. However, a camera was set high enough to scan the entire space, with a grill set directly below it. In that space, stood two white-coated technicians next to a humming machine from which various pipes protruded. But, more importantly, there was a line of uniformed guards, each holding what Ferguson now knew to be larger versions of projectile weapons. They snapped to attention as Thron and the captives entered, shouldering the weapons.

'Stand there,' Thron said, 'Four metres will be close enough.'

Allira and Ferguson obeyed slowly and stood on circular marks etched into the floor. They turned to face each other again.

'None of that!' Thron barked. 'The squad needs to get a clear view of your chests. Unless you want them to spend a long time on your execution, that is.'

Ferguson and Allira obeyed. They were still manacled and were sufficiently far apart they could not touch in any way.

'Take aim!' Thron commanded, and the weapons became horizontal, their muzzles trained on human hearts.

Ferguson spoke.

'Goodbye, Allira. I wish we could have had more time together.'

'Me too, Greg. You would have been a good father.'

Ferguson looked stubbornly at the guards, forcing his eyes to stay open. These creatures would not see him afraid.

They had but seconds left of life, but then a voice issued from the grill in the wall. It was a female voice, but one unlike anything the humans had heard before, except on one occasion. It carried power and authority, the voice of an individual who had witnessed earth-shaking events and had played a decisive role in their outcome.

'Guards, stand down! Thron, unchain the humans and have them sent to me. After I have dealt with them, I will call for you. You are relieved of all duties once you have delivered the humans.'

Vampires typically have pale complexions, due to the millennia spent as nocturnal predators, but Thron achieved something Ferguson would not have deemed possible: he went as white as a sheet of paper.

'Yes, High One, at once!' He waved frantically at the guards. 'Release them! Release them at once! Hurry up, you fools!'

Ferguson and Allira looked at each other uncomprehendingly; was this another example of vampire cruelty, pretending to free them, only to drag them back, again and again? However, the guards did unlock their manacles and then left the room, along with the technicians and their pleasantly humming machine.

Ferguson stood before Thron, rubbing the circulation back into his wrists.

'Who was that?'

Thron was looking at his feet for some reason, but lifted his face; a stricken, white face.

'What? That was Serafina Ginevra, of course. The Leader of the High Command.'

Serafina Ginevra!

The words thrilled! The one being that Ferguson most desired to slay. He was going to meet her!

His mind whirled crazily. How could he do it? How could he kill her? This would probably be his only chance to get to her. He must not fail!

He saw her in his mind's eye—the archetypal vampire, tall, raven-haired, emerald-eyed, nails like daggers, proud, imperious, mocking, contemptuous of everything human.

Well, we shall see!

He noticed nothing of the journey to Ginevra's office. He was dimly aware of Allira at his side, dimly aware of a silent Thron leading the way.

There was a door, a mighty door of metal so shimmeringly burnished that their reflections were clearly visible within it. It opened. Ferguson noticed it was immensely thick, as if designed to withstand the greatest imaginable forces.

They entered. Ferguson knew that Thron was no longer with them.

A huge desk stood before them, with a figure behind it.

Ferguson and Allira approached the silent figure. He saw what looked very much like a small human woman with short, mousey-brown hair, now streaked with white. But her eyes locked upon him as he came nearer, and he felt slightly dizzy for a moment. He shook his head and was himself again.

They stopped just before the desk.

'I am Greg Ferguson; this is Allira. We have come to see Serafina Ginevra.'

The female spoke in a quiet, assured voice.

'I am Serafina Ginevra.'

THIRTY SIX

Ferguson was astounded.

'You are Serafina Ginevra! But, you...'

'Are not what you expected? I'm sorry to disappoint you.'

'Your name,' Allira said, 'it's a human name, surely?'

'Yes. It's a name I adopted when I was working undercover as a human. A long time ago.'

'But you kept it.'

'Yes, it was the name he knew me by, so it has sentimental associations.'

Ferguson frowned. A sentimental vampire? Was this some kind of trick? Was he dealing with an actor?

'You are not a vampire,' he said. 'I know vampires, and you don't fit the bill.'

She smiled.

'I understand your confusion. I have followed your adventures since leaving Stralia, and you have been unfortunate in your dealings with my people. But I am a vampire.' Her smile broadened, and short, rather blunt fangs came into view. 'They are not what they used to be—but then neither am I.' The smile contracted but did not entirely disappear. 'But let me study you too, as you have studied me. It is good to see humans again; it's been a long time.'

Once again, Ferguson frowned. *Good to see humans?* What was happening here?

'I am confused,' he said. 'You don't want to kill me? You don't want to experiment on me? Have I done something wrong?'

Ginevra's smile became broader.

'Ah, humour. Such a difficult concept! That was the hardest part of my undercover work. I have missed it. But I'm afraid it may take me a while to respond; irony is the subtlest form of that discipline; only I and a few others have ever really understood it.'

Ferguson stared at what appeared to be a middle-aged woman. *Do not be fooled*, his subconscious warned, *this is the creature who exiled everyone to Stralia. The cruel tyrant.*

However, Ginevra was speaking again.

'Now, let me take a good look at you. Bear with me; you may find this somewhat intrusive, but no harm will come to you.'

Suddenly, Ferguson found that his mind was no longer entirely his own; something had infiltrated it. He could feel an intangible, immaterial *presence* alongside his own. It had a resemblance to what he had felt with Theondra, but this was not an attempt to control or even influence; he was simply being studied. But he knew he could not eject this presence, and somehow he also knew that it was just the faintest touch from something immeasurably powerful.

'Ah, I detect Gronz's work here. He has inserted a remarkable amount of material. You have done well to integrate it as well as you have; clearly the material he had to work with was finer, subtler than the average for humans.'

'You are in my mind—*mentalic fields?*'

'Obviously. I can detect not merely the data he inserted, but also the scars from the traumas you have experienced. You are remarkably resilient; no wonder Gronz wanted your brain.'

Abruptly, Ferguson felt the mentalic probe withdraw, and his thoughts were alone again. He saw Ginevra turn her attention to Allira.

'What have we here? You also have experienced great traumas, and at times you felt on the edge of madness. But you are not Ferguson; you are intensely female, with a great, persistent, driving need to reproduce, more than most humans have. Why is that?' She stopped, and a look of puzzlement came over her. 'Allira, there is something about you I have not encountered before. And I thought I had seen everything—but perhaps I have not. But what I can understand is how you two have survived all the worst that my kind could have thrown at you; I doubt any other pair of humans could have done it. But I must leave my investigations there; you are not lab rats.'

Allira, in turn, shook her head to clear it.

'You know me well; perhaps better than I know myself. You talk of reproduction. Did you have children with that male of yours?'

For a moment, a cloud dimmed the strength of Ginevra's gaze.

'You dig too deep, Allira.' She paused, then: 'As it happens, he and I did not have children; there was a biological incompatibility. But by other means, I now have two daughters. My dream is that one of them, or their descendants, will one day invade the higher dimensional universe, leading a great avenging army and finally put an end to the Vetusian menace.' Her attention snapped back to the two humans. 'But that is a dream for the far future.'

Ferguson shook his head to clear it. All doubts he had had about the veracity of the situation had been comprehensively demolished; he now knew he was in the presence of an immensely powerful being, one who could shred his mind as easily as if it were wet tissue paper. Ginevra was to Theondra as that tormenter had been to him. How was it possible to even think of slaying such a creature?

But he had questions to ask.

'You say you've been following our sufferings. Why didn't you intervene to save us?'

'That is a valid point, Ferguson. I could have done so at any point—and I would have done so, if I had thought your position was irretrievable. I have been monitoring Thron, Gronz and Theondra for some time. It is, of course, illegal to remove humans from Stralia, and it did not take me long to notice that was, in fact, happening. Gronz was a very respected scientist in our society, a renowned expert on the brain, and he had his champions. I am near the end of my career now, and I am not the power in the land I once was, and an antihuman faction has sprung up recently within the High Command. My tolerance of, if not actual affection for, your kind is seen by Kran and his followers as a side effect of my career, as early in that, I masqueraded as a human. And there was my partner, of course, the male who was a special case that straddled the human/vampire divide. Some vampires believed that there was genuine scientific knowledge that could be obtained from Gronz's experiments. I, myself, am of the opinion that individuals should be left to solve their own problems; only by struggle and endurance can we discover who we truly are. When it became obvious that you were in a problem which could not possibly be solved by you and Allira, no matter how courageous and resourceful you were, I acted. Your escapes from Gronz and Larn were entirely due to your joint courage and resourcefulness, and you are finer humans because of those triumphs. But Thron's firing squad was a problem you could not solve. And so I acted.'

'It is easy for you to say those things. You did not feel our pain; it was not your flesh that was torn. Have you suffered, Ginevra, sitting here behind your desk, behind your great door?'

She looked thoughtful.

'An excellent question. Perhaps only an outside observer could decide on the quality of my suffering and how it compares to yours.'

Ferguson could feel a righteous anger taking hold of him, shaking him.

'You vampires are not superior to us; in fact, in many ways, you're inferior! You need blood in order to live. However you obtain that blood, you cannot venture far from its source. You are not more intelligent than us; your machines, your technology, are no more than we could have created if we had been given the time. You are superior to us in one thing alone: your mastery of mentalic fields. There are people who believe some races of humanity, such as the Native Stralians, may possess those abilities to some extent, but if so, none have them as much as the weakest vampire. But that has simply made you the preferred prey of other, even more powerful beings, such as the Vetusians, who feed on your mentalities. And so, your one great strength is also your greatest weakness. As long as you use that power, you will have to defend yourselves against the Vetusians. Without that power, you are simply long-lived humans with a peculiar choice of beverage!'

To his surprise, Ginevra did not counter anger with anger; in fact, she seemed to be weighing his words in her mind.

'Fine words, Ferguson. I accept much of what you say. In many ways, we vampires are a tragic race; we were dependent on beings who in many ways resembled us, but we used them like you use cattle. But that was a trick played on us by biology; we no more chose that existence than you chose to have two legs instead of six. And as you say, it was our greatest strength that turned out to be our greatest weakness. If we did not possess our mentalic abilities, we would not be hunted by the Vetusians, just as you are not. It is your weakness that saves you from them, while we are locked in what may well be a literally endless war with our predators.

'But I reject your implication that I am somehow uniquely culpable for your present situation.' She leaned forward for the first time, and Ferguson started when he saw a backlit redness appear in her eyes. 'You have not studied all the information you now possess about the Third Vetusian War; you do not know how close we vampires came to complete subjugation in a prison of endless torment. I, my partner and his brother, saved us all at the very last moment, and as a consequence of that victory I held the survival, the very existence, of your people in the palm of my hand. A sentence, a phrase, a word from me, and me alone, could have brought about your complete extermination. But I chose not to do it, for personal reasons I will not disclose to you. Instead, I decided to let you all live and lifted the yoke of vampire predation from you by ordering the development of synthetic human blood! Many vampires complain that it is not like real human blood and long for the day when they have that returned to them; Renfield was one such vampire, Kran, another. But as long as I am in charge, that will not happen. And to save you—to *save* you, Ferguson—I placed you in Stralia, away from hungry vampires who would have re-enslaved you.'

'We deserved better,' Ferguson said, maintaining eye contact, even though Ginevra's gaze was becoming more and more intimidating. The middle-aged woman had vanished and had been replaced by a mighty vampire of the High Command.

'You deserved nothing other than what I gave you! Don't you understand—human and vampire cannot co-exist! We will always, always, subjugate you! You cannot defeat us any more than the lamb can defeat the tiger!'

'We are not animals,' Ferguson muttered. Allira was silent.

'Creatures who are not animals but nevertheless built Z0Z! Gronz put knowledge of that horror in your brain, Ferguson. Let me retrieve it for you!'

He felt Ginevra enter his mind again, but this time she was not gentle, moving slowly and considerately. She smashed down into the store of his new knowledge and dragged out the information about Z0Z.

And he saw it.

Saw the serried ranks of the ICBMs, the cruise missiles, the hypersonic vehicles of death; the vaults of viruses and bacteria carrying the promise of incurable diseases; the world-shaking bombs, the dirty bombs; the sick horror of a culture gone mad.

Ferguson quailed before that awful vision, all his pride withered as if by a blast from one of those weapons, and he fell forward, only saving himself from colliding with Ginevra's desk at the last moment.

Allira was less affected, for some reason, and asked, 'You have undoubtedly shown us how inferior humans are to you, and told us how you withheld the killing blow, but what about us as individuals? We have killed vampires; Thron made it clear there is no forgiveness for that crime.'

Ginevra was silent for at least a minute. Ferguson and Allira glanced at each other in growing alarm. And then she spoke.

'Yes. I have created a problem for myself. Vampire law is very clear on this: there is no justification for the act of a human killing a vampire; none whatsoever. There is only one penalty, and that is death.'

'Even for killing vampires who were torturing us?' snapped Ferguson.

'No.'

'If that is so,' Allira said, 'what was the point of you rescuing us from Thron? He was about to execute us, and now *you* are about to execute us. All you have done is give us a few more hours of life.'

'Your logic is impeccable,' Ginevra said. 'But you have not followed it through. For me to have rescued you and then kill you is illogical. So you have arrived at a false conclusion, meaning...'

'You are not going to kill us,' Ferguson said, his knees softening as hope returned to his brain.

'Yes. I will save you. Because once I loved a human.'

THIRTY SEVEN

'But by not killing us—surely that puts you in a difficult position?' Ferguson said, his mind grappling with the ramifications of Ginevra's words.

'Indeed. If I am caught, in theory, I could be the one being executed. However, I think it is more likely I would be expelled from the High Command and sent to a village in the Arktik. My name still means something, even in these degenerate days.'

'You are taking a great risk,' Allira said. Ferguson was annoyed by the undertone of admiration in the woman's voice. *Ginevra is the monster who exiled us to Stralia!*

'Not so much. I have done all I could possibly have done in my life, and spending my remaining decades as some kind of administrator does not appeal.' She leaned back in her great chair. 'Even vampires are not immune to nostalgia. I look back on the part I played at the end of the Third War, and sometimes I forget the horror and terror, the agony, the innocent lives lost, the death of my sister. I forget the rodent fear that gnawed away at the very marrow in my bones, until I longed for annihilation as the only possible release. But even so, I despise the quiet life I lead now, with every major problem solved.'

'The Vetusians are still out there,' Ferguson reminded her.

'Yes, there are problems with the Barrier, but they are not the kind that I could solve. Experts are working on that, and they will succeed, I have no doubt.' Her eyes lost their hold on the humans and became unfocused as she looked inwards, into the mysteries of her own mind. She spoke almost dreamily, as if reassuring herself. 'Some of the High Ones believe that mentalic forces can show us glimpses of events yet to come. My own powers are not minor, and occasionally I have visions of my descendants leading a great vampire army up into the higher-dimensional realms, to do battle with our great enemy in their own territory. I could want no greater legacy. And so, I no longer care what happens to me.' Her eyes regained focus as they returned to hold Ferguson and Allira in their grip. 'Vampire and human cannot live together. And so, now I must return you to Stralia.'

'Like you did all the other humans, you mean!' Ferguson said, his latent resentment finally breaking to the surface.

Ginevra stared at him for some moments. Then: 'Ferguson, you are becoming tiresome. Is it possible I have overestimated your abilities? Do you still not realise that I have given this tortured planet my *Pax Vampirica*?'

Ferguson looked away. He wanted, needed, to hate Serafina Ginevra, but was finding that increasingly difficult. If he had the chance to kill her, would he take it? But Allira had taken over the discussion.

'Is there anything we need to do? We are very anxious to get back home.'

'No more than I am anxious to get you off my hands. I would have severely punished Gronz and Theondra for removing you from Stralia, but you took that out of my hands by killing them. So, I can only end this problem by going against vampire law, and that had better be done as soon as possible before alarm bells start ringing in the High Command.' She looked away, shaking her head. 'I must admit, I never thought my career would end with a blatant defiance of my colleagues in the highest echelon of the vampire world. My mentalic powers did not foresee this!' She looked back at them, calm, controlled. 'There is nothing you can or need do, except follow me. There is a teleportation station that is not part of the main network and which Kran and his disciples do not know about. To reach it, we will have to pass through the Barrier Chamber.'

'Where the clones generate the Barrier against the Vetusians,' Ferguson said. Allira looked at him in surprise. Ginevra did not.

'Yes, Ferguson. You are integrating your new knowledge very well. I hope that one day we will not need the Barrier, but that day is far off.'

She stood. Ferguson was surprised at how short she was, accustomed as he was to physically imposing vampires. She saw his expression but merely smiled again.

'It's all part of the masquerade I was born to enact; the details are in your memory somewhere, Ferguson, but now is not the time to look them up. Follow me.'

The immense door opened silently and obediently at Ginevra's approach and then closed obediently and silently behind the ill-assorted trio.

'That is the elevator to the travelator, which in turn takes us to the Barrier Room,' Ginevra said, pointing at a nondescript door.

Allira giggled.

'That rhymes: *elevator to the travelator.*'

Ginevra stared at her, and she stopped giggling.

'Sorry. Nerves, I guess.'

Ferguson and Allira now knew the correct name for the "moving room" device, which was only just big enough for the three of them. It shuddered once, as if it had lain unused for a long time, but then began a swift descent, plummeting to depths not encountered before. When the elevator door opened, a wave of cold air swept over them, so cold that both humans gasped.

'It will get colder,' Ginevra said, showing no reaction to the temperature. The light was equally cold, blue-shifted, and unwelcoming. They walked a short distance to a metal surface divided into separate but contiguous plates.

'The travelator. Stand on it, please.'

She joined them and, after a slight jerk, the surface began to move, taking them down a blue-lit tunnel.

'The Barrier Room is not in the High Command building, but is not far distant. It is quite deep underground, however, hence the drop in temperature, which you appear to be finding unpleasant.'

'This is colder than a night under a clear desert sky,' Ferguson said.

'I'll take your word for that; I've never been in a desert at night. I'm not a great traveller, but I did go to Affrig once; mentally, that is.'

Ferguson did not understand the observation, but did not pursue the issue.

'Greg knows more about the Barrier than I do,' Allira said, as the travelator continued to whisk them through the tunnel; an emptiness the shape, temperature and colour of a shaft bored into a glacier. 'Something about *clones*?'

'Yes, there are hundreds of clones of the original vampire who first created the mental shield against Vetusian invasions. Their combined mentalic forces create our great defence.'

'Do they do anything else?'

'No. As you shortly will see.'

Allira took that as a request to stop talking, and the trio swept on through the arrow-straight tunnel.

The travelator slowed gently and emerged from the tunnel into a vast hall, equally cold and blue-shaded. Ferguson and Allira goggled at what it contained: row upon row of transparent cylinders extending across the floor of the cavernous expanse. But not just along the floor: there was row upon row of those cylinders above the lowest rank, and above them another row, and above them...

Each cylinder was bathed in a weird blue glow that appeared to emanate from a liquid inside each cylinder. It was an unpleasant blue; the blue of the heart of a glacier; the blue of the ocean depths before the last light from above is extinguished.

They stepped off the travelator and followed Ginevra until they were within the tremendous array of cylinders: to the left of them, to the right of them, in front of them, above them. Allira approached one, then gasped and recoiled.

'There's someone inside!'

Ferguson looked inside the cylinder nearest to him, seeing a naked humanoid floating in a blue liquid, a tube snaking out of its body.

329

'That is a biological copy of the vampire who saved you all?'

'Yes. Thousands of copies. But this is not the time for a history lesson; as long as I frightened Thron enough, he will not have reported your presence here in New Marinetown and we will all be safe.'

It was just then that Ferguson saw a movement in his peripheral vision, a movement where there should be no movement. He turned and saw a figure move out from behind one of the clone cylinders. As it came nearer, it resolved into someone Ferguson knew: Thron. Apparently, Ginevra had underestimated her enemies.

'But I'm afraid you did not frighten me enough, High One. My patriotism overcame my fear. You have traded on your past glory for so long you have failed to realise that you are no longer held in awe by younger vampires such as myself. And it grieves me to say that this episode will remove all trace of your glory, now and forever. You have sheltered vampiricides, given aid and comfort to them. But your crimes will be laid bare by someone much more important than I. Someone who will detail all the items on your charge sheet.'

Another figure came out from behind the cylinder and Thron stepped backwards to allow the newcomer to stand directly before Ginevra. Ferguson did not recognise the intruder, but Ginevra did.

'Hello, Kran,' she said.

THIRTY EIGHT

Ferguson stared at the newcomer, seeing a classic high-status vampire: tall, ramrod straight and with a glossy mane of black hair and an imperious attitude. He held a long-barrelled projectile weapon, pointed at Ginevra.

'Hello, Serafina. Good to see you again. I wonder if you could introduce me to your travelling companions; I don't believe I've seen them before.'

Ginevra did not reply. Kran looked across at Thron.

'You may go now, Thron. You have shown yourself to be a true patriot, something increasingly rare in these degenerate days.'

Thron lowered his head in submission, but not before a delighted smile had spread over his face.

'Proud to be of help, High One.'

And with that, he disappeared into the labyrinth of cylinders. Kran turned back to Ginevra.

'Serafina, Serafina, what has become of you? You have used that human name for so long you have forgotten your real name, haven't you? How could you have sunk so low?'

'I take it you are aware you are insulting the Leader of the High Command?'

'In name only, Serafina. Much has been going on beneath your attention, as you dozed your life away behind your big door. A whole new generation has grown up who are no longer impressed by cobwebbed stories of the past. You have relied too much on past glories, pretending it was you and you alone who defeated the Vetusians, neglecting to mention that you were part of a team.'

'I have never claimed that, never; I know what the others sacrificed, more than you ever can. I was there; you were not.'

'Of course, Serafina, what a great hero you were. But let's look at the other parts of your resumé, shall we? Was it not you who removed the crime of Human Loving from the statute book? I wonder why you did that? Oh, look who we have here! Why, it's two humans, I believe! Well, consorting with them isn't illegal now, is it, Serafina?'

'What do you want, Kran? I haven't all day.'

'Seeing as you asked, I want you gone. I want your position, so I can bring the vampire race back to the sanity that you have taken from us. I want your meddling completely erased. I want the factories churning out that artificial slop closed down. I want the humans brought back from Stralia. I want the Blood Farms reintroduced. I want the old days back! I want vampires to reclaim their rightful position as masters of the world! We were a great people once, before you emasculated us, and with me at the helm we will be again!'

'Humans deserve better.'

'Humans deserve nothing!' Kran screamed, the sound of his voice echoing and rebounding off the cylinders. The clones in the nearest cylinders stirred slightly. 'Nothing other than the restoration of the natural order, nothing other than that they become our property again, to dispose of as we wish!'

'How will you achieve that? I am not without allies in the High Command.'

A sly look stole over Kran's features.

'Yes, I believe you are. But what could bring them over to my side more than your death?' He whirled around, pointing the weapon at Ferguson. 'Your death at *the hands of a human*? Do you see the utter brilliance of it? I rid myself of you, and at the same time, turn the whole vampire people against the humans! It is so brilliant I could weep with joy!' He strode over to Ferguson and turned him so he was facing Ginevra. He waved the weapon at Ferguson's startled face, its ominous muzzle inches from his pupils. 'Now kill Serafina Ginevra, human!'

Ferguson looked at Kran, eye to eye; they were the same height.

'What's in it for me? After I kill her, you kill me; that's pretty obvious.'

Kran gave a smile reminiscent of the killing gape of a Great White.

'I promise I will let you live out your days in a safe house in New Marinetown. A special dispensation for services rendered.'

'And Allira?'

Kran looked across at her.

'Oh, the female? Well, you can keep her, if you want.' He pushed something into Ferguson's hands. He looked down—it was the projectile weapon. Kran withdrew slightly. 'There you are, you have everything you need now; just lift it, pull that trigger—and no more Serafina Ginevra! And Serafina,'—he gave Ginevra a quick glance—'don't try any mentalic tricks; I'm a lot younger than you, don't forget.'

Blood roared in Ferguson's head; he felt an electric thrill flash down his nervous system. This was the moment he had waited for, dreamed of! He had the cruel tyrant at his mercy. Now he could pay her back for scooping up the human race like dirt and depositing it in Stralia. One shot and all those human beings would be avenged! Such power!

He lined up the weapon so the muzzle was pointing at her heart. His own heart was hammering like an overloaded piston.

'Now we humans get our revenge! Beg for your life, Ginevra!' he said.

She looked at him calmly, untroubled.

'I don't think so.'

He heard a female voice calling to him from a long, long distance. What was it saying?

'Greg! Greg! What are you doing! She didn't imprison us—she saved us!'

The muzzle of the weapon wavered slightly. Ideas and their opposites fought madly for mastery in his brain. He glanced at Kran, saw the gloating on his face, the fire in his eyes. He looked at Ginevra, hands at her side, her face tranquil.

He lowered the weapon.

'No,' he said.

He heard Kran hiss in his anger, and then something cold jabbed into his right temple. It was a hand weapon.

'You kill Ginevra, or I kill you.'

The tumult in Ferguson's mind subsided. All the facts Gronz had input in his mind about those terrible days snapped together into a coherent whole. He understood exactly what Ginevra had done those long centuries ago, how it had not been an act of triumphant savagery, but the only way of saving the human race. His race, his people.

'No,' he said.

Without giving any warning, he spun around and smashed his weapon into Kran's face, and a second later had knocked Kran's weapon out of his hand. But Ferguson knew he could not win a fight with a creature who could rip his arms out without breaking a sweat. He had to shoot Kran.

He strove to aim the gun at Kran, but his intended target grasped the muzzle and forced it out of alignment. Ferguson kicked Kran's feet from under him, and the two went down, Ferguson on top. Kran was now holding the weapon at both ends and was forcing it up into Ferguson's face, while Ferguson was trying to push it against Kran's windpipe. A look of triumph was just coming into the vampire's features when Ferguson released the gun and rained a fusillade of his heaviest blows onto that grinning face. Under that salvo, Kran involuntarily turned his face aside and his grip on the gun weakened. Ferguson snatched it back, and the two rolled over. Allira was frozen into immobility by the desperate battle raging only a few feet distant, but Ginevra leapt forward to aid Ferguson. The two combatants struggled into a half-standing position, the weapon held between them.

Then suddenly it went off, once, twice; the sound of its reports was a terrible thunder in the great cavern. Allira screamed.

Ferguson heard Ginevra scream, but her scream was in words.

'The clones! You've hit the clones! The Barrier!'

Ferguson lost the battle to hold the gun; Kran grasped it. He fired twice.

But not at Ferguson.

The shots hit Ginevra full in her heart. For only the fourth time in his life, Ferguson saw rich, red vampire blood spurt out in a fatal spray. He fell backwards and landed on something hard. It was Kran's handgun. Ferguson clutched it and raised it as he saw Kran turn his own weapon on him.

He fired.

Kran fell.

And then silence.

THIRTY NINE

After the violent tumult, the silence felt unnatural; wrong. Ferguson lay on his back, the cavern spinning crazily around him. He felt, rather than saw, Allira bend over him.

'Greg! Are you alright? Did he hurt you?'

Mentally, Ferguson scanned his body, searching for dangerous wounds. Finding none, he sat up, aided by Allira.

'Kran, is he…?'

'Dead. But so is Ginevra.'

Ferguson finally made it to his feet; he spared one swift glance at Kran, and then walked to where Ginevra lay.

She looked peaceful in death; there were no expressions of fear or pain. Vampires do not have emotions precisely the same as ours, but Ferguson sensed a feeling of peace, of a burden finally relinquished.

He turned to Allira.

'Strange. For so long, I dreamt of killing her, of avenging the entire human race. But now I wish I'd spent more time with her; I could have learned so much; not just facts and figures like Gronz gave me, but how it felt to face the destruction of everything you believed in at the hands of real, live monsters.'

'Greg,' Allira said, 'I feel the same way about Serafina, but nothing of importance has changed for us. We're still trapped in a vampire city. We don't know where the secret teleportation station is or, if by some miracle we're able to find it, how to operate it. And now you have another dead vampire on your charge sheet. One who up until a few minutes ago was the most important one on the planet.' She gave a quiet sob, but stifled a repeat. 'Greg! We're still in a completely hopeless situation!'

Ferguson shook his head in what looked like defeat.

'I know; every time we think we're just about to get home, something worse happens.' He looked around the tremendous chamber. 'I wonder how long before Thron reappears. And this time there'll be no Ginevra to save us.' Then something caught his eye. 'The clone cylinders. She said the *clone cylinders*.' He walked over to the nearest and almost slipped as he came up to it. He looked down. 'The fluid—it's leaking.'

Allira joined him.

'Greg, look! It's half empty!'

Ferguson saw that Allira was right; only just over half of the mysterious blue liquid was left in the cylinder, but more than that, the clone inside was hunched up into a foetal position. Its skin had turned a dull grey, and the features were contorted in the rictus of a silent scream.

'At the risk of repeating myself,' Allira said, 'I think it's dead.'

'Not just this one. Look.'

The two humans traced the trajectories of Kran's bullets: two entire lines of cylinders had been penetrated and were busily emptying their contents onto the floor, leaving dead clones lying inside them, twisted into a variety of contorted postures.

'I suppose we'll get blamed for this as well,' Allira said, dully.

Ferguson did not reply but was looking around, his eyes screwed up as if he was not sure of what he was seeing. After some minutes of searching, he finally spoke.

'Allira, do you see a kind of glow in the air? A sort of purple shimmer over everything? Please tell me you can't and it's just my eyes playing tricks.'

Allira looked around, completing a full circle.

'Yes, Greg, I can. What's the matter?'

His face was grim.

'Allira, the clones. They generate the Barrier. The Barrier keeps the Vetusians out. Kran's accidental killing of a number of clones must have caused a local hole in the Barrier. That glow is them, trying to get in!'

Fear came into her face, but then she steadied herself.

'But they're not interested in us. They only prey on vampires; we'll be OK.'

'Perhaps. We can't be sure what real Vetusians will do if they break through. But we may well find out. All we know for certain is that they are incredibly powerful, and vampires are shit-scared of them.'

The purple-violet glow in the air intensified around them until there could be no doubt it was a real phenomenon. Allira looked at Ferguson.

'Should we get out of this chamber?'

'What's the point? We've nowhere to go." He leaned against a cylinder. 'Let's wait and see.'

Suddenly, a look of worried astonishment came over

him, and he jumped away from the cylinder. 'What the...'

'What's wrong?' she asked, in a *What Now?* tone.

'The cylinder. It felt...' He stopped, obviously looking for an appropriate adjective. 'It felt *spongy.*'

'*Spongy?* What in hell's name are you talking about, Greg?'

'*Spongy. Squishy. Springy.* Am I making myself clear?'

'Not in the least.' She joined him in inspecting the cylinder and extended a questioning finger against its surface. They both watched in amazement as the finger sank a short way into the supposedly rigid surface. They looked at each other.

'Am I going mad?' she asked him. 'If I'm not, what's happening?'

He was silent, and his eyes took on a faraway look; she knew he was accessing the knowledge given to him by Gronz. His eyes cleared.

'It's the breach in the Barrier; the Vetusians inhabit a world with a higher number of physical dimensions. They haven't broken through yet, but somehow their dimensionality is leaking in.'

'How can you know that?'

'Because something similar happened to Ginevra during the last war. It's all in my mind; the only problem I have is knowing where to look. It's not easy.'

'So sorry to hear that. But how did Serafina get out of this dimensional business?'

Ferguson shook his head.

'In a way that is absolutely of no benefit to us.'

'Oh.' Suddenly, she looked down at her boots. 'Greg, normally I wouldn't ask a question like this, but is the floor getting sticky?'

He lifted a foot.

'I'm afraid it's not a stupid question. In a higher-dimensional world three-dimensional obstacles are not obstacles.'

'That makes no sense at all.'

'I'm not sure how much time I have to explain this, but a two-dimensional being can't cross into a two-dimensional circle. But a three-dimensional one can. So to a being of dimensions higher than three...'

'There are no obstacles; no barriers. You can't imprison a higher-dimensional being in a three-dimensional cell.'

'You obviously didn't need a brain boost. But there's a worrying conclusion to what you just said.'

'I've got it. We're going to fall through the floor.'

'All the way down. Unless something else happens.'

'Which is?'

'I have no idea.'

They looked at each other, stoney-faced until Allira burst out laughing.

'Greg! This is so crazy I feel like I don't care anymore! Let's just get it over with, shall we?'

Before Ferguson could reply, he noticed movements some distance away beyond the edge of the cylinder array.

'Someone's coming. I doubt they're coming to help us.'

'You reckon?' Allira's voice was still flushed with laughter. Ferguson was starting to feel more than a little hysterical himself. They waited.

The movements resolved into a group of security officers; as predicted, Thron was leading the pack. But Allira noticed something.

'They're not right; they're slowing down, but not in a normal way.'

Ferguson agreed. The approaching vampires were slowing down, but not through changing their pace; all their movements were of individuals running extremely fast—but they were not running extremely fast. As the humans watched, the approaching group became slower and slower, and then froze completely, becoming a collection of lifelike statues.

'What...' Allira said, unable to complete her question.

Ferguson approached Thron, who had been leading the group. He turned to look at Allira.

'Watch this.'

And with that, he put his hand inside Thron's totally motionless chest, without any effusion of blood. He pulled the hand out, unbloodied.

'No need to explain,' Allira said, 'but party tricks can't help us. I guess the Vetusians run on different clocks from us.'

Ferguson was about to reply when events took yet another unexpected turn. He and Allira were suddenly enclosed in a shaft, a great cylinder of almost tangible violet light.

They heard a voice.

If thunder could speak in human tones, it would use that voice.

'Yes, I have them,' it said.

FORTY: THE VETUSIANS

There was dizzy disorientation: everything dissolved into a featureless blaze of violet-purple radiance. They had the feeling that some *force* was pulling them upwards, ever upwards, through an endless conduit to some vastly distant destination. Time ceased to have meaning; they could have been in that conduit for a second, an hour or a millennium. There were no yardsticks to measure time; there was only the apparently endless sensation of upward motion.

Then the violet radiance gave one last surge into a brilliance so great it could not be observed without pain.

It vanished, leaving whirling red-orange afterimages in Ferguson's sight. Gradually, his surroundings came into focus. And they were not pleasing surroundings; all he could see was a completely featureless plain. No, it was not a plain, it was a mathematical *plane,* of infinite dimensions. It looked as though it had been constructed from the same purple-violet light that had bathed them earlier, but changed into an adamantine solid. There was no horizon, for there was nothing on that plane to indicate a vanishing point; no structures, no features of any kind. The sky above had features, however; it

343

had great roiling masses of cloud, like mutant thunderclouds, and from those clouds great forks of lightning were regularly stabbing, but a lightning whose ominous bolts were of a deep crimson. There was no sound.

Ferguson involuntarily stepped backwards.

'This is a hell,' he whispered.

Allira was standing with her back to him; he could feel the pressure of her body on his.

'What are you talking about?' he heard her say. 'This is lovely!'

He whirled around and stood motionless, his mouth falling open.

He saw great snow-capped peaks, dimmed and softened by distance. He saw verdant trees whose uppermost branches were swaying in what could only have been the gentlest of breezes. Between the wood and the two humans stretched a carpet of soft grass of the purest green, everywhere dotted with multicoloured blossoms.

'Hell?' Allira said in an awed whisper, 'This is paradise!'

As one, they moved forward to experience this paradise in person, but stopped.

They could not move much beyond where they were standing. Ferguson put his hands up and traced the boundary beyond which they could not progress.

'It's a dome, a completely invisible dome.'

Suddenly, paradise seemed a long way away.

Ferguson turned so he was standing at ninety degrees to his initial position. His eyes narrowed as he surveyed the latest scene.

This one was nothing but abstract geometrical shapes: hexagonal prisms, octahedra, cubes, parallelepipeds, dodecahedra, and many, many more.

All were severely monochrome and without shadows or shading, as if they had been drawn by a giant pencil. He shook his head and turned again to the remaining compass point.

This one was purely abstract, comprising nothing but spinning multicoloured spirals and helices, on an ever-changing background of pulsing starburst patterns.

'None of this is real,' he finally said, with the taste of ashes in his mouth. 'None of it.'

Suddenly, Allira spoke, her voice tense with fear.

'Greg, there is something in here with us.'

Ferguson felt it too; an invisible *something* had joined them and now stood next to them in the confinement of their imprisoning dome.

Then there was a voice, not in their minds, but a normal, human-like voice, pleasantly modulated.

'Ah, you have detected me. Very good. I will make myself apparent.'

Before their disbelieving eyes, a form instantly took shape, that of a tall human male, with regular features and blond, curly hair. Ferguson felt Allira stiffen slightly, in admiration.

'And who are you?' Ferguson said.

The figure smiled, revealing perfect teeth, perhaps a little too dazzlingly white to be believable.

'I am what you refer to as a Vetusian, or perhaps, I could say I am THE Vetusian, as sometimes we are separate, sometimes we are united.'

'A Vetusian!' Ferguson gasped, 'But you're demons, monsters!'

'Indeed, we are,' the figure replied. 'We are all of those things, and none of those things. For instance, this is how the vampires see us.'

At that, the handsome figure instantly changed into a squirming horror, one that could not be observed, or even described, without madness. Allira doubled up, retching, and Ferguson covered his eyes. After a minute or so, he spread his fingers to see if the thing had disappeared.

It had.

'Which version is the real you?' he said with a mouth as dry as the Red Centre.

'Neither, of course. Surely that is obvious?'

'Are any of these landscapes real?' Allira said, in a voice still shaking with fear.

'None, of course. Now, this is becoming tedious. You are creatures from an impoverished three-dimensional manifold. Your nervous systems cannot interpret a manifold of higher dimensionality, so we created these images to give your eyes something to do.'

'Could you keep the living landscape version and get rid of the others?' she asked.

'Certainly,' the being—now returned to the form of the handsome young man—said. 'It is done.'

Allira glanced around, seeing pleasant copses, meandering streams, puffy cotton-wool clouds against a soothing, mildly blue sky.

'And now what are you going to do to us?' Ferguson said. 'I've studied the records of the most recent war with the vampires. Are you going to torture us, vivisect us?'

'That would be pointless, for reasons I may explain later. Normally, we (or I) have no interest in humans; you do not possess what we need.' His smile broadened. 'Which is extremely fortunate for you.'

Ferguson felt as if a heavy load had been lifted from his shoulders; his heart quietened from its hitherto frantic beat.

'Why can't we move out of this—bubble?'

'Now this is not good enough; you're really not trying to think, are you? You exist as three-dimensional structures, and such things cannot endure our higher plane of existence. I created a bubble of your spatial metric to keep you alive.'

'And what do you intend doing with us? Why did you capture us?'

'Always with the questions. The reason cannot be understood until you learn more about us/me. But I assure you we do not intend to treat you as we treat the vampires; not because we are compassionate—because we are not—but because we would obtain no value from such treatment.' The entity stopped suddenly, as if it had just noticed something. 'And yet...'

Ferguson saw Allira instantly go rigid, her face contorted with fear.

'Greg,' she whispered, turning her eyes in his direction, apparently unable to move any other part, 'there's something in my mind! It's him!'

Ferguson did not move. There was nothing he could do except stare at the now completely immobile Allira. Suddenly, she gave a groan and collapsed like a marionette whose strings had just been cut.

'She will be unconscious for a minute or so,' the being said, completely dispassionately. 'It would seem she is not accustomed to having her mind probed.'

Ferguson felt his fear come crashing back.

'You said you wouldn't harm us!'

'She is not harmed—other than a headache when she awakens. I saw something in her mind that I had not expected. But on closer examination, there is nothing there that would be of value to us.'

'And if there had been?'

'I would have extracted it in a way she would not have found pleasurable. Quite the contrary, in fact.'

'The vampires said you were monsters.'

'And we are. Have I denied it?'

Suddenly, Allira gave another groan and stirred. Ferguson helped her to her feet. She passed a hand over her sweat-streaked forehead and then reached for him, resting her head on his upper arm.

'Greg, Greg, it was horrible! There was this terrific pressure inside my head; I felt like it would fly apart at any moment!'

Ferguson glared at the image of the young man.

'If we are of no use to you, you should let us go! We are not animals!'

'Are you not? That rather depends on the definition one chooses, I think.'

'Tell us why we are here.'

Instantly, the figure transformed into a scaly, vaguely reptilian biped, whose raised arms terminated in vicious claws. Hungry red eyes blazed down on the terrified pair, while slimy drool dripped from its fanged jaws. A deep, menacing voice issued from those jaws.

'No commands; no demands! We are Vetusians; we do not receive orders!' Instantly, the smiling young man was back. 'Good, we have clarified that, I think.'

Ferguson and Allira said nothing, but held each other tighter.

'I can see you are frightened. Normally, I would enjoy that, but as I said earlier, I get very little value from human emotions. But never mind, I hope you are in a sufficiently calm state to listen to a lecture, because you are about to meet the Emperor. And he is not known for his patience.'

FORTY ONE

They had no sensation of movement, but the landscape changed as quickly as turning a page in a picture book. Gone was the pastoral idyll, replaced by another endless plane. This one had features, however: great sloping transparent shapes like huge quartz crystals. Moving soundlessly between those structures were things that Ferguson found impossible to categorise.

From some angles, they manifested as spheres of reddish light; yet, if the eyes moved slightly they were no longer solid objects, but more like apertures into another volume of space; ones composed entirely of blackness, as if absolute nothingness could become visible.

One sphere/aperture was larger than the rest. Ferguson felt that their bubble of 3D space was gliding across the plane, approaching the larger object. Or perhaps the object was moving towards them; it was impossible to say. It stopped, or they stopped, and it felt like they were then merely a few feet apart, but Ferguson could not be certain, as he did not know how large the thing was. When it was a sphere, Ferguson felt it was rotating; though how he knew that he could not say, as it was featureless. He decided to break the silence.

'I take it you are the Emperor.'

Once again, there was a physical voice, but it did not appear to be emanating from any particular direction. It was similar, but not identical, to their earlier visitor, who had now departed from their bubble.

'That is what the vampires know me as. But it is a meaningless term, as there is no hierarchy in the Vetusians. How could there be, when sometimes we are One and sometimes we are Many?'

'If I may ask,' Ferguson said carefully, remembering his recent encounter with the reptilian monster, 'why are we here?'

'I will answer that—in the fullness of time. However, you should reflect on the fact that you are the first humans to be physically in our realm. That is a new thing, and as Vetusians, we rejoice when we encounter new things.'

Allira and Ferguson sensed an oration was coming.

And so it was.

'As your presence is new, it amuses me to tell you of many things you do not know and could never have discovered. I sense that one of you possesses a great deal of knowledge, but it is only vampire knowledge, and as such, it is woefully lacking.

'I will explain that existence is expressed as a plenum, which contains everything that is logically permitted to exist. It is eternal, infinite, and indestructible. It is of higher physical dimensions, not those as postulated in your human Kaluza-Klein hypothesis, nor a temporal dimension as required by spacetime, but one of a dimensionality series such that each level encompasses the lower level, in a nested sequence. The plenum is infinite—

uncountably infinite—and it contains within it an infinite number of domains. Throughout the plenum there is a sea of churning, constantly changing probabilities. But it may help if you think of the plenum as a vast book that contains everything that can be, and this book contains an infinite number of pages. Each page is a separate universe, which separates out of the plenum whenever a probability of existence rises above zero. Do you understand?'

'No,' said Ferguson.

The Emperor continued as if there had been no reply.

'The plenum can be visualised as a sea of probabilities. Some are negative, some are zero. But whenever a probability becomes positive, a universe is born. Each is different, as the probabilities can be any real number in the interval between zero and one.'

To Ferguson's surprise, Allira spoke up.

'What does all this have to do with Vetusians?'

'We are immortal. Not *potentially* immortal, but actually immortal. Our memories only stretch back as far as the fateful decision our ancestors made in a universe that is now dead. We learned how to become immortal, and as our universe was fading out of being, we gladly chose that method. Our progenitors must have known the decision was irreversible, but they must also have believed that would not be a problem. And then our true, certain memories begin. And that is the curse that has made us what we are.'

'How is immortality a curse?' Allira gasped.

'Because when one is immortal, everything that can be done, has been done. Every thought in one's mind has been expressed an infinite number of times before. When nothing new occurs, there is no time, only an endless sleep. There are no discoveries, because in an infinity of time, either something cannot be discovered or it has been discovered, an infinite number of times. Infinite time ineluctably becomes zero time. That is our curse.'

Ferguson and Allira were silent as they tried to fully absorb the Emperor's complex words. Then Ferguson thought of something.

'What has this to do with your parasitism on the vampires?'

'It is very simple. Our curse is our memories. We can experience nothing new. Unless, that is, we absorb the mentalic energies of the vampires, because we discovered long ago that such energies erase a memory, so giving us the joy of discovery again, and the consciousness of time passing. Without the possibility of change, immortality becomes meaningless, and we sleep forever. The minds of the vampires give us that possibility.'

'Their suffering does, you mean!' Allira snapped, alarming Ferguson with her boldness.

'That is true. The irony is, the greater the mentalic struggle from them, the richer the harvest we reap. That is why in our most recent encounters, we adopted the personas of the Old Gods, to increase their fear of us. The fact that it created a whole swathe of religious beliefs in the Mesoamericans, who also observed us, was just a trivial side-effect.' The Emperor paused, then: 'In many ways, you humans are the most fortunate of the three types of races: we are locked into permanent dependence on the vampires, and they are locked into a permanent defensive war against us.'

'It doesn't feel that way,' Ferguson observed, bitterly.

'Understandable. It is open to debate whether it is best to be a cosseted sheep or the shepherd who eventually devours the cosseted sheep.'

'I would prefer to be neither,' Ferguson said, emboldened by the lack of hostile acts against him.

'There may be a way for you to achieve that,' the Emperor said.

Ferguson and Allira stared at each other, struck dumb by a new, vast hope.

FORTY TWO

'And what is this way?' Ferguson finally managed to ask.

'Every state that is not forbidden is actualised,' the Emperor replied. 'There are an extremely large, though finite, number of worlds which differ from yours by only a few trivial decimals in their probabilities. This state of affairs bears some resemblance to your theories of Multiple Worlds, the difference being that, as all of the domains are contained in a manifold below this higher-dimensional one, we can visit them all. Only a few contain vampires, which is why your world has an especial significance for us.'

Ferguson saw the implication.

'So the majority of this extremely large number of worlds does not have vampires.'

'Correct. As you know, your species and the vampires are closely related genetically. But evolution is random, and in some worlds the necessary mutations to produce the vampire race simply did not occur. In others, vampires arose but fell victim to various extinction events, unrelated to Vetusian predation.

'And there are worlds in which neither species came into being, and primates did not develop beyond the gorilla or bonobo.'

'Interesting, on a purely scientific level, but how does that help us?'

'It is a fact, demonstrated on all the worlds where both species exist, that vampires and humans cannot live together in equality. The situation is unstable and always leads to human subjugation. On most of the worlds, however, humans have been liberated by our conquest of the vampires. Your world is very unusual in that its vampires have succeeded so far in resisting us. We are not sure why that is, and because we are not sure, we know that we have *always* been unsure, for reasons I have already explained.'

'And do you expect this stalemate to always exist?' Allira asked, finally finding a part of the Emperor's speech she could understand.

'From our vantage point, we stand outside the timelines of all the lower levels. Their pasts, presents and futures are all open to us. Regarding your world's future, we have seen its vampires leave their dimensional level and engage in battle with us in this one. And we have also seen how that ends.'

Allira wanted to know more, but Ferguson interrupted.

'You still haven't explained how all this helps us.'

'Your presence here is unusual. It may have happened before in some slightly different form, but that may be in a memory that was destroyed by our recent attack on your world. This presents us with an opportunity. As long as the Barrier exists, we cannot penetrate it. It was weakened recently, but only locally. It was this temporary fissure that allowed us to collect you. But we did not do that for your happiness, but because I saw a new way to attack your world's unusual vampires. I calculated that a Vetusian essence could be implanted in your minds, which would act as a shield for that essence.'

'Don't understand.'

'Imagine your mind as a wrapper, with the Vetusian intelligence hidden within. The Barrier would only see the human mentality, and not prevent you from returning. Once inside, we could do many things.'

'You're asking us to act as infiltrators, saboteurs, against the vampires!' Allira said, sounding shocked to Ferguson's ears.

'But of course. How many vampires have treated you as sentient beings? Serafina Ginevra? Oh yes, I know her well. But she had very personal reasons for being different from the others.'

'I don't like it,' Allira muttered.

The Emperor's sphere blazed brightly for a moment, and the humans recoiled, fearful of what they might have awakened in that supremely potent being.

'You are the last hope of your people! Humans and vampires cannot co-exist! Serafina Ginevra thought she was being generous in exiling you to Stralia, but I know what lies ahead for you there. As individuals, you are not aware of it, but as a race, you know you are in prison and that hidden knowledge is eating away at you. Your birth rates are falling, and before long, you will be extinct. If you help us, I can help you.'

'How?' Ferguson demanded. 'How? All you have done is spout abstruse gobbledygook at us. How can you help us?'

'After the infiltration is done, I can transfer you to one of the Earth-like worlds that has no vampires.'

'What, just Allira and me? We will be very lonely, won't we?'

'If that is a problem, I can transfer the entire human population of Stralia.'

Ferguson's face showed an emotion it had not displayed for a long time: joy.

'You could? You can?'

'It must be done in a way that does not arouse suspicion; your Earth's vampires are very intelligent. It is possible that my plan may not succeed; I cannot foresee the outcome. But it will be done in a way that will appear to be your natural extinction, and the vampires will not intervene. I can harvest at successive points in your history so that the decline will be gradual from an outside viewpoint and thus mimic a genuine extinction. But I will deliver the entire population at the same time-point on the new Earth, irrespective of when they were collected.'

'There will be chaos,' Allira said.

'Of course, there will be. Do you expect me to solve all your problems?'

Ferguson was silent; in his mind, he saw the vampires trapped in an endless war with the Vetusians, a war that they might not win, despite their heroism.

And then he thought of the surviving scraps of the human race, dwindling away to nothing in Stralia.

He looked up.

'We'll do it.'

FORTY THREE

There had been a blaze of violet-purple light and then a feeling that some force was pushing them downwards, ever downwards, to some vastly distant destination. Time had ceased to have meaning; they could have been in the Vetusian conduit for a second, an hour or a millennium. There were no yardsticks to measure time; there was only the apparently endless sensation of downward motion.

Then the violet radiance gave one last surge into a brilliance so great it could not be observed without pain.

Their eyes blinked open.

They were standing before the door of the Kookaburra. Ferguson smiled and glanced at Allira, standing close to him.

'Great to be back!' he breathed. 'After all we've been through!'

Allira did not reply and looked uneasy.

'What's the matter?'

She grimaced.

'It's this Vetusian implant. I can feel it moving around in my mind. I don't like it; it's alien. I don't trust them, Greg. They say they're going to transfer people to this new world, but how do we know they won't just—oh, I don't know—just *evaporate* them?'

Ferguson did not reply for a while; he, too, had had similar thoughts about bad faith by the Vetusians. But, eventually, he spoke.

'We can't be certain of anything. All we know is that they don't prey on us. There's no reason for a double-cross.'

'Except for the fact that they're sadistic monsters.'

'They're not interested in us. And they're so powerful it's no big deal for them to do what they said they would. And what is the alternative? If they simply rub us out, we've lost nothing. We're going to die out if we stay here. Delgado noticed the birthrate is falling, so there's no reason to believe they lied to us.'

'Greg, you believe that the human race shouldn't die out, but what if no-one wants to move? Are we supposed to force people to go to some totally unknown place?'

'That's not how it works. All we have to do is get close enough to someone for the Vetusian power we carry to get into their minds. Once there, it makes them understand where they are and what happened to get them there. They will know they are prisoners of the vampires. And once they have a Vetusian implant, they will be like us, having the power to awaken others. It will spread throughout Stralia.'

'My people will not move. We are of this land. Without it, we are nothing.'

'That will be their choice. But some will move, I am sure of that.'

Allira looked unconvinced, but Ferguson decided they had argued enough.

'In we go!'

Ferguson looked around the bar as they entered. It was almost impossible to believe this had once been the centre of his life, only a short time earlier. So much had happened, he felt like the Ferguson who had frequented this place was another man, one who just happened to bear the same name.

The smell of stale beer assaulted his nostrils as he studied the clientele. He recognised no-one. He approached the bar.

'One Schwartz special, please,' he said, knowing Allira's opinion of Colonist beverages.

'Never heard of it,' the barman said. Ferguson studied him. He was a complete stranger.

'I'll have whatever's on offer,' he said.

The bartender pointed to a sign above his head. Ferguson read it in an instant and then laughed.

DO NOT ASK FOR CREDIT AS A PUNCH IN THE MOUTH OFTEN OFFENDS

He shook his head, laughing. Times had clearly changed.

'I'm Greg Ferguson,' he said, still laughing, 'my credit is good around here.'

There was a rather wizened fellow standing next to him, who up until then had been gazing morosely into his beer. He looked up at Ferguson, studying him intently.

'Ferguson? He disappeared about ten years ago. But you do look a lot like him.' He called the barman over. 'This guy's credit is OK. I'll stand his beer.'

The barman looked unconvinced, but slid a tankard across the counter to Ferguson. He took a long draught. The beer hadn't changed; it was still terrible. Just the way he liked it!

Ferguson, Allira and their new acquaintance moved to a rickety-looking table, some distance from the bar. The man ignored Allira and continued staring at Ferguson.

'You do look like him,' he said, 'but there's a different look to your face, in your eyes. Seems like you've been through the mill. Wherever you've been, it wasn't an easy-going place.'

'You could say that.' Ferguson paused; there was no point in delaying, either the Vetusians had lied or they hadn't. Time to find out. His enhanced mentality reached out and gently sank into the older man's mind, softly, soothingly.

Contact was established. Ferguson did not know how the knowledge transfer worked, but understood it was instantaneous. And so it was. He saw the man abruptly stiffen and his eyes go wide—with horror. Ferguson knew that the sudden understanding was too severe a blow. He reached back into the other's mind, forcing it into quiescence, dampening down the rush of adrenaline. He held the man's gaze in his own.

'You know now, don't you?' he said quietly.

The man lifted a face still lined with the shock of a terrible realisation.

'Yes, yes, I do! But what have you done to me? Who are you?'

'I am Greg Ferguson, just as you said. But I have been away. With *them*. And I have come back to tell everyone the truth. And now you also know, you will help me.'

'But there's nothing we can do!' The man reached across, grabbing Ferguson's hands. Spittle bubbled at the corners of his mouth as he gabbled his words. Other patrons looked around to see who this madman could be. 'We're helpless, just little farm animals! There's nowhere we can go to escape them!'

Ferguson shook his head.

'No, you're wrong. There is a way; there is hope. And I am here to tell you what that is.'

***

As Ferguson had predicted, the wave of knowledge, understanding, spread rapidly through the township. A palpable feeling of dread was detectable among all the inhabitants, old, young and even the handful of children.

By the evening of the second day, the awakening had finished its spreading, and everyone knew what was the true reality. The response was not always the same: some were angry, some despairing, and a few blamed Ferguson for shattering their illusions. But gradually, all of them coalesced together into a confused mass of bewildered people, anxious for answers. They sought out Ferguson.

There was a small hillock not far from the settlement, and he stood upon it as the people gathered below him. The sun had set, but a tawny shading still lingered in the west, while above in the clear desert sky, the first southern stars were appearing. All was still.

He stood there like an Old World preacher, ready to deliver the Law to recalcitrant followers. His arms were raised, his face unreadable in the gathering dusk.

'Now, you know the truth. I hear you ask what must you do to escape. The answer is you must trust me. A place, a world, has been set aside for you and I can send you there. Life there will not be easy, but when have you expected it to be otherwise? You are strong men and women who have survived in this most unforgiving land. You do not expect gifts to be handed to you. You are used to doing things for yourselves, finding your own proud ways. These strengths will serve you well in your new home, where you will finally be free of your oppressors.'

One man strode to the front.

'I knew you years ago, Ferguson—you're just an ordinary man! Why should we listen to you?'

'I've never claimed to be more than an ordinary man. It just happened that I got caught up in events I had never expected; it could have happened to any one of you. But you must realise I brought something back from those strange events; how else could all of you have discovered the truth at the same time?' He turned away briefly; a cold breeze had started to blow in as the desert yielded its heat to the darkening sky. 'But now you must decide; by the powers given to me, I can now send you to that refuge, away from the creatures who despise and abuse you. Stay where you are and you will be taken there. Doubt me, or decide you wish to stay here, and you can just return to your homes.'

The man who had spoken turned to the others.

'Come with me; don't listen to these fairy tales. The man is obviously insane!'

With that, he raised a fist and walked away, never to see Ferguson again. After some hesitation, two others followed. The majority of the crowd remained still, staring up at Ferguson and Allira.

'Thank you. We will meet again shortly. Do not worry.'

But Ferguson was worried; not until he walked the soil of the new Earth would he be certain he had not been cruelly tricked. But having come so far, made so many promises, he knew what he had to do. He sent the message to the implant, waiting patiently at the base of his mind.

'Now.'

Instantly, the scene was lit up by a powerful violet-purple radiance. For an instant, Ferguson thought he saw a great cylinder of luminous power descend upon the waiting throng. Then, it was gone.

And so were they. The wind lifted a few motes of dust from where they had been.

Allira touched him.

'Greg, have we done the right thing?'

'I don't know.'

'I could have stayed here with you in Stralia. You and me, Greg, that's all I've ever wanted.'

'You shall have me,' he said. 'In the new world.'

***

And so, the escape began.

Ferguson and Allira, by the power of the Vetusians, visited several more times over the coming century, to each and every part of the island continent of Stralia. Allira ceased to play an active part, as she said her implant was no longer responding. But with each visit, there were fewer people to convince and convert. And, as Allira had foreseen, many of the Old People refused to listen to his story of unseen oppressors and made clear their determination to stay on their land.

But even there, some followed Ferguson after Allira had convinced them of his sincerity. And so it came to pass that their work was done, and they sent the command to be taken. There was a brief blaze of violet-purple light.

FORTY FOUR

The transition was instant. The ochre aridity of the Red Centre vanished, to be replaced by soft shades of green. The ground beneath them did not have precisely the exact contours as the land they had left, and they swayed slightly as they adjusted their balance.

Ferguson knew something had happened to him and looked inwards.

The Vetusian implant was gone.

'Its work is done,' he said. 'I guess we're on our own now.'

'Mine stopped working a long time ago,' Allira said, but Ferguson was not listening. He was looking around at a landscape no human had ever seen before, on a world that was not merely in another solar system in another galaxy—but in a different *universe*.

One without vampires.

And Allira and he were the only sentient creatures on this new world. They had been sent to arrive some time before the other refugees, bringing their animals and their seed corn, arrived on this new world. Ferguson knew that the planet had a compatible biochemistry to Earth, so living off the land would not be difficult. They had an entire planet to themselves.

They were standing on a prairie dotted with small woods, stretching across a mighty, fast-flowing river of Danubian proportions. Green and gold flying things were swirling and wheeling above that river, occasionally diving out of sight, presumably hunting the local equivalent of fish. To their north stretched a great chain of lofty mountains, purpled by distance, but with their snow caps clearly visible in the westering sun. And in the east, the tremendous golden disk of a great moon was rising, its mottled surface twice as wide as their familiar satellite. The air was redolent with unfamiliar scents, odours to which they would soon become accustomed. Scattered all around them were flat stone slabs, the size of a standard sheet of paper, or less; some were jet black, others were brilliant white.

'We could use these like a blackboard,' Ferguson said, and then raised his eyes and looked around. 'It's beautiful. They did not cheat us.'

'It's not Earth, our Earth,' Allira said, with a touch of bitterness. 'We have lost that forever. The Red Centre, the Southern Cross, the wallabies, the quolls. We will never see them again. Never.'

Ferguson was angry at having his admiration brushed aside so easily.

'No more blood farms, no more experiments! We are free. Free for the first time in our history. The vampires have been preying on us since we lived in caves!'

'And what will we do with this wonderful freedom? Start wars again? Resume the killing? Build another ZOZ?'

Ferguson turned from admiring the landscape and faced her.

'No-one knows what humans are really capable of. Perhaps all our warring, our killing, was the result of us being prey animals. Perhaps here will be the new start we have always dreamed of, when the dead past can finally be forgotten.' He grasped her by the shoulders, almost shaking her. 'A new start, Allira! We have it here. Yes, the Earth is gone, but before long we would have gone from the Earth!'

'Have the Vetusians really set us free?' she said. 'What if they suddenly decide they could make use of us after all? They made it very clear they could find us wherever we were.'

'That is a problem we have no reason to think about,' he said. But even as he said that, he remembered how he and Allira had acted as infiltrators to smuggle Vetusian power past the vampires' Barrier. What mayhem were they inflicting on that race as a result of that bargain? He shrugged. He did not know, nor would he ever.

'When will the others arrive?' she asked, her voice sounding flat and uninvolved.

'A day or so. I believe the rotation period of this world is about twenty hours, so it's not long to wait.'

'And will they materialise six feet under, or in the middle of a tree?'

'What is wrong with you!' he snapped. 'We didn't do either of those things, so why should they? Allira, we are living in wonderful times; for the first time ever, we are living a life free from the shadow of the vampires. Who knows what we can achieve! And yet you sound as if everything is a terrible mistake, instead of being a wonderful opportunity!'

She looked away towards the mighty rising moon, now well clear of the horizon.

'I feel some crisis is approaching,' was all she said.

He felt the need to comfort her and pulled her against him, smoothing her abundant hair.

'Allira, Allira, I know life will be hard here. We will live out the rest of our days in a simple, even primitive, agricultural society. But that's not too different from what we had in Stralia. We'll lose the assistance with our bodily health that Ginevra gave us; there'll be no Renfield, but don't forget the knowledge I got from Gronz. We'll make rapid progress, just watch!'

She did not respond to his encouraging words, nor did she look at him. Instead, she merely said, 'I want to walk.'

Now seriously worried, Ferguson watched her walk past him in the direction of the brilliant rising moon. He caught up with her and reached for her arm.

'Allira, please stop being like this. I don't understand you. Think of all we've gone through, all the trials we've overcome. We have endured, dammit!'

'Yes,' she said. 'We have endured.'

They walked on; the evening became cooler as the sky darkened. Strange stars were beginning to appear, forming constellations never seen before by human eyes. Abandoning his attempt to get Allira to talk, Ferguson spent some time looking at that sky. As the deep blue turned to blackness, he began to see a dim frosty radiance becoming visible. It was faint and milky in the refulgent moonlight, but he could see it was tracing a magnificent ethereal whirlpool shape

369

against the darkness. He stopped Allira from continuing her silent walk.

'Look, Allira! Remember how we used to look at the night sky, and how you told me about the great god Nepelle who lived in the river we could see there?'

To his relief, she said, 'Yes, I remember, Greg. Such a long time ago. It is like it happened to two different people.'

'No, Allira, it was us! Even then, I knew there was something special about the two of us!'

They stood for a few minutes, looking up together as the milky radiance took on the unmistakable shape of a tremendous Catherine Wheel.

'We must be orbiting a great spiral galaxy, and we're seeing it face-on, unlike what we saw from Earth. Allira, just think! Maybe our descendants will invent fables about who lives up there, just like the Old People did!'

'Yes,' she said. 'Our descendants.' Suddenly, she looked down. 'It's just as well we stopped when we did. Look.'

Ferguson looked, and despite the darkness, saw that they had stopped just on the lip of a great cliff. He leaned over the edge. The tremendous moonlight was striking into the chasm, illuminating a mass of jagged boulders, dizzyingly far below.

He smiled.

'You haven't lost your vigilance, have you?' He straightened and retreated slightly from the edge. 'You know, everything is new here, waiting for us to give them names. I think I'll name this "Allira's Leap." Would you like that?'

'*Allira's Leap.* Yes, I would. Something to remember me by.' She turned away from the abyss.

'It's getting too cold; we must find shelter. The Vetusians didn't think to send a house along with us.'

Ferguson had noticed the humour, but not the ominous implication. He laughed.

'I shall register a complaint! Let's go!'

They found their way into a small wood and covered themselves with the giant fronds of a fern-like plant. The other Stralians would be arriving before long, and the building of proper shelters would soon be underway.

He stroked her arm as she lay beside him.

'It will be very hard for us in the beginning, Allira, but we'll make it; I know we will.'

He could not be certain in the darkness that she was smiling, but he assumed she was.

He had never had trouble sleeping, and it was the same on the new world as it had been on the old. Allira lay there, listening to his rather raucous snoring. Then she lifted her head. There was a strip of dark sky visible between the dark boughs of the tall native trees. Unknown bright stars sparkled in the rich blackness.

She spent a long time staring at the sky.

FORTY FIVE

Ferguson woke with the sun in his eyes. He looked up to see golden shafts of mote-crowded sunlight shining through the spaces between the boughs. He smiled and stretched. His muscles were a little stiff from the night's cold, so he stood and flexed his arms and legs. His motions woke Allira.

'How was your night?' he said. He lay back down beside her, and they kissed.

'I was cold,' she said, 'and I dreamt of vampires.'

'You'll soon forget about them. Hey, we can't sit here all day; I can't remember when we last ate!'

'There should be fish in the river. If they won't poison us.'

'They won't. Stop worrying about everything. The Vetusians got what they wanted and we've got the reward they promised. When will you accept they haven't tricked us?'

'Perhaps never. And what happens if the rest of the people don't arrive? You can't build a world from just two people.'

'Be fun trying, though, eh?' Ferguson grinned, but Allira did not respond.

The river was farther away than it looked; its great size had deceived them, but they were soon looking down into a calm side branch of the main current's powerful flow.

'Look, there's one!' she cried, pointing into the green water. Ferguson scooped it out and flung it onto the grass-like vegetation.

It bore a strong resemblance to a Terrestrial fish; convergent evolution requires that all active waterborne animals adopt a similar body plan. The fish-creatures showed no fear of humans, and appeared not to notice that their numbers were decreasing, and so the two fisherfolk soon decided that they had done enough angling.

'Now what do we do?' Ferguson said. 'There were no fish where I lived. I've never eaten one.'

'You have to eat them raw,' Allira said, and waited for the reaction. After his look of disgust had faded, she allowed herself to laugh. 'Didn't Gronz give you the method of making fire?'

'No, just a lot of physics.'

'That won't feed you. Let's take them back, and I'll show you how we Old People make fire.'

After they had eaten enough and wrapped the surplus in the large fronds for later, they lay side by side again.

'It was good to hear you laugh again,' he said. 'That's the first time you've laughed since we got here.'

'Maybe I've forgotten how,' she said, looking up into the branches.

'Allira, please try to shake off this gloom you've wrapped yourself up in. Can't you accept that we're safe now, that it's all over? As soon as the others arrive, we'll have a whole community again. We'll plant crops, tend the sheep and pigs, build proper houses. And we'll begin the long climb back to where

373

we were before the vamps enslaved us. And there'll be children, lots of children. We'll make this place a paradise.' He paused. 'Perhaps you and I could have children.'

She continued to stare up into the canopy.

'Perhaps I don't want children.'

He frowned.

'Now, don't say that. There must be children.'

Now she looked at him.

'Why must there be? It's my duty; is that what you're saying?'

He stroked a dark-brown arm.

'Now, you know that's not what I meant. All through this, it's been you and me against everything that's been thrown at us. Everything. We're a unit that can't be split up.'

She pulled some leaves from the undergrowth and spent some time staring at them, rubbing them between her fingers.

'Perhaps we're not as alike as you think.'

'We're not that alike,' he grinned. 'I'm a man and you're a woman.'

He reached across and began kissing her, fondling her breasts as he did so. At first, she did not react, but as his caresses became more ardent, she began to respond and pressed herself against him, as if trying to fuse with his firm whipcord body. The clothes Gronz had given them were soon discarded and Ferguson rolled on top of her, his weight pushing her down into the sward. She felt his manhood prodding her belly and then the movement of his hips downward.

'No, Greg!' she cried. 'Remember what we promised!'

'I made no promise!' he grunted, and an instant later she felt his penis drive deep into her. For an instant or two, she tried to push him away, but as his rhythm intensified, her struggles stopped, and she began to match his thrusts with upward lunges of her own. Then, after an unknown time, he gave a deep groan from the depths of his being, and she felt his entire body go rigid as he gave her his essence. He lay heavily upon her, taking in great rasps of air. She lay still for a while, and then began to try to throw him off, her small fists hammering on his great chest.

'Get off me! Get off me! You promised!'

He came to his senses and reluctantly withdrew. She struggled into a sitting position, her back to him. She was sobbing.

'Why did you do it?'

He shook his shaggy head.

'Why did I do it? I did it because I wanted to, because I'm a man. That's what men do. Don't tell me you're afraid of pregnancy! How can you be afraid of anything after all we've done?'

'I don't want a child. I must not have a child.'

Feeling his lust replaced by anger, Ferguson crossed to her and pulled her upright.

'That's nonsense! You drooled over Brin, and Ginevra read your mind and said you had a strong desire to bear children.'

She sniffed and rubbed her nose but did not reply.

'Alright, you're not telling me something! You're hiding something!'

She shook her downcast head.

'Can't tell you, don't want to tell you.'

Ferguson stared down at her, and a strange, fearful look came into his face.

'I've tried to hide it from myself, but all through our time together, odd things have happened when you're around.'

She made no answer; her head remained downcast.

'Let's see if I can remember. When the Cat was about to kill me, you were suddenly there. And the Cat didn't kill me; it just lost interest and walked off.'

Allira made no comment.

'When I was about to fight Renfield, you said something about not being able to hold him for much longer.'

No comment.

'You said something to Gottlieb and, all of a sudden, he woke up and was on our side, fighting like hell itself.'

Nothing.

'The ease with which you fooled Sran.'

Another sniff.

'You were able to throw off the effect of Larn's drug and somehow contact me through the mind.'

Her head remained bowed.

'When we met the first Vetusian, he said he saw something in your mind, and the Emperor's implant wouldn't take hold with you.'

At last, she raised her head.

'And what does all that mean?'

'It means you have some control over mentalic forces. Something humans can't do.'

A strange smile from Allira.

'And therefore?'

He took two steps backwards.

'You're a vampire.'

She laughed, but it was a sound of a tone and timbre he had never heard from Allira before.

'If only! My life would have been so much simpler. I would have killed you and joined the fight against the Vetusian monsters! But instead of being your executioner, I am simply and utterly in love with you.'

He shook his head in bafflement.

'I don't get it. If you're not a vampire—what in the name of all the hells are you?'

'Let's put our clothes back on. This may be a long explanation.'

After they had dressed, Ferguson sat on a fallen log, looking up at Allira, who stood over him like a contemptuous headmistress.

'What am I? It's a relief to finally be able to tell you. I often wondered if I were giving myself away, but despite all that physics, you're not the brightest of men.' She took a deep breath. 'You know that vampires and humans have a common ancestor?'

'I do now.'

'The differences between them are not great as genetic relationships go. And some genes are key in determining what kind of hominin you become. And these genes are very dominant, very powerful. They make all the difference; once they get into a population, they drive it inexorably to vampirism.' She took another deep breath. 'I am a kind of throwback—I carry some of those potent vampire genes. I am neither fully human nor fully vampire, a kind of carrier, a Trojan Horse, like we were with the Vetusian implants.'

He shook his head.

'I haven't heard of that kind of horse.'

'Never mind. It was only an allegory. The point is, I am a deadly danger to regular humans. If I breed, I will begin the process of spreading those vampire genes throughout my host populations. That's why I could never have a permanent Old People tribe; they knew I was different, and I would always be asked to move on. So you see my problem; I wanted to be your lover but, at the same time, I didn't want you to be the father of my child. Or to have any father of my child.'

'But Ginevra said you have strong maternal instincts.'

She threw back her head and gave a raucous laugh; another sound he had not heard before.

'Oh, the irony! These genes control the mind—they want to be duplicated, they want to spread, they *want* to turn a population into vampires. That's why humans have never stood a chance against us.' She shook her head and corrected herself. 'Against *them*.'

She approached Ferguson and pulled him to his feet. He noticed she seemed stronger. 'You have no idea how powerful is the demand those genes create. Do you remember when Gronz took me away after your ordeal in the cylinder? You were worried, and, Greg, you were right to be worried. I had sex with him—and I loved it! I pretended to myself I had not, but he awakened my need to side with the vampires, and ever since that moment, the more urgent, the more irresistible the need to reproduce becomes. You had no idea how I lusted after Thron and Kran, strong, powerful vampires, ideal as consorts, ideal for vampire fatherhood, much more than sterile old Gronz. But I held out; they were your enemy, so they were my enemy. But if I had revealed my true nature, they would have taken me in, and I would have watched while they killed you. And soon, I will not be able to control this biological imperative to reproduce. I will seek out males—*any male*—and seduce them. I will be the whore of this new world, spreading vampire genes in all directions!'

Ferguson stood aghast, looking helplessly at Allira, seeing a stranger who, even when they had stood shoulder to shoulder, had almost been his enemy.

And might still be.

She came to him and whispered in his ear.

'And I can tell you something else, Greg Ferguson: you have got your wish. While we have been talking, I have become aware you have impregnated me; you have fertilised the vampire garden. Congratulations, you are a father!'

He fell back, his face transformed into a mask of horror.

'Your new world, Greg, you have destroyed it before it began! Before long, the vampires will rule again, and all your pain, your endurance, will have been for nothing. Nothing!' She followed him, placing her hands on his chest, looking up at him with a vampire smile. 'With every passing second, now I am pregnant, I will be more vampire and less human. So, you know what you must do now, don't you, Greg?'

He shook his head.

'You must kill me, Greg. Only that can save your new world.' She pointed to the position of her heart. 'Stake through the heart. The vampire way.'

He screamed and covered his face with his hands.

'I can't do it, Allira! I can't kill the woman I love! The one who stood shoulder to shoulder with me through all the horrors we have endured! I'd sooner kill myself!'

She shook her head.

'Typical human weakness, human sentimentality. That's why human and vampire cannot co-exist because the human must always give way, go under.' Suddenly, her face changed; strange, mixed emotions battled each other in her features. 'There is a way,' she whispered. 'If only I can hold out a little longer. Just a little longer!' She ran a hand over a sweat-streaked forehead, and for a few moments, Ferguson saw the old Allira. 'Greg, get me two of those stones!'

He looked at her blankly.

'The black type and the white type. A blackboard. I want to leave a message for posterity!'

He ran to obey, but after he had returned, the import of her words finally hit him.

'For *posterity?*'

She took the stones and turned her back, scribbling on the black stone with the tip of the white one. She placed the black stone under one of the fronds that briefly had been their marital bed.

She came up to him, and she was the old Allira, strong, resolute, loving. Human.

'I think I can do it, but only if I go now! Quickly, quickly!' The old smile returned, briefly. 'I have loved you so much, Greg Ferguson, so very, very much.'

She kissed him and was gone.

It took him a while to realise she was heading for Allira's Leap.

FORTY SIX: CODA

Ferguson swore as, once again, his right knee refused to bend. His arthritis was definitely getting worse. The herbs from the banks of the Great River certainly helped, but they were no cure. Neither was all the physics information Gronz had implanted in his brain. He knew that New Stralia was a world orbiting in the halo of a grand spiral galaxy, and that it had likely been flung there after an encounter with a heavyweight star—but that didn't help with his arthritis.

The biological knowledge was of some help; at least they wouldn't have to rediscover the germ theory of infectious diseases and start believing in demonic possession. He gave a quick smile: there were no demons on New Stralia.

Or vampires.

There were no vampires in this entire universe.

From his position atop the little hill, he could look down on the thriving settlement. If only the refugees hadn't insisted on calling it Fergustown! That still embarrassed him.

From his not particularly lofty vantage point, he could see the well-constructed log cabins and their vegetable plots. The pigs were rooting around as happily as pigs always will. More importantly, he could see the children playing near their parents' cabins. All the children were growing up healthy and strong. It was as if somehow their bodies knew that they were in no danger of vampire predation.

Humans and vampires cannot co-exist.

How many times had he heard that sentiment? He absent-mindedly rubbed his beard, snow white, just like his still abundant hair, while images from the past flashed briefly through his mind. Sometimes he could not believe that all those events had actually happened, or if, they had indeed happened, whether it had been him they had happened to. And he knew that the younger members of Fergustown found it increasingly difficult to believe his tales. Those who accepted the reality of vampires were an ever-dwindling minority.

Fergustown was a thriving little township with a burgeoning population. Already, young families were moving away to set up new homes on the other bank of the Great River. A few trailblazers were even talking about discovering what lay on the other side of the mountains.

Occasionally, Ferguson wondered if he had relaxed too soon. There was still the possibility that all this was part of a cruel trick by the Vetusians, and that somewhere on this world they would come up against some new threat. Could one really trust monsters?

He buried that thought, forcing it down into his subconscious. There was absolutely no evidence for such a betrayal.

He looked around at the beauty of New Stralia, especially the mysterious purple mountain range. He knew he would never explore beyond it. Hells, it wouldn't be long before he wouldn't be able to get to the top of this puny little hill!

He returned his gaze to the settlement and, once again, he smiled. His wife would be wondering where he had gotten to if he didn't show up soon!

But before he began the descent, he would do what he often did when he was alone.

He fished in his pocket and took out a flat black stone. The blackness had turned out to be simply a thin coating, and so Allira's writing had been more permanent than she expected.

He looked at the stone and read those simple words yet again. And yet again, he felt the tears start as he saw the simple message:

Remember me.

ABOUT THE AUTHOR

Martyn Rhys Vaughan was born in the World Heritage steel town of Blaenavon which nestles among the green hills of the south Wales valleys.

From a very early age he was interested in how the Universe works and what it contains. He listened to early space travel adventures on the radio, such as Journey Into Space and devoured the few American magazines of unusual and unlikely adventures which happened to come his way. Early examples were the Classics Illustrated versions of H G Wells' The Time Machine and The War Of The Worlds. He soon developed an undying interest in "speculative fiction" and began to write fiction for his own consumption at an early age.

His career took in a wide variety of roles including working in the Agricultural sector and in various laboratories in the worlds of heavy industry and organic chemicals. His longest period of employment was working as a statistician in the Government Statistical Office, concentrating mainly in Balance of Payments issues.

Throughout his time he has remained a passionate advocate for the value of rationality and science in human affairs, one which he sees as of paramount importance in the increasingly turbulent times in which we live, as all of us may soon find ourselves in one of the Dystopian worlds so beloved of Science Fiction.

His works to date are all in the realm of speculative fiction and have received critical acclaim amongst those who love stories which probe the bounds of possibility.

looked at from a lot of angles, so there is still more to puzzle over. I recommend this book to dystopia, suspense fans, and those who love well-characterized, explored and thriller tales.'

Tejiri Enimu – Online Bookclub

No Truce With The Vampires: Those Who Wake

One thing that struck me about this book is how detailed each scene is, thereby making it easy to paint a vivid mental picture of every action. I was also mesmerized by how much this author had me glued to the pages of this very book ranging from jaw-dropping revelations, adrenaline-pumping cliffhangers, and new enemies. It was nearly impossible to put down this book. What about some of the villains; Serafina's sister Eleonora and Charles' brother, Edward? I enjoyed every bit of the last-minute twist of events and the suspense that re-emerged.

I must also commend this author on the steam he created between Charles and Serafina. Serafina fights silent battles between her professional duty as a guardian and her feelings towards Charles, desperately wishing everything is over so she can take off her mask and show him how vulnerable she really is around him.

On a final note, I would like to acknowledge the writing style adopted in this book. It was neither too ambiguous nor too simple. It simply had a perfect touch of everything ranging from suspense, drama, romance, and fiction.

Hence, to every lover of a good book, this masterpiece is for you. Vaughan, Martyn Rhys did it yet again!

Anthionette Ejimofor - Amazon reviewer

The author's descriptive talent is spot-on and evident throughout. I could easily envision the Vetusians as well as the special transportation laser created to transport the vampires to chosen destinations.
The vocabulary implemented paints a picture of each fantastical scene from the Elite headquarters to the strange joined visions Charles and Serafina have throughout.
My favourite element of this book other than the plot and the fantastic twists and turns is the character development. For instance, Serafina begins as a strong female leader but becomes a more loving and thoughtful individual as the chapters continue.
I am excited to announce there will also be a third and final instalment of the No Truce saga so stay tuned!! I give book two of this series five out of five stars and recommend it to lovers of vampires and the unknown and for ages high school and above.

Jessica Rainstein – Amazon reviewer

Vaughan did an incredible job. The writing is superb and descriptive. The book also has expert world-building. It transports readers to a world where humans are seen as sub-par, where vampires rule, and evil looms. Through Serafina's eyes, we see the almighty vampires brought down. We see their fight for survival and drive to protect their own.

The book balances fantasy, horror, and suspense. Vaughan knew the exact time to increase the tension, when to slow it down, and when to add a twist. The action and mental battles are intense and exciting. The relationship between Charles and Serafina was, without a doubt, the highlight of this book. It added passion and spice to the book, which kept me eagerly turning the pages. Their romance was fierce and tender, and their interactions were engaging. Their relationship was woven into the plot and didn't feel forced; it complemented the plot. The passion between them was undeniable and intense.

This is a gripping and unforgettable story. There is absolutely nothing to dislike, and this book deserves 5 out of 5 stars. I found a few errors while reading. I recommend it to fans of fantasy and horror stories, particularly to readers who enjoy books about vampires.

Chris Sharon – Amazon reviewer

Hideous Night

'Reading this brilliant novel was just like riding a scary roller coaster! I found myself hanging on with an enjoyable sense of dread throughout the many thrilling plot twists and turns, as I the reader was propelled along with each new page towards what seemed like an unavoidably hideous climax. However, I needed to know what happened next so I devoured the book like the hungry monsters that are the villains of this extraordinary story! This thoroughly entertaining book has reminded me how much fun reading good sci-fi can be and I will certainly be ordering the rest of Martyn Rhys Vaughan's back catalogue in the hope of experiencing similar thrilling adventures. In the meantime I will be reflecting on the writer's astute observations of the privilege of modern lifestyle choices and how flawed people can choose to be heroes when forced to fight seemingly overwhelming odds to save (a perhaps undeserving) humanity.'

Wayne Edwards – Amazon Reviewer

Doom Of Stars

'So much happens in this book, but it does not have that overcrowded or rushed feel to it. We get the whole scope and view of events without the drawn out, lengthy series many SciFis turn into. In the story we follow Kalli, a young woman living in a small village just outside of London, who, along with her fellow villagers, hunts seals and trades goods in London to survive an Earth with sweltering summers, frozen winters, and out of control tides. Her grandmother is legendary, a renowned scientist whose name has become akin to a curse. She brought about these end times, the Doom of Stars. Or did she?

There's something so refreshing and wonderful about the idea of humanity fighting to survive without the influence of money and wealth or debt. Watching people who have been cut down the bare basics use their skills to find food and survive, working to learn new skills to better their survival, is wholly entertaining. It's a reset button many desperately want.

On top of that, the story is full of strong, incredible, and intelligent women. It skips the usual tropes you see with strong female characters. They have believable insecurities, they aren't infallible or perfect, and they aren't described as being some version of a perfect dream girl. There's barely any emphasis on looks for the purpose of driving their personality. These women feel human and real.

If you enjoy SciFi with real feeling science (I say this as I'm no scientist and couldn't tell you if there's anything real to it or not), great female characters, and the end of the world, definitely give this a read. You won't be disappointed.'

Chelsea Hauth – Reedsy Reviewer

Resolution Of Stars

'Martyn Rhys Vaughan delivers another enthralling read in his new SF novel and the sequel to Doom Of Stars making environmental themes and the human condition in a fascinating post-apocalyptic setting…Martyn Rhys Vaughan has created a fascinating world for readers to navigate and characters that are complex and multi-layered…The story is hauntingly intoxicating and readers will find it immersive…Resolution Of Stars is a twisty story with right-angle turns, fast pace and suspenseful. It is not one to miss.'

Franklin Bauer – The Book Commentary

Culmination Of Stars

'The Doom Of Stars is finally here. Five lightsail ships depart from the familiar confines of the solar system, embarking on a voyage towards the distant Centauri…The writing dazzles with brilliance, skilfully portraying the journey in captivating detail and flawless execution. Each part remains vibrant and engaging, avoiding monotony while installing a sense of wonder. Delving deeper into scientific concepts and exploring dystopian adventures, the narrative pushes boundaries…The characters in this gripping space odyssey are vibrant and dynamic…The author's skilful storytelling is evident throughout, while the writing itself is commendable, capturing the reader's attention from start to finish.'

Saima Rahman – *The OnlineBookClub*

9 781036 934477